Hullabaloo
in Huron Shores

An Ellie & Lucy Wilson Mystery

Eleanor Wood Mason

Hullabaloo in Huron Shores

An Ellie & Lucy Wilson Mystery

By Eleanor Wood Mason

ISBN-10: 0990724018

ISBN-13: 978-0990724018

OptiMystic Press Inc.
P.O. Box 6
Woodburn, IN 46797
www.om-press.com

ACKNOWLEDGEMENT

Thank you to my very special daughters. Without their loving support and encouragement this book could never have been written. Extra special thank you to WRPBiTV.com for support, encouragement, contacts and so much more.

CONTENTS

Prologue.. vii

Chapter 1...9

Chapter 2...15

Chapter 3...27

Chapter 4...35

Chapter 5...41

Chapter 6...45

Chapter 7...53

Chapter 8...61

Chapter 9...69

Chapter 10...77

Chapter 11...87

Chapter 12...99

Chapter 13...115

Chapter 14...127

Chapter 15...137

Chapter 16...147

Chapter 17...157

Chapter 18...167

Chapter 19...181

Chapter 20...197

Chapter 21...209

Chapter 22...223

Chapter 23...233

Chapter 24...243

Chapter 25...257

Chapter 26...269

Chapter 27...279

Chapter 28...281

Chapter 29...293

Epilogue..307

About the Author...309

PROLOGUE

The thief caught the back of the pint sized runaway's shirt in his strong hands. He pulled the squirming figure close, his gloved hands slipped on glossy fabric. He felt his captive's intake of air preface a scream. He grabbed a handful of the interloper's short, cropped hair, and with one powerful thrust forced the face into the soft, yielding, floury heap.

His huge hand pushed her face deep into the spongy mass of rising dough. I can't die, not here she lamented as soft, moist dough clogged her nose, filled her mouth, and crept down her throat.

The thief pulled his captive's face from the gooey mass. Her head flopped back, the thief shook her. He laid her down, felt for a pulse, and sank to his knees beside her body as tears of self-pity coursed down his face.

ELEANOR WOOD MASON

CHAPTER 1

"Blast," Ellie Wilson muttered, slapping her small fist sharply against the scared pine table, "It's only August and the 'Harass the Baker' Committee is already at it."

"Jake," Ellie called, beckoning to the baker's best friend, "Those selfish people, who understand nothing about business, started their campaign early. They have convinced that exhausted man to keep the bakery open when good sense and business sense tell him he should close." Ellie gasped for breath, and continued in the same vein. "Those inconsiderate, self-centered people have triumphed long before we could reasonably have expected them to start their annual campaign. You know he could make a lot more money teaching. The college has been after him for years. What are we going to do to stop this senior moment Baker is having?

"Senior moment," Jake feigned indignation while threading his way through packed tables. "What do you mean *senior moment*? Baker and I are the same age; and we, like fine wine and old cheese, improve with age." Jake grinned and sat across from Ellie at a table that Baker called the executive seats; a table reserved for friends.

"So he's being stupid." Ellie frowned, "He works ridiculous hours all summer only to lose those hard won dollars to autumn costs," Ellie shook her head, setting her auburn curls bouncing.

"You're right," Jake agreed, "but if there's any convincing to be done you'll have to do it. He doesn't hear me anymore."

"Well, I suppose I could talk about threats to his health from overwork," Ellie stalled. She had been invited to sit at the baker's table shortly after her return to Huron Shores and was loath to risk losing her privileged spot. She was opinionated and spoke her mind, and strangely

Baker admired that trait, strangely, because Baker, a product of his upbringing had a streak of chauvinism that while charming and often amusing, spawned many a good natured, boisterous debate.

The control that was usually natural to her fled when she engaged in any discussion, on any topic, with the irascible baker. He knew how to get her goat. She wondered if he watched where she tethered that goat, because he unerringly located and freed it. Ellie giggled at the image of Baker and the goat prancing through fields of misspelled quotes. She forced herself to focus on her current problem. If she alienated the volatile baker, she might lose her opportunity to convince him that she could, and would, treat his apple fritter recipe and his cinnamon bun formula with the respect they deserved.

Jake interrupted Ellie's musings, "When is Lucy coming? Your daughter's a sensible girl and Baker says she was his best manager ever, until now that is." Jake frowned at Ruby, Baker's new manager. He sipped from his personalized coffee cup, and continued, "So there might be an off chance he'd actually listen to Lucy."

"He just might at that," Ellie said, her brow furrowed, "though why he thinks of my Lucy as an astute business consultant with her obvious artistic temperament, I'll never understand," Ellie spread her hands. "Though to be fair, maybe he sees something in Lucy that I don't." She grinned, "However, to answer your question, I'm picking Lucy up at the airport later tonight."

"Shouldn't you be on your way?" Jake asked, checking his Rolex. "The traffic down that way is terrible. I could drive you to the city."

"You sound like Lucy! I have been driving myself around this continent for thirty years and expect to continue doing so for the foreseeable future. I am fully capable of driving in any city, in any traffic, anywhere, anytime, thank you very much," Ellie snapped, realized she'd over-reacted, and grinned sheepishly.

"Anyway," she continued, "Lucy is arriving via private plane at that little airport just upcountry."

"Oh well, that's alright then, but Ellie, when you said city, I thought you meant that place we love to hate down country, the one with a couple of million people," Jake said hastily. "I didn't mean to impugn your driving. I thought you might like company on the drive. I know I would have enjoyed spending the time with you."

"Do you think there's a chance Baker might part with his Chelsea bun recipe?" Ellie asked brightly, ignoring Jake's transparent attempt to advance their relationship. "They are head and shoulders above any I have tasted and his lemon cakes are, or should be, world famous.

Whatever it takes to be a great baker, he has it, and yet he panders to his friends and stays open instead of using his God given talent to teach."

Jake gazed out the window, "Oh crap, that's the health inspector's car pulling in across the street." Jake sighed heavily, "That'll make Baker's day," he upset his chair in his haste to warn the baker.

Ellie watched Jake take off like a scalded cat. She thought ruefully, did my unfailing charm scare him off? Maybe not this time—that health inspector is after the baker's goodwill ambassador, Rex again. The poor cat has nowhere else to go, and if she bothered to ask she would understand that when Baker took Rex home, he disappeared for three weeks before he returned to the bakery, sick and hungry. It is as hard to teach an old cat a new trick as it is to teach a man. Baker did not have a choice, his kind heart, his most endearing trait, would not allow him to abandon any tormented soul.

Rita Russell, district health inspector, smiled evilly. "I've got you, seven long years I've waited to close your dingy diner, and today's my day. I got my promotion, and I am top dog. I may have been a little over zealous before I got transferred to this backwater; maybe closing half the dives I inspected was a bit of overkill, but rules are rules; obey, or take the consequences. Not my fault if some of those skanky dumps closed permanently. They got what they deserved. No one, especially no donut dunker in a forgotten resort town will get the best of me. Not for long anyway."

She reached for her clipboard, her keys slipped from her sweaty hand. Rita breathed deeply; no need to fret, it's all set. Today I close him down, she exhaled, I'll red card him and chain the damn door, this is my greatest achievement, my victory, my *raison d'être*. That damn baker and his disregard for rules have been eating at me for years. He's my one failure, and today that ends.

Tsk, tsk, Rita thought, snatching up her clipboard and climbing from her government issued white Ford sedan. Peeling Paint-Infraction Number One; and I haven't even stepped inside the door. She tiptoed over the packed gravel parking lot to keep her stilettos pristine.

The place is jumping. Good, I like an audience. There's the old buzzard and my snitch Ruby; she's smiling at me while cuddling up to him like she's his friend and not his Benedict Arnold. She cost me a few bucks, but having a spy and proof that the cat lives here is worth every cent. Rita Russell jerked open the door and stalked into the bakery.

Jake stepped between the seething baker, and the tense inspector, he held out his hand. "We see a lot of you these days, Ms. Russell. Not that we're not happy to see you of course." She ignored him and focused on

Baker. Jake clasped her clenched fist and towed her away from Baker and toward Ellie.

"This is our local celebrity Ellie Wilson," he said cheerfully, "she writes cookery books; her column is syndicated in over sixty papers worldwide. Ellie meet Rita Russell, our local health inspector. Ms. Russell, Mrs. Wilson," Jake stopped talking, no one was listening anyway. Baker bristled, rude Rita ignored exasperated Ellie's out stretched hand, and he, well, he was out of ideas.

"Let's get on with it," Rita said flatly, and stalked into the kitchen. "Crumbs, flies, definite infractions here, here and here," she wrote furiously pausing only to gesture vaguely. "Tables not bused, floors dirty, covered with sand. That kid didn't wash her hands, and no hair nets. I warned you about that," Rita snarled, "Those racks haven't been cleaned today," she continued to list every infraction; some so obscure no one remembered them, but no sign of the cat . . . yet. She flounced down the stairs, glanced quickly at Ruby, and waited a moment as if for a cue.

Rita's eyes scanned the baker's domain. She checked the fryer, the proofer, and the high flour-covered work bench, all the while writing furiously. Red, her favorite color, bloomed like blood spatters on an axe victim's wall, "No paper towels in the staff washroom. I've warned you about that. Fix it! I told you new regulations say hand sinks on all floors."

The baker angrily marched toward Rita, but Jake's up raised hand stopped him.

"Yes," Jake said patiently, "we understood you, and over there," he pointed, "are two new sinks ready for installation, but summer is our plumber's busy time. Its nine days since your last inspection, nine days, when we need three weeks." Jake drew a deep breath and rushed on, "However, Baker has made every effort to comply with the new regulations."

Rita Russell scoffed, "This isn't the first time you've been warned and ignored an order."

Baker snapped, "We've got eight sinks, any more and there won't be room to swing a cat without hitting a damn sink."

He's taunting me, Rita thought, I'll show him, "The time limit on that form is seven days." Ignoring Baker, she turned to Jake, "The owner must comply or be cited." That and the cat will be enough to close him temporarily.

Partially hidden behind a skid she found bagged cat food and litter, but still no cat. Rita looked at Ruby. Ruby looked at the ceiling.

"This screen is ripped. Fix it. The cooler is set two degrees too high. Fix it." Rita zealously counted offenses, but she needed the cat. Ruby looked anywhere but at Rita who diligently inspected each sheltered corner and shadowed space. She found cat marks, but no cat. Obviously her informer forgot who paid her and informed the wrong person. But how did Ruby do that without incriminating herself? Rita fumed; I didn't wait seven years to be double crossed by a backstabbing, two-faced tramp. I'll get her for this.

"I need a water sample," Rita snarled, she snatched a sterile bottle from her briefcase; chose an unused sink piled with boxes, there's more than one way to skin a cat. She rhapsodized, a hint of fecal coliform, or the mere suggestion of E. coli will cook his goose or glaze his donut, so to speak. Contaminated water, she shrugged, probably not, so it's the cat, and its here; I can feel it and I will find it. She flung a copy of her report at the cat-less, smirking baker, waited for his signature, and stalked out the back door through the newly mown grass, across the gravel lot and with gears grinding sped away

Jake seized the baker's arm, and hauled him away from Ruby. He knew her kind of woman, always standing a little too close, always eager to add fuel to any feud. Baker's dispute with the health inspector was to her, like breast milk to a baby. Ruby's spiteful nature shone brightest, at least to Jake, during times of trouble.

Thwarted by Jake's intervention, Ruby claimed distress, manufactured crocodile tears, slammed out the back door and smack into a dark-haired, handsome youth. Distress and tears miraculously gone she grasp his arm and shoved him into the cedar hedge. *"We do it tonight,"* she snarled, "The baker trusts me now, but if that old hag squeals I'm toast around here."

"What are you yakking about Ruby? If who squeals? What old hag?"

I've been taking money from Rita Russel, the health inspector, to spy on Baker."

He smirked, "You're shittin' me! Somebody's actually paying you to watch a boring baker? Why?"

"Never mind that, I think Jake knows, but I can handle him."

Bending nearly double he whispered, "Jake won't be the easy sell you think. He knows women, he managed of a bunch them working down country, and he's nobody's fool. He'll see through anything you throw at him."

Ruby scoffed, "All men are stupid, you'll see Jake panting after me like all the rest," she pulled the elastic band from her long, blond hair, her braless breasts clearly defined under her tight red sweater.

His eyes firmly fixed on her heaving chest, the lusty youth believed her.

"What Jake thinks doesn't matter anyway. You need to listen to me. It's a long weekend and the money is rolling in and Baker can't bank it."

"He'll make a night drop." The toff scoffed, running his tanned hand over his shining brown hair.

"No he won't, he doesn't trust night drops. Shush," Ruby whispered slapping her hand over his mouth. "Someone's coming." She towed him to the gleaming, cherry red, Chevy Corvair classic that her guilty father gave her on her last birthday. Propelling him in through the passenger door, she scrambled over him. "Close the door quick before the cat gets out. I hid him after she called; but don't worry he never repeats a thing I tell him. He's a cat of few words, and not worth the money that crazy, old bitch is paying to find him."

"Duh, no shit. What do you want? I gotta get back to the store. They're questioning my sales slips again so I'm buying the coffee and donuts until they stop looking so close." He smirked, "When they say jump, I don't say, who do you want me to jump, I say, great idea boss," he fluttered long lashes over guileless, blue eyes. "Speak up, because I gotta get back to work."

"Okay, okay, fine," Ruby pouted; her voice gained strength and became strident, "Just shut up and listen..." she continued to detail her plan, all the while stroking Rex's soft ginger fur.

CHAPTER 2

Betty Archer waited patiently while the airplane taxied to the terminal. She waited until her seatmates deplaned, then tried to wrestle her familiar old Louis Vuitton suitcase and plastic duty free bag from the deep overhead compartment.

Masculine hands easily reached over her head into the extreme back of the compartment where, in any case, she hadn't a hope of reaching them.

"*Merci beaucoup*," Betty responded automatically to the steward's kindness. Her plump hands unconsciously smoothed the wrinkles from the skirt of her Chanel suit, the suit the elegant Parisian saleswoman said would never wrinkle.

"No problem. *Bonsoir* Madam," his smile revealed deep dimples while his eyes showed appreciation for Betty's rounded figure and pretty face.

Where do the airlines find those handsome fellows who without a word make a woman feel beautiful and desired? Betty wondered wearily towing her case toward the customs checkpoint. She waited uncomplainingly as no one eagerly awaited her arrival, truth be known, and she was reluctant to reach either home or husband. Michael, her business partner, would have met her had there not been an important estate sale they could not afford to miss.

Ten minutes later the clerk asked the requisite questions, and like an unanimated golem she answered, was summarily welcomed home, and dismissed.

She joined the jumbled migration to the baggage claim area where two large boisterous families parted as had the Red Sea at Moses' command. Betty saw all of her luggage, miraculously together, gain speed as it rounded the corner and bore down upon her. Unwilling to ignore the wondrous, new experience of her luggage in tandem on the carousel at her arrival, she squeezed into a space big enough for a pixie and grasped both cases, strong arms relieved her of her burden.

"Looks like you could use a little help there, Mrs. Archer," Betty's savior, said grinning widely. "It looked to me like you were going to ride round on that belt with your bags." His bright eyes and toothy grin made her smile, "Sorry I missed you coming out," he set the bags on the cart and steadied Betty, "looks like you need me."

"Yes I do," Betty panted, "and like the angel Gabriel, you appeared in the nick of time."

"Ma'am, no one in my entire long life has ever accused me of being angelic," he laughed uproariously."

Betty trailed the bulky porter. They slowly wended their way through the horde of weary, happy people rushing to meet loved ones who waited for only them. She grimaced, and wished she shared a fraction of their excitement.

"There's my driver," Betty announced, pointing to a sharp nosed, middle aged man holding a large pink card, 'Welcome Home Betty Archer' it read. At least someone is happy to see me home, she sighed.

The limo service with its many stops will delay her arrival by two hours, and she did not mind a bit. Betty thought of earlier times when she'd run through the airport, and into her husband's loving arms.

She'd been angry when her father bought the antique shop, the shop that today was her link to sanity. Father had a premonition as he foresaw chaos in her life, and the shop was his solution. Profoundly sad, she regretted the chance for independence she'd blithely thrown away when she'd accepted Derwood Day's proposal short months after Robert's untimely death. Derwood, who seemed an answer to her prayers. Derwood, who did not care enough for her to meet her at the door, let alone the airport.

Driver and porter struggled to heft Betty's suitcases into the cargo bay, "These bags are real heavy. You got your usual load of contraband bricks, Mrs. Archer?"

"No Roy, just the usual icons pilfered from various churches throughout the Old Country," Betty said and forced a laugh. She climbed gracelessly into the high, red, Ford Econoline van with the words 'Airport Limousine' incongruously printed on the side.

"Thank you for your help," Betty leaned out to tip her porter.

"My pleasure," the happy porter replied with a covert glance at the folded fifty dollar bill tucked in his hand. "I'll keep a sharper eye out for you next time, be sure of that," he promised.

"You think you might have over-tipped just a little," Roy asked, settling into the driver's seat. "You're never that generous with me," he laughed, "and I risk jail time transporting all your stolen stuff," he continued with the interplay they both usually enjoyed.

Betty giggled, because Roy expected her to. "I won't tell if you don't," she promised, leaning back and closing her eyes, effectively ending the ritual.

She wondered why she could interact with the porter, her driver, and the boys at the donut shop while despite her best efforts, life with Derwood deteriorated. Perhaps she was as shallow, selfish, and stupid as Derwood claimed. But if that were true why did the men who liked to start their day with coffee at the bakery welcome her? They always seemed happy to see her. Betty happily anticipated her visit to the bakery each morning.

Doubt and sadness overwhelmed her. That was a pleasant dream. She could no longer face her friends now that everyone knew of Derwood's abuse. She wasn't strong enough to endure the shame, the sly digs, or worse the pity from friends.

Ellie had kept her secret, but Zack, when he saw her injuries, was incensed. He would talk to her old friends at the bakery, and they would reach the only logical conclusion; she had driven Derwood until he hit her.

She could not go to the bakery. Derwood had ruined that too. Think of something else, anything but Derwood, something pleasant. Think of the bed Ellie's daughter, Lucy located. Lucy's exhaustive efforts had finally paid off. She'd found and purchased the elusive bed. The expense had been almost obscene, though Lucy had worked for expenses only and not asked her usual finder's fee. Lucy understood the importance of the bed to her; perhaps she guessed it was their honeymoon bed.

It was beautiful and ancient and she'd needed a stool to climb into it. How Robert with his long legs had laughed. They'd spent many hours fanaticizing and spinning stories around all the people, famous or infamous who might have slept or whatever, in that magnificent Renaissance bed. Betty smiled her first real smile since her plane had lifted from Charles de Gaulle Aéroport in France.

I know when I sleep in that bed, I'll feel close to Robert. He'd often said, only half joking, that the twin cherubs on the headboard would bless our union every time we slept. We were sure God would gift us with children. Robert was careful to hide his disappointment as each barren year passed. I do not feel cheated; we had love, and I am grateful for that love, a love one experiences only once in a lifetime. I am grateful though Robert will never physically join me in our bed, I'll feel his presence, his breath warm on my face as if he were with me and I will be happy. My bed's waxed walnut sheen and aged patina will give new life to my memories. Perhaps I will hear Robert's voice whisper to me as he did in life. Betty wrenched her mind from her thoughts, and back to practicalities.

Michael said our container passed through customs two weeks ago. He was so excited by the shipping manifest that he unpacked it immediately. He had delivered the bed and assembled it in her room ready for the special order mattress due to arrive from Greenville next week. He gave her his cherished circa 1725 brass bed warmer to celebrate the occasion. An occasion he appreciated as few others could, because she and Robert had given Michael a home and unconditional love when he'd lost his father.

Again Betty pulled her mind from Robert and back to the bed. I cannot wait to see my bed in my room. Michael said it looks magnificent with the soft cream walls and pale pink, Italian silk drapes. I'll have a bedspread made from the fabric Lucy and I found at the Marché St. Pierre in Paris and the ensemble will be perfect, although Michael insists it is perfection now. Dear Father, thank you for bringing Michael into my life, amen.

Betty eagerly anticipated the comfort and safety she felt in the only 'Derwood free zone' left to her in Huron Shores. Her bedroom, her sanctuary, was exclusively hers, and there she could forget that she was tied to a cruel Philistine.

Derwood, all thoughts brought her back to *him*? Betty sighed, and made a promise to herself; if he mistreats me again, I'll throw him out, and I'll get a court order to keep him out. I will divorce him.

She shivered; she feared her husband and she could not fight him alone. Memories were fine, dreams necessary, but what she needed now was a backbone and a friend.

Robert would want me to be happy and I will be happy. I'll change my life. My friend Ellie will lend me strength and I will beat *him* and get my home and my life back.

Ellie, Betty smiled, Ellie would stand with her. Ellie was her oldest friend, her chosen sister. They'd grown up together, and there were no secrets between them. Ellie offered to meet her plane, but Lucy was arriving tonight so she'd refused Ellie's kind offer, she could never ask Ellie to choose between daughter and friend.

Betty and Michael had a mother son relationship she cherished, but the bond between Ellie and Lucy was different and special.

We three will be together and whatever happens with Derwood I will have a safe haven with Ellie and Lucy.

Lucy, eyes squeezed shut, clutched Harv's arm as the tiny Cessna swooped through the twilight toward the ripening grain field that boasted the misnomer airport. Time slowed to a crawl while Lucy, certain it would be her last, savored each breath.

"Open your eyes Lucy," Harv said through stifled laughter. We've landed."

Lucy cautiously opened one green eye, "Are you sure?"

Harv patted Lucy's hand. "I'm sure because I'm a pilot who just landed an airplane one handed, so I'm pretty sure."

"Okay, if you say so Harv, can we get out now?"

"Sure we can. Lucy, but you have to let go of my arm."

"Are you sure it's safe," Lucy moaned.

Harv jumped down, opened the passenger door and grinning widely said, "I promise if you stop imprinting my upholstery with your nails I'll get you down safely." He gingerly rubbed five red nail marks on his forearm.

Lucy opened both eyes, saw the ground, and launched her body like a missile. Harv caught her, won the struggle to stay upright, and folded his arms protectively around her; he murmured against her hair "You're fine now honey. I told you I'd keep you safe."

Lucy gazed into her champion's hazel eyes; she struggled to control her breathing as Harv's mouth descended toward her waiting lips.

Ellie's high beams illuminated entwined figures that leapt apart like startled fawns or maybe a faun and an innocent wood sprite, Ellie thought amused. She gasped, that is my innocent fawn in the arms of a satyr, my Lucy in the arms of the Spencer scion.

"I'm here honey." She called; slipped her powerful car into gear and surged toward the startled duo.

"Careful Mom," Lucy yipped, "You almost ran over Harv's foot."

"Lucy," Ellie said, "it's quite late."

"Uh, Mom, don't you think I might need my luggage? Mom, meet Harvey Spencer, Harv this is my mother Ellie Warden Wilson."

"Good evening Mr. Spencer. Thank you for bringing Lucy home. It is nice to meet you," Ellie lied. "You look tired Lucy, we should go." She tugged on her daughter's hand; the one Harv wasn't glued to.

"It's nice to meet you Mrs. Wilson," Harv said, and whispered in Lucy's ear, "I'll call you." Then to Ellie, "If you open the trunk I'll load Lucy's cases."

He stepped into the bright lights; Ellie saw him clearly for the first time, her knees buckled. "Lucy we have to go right now."

"This is the way to travel, eh mom?" Lucy enthused, distracted by Harv's rippling muscles, she did not notice Ellie's pallor.

"Sorry about the short notice," she said, "but I didn't think you'd mind not driving all that way to the city."

"Lucy, you know I can drive…" Ellie began in the voice Lucy knew heralded the, I can drive anywhere diatribe.

"I didn't say you can't drive in the city mom, but it's three hours each way and Harv offered me a lift and I'm here seven hours early." Lucy leaned close, "I like him a lot and you will too when you get to know him better."

"Will I?" Ellie said, skeptically, but softly. A reckless ne'er-do-well playboy with an aircraft, no I will not, with a noticeably stiff spine she stalked to her car. "Let's go Lucy."

Harv smiled at Lucy, waved to the night watchman and sauntered to a low-slung, black sports car. The squeal of tires and smell of burning rubber coupled with the earsplitting roar of dual exhaust made Ellie doubly glad she had arrived in the nick of time.

"Mom," Lucy wailed, "don't I even get a welcome home hug?"

Disapproving mother was instantly replaced by loving mom, "I am so happy you're home;" she clasped Lucy's willowy form protectively."

Lost in thought Ellie maneuvered the inherited Lincoln town car over dark country roads. Harv is the image of his father she mused, and while I should not blame him for his predecessor's misdeeds, I do.

Lucy watched her mother's expressive face, and wondered what demon took Ellie and left this irrational person behind. "Okay mom," she said reasonably, "let's start over. Why are you upset?" She waited a moment, "It must be me riding in that tiny plane." Lucy grinned happily, "Because it can't be Harv. He's got a super job, a great car, and," she sighed, "a trust fund. He's never been married and has no children so he's the kind of guy *we* have been looking for." Lucy studied Ellie's face, then dropped the clincher, "Just imagine, in no time you will have handsome grandchildren to spoil." Lucy knew her mother would like that aspect since she had been pushing every eligible bachelor within a country mile at her since she'd turned twenty one.

"Lucy," Ellie said frowning, "Playboys do not make good husbands. Harv, like his father, his uncle, and his grandfather, is a pleasure-seeking man. The fancy car, the plane, the trust fund, the unearned place in his great grandfather's purloined company all add up to an unsuitable match. I admit he is a fine looking . . . boy;" she said disparagingly, "but Lucy, looks are the least important thing when selecting a mate. I know all you youngsters have hormones rampaging through your blood, but you must think of the future. Harv is simply not the one for a sensible girl like you," Ellie slapped the steering wheel thus ending, she hoped, all discussion.

"Mom I'm twenty-nine, and Harv is thirty, it's cute that you think of us as teenagers with hormones running amok." Lucy grinned, and she kissed Ellie, "You are one of a kind, but I think Harv is the one."

"That's nice Lucy, but Harv is from a long line of adulterous, amoral unethical profligates who could not understand the word faithful if God our Father explained it. He will abuse or abandon any woman who trusts him; remember the rotten apple never falls far from the diseased tree." Ellie snapped, "He is a piece of work not worthy of your notice."

Lucy giggled.

"This is not a laughing matter Lucille Warden Wilson."

"I know you mean well mom, but Harv is different, and that last bit sounded like a Dreadful Derwood quote."

The more I speak against Harv the more Lucy has to defend him, Ellie thought, and forced a laugh, "Did it? How awful! If I do it again either shoot me, or lock me away forever."

Ellie turned from the winding back road to the highway and thought how empty her life would be without Lucy. Her child bolstered her confidence when it lagged, as it often did. When she was stuck with her cookbook or column, Lucy offered not only moral support, but innovative recipes, or outrageous ideas for a forum, a column, or a book. If I could live my life over, I would change nothing past or present, Ellie vowed.

Lucy watched the trees, mysterious and brooding silhouetted against the midnight blue sky. The velvet darkness relieved only when solitary farm lights cast a warm glow over the buildings huddled beneath them. She sighed and closed her eyes, the pressures of her career fled like dandelion fluff blown on a gentle breeze. She saw the secluded beach where she could swim and sketch to her heart's content, and renew her tan while reclaiming her sanity. Quiet beach time without stress was unlike her normal day where temperamental artists and craftsmen vied with demanding clients for the obnoxious award. Placating wealthy, spoiled clients was her life and most of the time she loved it, but at home in Huron Shores people accepted and loved her for herself. She sighed, "It is so good to be home."

"It's wonderful to have you home honey. Betty, Uncle Rodney, Michael and Brad all miss you. The baker's been asking when his best biscuit eater gets back. Did I tell you Baker has a new helper? Jake Carlton is our newest resident and a very nice man."

"Hmm," Lucy chuckled. "Talk of Mr. Wonder's cheese biscuits started my stomach rumbling. I wonder if the baker has an old, dried up, cheese biscuit hanging around the shop. Let's drop my stuff at the house and check. It will be like old times, coffee and cheese biscuits at midnight. That will leave tomorrow to lie on the beach and rest."

"Uh, Lucy," Ellie interrupted, "You know men are retiring earlier than their wives, and there's an increased interest in cooking and baking. I've been approached to run a men only culinary class. What do you think of that idea?"

"Ah, Mom, say you didn't commit us again this summer," Lucy groaned. "Don't you remember how it messed up all our plans? Please say you aren't doing that again."

"I'm not doing quite that same thing again Lucy. Are you happy now?"

"Not until you tell me the rest." Lucy grumbled and waited for the proverbial other shoe to drop.

"I did sort of say we *might* teach it." Ellie admitted, "Mrs. Rochet misunderstood, and to make a long story short we are teaching four classes. They wanted eight but I held to four. At two sessions a week we will be done before you know it," Ellie said hopefully.

Lucy pulled her fluffy, angora cardigan up over her head. "I am not listening. In a minute I'll wake up and this conversation will have been a really, really bad dream."

"Uncover your head and tell me you're not angry. Ninety percent of the fellows that signed up this time are single. Remember all the nice men you met last time."

Lucy sighed, "Yeah I remember I met Artie, and he was nice, but after a few dates with me he ran back to his wife."

"That was just one fellow. This time there are more to choose from. That's a good thing isn't it?"

Lucy giggled, "It's a thing alright, but if the guys are single there's less chance of some dude's wife chasing me with a frying pan, like last time."

"The wives wouldn't be upset anyway. Women who have cooked for families all their lives and are happy to have someone cook for them. The women will have time to do the things they always wanted to, like painting, writing or just watching the news uninterrupted. Imagine yourself in that situation. Wouldn't it be wonderful to have dinner put on the table by someone else, anyone, who wasn't you?"

"You might be right," Lucy agreed, "but I wonder if the guys would be so keen to cook if we took away their dishwashers."

"Local scuttlebutt says the baker is thinking of retiring," Ellie said. "Consequently, the boys at the bakery, old and young, will lose their source of sweet treats. I wonder if they'd like to learn to make their own. Perhaps we should base this class on baking."

"The baker has been retiring for as long as I can remember, and twenty years before that according to Grandma. Is he serious this time?"

"I certainly hope so. When Jean Pierre, your favorite French chef, was our mystery guest everyone loved him," Ellie paused to collect her thoughts. "What if the baker agreed to teach our class to make his wonderful apple fritters? That would be a *coup de grâce* for us, and if he's retiring anyway, it could be an opportunity for him, I know he will love teaching," Ellie, ever the optimist, predicted.

"To hell with the fritters," Lucy said irreverently," get him to teach then to make cheese biscuits."

"Lucy despite of your colorful phrasing, you have a point. Most men enjoy fresh, hot biscuits. I think they would love to learn to make them at home, don't you agree?"

"No Mom I do not agree. Remember the last all male class? All they wanted was to eat what we cooked and hit on us. You must remember that group."

"Yes, but this time will be different. We will issue a list of ingredients and utensils that every participant must bring to class. If they don't bring the required materials, they cannot stay. Uncle Rodney has promised to evict all nonconformists." Ellie sighed, "But Lucy, if you really do not want to help, I'll manage on my own."

"No, I'll do it. It's always fun working together, even when I'm press ganged into doing it. Maybe I can write my trip off as a tax deduction. So tell me exactly what are we teaching the greenhorns to burn?"

"I think we should look for recipes with a limited number of ingredients."

Lucy smiled impishly, "That's a great idea, the thinking part I mean. Most bakery type dishes are too complicated for the greenhorns. They think buying pizza and taking it out of the box is a two-step meal. Add a coke and they have a two course meal. If the pizza has more than two toppings, it's a gourmet extravaganza."

Ellie laughed heartily, "I bow to your experience, though you might have exaggerated a tiny bit."

"You know Mom, tired as I am, all this talk of food has made me want a cheese biscuit."

"Of course dear, if that's what you want, but after that long exhausting flight you must be tired."

"I never can sleep when I get in; the time change messes me up. But I know a couple of the baker's biscuits will drive me right to dreamland."

Ellie laughed, transported back twenty years to when Lucy, age nine, told amazing stories to avoid bedtime. "I should insist you go to bed; but since you're not sleepy, let's look at the restored lighthouse, it is quite a sight," she pulled onto the smooth sand and parked next to the gently lapping waves.

"I forget how clear the sky is here," Lucy, unwilling to disturb the tranquility whispered. "There is no place like home. The air is so clear I can see every star, no smog, no dirt, and no pollution. It's wonderful. The lighthouse changes the skyline. I'm not sure I like any change here, even if it's a good change."

"I know," Ellie agreed. "I often sit on the shore at night and watch the water splash against the rocks. I wonder how many men saw that radiant light as a beacon of hope while their ships were driven ashore by relentless waves. I think of women watching from their widow's walks and I hear their weeping, their hearts breaking as their hopes and dreams are buried beneath tons of foaming, wind-lashed water." Ellie absently placed a metal shard above the tide line. "I hear barrels of molasses, whiskey, or salt pork break free of their lashings and batter fragile wooden hulls. I hear the desperate cries of men crushed beneath shifting cargo as ghost engines chug, gurgle, and breathe their final breath, a hopeless sigh. The captain, his soul burdened, orders the lifeboats lowered knowing most will not reach the shore. I hear the prayers of wives meet those of their men over wild, foam topped waves, prayers for mercy that go unanswered." Tears streamed down Ellie's face and her voice faltered.

Lucy gathered her mother in a tight embrace. "Let's go home Mom. Daddy would want us to remember only the happy times." Charles Wilson, Lucy's father died on this lake, and she had too few precious memories of him.

"I'm sorry, Lucy. I know I should get over it, but sometimes I wonder if Charles might be alive, if the lighthouse had been functioning."

"I know Mom, I know, but it's shining now so maybe no one else will have to endure a loss like ours. Why don't we focus on the ships that didn't sink because the beacon warned them off?"

"I've ruined a happy event with maudlin memories."

"No you didn't. I love the way your mind works, but it's time to go home," Lucy slid behind the wheel and sought an upbeat subject. "Did you know that Harv's dad is directly responsible for the lighthouse restoration? Harv said his dad is head of the restoration committee they are going to repair all the rundown lighthouses. Mr. Spencer made a substantial financial contribution to the renewal fund. You've got to admire a man who puts his money where his mouth is." Lucy glanced over at her mother.

Ellie, put aside the grief that was still fresh after twenty years, and listened to Lucy extol Harvey Spencer Senior's dubious virtues.

"Let's drop your belongings at the house. When you're stuffed with cheese biscuits, you won't be able to lift anything. I was so excited to have you home, I forgot to lock up, and it's on our way."

Lucy loved the yellow brick house, the ornate gingerbread trim, and the wraparound porch where so many wonderful memories lingered. She loved this old house where she'd spent so many happy holidays with her grandparents. She loved the calm she felt in this town, her home town.

Lucy dropped her bags in the foyer, nodded to the ancestors whose portraits lined the walls and sighed, home at last.

"There's a message, want me to see who it is?"

"It's probably my editor; I've been a little lax with deadlines. I'll let him nag me tomorrow."

"We may as well get it over with. I'll put it on speaker," Lucy giggled, "so we can have a group nag."

CHAPTER 3

"Oh," Betty gasped, "what are you doing?"

"I'm fixing this piece of shit," Derwood kicked the mutilated, ancient bedpost. "More useless junk," he punctuated each word with a thrust of his heavy boot. "If you had a brain, you loony old bitch, you'd know the mattress won't fit." Derwood's voice grated menacingly. "This better be the last time you waste *my* money, the last piece junk you bring into *my* house."

Through a haze Betty saw her dream bed shattered, desecrated by Derwood's viciousness.

Derwood stood proud and self-righteous amid the wreckage of her beautiful antique bed his smile belligerent and smug, pleased by the depth of pain he read on her face.

"I sawed down the center of the headboard, had to rent that," he pointed to the oily chainsaw staining her Persian carpet. I ripped those ugly angel things off, bloody romantic crap. And who needs six foot bedposts," he sneered. "I shortened them so a sawed off runt like you won't need a damn stepladder to get into bed." He grinned evilly. "You stupid loony old bitch, were you drunk when you bought this monstrosity"

Betty saw Robert's cherub lying butchered, its delicate Renaissance face deliberately disfigured. She knew that *his, Derwood's'* goal was to erase Robert's memory. She pictured the Norman dish armoire, Robert's favorite piece; striped of its ancient patina and painted garish orange; the delicate inlaid table, Robert's last gift to her, altered beyond recognition; the Flemish still life, another gift from Robert, reframed in shining steel. The garish colors *he'd* used to stain her ancient treasures and walls; until her house was no longer her home. But he'd gone too far, *he* violated her bedroom, her sanctuary. Tears streamed from her pain filled eyes.

He smiled; his plot would work. She would run away as she always did and leave him to complete his final project.

Betty hugged a piece of her mutilated bed, "Oh God," she begged, "help me."

He kicked Robert's cherub against the wall then with *his* dirty boot he ground a tiny cross into the rug.

The black rage of a gentle soul driven beyond endurance overwhelmed her. Her arm rose of its own volition. Derwood, his fists balled, lunged, Betty swung. The jagged edge of the maimed bedpost obliterated *his* sneer. All his calculated evils lent strength to her small body, she swung again and again, and again past caring where her blows landed. Then as *he'd* planned, she ran away. *He* lay ominously still amidst her ruined bed. She ran blindly down the spiral staircase and out the door, down Feder across 2nd Avenue and onto Main. She stumbled over a broken curb and cursed the town council for neglect. She giggled hysterically…what was a broken sidewalk compared to what she'd just done?

"Betty? Betty Archer is that you over there?" the baker called shielding his eyes against the glare of the bright halogens. "You back from gallivanting over Europe? Come join Jake and me in a coffee."

Betty's aimless flight had brought her to the bakery's warm welcome; she steeled herself and crossed the street. Baker had a steaming cup of coffee in hand. "Anything interesting in the sky tonight," she asked, trying to appear normal.

"Not tonight, so we're enjoying the night and listening to the radio," Jake said, "Tell us about your trip."

"Jake," Baker said, "turn that radio down so I can hear this lovely lady's dulcet tones."

"Betty, you should be resting, got to be sharp for tomorrow's discussion. The guys miss you. What are you doing out alone this time of night anyway?"

"I just got in and I couldn't sleep."

Baker saw her tear stained face and handed her his handkerchief, "You know Betty you can tell me anything. It won't go farther, and maybe I can help."

"I have to go," Betty whimpered, she dropped her coffee and ran down the street.

Jake slammed out the bakery door, "What did you do, Baker? Scare her away with your usual half-witty conversation?"

"That bastard Derwood's been beating on her again. She was crying and she had blood on her face." He sighed, "Remember the old days when we knew what to do with wife beaters?"

"Yes Baker, I do remember, but those days are gone. Today's women think they're different, and it can't happen to them; when in fact they are more vulnerable to than ever. I don't know about you pal, but that leaves me feeling old and bloody well impotent."

"I know, but I am responsible for this one. Betty's first husband, Robert, expected his friends to look after his widow. I should have been there for her, and I wasn't. I'd better go after her."

"Wait, Baker. That's not good idea; give her time to compose herself. She knows you're here." Jake picked up the H.I. report, "Let's discus something we might actually be able to fix."

"I know what you're going to say," Baker muttered, "so go ahead, talk about the harpy health inspector."

"I think I know how to spike her guns. You hire me to do maintenance, at my same salary," Jake grinned. "Only take a couple or three days to fix all the problems. Then when she finds Rex she won't have much of a case, will she?"

"I'll not let that battle-axe tell me what to do," Baker snarled.

"Then get ready to close, because she will shut you down. If you're serious about retiring, a working business will sell faster and for a better price. You know I'm right."

The baker grumbled before he grudgingly agreed, "You're right, but I hate to let her beat me in this. She's a menace, a proper pain in the aspidistra."

Jake asked, "She's a pain in the what? Aspi . . . what? Maybe you are old enough for those senior moments Ellie suspects if you remember that old Gracie Fields' song.

"Don't try to jolly me off a subject you brought up," Baker groused. "That witch has all the power now that she's district supervisor."

"What was that sound?"

"Just raccoons, I shouldn't have thrown chocolate creams in the dumpster. Those pesky bandits can't resist them"

"They're not pests," Jake said grinning, "but rather animals with discerning tastes who patronize the best dumpster in town."

"Did you see that?" Baker pointed excitedly toward the lake. Six bright objects stopped abruptly, hovered, and then moved horizontally across the sky, "It stopped dead in its tracks."

Jake grabbed his binoculars and gazed in wonder as the U.F.O crept slowly across the night sky. He thrust the glasses at the baker, "I'll call the radio station so they can clock the time, and broadcast our sighting in case anyone else spotted it." He chuckled, "You keep watching and don't let them get away."

"By gosh it's a genuine unidentified flying object; an actual UFO." Baker exclaimed. "Maybe it's not an alien space craft, it might be a satellite or some secret prototype aircraft, but we spotted it; just goes to show persistence pays off."

Rita Russell parked her car in inky obscurity behind the closed library. She peered through the thick, cedar hedge that shielded the quiet library from the busy bakery.

He thinks he's won, but not this time. I did not spend seven boring years clawing my way to the top to have a donut dunker get the best of me.

I'm obsessed and being a total moron. I know it, so why can't I let go? I would if it was only the cat, but his flagrant disregard for the rules gets to me. He's like an irritating monkey riding my back. Rita grinned. *Revenge*, someone clever said, *is a dish best served cold*, and I'm about to enjoy an icy treat.

Rita studied her clothing to ensure her black silk blouse hid the white satin shell she'd thoughtlessly chosen for contrast. She was as invisible as any other burglar. Lacking a pocket, she tucked her wallet into the waistband of her black leggings. The soft soled shoes she'd selected for color and not stability she slipped off, she hung her silver digital camera around her neck, scowled when the moonlight hit it, and tucked it inside her blouse.

Shoes in hand Rita eased the door of her borrowed auto closed, and crept toward a gap in the cedar hedge. She crouched among the scratchy, clipped branches, and listened to the cacophony of night sounds. Rita jumped when she heard, "Come join Jake and me for coffee." She straightened wondering how to explain her presence, saw a woman cross the lot, and ducked behind the prickly bushes.

There they sit on that rickety porch, radio blaring while they discuss stars and U.F.O's. At least Ruby didn't lie about that. Two half deaf, old fools drinking coffee with some whiny woman, probably that nosy old bag with the syndicated column. Was that introduction supposed to impress me? It didn't. The voices grew faint, and Rita stopped listening. I have to be quiet; the woman likely isn't as deaf as those two old duds.

As she slipped from the hedges shadow to the malodorous dumpster Rita saw a dim light in the proofing room. If Ruby wasn't lying, she had thirty minutes to find the cat before the baker checked his rising sponge.

He's so damn arrogant. I know he ridiculed me to my staff. If I don't shut him down, I'll lose all credibility. It's hard for a woman in this trade. If I do my job, I'm a bitch; if I don't, I'm incompetent. All the pathetic fools have to do is follow the rules; granted there are a lot of rules and some of them are silly and antiquated, but my job is to protect the public. Rita moved a few steps away from the reeking dumpster to duck behind a discarded freezer next to the screen door.

She fondly recalled the day Baker Wonder asked his friend, her former boss, for another favor. She'd used that favor to launch the inquiry that culminated in his dismissal and her promotion to his job. It took a little digging and some fabrication, but he broke the rules and deserved what he got. I don't even want the job. What I want, what I need, is to shut this place, and then I can get on with my life.

Rita tiptoed to the back door, noted the mended screen, slid through the tiny opening. She inhaled the mingled scent of yeast, cinnamon, and remembered she'd forgotten to eat dinner.

There it is. I knew it, I knew it; she hummed softly though she wanted to shout.

"Here kitty," Rita whispered, she set her shoes next to a skid, and tugged her camera from under her blouse. "Smile for the birdie," she instructed carefully focusing to include bags of flour and the cat's red collar conveniently inscribed, Rex.

Rita heard the screen door spring stretch and contract. She kicked her shoes under the pallet, darted down the short hall, and into the dark office, she shoved the shiny camera onto a sagging shelf, she crawled into the kneehole beneath Baker's old desk, and tugged the wheeled oak chair close. Flanked by banks of worn drawers Rita huddled and shivered glad she'd shed those extra pounds as her former chubby self would not have fit easily into so small a space, especially since she shared it with a softly purring cat. There's a weird kind of irony happening here. Rex mewed softly, and snuggled against Rita's cramped legs, she pulled the tomcat into her lap, and stroked his long, soft fur, and prayed.

In a flash sanity returned, by not announcing herself to Baker she had violated one of the rules she was paid to enforce. If caught, her profession, her pension and her self respect were gone.

The ludicrousness of her situation hit her like a bolt of Florida lightning; she visualized her mind as an enormous, seething mass of obsession surrounding a minuscule nucleus housing a sop of sanity. She saw the throbbing core engorge and explode over the diseased mass transforming the swirling mess into healthy pink cells. That silly cliché, 'what's a nice girl like you doing in a place like this,' came to mind, and in spite of her dicey situation, she grinned. If I get out of this mess with my career intact I'll take the next promotion, leave this burg, and never look back. Here I sit under a desk after chasing a harmless, affectionate feline, and yeah I am dumb as a stick. Rita shivered and hugged Rex.

"Man its dark," the interloper whispered.

Rita clamped her lips over chattering teeth as a flashlights tight beam paused inches from her right foot. She saw enormous white sneakers stop, she hugged Rex tight and prayed the flashlight-wielding trespasser would find what he wanted and leave before the baker returned.

The owner of the sneakers opened a drawer and gasped. He set the light on the desk; paper money rustled and was quickly stuffed into the zippered bag Ruby had provided.

Every nerve in Rita's panicked body screamed *run*! Rex rubbed his face against her cheek and she relaxed a little.

"Shit," she heard, "there's gotta be twenty thousand here," he cursed softly while trying to tuck the bulky bag behind the band of his tight denim shorts, the flashlight rolled slowly off the desk and onto the chair fully illuminating Rita.

Rita's legs with a will of their own, straightened.

The chair shot toward the thief, "What the hell," the thief exclaimed when Rex yowled, vaulted over the chair and as if it were his duty to protect the health inspector dug every hooked claw into the thief's tanned legs.

Rita sprinted out the door, down the hall and into the proofing room. She stumbled, grabbed for the prep table, caught the protective cloth, and dragged it off the huge mound of risen dough. The thief's strong hands caught the back of her shirt. His gloved hands slipped on the glossy fabric Rita threw caution to the wind and opened her mouth to scream. The thief panicked, grabbed a handful of her short hair and with one powerful thrust forced her face into the soft, yielding, floury mass.

Rita tried to scream, but her assailant forced her face deep into the spongy dough.

"Did you think you'd get to the money before me?" the thief hissed.

Not here, not now, Rita moaned as soft, moist dough clogged her nose, filled her mouth, and crept into her throat.

The thief waited while his victim writhed and then quieted, "About time you smartened up." He jerked his competitor's face out of the dough; her head flopped against his chest, the thief shook her, felt for a nonexistent pulse; and sank with her body to the floor, tears of self-pity coursed down his face. Moments later he carried her lifeless body to the discarded freezer outside the back door, tossed her in, and quietly lowered the lid. His feet propelled by panic as he ran to Ruby. She would know what to do

NO! He thought this is all Ruby's fault, her idea. If he took the fall for this, she'd go down with him. This time she wouldn't come out smelling like a rose.

ELEANOR WOOD MASON

CHAPTER 4

Derwood awoke, heaved his aching body upright, waited for the dizziness to pass, and staggered to the bathroom. What he saw in the mirror amazed and appalled him, "I underestimated that loony bitch." His parted black, curly hair showed a two inch gash as he moaned piteously. Blood trickled in a zigzag line over his forehead, a clotted mass swelled below his ear and his chin was on fire. She'll pay for this, he promised. Furious, he cranked the brass tap to hot, rummaged for the bandages, salve, and tape. Why can't the stupid old loony bitch have a medicine cabinet like normal people? He dumped the drawer's contents onto the floor and the adhesive tape rolled under the counter. He bent to retrieve it, the scorching water streamed over the sinks rim and onto his head, and his rage intensified. The hot tap burned his hand; he cursed, dried his scalded head, threw several towels over the mess on the floor, and bandaged his wounds.

His reflection in the ornate mirror somewhat appeased him; the stark white tape gave his features a menacing aspect, but enhanced his tan. He grinned evilly and dialed a familiar number. "She's here; bring the money." Derwood slammed the phone home, went to the study, poured Bourbon over ice and waited.

Rodney Wilson cursed and cradled the phone. I did everything wrong; she came to me black eyed and bleeding and I allowed her to talk me out of killing him. She cried in my arms while she told me how he hurt her, and I did nothing. I said divorce him. She said she could not stand the humiliation.

By not calling the authorities, I played into the bastard's hands. I confronted him but he denied hitting her. Rodney stopped pacing to recall the liar's exact words, 'Stop disciplining my wife for a gift of twenty five thousand dollars, cash of course.' I thought it a small amount to ensure Betty's safety. It was the first of many such 'gifts', but over his dead body or mine this will be the last.

"All you sniveling wimps talk, talk, talk, talk," Derwood snorted, "then you pay up." He fingered the sloppy bandage near his ear. "But I'm a nice guy, so let's drink a toast to our continued association. I made martinis, dry and shaken, not stirred just the way you James Bond type poufs like them."

Rodney Wilson, the quintessential English gentleman automatically accepted the murky glass Derwood proffered.

"I will not drink with nor associate with a barbarous Philistine," Rodney said quietly. "Incidentally, one uses olives, not onions in martinis. This, old boy, is a Gibson," he placed the untasted drink on a side table.

"Trust a pseudo-intellectual in an outdated, double breasted, pinstripe to know the pansy stuff," Derwood mocked gleefully, he did not often get to insult Rodney's personality, dress, and manners in one shot.

Accustomed to Derwood's insults, Rodney ignored them. He endured Derwood's abuse to protect Betty. If he'd done his duty after Roberts's death, Betty would never have succumbed to Derwood's dubious charm and married him. Thus in his eyes, Rodney failed her, and she'd been deceived by an unscrupulous fraud.

"Fork over the cash," Derwood demanded. It was his duty; he felt to relieve Rodney of as much of his undeserved, inherited wealth as he could manage.

"What happened to your head?"

"Shut your damned trap, you perverted faggot. Leave the money and get out of my house."

"You are an unprincipled swindler and I am done with you. I shall insist Betty leave you, and charge you with assault and battery. I will see you arraigned and jailed for extortion. That will put you away for a good long time, I'll wager."

Derwood leered, "Yeah, I'm sure you'd both like to see that, but it ain't gonna happen."

"I have all the evidence I need."

"Funny you should mention evidence. Ever wonder how Robert died? Convenient wasn't it? Remember we all had a drink together before you flew to England?" Rodney frowned, "Sure you do, you handed him the drink I fixed then you carried the glasses to the kitchen, just like mother's little helper, you left a perfect set of prints."

"What are you saying?" Rodney snapped, "Robert had a heart attack."

"Ah, but Betty saw the suicide note."

"I do not believe you!"

"It was so easy," Derwood said. "Darling Robert had to be buried in hallowed ground, last rites muttered by a dithering old fool. The blubbering old cow couldn't stand the idea of," Derwood imitated Betty's voice, "Dear Robert's eternal soul condemned to purgatory."

Skeptical, Rodney waited.

"But," Derwood continued, "We know Robert didn't commit suicide. We know you poisoned him." Derwood laughed, "The goblet is in my safe with crystallized residue and your fingerprints. That's enough to hang you high. So don't threaten me."

"You bastard, you murdered my best friend."

"No," Derwood jeered, stabbing a finger at Rodney's chest. My prints aren't on the goblet, yours are and everybody knows you're hot for Betty, so you can't do a damn thing about it, not a damned thing," he reiterated. "Who comforted the grieving widow? Me. Who covered up Roberts's suicide? Me. And," his lip curled, "she came to me like a lamb to the slaughter, and now I-Fleece-You." Derwood chortled, "And you can't do a damn thing about it."

Rodney said quietly, "No Derwood, You-Will-Not." He pictured a bull's-eye on Derwood's nose and with three years of suppressed rage behind each fist, threw a left jab followed closely by a right cross.

Damn I underestimated the pouf, Derwood thought and dropped like a polled ox.

With Derwood at his feet, unconscious and bleeding, Rodney dusted his knuckles on his jacket, smiled his satisfaction, and left without a backward glance.

Betty wandered, oblivious of the tall pines that like guardian sentinels shaded her path. She did not hear the susurrus waves, nor see the family of deer frolic in the roadway. But she understood, finally, why she'd drifted like a ship without a rudder, when Robert, a man careful of his health, died suddenly. Betty stopped abruptly, "Say it out loud, you sniveling fool. Robert killed himself!" And you didn't even see it coming. Why didn't I know he was unhappy?

Betty took a breath, Robert you handled all things financial, while I dealt only with my shop. You made my life effortless, but you left me vulnerable. I was suffocating under a mountain of responsibility; when all I wanted was to be left alone to mourn.

When our lawyer asked for papers, tax receipts, your will, I couldn't locate them. I couldn't even find our checkbooks. I was stupid, naive, and a fool.

Enter Derwood, kind, consoling, helpful. Derwood took over my life, and I let him. Derwood understood your business you apparently told him what you should have told me? But that's not fair. The truth is I wasn't interested.

Derwood took over my life, he said sign, and I signed. He arranged Robert's funeral, and when I couldn't face the world; he sheltered me. He took the calls I couldn't, and when I asked, he sent everyone away. He cooked the meals I couldn't eat, and he gave me addictive pills when I couldn't sleep until I couldn't live without the pills, or without him. When he proposed, I mindlessly accepted. We were married that week.

Derwood's metamorphosis was as sudden and startling as it was terrifying. I, who had never been touched in anger, was yoked to an abusive beast. I ran away, I traveled, increasing the frequency, and extending the duration of each buying trip. Each time I returned my home was grotesquely altered, one pint of garish paint, one stroke of the saw, one more missing or reframed painting, and one more empty space where a treasured object had been, one by one he expunged every trace of Robert and of our life together. When I objected, he hurt me.

My bed was a tangible symbol of the love Robert and I shared. Derwood knew about the bed he'd seen our honeymoon pictures. That is why he destroyed it.

Betty sat on a cedar stump beside the road. I was an easy mark for Derwood; I'd gone from the security of daddy's house to cosseted indulgence with Robert, with never a worry between. Betty studied the jeweled, night sky, so peaceful and beautiful, she knew God must be listening.

"Thank you, Lord for the time you gave me with Robert," she prayed, "But why didn't you show me how depressed he was? Why? Why? Why?" Betty begged an answer from above. "God, please help me, I need help, I don't know what to do," she sobbed into Baker's handkerchief. "What is wrong with me that Robert couldn't talk to me instead of leaving that dreadful note?"

Betty prayed silently until bright headlights illuminated her. She quickly signed the cross, and used the baker's formerly pristine handkerchief, to scrub her face, Derwood hated crying.

"Can I help you ma'am? Whoa Betty, that you? What are you doing way out here?" He leaned over to open the door, "Hop in, I'll run you home." Betty's old friend, stolid, stoic Eric Platt studied her face, "You look real . . . tired," he said, eyeing her streaked mascara. He noted her distress and how it embarrassed her. He talked about nothing, murmuring meaningless platitudes, knowing Betty's thoughts were elsewhere.

Derwood first punched and kicked her two days after their wedding. She gazed blindly through the windshield. Shocked, humiliated, and ashamed, she'd attempted to cover the bruises, and run to Rodney. Derwood called her cell phone almost immediately. He apologized and said dealing with her complicated financial affairs had stressed him. She forgave him, accepted his excuse, and believed him when he said he would never hit her again. He lied; he hit her each time she came home.

Eric was reminiscing; she dragged her mind back and listened.

"Remember when a bunch of us, Robert, Baker, me, you, and Ellie, and what was her name?

"Susie," Betty supplied.

"Oh yeah, wonder what happened to her?" Eric mused. "Doesn't matter, anyhow we went skinny dipping at the old quarry. Nothing happened, except swimming, I mean. I was only fourteen. You guys were younger because I was kept back in grade two, remember? God were we innocent. Lucky we didn't know what life would hand us." He glanced at Betty, huddled in the seat beside him. "Old friends are still the best friends and I've missed you."

Betty nodded; unable to speak past the lump in her throat.

"You know Betty, I'm sorry I wasn't here for you when Robert died. I let you down on that, but you know, I was out of town on a training course and when I got back I called, but Derwood said you didn't want to talk, then you two married and I didn't want to intrude." Eric, never the most articulate kid in the class, tried to explain. "Betty, what's wrong, you're crying? I'm sorry. I'm real sorry. Betty, please don't cry." Eric pulled onto the shoulder, put his arms around Betty, and held her. "I've missed you my old friend. Tell me what's wrong Betts? Maybe I can help."

No one else called her Betts, and his kindness opened the floodgates, and she sobbed.

CHAPTER 5

The thief sprinted past the hairdressing salon, the new Mega-Grocery, slowed to skirt the open back door at Darcy's Diner, wove between closely-packed, rental cottages, and slid to a stop behind the Snack Shack, gasping for air. The money bag was an irritating reminder of what he'd done and what he had to do.

Where the hell is Ruby? This whole screw-up is her fault. Angrily he circled the small building. She's supposed to be here, we'd go back to the bash messed up, like we were making out, no questions asked. He scanned the beach from the shadows and considered his options, the rave is heating up, some old biddy will call the cops, and they'll do a drug search, find the money and I'm dead. Dad will search me first to prove he's fair. He won't suspect me, Jordan Platt grinned, I'm the good kid, never take drugs, sell yeah, but never use.

But this isn't drugs; murder, even accidental murder means hard time. What the hell am I going to do? He made another worried circuit around the shack, stopped abruptly, grinned, and imagined a light bulb over his head. Pain in the ass, fish-gutter Bradley will take the fall. I'll hide the money on his boat, toss her body in the water, and, the thief sneered, teach that pain in the ass a lesson. His mind churned as he schemed. I don't need Ruby I need her ride, she hides a key under her front fender. His mind segued to the time the play had gotten a little rough, and she'd lost her car key in the sand; the rape wasn't his fault either, she led him on and never told anybody so it was no big deal.

Lucky for me she's not too smart, he unlocked the door, pushed the seat all the way back, took the car out of gear and let it roll down the incline, cranked the engine over when it hit the pavement. Without lights he took the back way to the bakery, parked as close to the freezer as he dared, crept from the car, and unlocked the trunk. An icy chill raised the shaved hairs on the back of his neck; he froze, listened, but heard nothing. Must be the cat, I'll flatten the damn thing next time I see it crossing the road.

He quietly lifted the freezer's lid, wishing it empty and the episode a weird dream. He shifted the scratchy money bag, a reminder of his new reality; and put the small body in Ruby's trunk. Tears of self-pity made the task more difficult, he swiped at his eyes with the back of his hand, surprised that he still wore the surgical gloves he'd put on at the beginning of the evening. He tossed a plaid blanket over the body so small it was lost in the cavernous trunk; quietly lowered the lid until it clicked, and drove fast toward the pier where Brad's fishing boat waited.

Zack angrily knuckled sleep from his gritty eyes, and wiped the sweat from his brow with a corner of the sheet. The new meds killed the pain, but the flashbacks could kill him. Doc mentioned aggravated sleep patterns; and meant flashbacks, and that's fine, I can handle old memories, but these new refinements; not so much. Zack shifted from his bed into his motorized chair. The usual routine failed to kill the nighttime memories. I better keep these dreams to myself, or some self-styled shrink will analyze them to death and that last one is just too crazy. I'll go over to the bakery and talk with the guys, mechanically he jabbed at the big red button that electronically operated the door, and missed. Irritated he aimed and poked again, shook his muzzy head, and zigzagged through the door, down the drive and into the roadway.

He heard his sister's voice screech, and pulled up short. "Get out of the street moron, do you have a death wish, do you want to get hit by a car, are you blind?" all in one long shrill sentence. Zack nervously checked the empty street awaiting the slap to the back of his head that inevitably followed. 'Remember the rhyme.' How did that old verse go again? He sighed, I can't remember, Dot screeched it a thousand times, and I cannot remember. It's got to be the new meds, he decided and wheeled onto the sidewalk bumped over cracked concrete slabs, and wished the town would use a few of his tax dollars to fix the damn sidewalk. Not everybody was thoughtful and kindhearted like Baker.

No one knew all that Baker had done to help him; small thoughtful things, like cutting this arch in the hedge so he could get to the bakery without coping with gravel or the busy parking lot.

Damned medication is making me woozy; he winced as prickly cedar twigs scratched his arms, focused and tried to merge the two images into one easily navigable space, then waited impatiently for it to happen.

He strained to hear Baker and Jake's conversation, but the thumping bass from the beach party drowned them out. I'm early, but the night's warm and the guys will be down soon, I'll wait.

Ruby must be drunk again, she forgot the headlights. Concealed by the hedge, Zack watched the classic car stop behind the bakery. He willed his eyes to see only one control on his armrest and jockeyed his chair into a better position.

Ruby never lets anyone else drive her baby, but that's not her. Zack rolled his softly humming chair forward, still in shadow he watched the bakery's back door.

Dazed, Zack shook his head. A kid I've known since . . . forever, couldn't . . . nah, it's the new meds. I'm stuck in a darn nightmare. He backed his chair through the hedge and went home. It was only a drug induced nightmare, but one impossible to wake from. Fully clothed he swung from his chair and slid beneath his cool white sheets.

Fastening his seat belt, leaving one less reason for the cops to stop him, the thief left the bakery, drove toward Lake Shore Road, flicked on the headlights and turned toward Indian Wharf. The car windows reverberated with the sound of another stereo booming on the beach. All the old biddies will start yelling soon, he forecast, and the cops will arrive.

He brought Ruby's car to a sliding halt near the ramp where Brad's boat, The Cal-o-crow was docked in the harsh glare of halogen lights. The thief's anger and resentment grew; damn Indian got it handed to him. Indians get everything on a silver platter, he echoed the prejudice he'd heard all of his life.

Those young guys are steady workers, he thought with a twinge of conscience, so unfamiliar it stunned him. Get over it! You know you don't give a damn about fair. Life's not fair.

Wrenching open the unlocked door to the enclosed cabin, the thief experienced serious misgivings. He didn't see the messy rat's nest he'd expected; the gear was neatly stowed, maps and charts were labeled and organized, communication equipment glowed with newness, even the small head, though crowded, was spotless.

Stop gawking, and dump the cash. He ripped a neat piece of duct tape off the seatback, found a jagged tear, pulled hands full of foam stuffing out, threw it overboard, and stuffed money in the gap. He sealed the slit with new tape liberated from a handy toolbox, stuffed the money bag back under his shirt, and fled the boat. Now I'll dump the body, he smirked, flinging open the trunk. I'll stash her under the pier. With luck she won't be found until the boats come back this afternoon. Abruptly the thief slammed the trunk, leapt into the driver's seat, gunned the engine, threw the car into gear, and heart pounding, raced along the rutted drive onto Lakeshore Road.

That was close, if the savage caught me messing around his boat he'd kill me. He flipped the headlights to bright, to blind the oncoming driver. Relief at his narrow escape was fleeting; the body was still in the trunk. He swerved to the shoulder, laid his aching head on the steering wheel, considered, and discarded options until he had a workable scheme. Act now, worry later. He turned down the winding dirt road to the reservation.

Baker's eyes scanned the starry sky, "Whatever was up there in the sky is gone."

"But, the radio station aired our sighting and invited others who saw it to call in," Jake responded, sharing the baker's enthusiasm. "We ought to hear their count tomorrow night or tonight," he corrected with a glance at his watch.

"It's time to get back to work," Baker said, "the dough should be ready and we should hustle because we'll be interrupted sometime tonight.

"Zack will come by, but you can't mean him, so who else are we expecting? Jake asked, not nosey, just wanting to be in the know.

"Remember I told you we always made an extra tray of cheese biscuits when Lucy worked here? And remember you said Ellie was collecting Lucy tonight?"

Jake nodded.

"Well if I know Lucy she'll insist Ellie stop in for cheese biscuits. They'll be here, she and Ellie," Baker teased grinning, "So you'll want to stay spiffed up Jake."

Jake took Baker's teasing good naturedly, "Guess I better start with the cheese biscuits then."

CHAPTER 6

When he spotted Ruby the thief swigged whiskey from the bottle and doused himself with the rest, then staggered around the Snack Shack.

Ruby muttered hasty goodbyes to the raucous group with whom she'd spent the evening, hiked up her hipsters and strolled to meet her sometimes boyfriend. "You're late and you stink of booze," she hauled him deep into shadows. "Where's the money? Come on give it here," she held out her hand. "I'll take it from here."

"I didn't do it. Your plan was way too risky."

"It wasn't risky. You turned to that for courage," she glared at the whiskey bottle clenched in his fist. "And you just blew it off, didn't you? You drunken jerk."

"Wait Ruby, it was so risky and I had a few, but I'm not drunk." He gripped her arm, "Shut up Ruby. The whole town will hear you! I told you I didn't do it."

"Who are you kidding, you liar. You're trying to cut me out."

"Honest Ruby, I'm not lying. I didn't do it, but I got a better way to get dough," the thief grimaced, bad choice of words. "You wait here and I'll get us some cash."

"What kind of sucker do you think I am? You ain't going no place without me. Not on your sneaking, lying life."

"Read my lips, I. Do. Not. Have. The. Money," he pulled her against his chest, and whispered, "We don't need the bakery money. I got my own bank."

Ruby snorted, "Yeah right, and I'm Mrs. Got-Rocks."

"Listen, I'm serious. Remember last year I worked for Sneed, Brown, and Fiskar, Attorneys at large?" the thief joked feebly. "Old man

Sneed's a moron. He used his kid's names for his password. It would have been a crime not to access his files."

"What the hell are you yakking about? Sneed is a tight-assed pillar of the community, you got nothing on him, but go ahead, lie some more." Ruby rolled her eyes, "We've got until the cop's raid the rave."

"You're right. Sneed is clean, but Ruby, somebody else isn't." Ruby sighed disgustedly, and he rushed on, "Derwood Day is robbing Betty Archer blind."

"That's news? Everybody knows that. Why else would a hunk marry the rich old bat?"

The thief dropped his bombshell, "That's the good part they're not married, not legally."

"This sounds like a soap opera, but keep talking," Ruby followed him through the dark streets.

"Let's go. You think you can walk and listen at the same time? A couple of days ago a tall blond came into the shop looking for her husband, she whipped out a wedding picture."

"So she had a wedding picture, so what?" Ruby asked, and followed him across the Smyth's close cropped lawn.

"Ruby shut up and listen; she called him Daniel, but the guy in the picture was Derwood Day."

"You're shitting me!"

"No I'm not, with that and what I got from Sneed's files, Derwood or Daniel is going to cut his losses and run real soon." The thief chuckled, "You gotta love a guy with that kind of guts."

"Yeah Jordan, trust you to admire a scumbag. So he's a bigamist. How does that help us?"

"Well he's scared I'll tell my dad. Being a cop's kid has its advantages," he led Ruby down Short Street, they stopped beneath a burned-out street lamp. "You be quiet and let me do the talking." They slunk across the road inched along a high, board fence; fought through Betty's award-winning, perennial bed, and slid along the front of the house to a low, bay window.

"Come on Ruby. It's---Show---Time." The thief dropped onto his hands and knees and crawled under the window.

"Maybe this isn't such a good idea," Ruby peeked over the sill into a sumptuous study. "I can't see anybody."

"Look again Ruby. He's home alright and his face is bloody, somebody beat the shit out of him. You still think he's a hunk?"

"We better go, he didn't beat himself up ya know." Ruby shivered, "He probably already called the cops."

"Go if you want, I'm not going. He's primed and ready."

"Get down!" Ruby hissed, "If he catches us we're in big trouble! You can hit the bakery tomorrow, there'll be even more money. Remember the baker can't make a deposit until Tuesday morning."

"I'm not going anywhere. Somebody softened him up for us, and the door's open that's gotta be a good sign."

"What if his old lady's here?"

"Get real, he'd be yelling, and beating on her if she was. The thief pulled Ruby toward the open front door.

Ruby shook him off, "I almost fell. Jerk!"

"Shush, listen, he's upstairs."

"I'm scared Jordan, what if he's waiting to jump out at us with an axe or something?"

"Come or don't come, I don't care," he bumped the door with his hip and tiptoed inside, "More for me."

"Wait, I'm not staying out here alone in the dark."

"Ruby," he beckoned from the study door, "the safe's open. I'll get the stuff; you find something to put it in."

"Use the bag I gave you."

"Just do what I tell you for a change." When she sees all this cash she'll forget the bag.

"I'm scared, let's go."

"Find us a bag and stop worrying." He turned her around and shoved her toward the hall.

Ruby plunked herself down on a heap of luggage next to the stairs. She plucked a duty free bag from the pile and threw it at him. "Use this."

Ruby's gasp alerted the thief who reluctantly tore his greedy eyes from the papers he perused; he could not make his hands release the banded bills.

Derwood rushed down the sweeping staircase, in his hand he clutched the decapitated bedpost that had recently, and unexpectedly, been used on him. "You put that back and get out!"

"Right old man, you gonna make me?" The thief flung the safe's contents onto the foyer's marble floor.

Derwood snarled, "I'm going to enjoy this," his stiff arm knocked Ruby flat. He stalked eagerly toward the more challenging intruder.

The cocky thief reached lazily to pluck the weapon from Derwood's unsteady hand. He slowly forced Derwood backward one step at a time. The fear he saw in Derwood's eyes gave him courage.

Ruby clung to the newel post; Derwood spun and with a vicious chop, knocked her flat again, he leapt over her and ran up the stairs.

Ruby picked herself up with the aid of the newel post; the thief stiff armed her out of his way. She yelped, he ignored her and charged after Derwood.

Derwood threw his body against the bedroom door, the thief unable to stop, rammed on through; Derwood off balance stumbled over the mangled bed's sorry remnants and fell flat on his back. The thief, also off balance, flung his hands out to break his fall. The cudgel he held bounced off Derwood's head and hit the floor; the sound reverberated through the house.

Ruby again used the newel post to haul her battered body upright, and spurred by the sounds from above scooped the cash into the duty free bag, and added the documents. The loud crack of cudgel hitting wood gave legs to the flee impulse she'd resisted since leaving the beach, and she took off running. She paused only to jam the overstuffed bag as far as possible under the Smyth's partially constructed deck. If Derwood didn't press charges, she could get it later, if he did, she'd never seen it. She joined her friends on the beach.

Derwood's eyes rolled back in his head.

"Ruby, get up here," the thief whispered. "Shit, he's not moving. What am I gonna do? Ruby! Where is that bitch? He peered over the balustrade, she's split and left me holding the, his thoughts slid—the bag! He flew down the stairs and gaped at the empty foyer.

She's gone, his bravado leaked away. He stalked into the gourmet kitchen where he'd often brought groceries for Betty, and usually liberated an extra ten or twenty from her cookie jar. He lifted the familiar lid and tucked the bills into his pocket. Retracing his steps, he carefully wiped everything he had touched, and just as carefully left Ruby's prints intact. He used the towel to open the French doors leading to the terrace, ran to the fence, wrapped the bedpost securely in the towel, and threw it into the woods. Then he ran home and, tired from his exertions, slept soundly. Later his father was relieved to find him safe in his bed.

Zack woke with a clear mind; his decision to cut back on the mind-bending drugs was the right one; he could endure pain in real time if it meant less nightmare episodes like that last one. People he'd known his whole life did not hide bodies in freezers. That was big city stuff and did not happen in Huron Shores.

Baker and Jake would be baking up a storm, the coffee hot and fresh the conversation feisty; exactly what he needed. He hit the large, red door-release button, dead center first try, Zack grinned, all was well, and what he saw was a nightmare, and nothing more. I wonder what the guys will make of my weird dream. Should I bill it as a vision or an apparition, both Jake and Baker are into that supernatural mumbo jumbo, but then maybe drug induced dreams don't count.

"It's feet," he hollered, stopping at the curb. "The rhyme goes:
Stop, look, and listen before you cross the street.
Use your eyes, use your ears before you use your feet."

His sister's familiar verse convinced him that he was awake and delirium free. "Now," his voice echoed in the night, "Stop feeling sorry for yourself and while you're at it, you might want to stop talking to yourself and awaiting an answer." He chuckled, "people will think I'm nuts." Inhaling deeply, he thumped into the bakery and yelled, "Where's my coffee?"

"Glad you finally got here," Baker said, grabbing Jake, and while both guys woofed and barked the melody of the Blue Danube, they waltzed to where Zack waited.

Zack laughed, "You two sure are lit up. What's all the excitement?"

"We saw a genuine unidentified flying object," Baker whooped. Zack looked disbelieving, "Scoff if you want, but we know what we saw."

Jake nodded vigorously, "We called it in to the radio station and . . ."

"And," Baker seized control of the story, "then we came down here and found a pronounced face print in my dough. It's a female face," he hypothesized. "Jake here, quick-froze it with the CO_2 from the fire extinguisher and made a model with that rapid-set plaster we keep for mock-up wedding cakes. So scoff now," the baker challenged breathlessly.

Zack, a mulishly-intractable, dedicated skeptic peered at the plaster cast, then at the depression in the air-dried yeast dough. Both were oddly compelling and eerie. Horrified, Zack thought I'm stuck in a nightmare.

"You okay buddy? You don't look so good, is that new 'script not working? I got just the thing. Jake, bring him a cup of coffee with some of that French Armagnac Lucy gave me last year." Baker gingerly felt Zack's forehead and found it ice cold, "That's what you need to perk you up."

"You're right Baker it must be the new meds." Zack wheeled out the bakery door and disappeared into the night.

"Never knew Zack to refuse a free spiked coffee," Baker said. "I thought he'd have all kinds of reasons why the face couldn't be a genuine paranormal phenomenon. I thought he'd say it was a prank," Baker placed a pan of perfect doughnuts into the proofer.

"And," Jake said sensibly, "it could be. Most of the kids whooping it up on the beach worked here and know your habits and your interest in the paranormal. Two of them could have pulled off this trick, they'd see it as a great practical joke," he examined the imprint, "if it is a hoax it's at least creative."

"I guess you're right," Baker said distractedly. "I'll go make sure Zack got home safe. You can do without me for a few minutes, can't you?"

"He was acting strange," Jake agreed, still studying the imprint, "You go ahead, I'll hold the fort."

Baker hurried across the back lot, the dumpster reminded him of the thump he and Jake heard earlier. Maybe it wasn't sugar addicted raccoons, but instead as Jake suspected, kids playing a practical joke. It'd be a darn shame if it was some elaborate prank. It'd be a lot more interesting if it was a real specter or at least remained unexplained.

Jake got a pail of the famous biscuit mix from the cooler. Baker prepared vast quantities of his formula, once or twice a week, according to demand, thus allowing anyone with minimal skill, like him, to add cold water and fruit or cheese for perfect biscuits every time.

Seeing Baker work was akin to watching a sculptor coax an image from stone. He loved his craft and in a time of thaw and bake bakeries, his hand made, always fresh products were unique.

Baker had a routine, or 'blueprint', Jake thought, unconsciously updating the baker's craft. He weighed all-purpose flour, added sugar, and milk powder, some ounces of baking powder and salt, finally mixing in room temperature shortening lard with dexterity and patience until, Jake shrugged; until it felt right. Explain 'feels right', Jake had asked with never a satisfactory answer.

He thought he remembered enough to duplicate Baker's flakey biscuits; biscuits so light that once baked, they needed secure storage lest they float away. Jake smiled at the fanciful direction his thoughts had taken. He scooped mix onto the antiquated scale, who would have thought I'd get such pleasure out of a few natural ingredients? Not the guys I climbed over or those who blithely scrambled over me to scale that legendary corporate ladder. None of them would believe how little it actually takes to make a guy happy. He shredded extra medium cheddar for the extra tray of cheese biscuits needed to hail Ellie's daughter's arrival. He anticipated with pleasure, meeting Lucy and serving her biscuits he'd prepared.

He wondered, while he worked, how much the flavor and texture would change if he substituted one third whole wheat flour, aged cheddar cheese and a few of the fresh herbs, thriving in his new garden patch.

'Don't mess with perfection' add the cheese and fold, (do not knead, fold) fifteen times, turn it one quarter after each fold to a total of fifteen folds. Then using the massive rolling pin that had belonged to the baker's father, he rolled and patted the dough into a large rectangle exactly one half inch thick. With a floured two inch cutter he cut and placed round after perfect round onto parchment covered trays until his final not so perfect mound-like bun was all that was left. That one, he'd taste to be certain of a quality equal to Baker's.

Jake carried the biscuits to the preheated oven, but quickly returned them to the bench, brushed them with beaten egg and put a smidgen of cheese on top. He set the timer by rote, while his mind strayed to his new life in Huron Shores, a life encompassing comfortable friendships, a flexible time clock, and peace. "As little as ten years ago, if anyone said I'd be doing this I'd have laughed," Jake lopped off a hunk of rested dough, what was the catalyst? "Definitely losing my wife unbelievably fast had started it." He rolled the dough for cinnamon buns. "The young talent pushed me out, and I didn't care enough to fight. Why did we join the rat race in the first place? Did we need the huge house, the new cars the club memberships we were too busy to use? Money and possessions didn't save Mary, nor did they provide us time together."

He gently flattened the dough imitating, he hoped, Baker's method. Generously brushing melted butter on the rolled slab, his thoughts turned to Zack, Baker should be back. Zack must be really troubled. Jake spread brown sugar over the butter and scattered raisins over that, then liberally sprinkled cinnamon over all, finally he rolled it, jelly roll style then sliced the roll into ¾ inch pieces, he settled the rounds close, cozy but not intimate, as the baker always joked. Jake wondered how cozy things that looked like wagon wheels needed to be.

Baker returned as Jake took the first batch of trays from the proofer, "Sorry I was gone so long."

"Don't apologize for being a good friend."

"Good man," Baker said surveying Jake's efforts while he surreptitiously checked the timers.

Jake accepted Bakers praise with a smile, "How's Zack?"

"We talked a while, but not about what's bothering him." Baker tested the fryer temperature. "I tried to get him to talk about it, but he wouldn't. Said he needs to get his mind around it before he shares," he slide donuts into the hot oil. "Oh, I almost forgot, I saw Lucy in Betty's study. Since Ellie won't let Lucy out alone on her first night home, Derwood won't be knocking Betty around tonight."

Jake shared Baker's relief, as he made tray after tray of perfect muffins.

Baker teased, "You might as well go on home Jake, looks like the ladies aren't coming."

"To be honest Baker, after doing all of your work, I'd better shower before I see anybody."

"You're not getting all reticent and shy on me, are you?"

"Never happen," Jake said, "You need me to pick anything up for tomorrow?"

"Check the list. The kids ran out of some stuff. They wrote it down, I hope."

"Yeah," Jake confirmed scanning the long list, "they need supplies alright."

"Wait, I'll give you some money."

"Never mind, pay me when I give you the receipts."

"No, let me get the money for you now," Baker insisted. "Jake!" he bellowed, "Come here!"

The drawer that held the weekend's receipts, hung out from the desk like a panting tongue. The unlocked strong box yawned open and empty.

"That was the best weekend we ever had," Baker whispered dropping onto the chair.

"We better not touch anything," Jake cautioned, he scanned the scene, there may be fingerprints."

"Who could have done this?" Baker asked. "Forty years, I've been here. Forty years without a robbery. Jake, who would steal from me," his eyes begged for an explanation he could accept.

"Come upstairs Baker," Jake urged, he knew that Baker's unshakable trust in his fellow man had taken a potent blow.

"I'll lock up and call Eric Platt; he'll take care of it."

"I've got to answer that call," Chief Eric Platt alluded to a burst of incomprehensible static issuing from his radio. "Betty I'll take you home now, okay?"

Betty nodded.

"I'll let you out at the corner and watch 'til you get to your gate," he offered, knowing Betty would get flack from Derwood if he saw them together.

CHAPTER 7

Her feet dragging, Betty plodded the half block to the house where a man, obscured by murky darkness, waited on the porch swing. She fought an impulse to run away and resolutely forged ahead. She had to face Derwood, and now was as good a time as any. She waved to tell Eric she was home, and went to meet her fate.

She paused to ask God for courage, and chin up, shoulders straight marched to the veranda.

"Michael?" Betty gasped her relief palpable. They exchanged hugs, "What are you doing out here so late?"

"I wanted to be here when you arrived, did I get the time wrong?" Michael asked, looking questioningly at his business partner's empty hands, "Where's your luggage, and why are you walking?"

"I arrived early and went for a walk."

"Then you've seen it?" Michael smiled, "the bed I mean. Don't you just love it? It's wonderful, perfect in your room and best of all," he paused, drawing out the suspense, "the mattress came early. It's at the store," he announced, with a sweeping flourish, his face alight with pleasure.

"That's . . . great," Betty whispered.

"What's wrong? I thought you'd be pleased."

"Of course I'm pleased, but I haven't seen the bed yet," she stammered, the lie rough on her tongue. "Michael, I can never fool you can I?" she shrugged, "The truth is simple. Derwood was unpleasant when I arrived, so I went for a walk and I've decided to divorce him."

"Hooray!" Michael grinned, "I'd say that's the best news I've heard this year, or this decade. Let's throw the bum out. Strike when the irons hot."

Betty eyed her partner's slim, fine boned physique, and then looked down at her own short, slightly plump figure; together they couldn't match Derwood's strength. "Thank you Michael, but I think I'll talk to my attorney first."

"Okay if you insist," Michael said grudgingly, "but right after that we toss him out. I'll call Fraser of the Royal Canadian Mounted Police and his faithful wolf Diefenbaker, first thing in the morning. I hear the Mounties always get *rid* of their man, right?" he joked. "So I'll stay with you tonight and go with you to the lawyer first thing in the morning. Or, even better, you stay with me tonight."

"I'll be fine," Betty insisted. "I need a little time alone to plan."

Michael shook his head, "That is not a good idea."

"Please go," she pleaded, "I know him, he will have calmed down and be full of remorse. And if he hurts you I will never forgive myself."

"If he is troublesome I'll call, I promise."

"I still don't like it." Michael snarled, "Use the downstairs guest room, your dyslexic decorator has ruined all the rest."

"Goodnight Michael," Betty squeezed his hand, "thank you for your support."

"I'll be back as soon as it's light."

"Till tomorrow then." Betty watched him stroll out of sight before collapsing to the porch swing. How am I going to tell Michael and Lucy about the bed? They will kill Derwood for ruining it.

Her new found courage firmly in place, Betty searched for the key she kept in her favorite antique brass urn, the urn Derwood relegated to the open porch. When she touched key to lock the door swung wide. Derwood always locks the doors when I run. Shoes in hand she crept silently through the foyer and started up the stairs. She stopped abruptly, put her shoes on, and finished the climb. Old habits die hard she thought, and was comforted by the cliché.

Is Derwood hiding behind the door? He likes to catch and *punish* me for defying him. Nice turn of phrase Betty thought wryly. Thumping him several times with a chunk of wood might be a little more serious than defying. Fear knotted her stomach, her head ached, her bowels threatened to empty; I am an adult woman and I will damn well act like one. Tomorrow I will have him removed from my home. Tomorrow I will start divorce proceedings. Tomorrow I will get a restraining order and the police if necessary. And it will be necessary clanged in her mind like the bell on St. Peters church. She hesitated in front of her bedroom door forced her hand to turn the knob; saw Derwood and knew her life was over.

He lay sprawled amid the refuse that only yesterday was her cherished bed. Betty approached warily, Derwood often played possum until she was close enough to grab. This time he won't stop at black eyes and dislocated shoulders. Betty poked his hand with a handy piece of her mutilated bed. Reluctantly she laid her fingers against his neck. Derwood's dead eyes glared at her reproachfully.

Betty swayed and fell to her knees; she crawled out of the room, her new found strength gone. "I killed him," she said, tears coursed silently down her cheeks while she prayed for guidance.

Lucy rewound the tape in grandma's legacy, antiquated answering machine.

"That can wait for morning," Ellie said. "It will be James. I've been a little cavalier about deadlines lately."

"Might as well get it over with," Lucy pushed the button prepared for a harangue; instead she heard Aunt Betty's anguished voice.

"Ellie, I need you. Please hurry. I'm at the house."

"I'm coming Betty," Ellie called into the machine. "That filthy swine has beaten her again," Ellie fumed. She pried the keys from Lucy's fist.

"Mom stop, I'll drive. We want to get there alive."

"We have to hurry." Ellie remembered Betty at the clinic, her right shoulder dislocated, her eye blackened and new bruises caused by Derwood's fists purpling over yellowed older welts. *He* had the temerity to follow with a specious explanation for each injury he'd inflicted. The liar left when I accused him, but waited outside to threaten me. Zack heard and saw everything. Betty was mortified and left the next day. She's home and *he's* hurt her again.

Ellie jittered, seethed, and worried while Lucy piloted the powerful Lincoln through sleepy streets.

"Betty! Betty," Ellie shouted, leaping out before the vehicle stopped.

"Mom, wait for me," Lucy yelled, forced the shift into park, stomped the emergency brake, and dashed after her mother.

"Mom, Lucy panted, snagging the back of Ellie's jacket, "Wait! We have to be careful. He's dangerous."

"All the more reason to hurry. Betty!" Ellie shouted.

"I'm up here."

Lucy followed Ellie's headlong rush up the serpentine staircase, and slammed into her mother's stalled figure, driving them into Betty's ruined bedroom.

All the scenarios she'd envisioned could not prepare Lucy for what she saw, Aunt Betty, petite, pretty, and incoherent, sat next to Dreadful Derwood's motionless body.

"It will be alright," Ellie said irrationally, and pulled Betty upright, hugged her, and while murmuring inanities led her through the shambles and into Lucy's waiting arms.

"Take her downstairs."

"What about *him*? Lucy said, pointing the appropriate finger at Derwood.

"Not now Lucy. Betty needs us."

Ellie urged Betty onto an overstuffed loveseat, "Can you tell us what happened?"

Betty sat quaking, but silent. Ellie wrapped her in a crocheted afghan. "Lucy, she's in shock. Please put the kettle on for tea and then call the doctor and the police."

"No!" Betty said vehemently. "No doctor! No police!"

"We have to call a doctor," Lucy insisted.

"It's too late, he's dead. I killed him."

"You killed him?" Lucy sputtered. "That's like saying Little Red Riding Hood ate the wolf. Pussycats like you don't kill rabid skunks like him."

"But, I did," Betty said with a certainty that defied argument.

"We, I mean I need something stronger than tea," Lucy said and poured two generous goblets of Amrut Sherry. This Sherry must be left from Uncle Robert's stock; *Derwood* wouldn't know fine wine if he drowned in it. She poured a large tumbler of scotch for herself. Yuck, a cheap blended scotch; depend on Dreadful Derwood to stock inferior booze.

Ellie with her arms around her silent friend, waited patiently.

"I'm not sorry he's dead," Betty whispered.

"I'm not either," Ellie murmured. "How can we help?"

"Help me get *him* in the car. I'll hide *him*," Betty said vaguely, "somewhere."

"Are you two stark raving mad? You can't hide a body, we aren't even sure he's dead." Lucy dragged her mother out of ear shot and whispered, "Mom we have to call the authorities."

"Then what," Ellie demanded. "Betty goes to jail for killing the serpent that beat her, robbed her, spread vicious lies about her, and he did all this while swindling everyone in town."

Lucy's mouth hung open, "How do you know all of this Mother?"

"This is a small town. Everybody knows."

"Okay," Lucy sighed, "let's suppose we help Auntie lose the body, how do we do it and not get caught? This, as you so astutely noted, is a small town."

"Let's get back to Betty. She shouldn't be alone." Ellie wrung her hands, a worry sign Lucy shared and understood.

Betty slammed her empty glass onto the coffee table. She stood, shook her head, and straitened her spine, "What am I doing, involving you in my crime. Go home, forget you were here. I'll call Eric when you're gone."

"Let's think about it," Lucy said while she paced, belying the calm she tried to project. "Nobody should go to jail for doing this town a public service. You make tea. I'll take another look at the . . . room." She climbed, placing one foot on a step and then slowly dragging the other up to sit exactly aligned to its mate, as a small child climbs stairs, thus she disassociated herself from what she was about see and do.

Lucy's heart pounded like a butcher's mallet. Derwood's battered head nestled obscenely amid the remains of Betty's ancient Renaissance bed.

Lucy the artist was affronted by the mess Derwood made of Betty's formerly beautiful room, while her saner self saw a sequence of poignant scenes. Betty bringing injured wild animals, abandoned dogs and cats, a motherless fawn, and a tortoise that lost an argument with a car, to Uncle Rodney. Each creature artfully bandaged, with scads of provisions, meticulously researched and purchased without Derwood's approval.

Why would Derwood marry and abuse a woman, incapable of causing harm to any living thing, including, until now--- him?

Ignoring Derwood's open eyed glare; Lucy felt for a pulse. Rigor mortis hasn't started. Rigor sets in three to four hours after death, she remembered Valerie, a mortician's daughter saying in reference to a carefully contrived college prank. It lasts for several hours and is complete within twelve hours, depending on the conditions, temperature, et cetera, et cetera, et cetera.

Grateful for gratuitous information dispensed by old friends, Lucy brought out her Blackberry and snapped several quick photos and then decisively closed the door. If Betty did the damage to Derwood that Lucy saw, it was justified, and she should be seen as a heroic righter of wrongs, and deified not crucified.

We need a plan and it better be a good one or we'll all end up living off the government's largesse, wearing those awful orange jumpsuits and none of us wear orange well, Lucy thought facetiously. Pull yourself together, she ordered. Those two defenseless women are depending on you for strength and sense. Find some!

"Where shall we put him?" Ellie asked between sips of tea.

"I've thought this out," Betty, organizational skills in place, said. "The car is in the garage. We'll put him in the trunk; I will drive him somewhere and drop him off." She spoke calmly as if she were about to leave her dead husband at the bus stop.

"Okay ladies," Lucy interrupted, "if you have a plan, we need to get busy before *he* uh stiffens," she said as delicately as possible.

"Oh my, you mean before rigor sets in, don't you dear?"

"Yes," Lucy said edging toward Derwood's inferior scotch.

"Lucy!" Ellie admonished.

"Well, how does she know that?" Lucy whimpered.

"Murder mystery novels, dear," Betty piped up.

Lucy sighed, an extended exasperated sigh. "When rigor sets in, he'll be more difficult to stuff, I mean situate in the trunk. We'll need something to wrap him in, a tarp maybe. No wait, we'll use the blankets from his bed, they have his hair and dead skin, and nasty stuff already embedded, but plastic would be better to prevent uh leakage."

"Lucy," Ellie asked, exercising her mother voice, "you haven't done this before, have you?"

"Of course I haven't. I'm just trying to think of everything, Aunt Betty do you have a plastic leaf bag, one of those really big ones?"

Betty scurried through the kitchen to the garage and soon returned with the requested bag and three pair of florescent pink, plastic, kitchen gloves.

We look like a female version of 'The Three Stooges,' Lucy thought as she, her mother, and aunt crept up the stairs.

Lucy groaned. "It's a leaf bag alright," she spread the enormous, orange bag with its gigantic, smiling pumpkin face next to Dreadful Derwood.

Betty and Ellie, overtaken by fits of hysterical laughter held each other up.

Damping an almost uncontrollable urge to join them, Lucy glared, "Don't suppose you could give me a hand here?"

"Sorry Lucy," Ellie sobered, and knelt beside Derwood's boots. Betty obediently took up a position near his belt, leaving Lucy to handle his bloody head and battered shoulders.

"On the count of three," Lucy directed, "roll him onto the bag, one, two, three, push!" Derwood cooperative in death, as he'd never been in life, flopped over to lay face down. "He's a tight fit," Lucy grunted, wrapping the bag around him.

Betty fetched a roll of silvery duct tape from her bedside table, "Use this to fasten it."

Do I really want to know? No! Lucy's mind screamed as she accepted the tape.

"Derwood wears orange very well. How appropriate is that." Lucy said, using humor to escape reality. "Now comes the hard part. We have to get him downstairs and into the trunk and dump him in a dumpster, or maybe we could just drop him beside one."

"Oh no Lucy I couldn't just leave him like that," Betty objected.

"Why not, he was trash alive and he's still trash dead." Lucy struggled with the head end of the bag, while Ellie and Betty each fought with a leg. Together they bumped and bounced their gruesome bundle down the stairs, the plastic pumpkin face continued to smile bright and cheery as if delighted to shroud Derwood.

Maybe it understands the appropriateness of Derwood in a trash bag, Lucy thought factiously, as they hauled the macabre bundle across the foyer, through the kitchen, and into the garage.

"This is thirsty work perhaps you could make some tea, Betty," Ellie said, and closed the door with Betty on the other side.

Lucy sat on the bumper next to the open trunk, "Is this real Mom?"

"I'm afraid it is," Ellie whispered. "Once *he* is settled in the trunk we can decide what to do with *him*."

"Ellie, Lucy, come see who dropped by," Betty's flustered cry urged haste. "Officer Platt, Lucy is home for the holidays."

Lucy eased the trunk lid down until it clicked.

"Hello Eric," Ellie rushed to greet her old friend. "Look who I brought to see Betty." She tugged Lucy from behind the sheltering kitchen door

"Hi there Officer Platt," Lucy said brightly. "What are you doing out at this time of the morning?"

"Just checking," he stalled; "There's been a robbery over at the bakery. I just thought Betty should make sure the house is secure."

"We're having a girl's night, and I'm fine now. Thank you so much for dropping by." Betty almost pushed Eric through the door.

"We were just about to make fresh tea," Lucy said. "Would you like a cup?"

"I'd love one, but I've got to go down to the beach. The bakery thief is probably hanging around down there, full of himself, bragging about his windfall."

"Baker must be devastated. You'd better go catch the culprit and recover the money," Betty said inanely. "Goodnight Eric, don't let us keep you."

"Glad to see you're well," Eric said straining to see past Ellie and Lucy. "Call if you need help . . . any kind of help."

"Thank you Eric, but I'm fine now that my girl friends are here."

"Goodnight ladies. Don't forget to lock up." Eric hustled down the path to his patrol car.

Betty sagged against the door.

"Don't you dare faint," Lucy snapped, "and lock that damn door! The package is safely in the trunk."

"Maybe I could leave him there and move," Betty tittered.

"Or put the car in the yard and plant petunias in it," Lucy sniggered.

"This is not a laughing matter," Ellie chastised, quashing an uneasy chuckle.

"Mom's right, what happened to the bed?"

Betty fought tears. "He destroyed the bed and he was awful," she drew a large rumpled handkerchief from her pocket. "He was laughing, and contemptible. I didn't mean to hurt him, I just wanted him to stop taunting me and demeaning Robert's memory, I hit him and hit him and then I ran away. I knew he would . . . well, Ellie you know what he was like." Betty drew a deep, breath and continued, "I walked out the door and kept going. I saw Baker and Jake, but it must have been before the robbery because they weren't upset," she paused twisting the stained handkerchief. "I knew I knocked *him* down. I didn't know I k...k... killed him!"

Ellie soothed her with a hug. "Go on."

Betty sniffled, "Eric came along. He knows about Derwood's violence now. I guess everyone does. He, Eric, I mean, comforted me and brought me home."

Oh great! Lucy thought. How are we supposed to get her, Aunt Betty, she reminded herself, out of this mess. "Let's get out of here," she said and pushed Betty's small suitcase at Ellie. Visions of Harv's rippling muscles came to mind, as she lashed Betty's heavy bags together and laboriously towed them to the car.

Ellie fastened the seatbelt around Betty, whose manner was now reminiscent of a marionette with no will of its own. "Lucy will follow us in your car Betty. You will feel better when you're settled."

CHAPTER 8

"I'm going to shower, and when you two are snug and cozy in bed, I'll bring you hot chocolate." Lucy held Betty's arm while her mother searched her cavernous purse for the house key. "I'll make the guestroom bed?" Lucy asked, eager to have her mother and aunt settled so she could revisit the crime scene.

"Thank you dear, but I'll keep Betty with me tonight. It will be like old times," Ellie explained. "We would beg our parents to let us have sleepovers, and inevitably we slept in the same bed and whispered together all night," Ellie reminisced. "Remember Betty?"

"I wonder who my cellmate will be," Betty said, sinking onto the rocking chair next to the old-fashioned stove.

Lucy gently tugged Betty toward the stairs, "You need to sleep. There is no prison in your future. I want you around for my wedding. I've met the perfect man. The only fly in the ointment is mom, she hates him, but don't worry, I'll bring her around," Lucy chattered. "I want the kind of wedding you and Uncle Robert had, that way I know we'll be as happy as you," she winced . . . "were," Lucy said, and promised herself a good swift kick.

Betty hugged Lucy, "You've finally met the right one? That's wonderful. I've had the color scheme for your wedding planned since the day you were born," Betty enthused, then sobered, and whispered, "I hope I'll be there."

Lucy, fresh out of encouraging words, welcomed Ellie's arrival.

Ellie mouthed, "Honey, never mind the cocoa."

Released, Lucy raced down the hall.

While she stood in the old claw-foot bathtub basking under a spray of deliciously hot water, Lucy fumbled for a feasible plan to deal with

Derwood, better to think of him as *the body* or *it*, she decided, while the water soothed away tiredness.

Tomorrow night we'll toss *it* in the lake, and be rid of *it*. But it's Derwood the windbag, and it'll hover like a fishing float. She giggled at the morbid image of Derwood clothed in red and white stripes, gently undulating in the waves, amusing maybe, but impractical.

What if we sat *him* on a rock deep in the woods? If we're lucky bears will eat him before *he*'s discovered; she adjusted the old shower curtain that let out more water than it contained. But those old logging roads are virtually impassable and anyway the animals would probably get sick since Derwood was a rabid little man.

We could drop *him*, not him, *it*, off in a seedy part of the city. They've got lots of bodies and probably wouldn't mind another one; she rinsed aromatic herbal shampoo from her long, blond hair. But we don't want their trash so it's not fair to leave them ours.

Trash now there's an idea. Put him in the landfill. I can use the bulldozer to push garbage over it. How hard can driving a bulldozer be? Bad idea, if Aunt Betty won't go for a dumpster drop an actual dump won't work either. Ridding ourselves of a hundred and eighty pounds of Dreadful Derwood isn't going to be easy.

Lucy braided her wet hair, pulled fresh clothing over her damp body, and slipped silently down the hall.

She heard hushed voices coming from Ellie's room and paused to listen.

"I hate to involve Lucy, she's such a sensitive child," Betty lamented.

"Are you talking about my Lucy?" Ellie asked. "She's artistic, perceptive, capable maybe even levelheaded, but not sensitive. However she will be hurt if we exclude her. And besides we cannot hide the body without her help."

"You're right Ellie, but, it's not fair to spoil the child's vacation." Lucy heard a deep sigh, "Should we hide *him?* Don't I have to file a missing person report if he's just not there tomorrow?" Another sigh. "But its Lucy I'm worried about, she's so young and innocent."

"I told you Betty, she'd be hurt if we excluded her."

Lucy rolled her eyes and tiptoed down the stairs, retrieved car keys from a hook in the cupboard; reconsidered and took both sets, just in case Betty forgot the package in the trunk.

She parked the town car on the grassy verge behind Betty's property. Saw signs of false dawn and hurriedly skirted the natural area, picked her way through gardens thick with perennials, and slipped through the French doors into Betty's kitchen, and up the familiar stairs.

How did Aunt Betty, a four foot eleven, and three quarter inch, forty nine year old woman kill an abusive hundred and eighty pound husband who worked out and not even break a nail? Lucy closed her eyes and tried to picture the room as she'd first seen it complete with dead Derwood's corpse.

After a frustrated moment she opened her eyes, saw the room, and was angry all over again, "For this alone he deserves to rot in hell." She saw walls painted eye-assaulting red, handcrafted, ancient furniture splashed with thick blobs of lacquer, the high beamed ceiling sported a smeared coat of lilac paint. As Lucy picked her way through the forlorn remnants of Renaissance splendor defaced cherubs huddled amidst the debris peered up at her, "You I will save," Lucy promised. She wrapped each angel in a soft blanket retrieved from an early American cedar chest, now a ghastly orange mess.

Lucy wrinkled her nose in distaste, and almost missed the handprint on one door in a row of seven identical doors. The bathroom door, she jiggled it open carefully avoiding the bloody palm print, she edged around a mound of sodden towels, and piles of soggy cotton swabs to the blood stained sink. Aunt Betty did not kill Derwood; he was alive to clean his wounds so her blows didn't kill him; at least not immediately.

The marble counter held a jumbled mass of salves, bandages, cotton, gauze, and incongruously, make up, which proved Derwood was alive after Betty fled. Lucy used her phone to photograph the bathroom, firmly closed the door, and her mind awhirl, recorded every inch of the vandalized bedroom. "Ain't technology grand," she snickered using humor to lessen horror. Lucy hesitated, something didn't add up, but what? It'll come later she thought on her way to the study. She shrugged tiredly; I'll show the pix to Mom, with a fresh eye she'll find what I missed.

Lucy found rusty spots on the hardwood floor, more proof. Derwood was downstairs after Aunt Betty left. The safe stood open and empty except for a paper bag. Lucy gently teased the bag open. Why would Derwood keep a dirty wineglass in the safe and why is the goblet the only item in the safe? Betty had stocks and bonds, even if he sold them and all of her jewelry, he would have had scads of cash in the safe. *He* was a secretive guy with sins to hide, so why an open empty safe? And how do blood spots and a dirty glass tie in to *his death*?

Too weary to think strait Lucy threw her arms wide and knocked a full goblet off an occasional table to shatter on the hardwood floor. Talk about messing up evidence, but wait there's another glass. Who other than Aunt Betty and the safe cracker were here? He wouldn't have prepared cocktails for wife or thief so who did he entertain while Betty was away?

My mind is like molasses. I guess that's why the police have investigators for this sort of thing; she ignored the broken glass, and shifted her attention to the desk she still thought of as Uncle Robert's.

Liberating a nail file from a maltreated Spode, dollar pattern saucer Derwood cavalierly used for odds and ends, she blessed the schoolmate who'd taught her lock picking. Never know when a skill will come in handy. She smirked, slid the large center drawer open, and found Derwood's laptop computer. She put it and all the checkbooks, stubs, bank statements and as an afterthought the paper bag from the safe into a black leather carrier she found under the desk.

Straightening her back she spied the last gift from Uncle Robert to Aunt Betty before his heart attack. Why would Aunt Betty reframe it? Lucy distinctly remembered Betty waxing poetic about how the dark, wooden frame was so like the desk it might have come from the same tree. Undoubtedly Dreadful Derwood's work; only a cretin would frame a Flemish Masterpiece in steel.

"It's a damn fake!" Trusty pen light in hand Lucy toured the house. Uncle Robert's carefully amassed originals were gone, replaced with mediocre reproductions. How did Derwood get away with it? Why didn't Aunt Betty notice? Dumb question, *he* made her life so miserable she stayed away.

Juggling the cherubs and Derwood's computer bag, she left the house, carefully locking the French doors. So what did I learn? She pondered while stumbling through a patch of hacked off foxglove. Derwood, the wife beating art thief was alive when Aunt Betty ran out. An unknown individual entered the house with robbery in mind. Derwood interrupted that person, and what? They had cocktails? Yeah right and then Derwood obligingly carted himself back upstairs and died where Aunt Betty left him. Or, a darker part of her mind supplied, Aunt Betty returned, set the study up to look like a robbery had occurred, found Derwood upstairs treating his injures and finished him off. Lucy frowned, as unlikely as her last scenario was it had to be considered since it was the more plausible of the two, however painful, she added weaving her way through dewy gardens.

Lucy climbed onto a pile of firewood and over the fence, an easier feat when she was ten, found the tree shaded path and hurried along until she landed face down on a pile of musty mulch. She sat for a moment rubbing her ankle, then pawed through leafy debris to retrieve the purloined computer bag, the cherubs in their protective wrap, her still shining penlight, and the section of Renaissance bedpost she'd tripped over. This is what I missed; there weren't enough pieces to reconstruct the bed. This chunk of polished wood will exonerate Aunt Betty, because she couldn't have thrown a chunk this size this far. And she hasn't been in these woods since Uncle Robert contacted poison ivy. The memory of her uncle swathed in foul-smelling poultices supplied by grandma brought a smile. That memory when combined with this proof of Aunt Betty's probable innocence was worthy of a smile. But I can't leave it here. What can I do with it? She flashed her light on the tree where she'd hidden letters to her dad after he was lost to the lake. Her nine year old self knew he'd read them and leave her an answer. She hobbled to the lightening-blasted tree and used the blue and white cloth she found on the path to stuff the bedpost deep into the cleft, added the paper bag encased glass from Derwood's safe, and was wryly amused to see tattered remnants of her letters. "Take care of this for me dad, I think it's important."

Brad kicked off his running shoes, flicked off the porch light, and closed the door. "I'll never get used to the silence." Crouching, he patted Foster. "Poor old guy, you don't like it much either do you boy?" He ruffled the dog's ears.

Before there'd always been sound, all the sounds associated with a large, vibrant family busy with life. Then the accident, he sank onto a straight backed chair only to hear his mother's voice, scold, 'Don't you sit your dirty butt down at my table until you've had a shower, hurry up dinners ready.'

Brad smiled sadly. There would be no more lovingly prepared meals, no familiar face eager to hear about his day's bumps and triumphs, no more boisterous family gatherings, no more anything. The things he'd taken for granted, all gone, eradicated by a drunk driver in less than the time it took to feed Foster.

It should have been a festive time, the parties planned, the wedding food prepared; the entire excited family, all except him going to the airport to meet his sister Nancy and her fiancé. A drunken teenager passed five cars and Dad had hit the ditch to avoid a head-on collision. It was so like Dad to avoid trouble, Brad thought.

"At least I still have you," he muttered, automatically scratching Foster's ears. The ancient dog whined as if its animal thoughts paralleled Brads own. "Come on mutt, let's get your breakfast."

He filled the dog's dish with soft, senior-friendly food, and returned the remainder to his empty refrigerator. It was never so bare when momma was alive. The day of the accident the fridge had groaned with dishes intended for the wedding. That food, prepared for celebration had ironically become funeral fare.

"I know it's too late for dinner and too early for breakfast," Brad spoke softly to his puzzled dog, "but you've had time to get used to the new schedule and the doctor says this shoulder will be fit in another week or two. Then you'll miss me. I won't just be running the guys to the boat, I'll be back out there with them," he said smiling at the dog's wrinkled brow. "Don't worry, Stan's a good first mate, he'll find the fish." The boat had been his father's dream, and he'd used the insurance money to buy it, Brad thought sadly.

"I should be frying eggs, not standing around wallowing in self-pity," Brad told Foster what he needed to hear.

Nothing in the refrigerator tempted Brad enough to cook it and quiet his grumbling stomach. I'll call Jake. He likes to breakfast at Darcy's Diner, the thought cheered him. An unexpected friendship had grown between him and Jake. They'd started talking in the bakery shortly after Jake came to Huron Shores. He'd opened up to the older man as he hadn't to anyone else; he'd cried for the first time since the accident and the tears had cemented their friendship. Now when Brad's personal phantoms haunted him he called Jake who let him talk and listened, never offered advice, he just patiently listened.

When Jake didn't answer his home phone Brad dialed the bakery, "Good morning Jake. I thought you'd have been home by now. Do you want to meet me for breakfast at Darcy's, my treat?"

"The police are here Brad; somebody robbed the bakery last night. We can't leave until the police finish with us, so it may take a while. I'll drag Baker along if that's okay."

"Sure that'd be great," Brad replied, "You guys are alright aren't you?"

"We're fine. I was going to call you, I'm having my house painted and I wondered if you'd put me up for a few days."

"My guest room is always open to you Jake; I'll pick you up in thirty minutes or so."

"Okay, see you then," Jake said hanging up the phone. "You won't need us for more than half an hour will you Eric?"

"I have a few more questions," Officer Platt replied checking his small black notebook. "Then I'll interview the staff as they come in, but you two don't need to be here for that."

"Ruby will be here at seven, she knows the schedule." Jake handed him the employee list, "Or use this."

"It wasn't one of my girls," the baker muttered.

"Baker you know everybody's a suspect in this kind of thing, even Jake here," Chief Platt explained beckoning Jake closer. "Where were you last evening anyway?"

"He was with me all night and he wouldn't steal!"

"That's not exactly accurate. The being together all night part I mean, but he's right when he said I don't steal," Jake clarified and when Eric's cop-stare intensified, he explained. "Baker was out for about forty five minutes visiting Zack just before we discovered the robbery so I guess that makes me a suspect."

"It does," Eric stated.

"Wait a rock picking minute," Baker challenged, "Jake worked the whole time I was gone. Look at that," he pointed to racks resplendent with biscuits, donuts, Chelsea rolls, and muffins. "Jake made all those while I was gone. You crazy bugger you're looking at the wrong guy."

"It's okay Baker, Eric is just doing his job and if you think about it from his point of view, I am an outsider and I could have taken the money, hidden it and be at this very moment planning to recover it and run off to Europe to open a secret Swiss bank account with the proceeds of my nefarious act."

Eric smiled; Jake had opportunity, and knew where the money was kept, but he was not a likely suspect.

"Jake, is that Indian waiting for you?" Eric snapped when a rusty pickup disgorged its lone occupant.

Jake bristled, "Yes officer, Brad Talltree is my friend."

"Uh huh," Eric grunted. I'll check Jake and his little friend out very carefully. It was a well known fact, that Indians, like gypsies, would steal anything that wasn't nailed down. His son, Jordan saw Brad steal money when they were together in High school, once a thief always a thief. "Go but come right back."

"Brad is here to treat Baker and me to breakfast," Jake said. "We'll be back when we get here."

CHAPTER 9

Ellie abandoned the relaxation techniques she relied on and opened her eyes; she slipped out of bed envious of Betty's soft snores. She shoved Derwood's death from her mind, and replaced it with thoughts of hot coffee, warm showers and the recipe trials for her autumn casserole column.

Drawn by the energizing aroma of dark roast Brazilian coffee, she rushed through her morning ministrations and filled her mug, thankful for automatic coffee makers and daughters who insisted on them. Then, rocking gently to and fro in her mother's old rocker, she scrutinized her daily planner that made Lucy, an advocate of everything electronic, laugh.

Today she'd make Lucy's rabbit stew and test her ideas for substituting poultry. She sipped coffee while she compared the herbs and vegetables she'd change in the more subtle flavored chicken version.

Rodney, Ellie's brother-in-law was coming, and Michael, Betty's business partner was a regular, Zack, hopefully to tell what worried him, Jake, Baker and his lady-friend Katherine, Lucy, and of course Brad. Because Michael had responsibility for the store she'd have to be sure to put aside a serving of each dish as well as a substantial piece of raisin pie. He'd grumble if he missed his much-loved favorite.

Ellie trekked back upstairs, a cup of coffee for Lucy in hand. When a light tap on the door elicited no response she called softly, listened, and then alarmed, pushed the door open and flicked on the bright overhead light.

All too familiar with the look of a bed deliberately mussed to appear slept in Ellie checked for the note she knew would be there. A scrap of a note paper was pinned to the pillow.

MOM - GONE TO CHECK DOORS LOCKED–AUNT BETTY'S LUVYA - L

All in capital letters, with no consideration given to syntax, punctuation, flow or spelling. Ellie shook her head and pocketed the note to add to all the others carefully saved along with report cards and conduct evaluations. Someday they might spare her much anticipated, similarly precocious grandchild grief. Ellie's smile evaporated, stripped away by visions of Lucy alone in that gruesome bedroom.

She peeked in on Betty and removed the clothing she'd worn, added it to the dry cleaner pick up box, and marched back to the kitchen where she, like her mother and her grannies before her, worried best. Ellie knew her daughter and Lucy, dissatisfied with Betty's version would need to know the exact sequence of events.

She sank into the rocking chair, but quickly hopped up as the words embroidered on a sampler hanging where she or any other soul, slothful enough to want a sit-down couldn't miss it. 'Idle hands are the devil's tools,' glared at her. Was that her mother's work or the incessant nagging of some earlier ancestor? Whoever, the effect, Ellie decided as she assembled the ingredients for the casseroles, was the same.

With kitchen shears she snipped a half pound of smoky bacon into inch long pieces and set it to gently sauté in a high-sided skillet. As the bacon began to sizzle, she sharpened her knife and quartered the rabbit. Absently adding the sections to the pan, she wondered how a petite woman like Betty could possibly have killed violent, angry, not to mention physically powerful, Derwood. What if Betty was mistaken? Her story was rather vague. Maybe she didn't kill him, but if she didn't who did? And since they disturbed the crime scene would the truth ever be known?

Coaxing her wandering mind back to the task at hand she said, "I'll call it Lucy's Lapin." She coarsely chopped onions, carrots, celery, and aromatic leeks; paused over the browning rabbit as an unwelcome thought arrested her hands. Michael was at the house that evening, but no, it could not be gentle Michael. But even gentle people have a breaking point. I would never have believed Betty could strike back, but she did. Pay attention, she admonished, or this dinner will be a burnt offering and I want no part of a sacrifice on Derwood's behalf.

Scooping the bacon from the skillet to cover the browned meat in her trusty cast iron Dutch oven, she carefully added the vegetables to the rich meat flavored fat, adjusted the gas and stirred for ten absent-minded minutes while she worried. Lucy was out there running around in the dark with whoever robbed the bakery on the loose. Hadn't Eric warned them all? Would Baker and Jake be able to attend her tasting tonight? I'll call to find out as soon as I finish, she spread the sweated vegetables evenly over the meat portions.

Where is Lucy, she wondered and for the hundredth time checked the clock with Ellie's Kitchen prominently printed on its face. Michael's birthday gift usually made her smile but this time rather than a fond smile it evoked anxiety.

Ellie added a bay leaf, a scant teaspoon of dried thyme, a handful of fresh chopped sage, a grinding of black pepper and then sprinkled flour and a crumbled chicken bouillon cube over the contents of her casserole, added several cups of water and the wine before bringing the stew to a boil. As she stirred, she visualized Betty's bedroom; Betty's previously perfect wonder-ful bedroom. The room Derwood turned into an abomination. She tasted the bubbling stew, added a little sea salt to correct the seasoning then turned off the fire.

"Coffee," Lucy panted rushing into Darcy's Diner, "and muffins," she added, when Darcy grinned.

"When did you get home?" Darcy asked.

"I got in yesterday," Lucy said heading for her favorite booth in the back.

"Valerie, is that you girl? What a coincidence, you here in my booth when I've just arrived. It's so good to see you," Lucy exclaimed sliding onto the bench across from her old college roommate. She reached to grasp Valerie's hand, "Tell me everything that's happened since the last time we met. How long has it been? No, don't answer that; I feel old enough already."

"You haven't changed a bit Lucy. You still have a great figure and no wrinkles, while I," Valerie hunched her shoulders and made her voice high and shrill, "have been through the mill and become a shriveled old hag," she ended with a convincing witch's cackle. "What have you been doing since we last met, other than that face lift, hair extensions, dye job and body sculpting surgery, I mean?"

"Well friend," Lucy stressed the word, "all that kept me very busy but since you've covered it all evil twin," she smirked, "there's not much to tell, though I see you still use the same cheap, brassy, strawberry blond dye you always did. Nice to see some things don't change. Though it's too bad you didn't take the hint when I e-mailed you that info on tummy tucks, but c'est la vie! Let's go from there. You first. Tell me everything."

"I always have to go first," Valerie whined, remembering university where she and Lucy shared a room. Valerie got up first and quickly cleared the bathroom before Lucy tumbled from bed at the last possible moment and charged into the shower whether it was free or not.

"Spill it Ms. V. and stop whining," Lucy prompted. "No one likes a tall, thin, drop-dead-gorgeous woman who spends her entire day sniveling, except me of course." Lucy crossed her eyes, a childish trick that'd always made Valerie laugh, but this time she saw Valerie's eyes brim with tears.

"That didn't work quite the way I planned," Lucy said nodding yes to Darcy's offer of coffee refills. "Tell me what's wrong," she urged, though crying made her cringe. "It must involve a man; it always does," she joked to fill the awkward silence. "Let's find somewhere quieter to talk."

"Here we are," Brad announced, "Looks like we're the early birds." Jake selected a front booth far from the patrons clustered in the rear.

"How are you guys this morning?" Darcy asked cheerfully, deftly juggling three mugs of steaming coffee, napkin wrapped cutlery and the menus that the locals never opened but always demanded. "You boys need menus?"

"No thanks Darcy," Jake responded.

"Cat got his tongue?" Darcy inquired jerking a thumb at Baker. "Stop sulking," she playfully demanded and failing to get the expected acerbic response, asked, "What the heck's wrong with him today?"

Jake acquainted Darcy with the past nights events.

"So why are you moping? Silly fool," Darcy scolded adding cream and sugar to Baker's coffee. "I'd be madder than a wet hen. Stop wallowing," she ordered with an affectionate glare.

"He's afraid that one of his young staffers took the money since they were the only ones who knew where the receipts were kept," Jake said.

"You got to be kidding. Everybody knows he keeps his cash in an unlocked box, in his unlocked desk, in his unlocked office," Darcy smirked. She sat next to Brad. "Heck, I've even offered to take his loot to the bank with mine, to do a night drop, you know, but no, the silly old fool wouldn't listen. Now he sits here in a blue funk because he got ripped-off." She held Baker in an unwavering glare, and added, "You asked for it, you got it, snap out of it."

"If I'm an old fool," Baker responded in his customary style, "What does that make you? An old fool-ess remember you're two long days my elder."

"Anymore of that talk and you won't be getting the usual tastefully chosen gift from me," Darcy threatened, while she anticipated the joint party she and Baker always held to celebrate their birthdays.

"Darcy?" Baker ingenuously asked. "If you are finished abusing your limited," he left the word hanging to stand and peer shortsightedly around the restaurant, "customers, do you suppose you might consider taking our order? That is if you're not run off your feet."

"Humph," Darcy sniffed. "What can I get you Jake, Brad?"

"The usual, thanks," Jake said.

"The usual," Brad echoed, smiling as Darcy hopped up, and charged to the kitchen.

"Don't forget my order," Baker yelled. "She'll probably fry my poached egg and poach my sausage," he complained good-naturedly. "I hope she doesn't expect to be paid now that I'm poverty stricken."

"Don't worry Baker, I'm treating," Brad reminded him. "Do the police have any leads?"

"Nothing plausible, unless you consider Jake a suspect," Baker said disgustedly.

"You must have some ideas Baker. It might help to talk it out," Jake tentatively suggested. "No," Jake said furnishing his own answer as Baker silently studied his coffee cup. "Okay then, let's talk about something else. How's the fishing Brad?"

"I don't know about today yet," Brad responded, flexing his injured shoulder, "yesterday the lake was a bit rough, but the catch was well worth the effort."

"When does the doctor say that shoulder will be healed? I bet you can't wait to get back out on the water."

"You said it," Brad agreed. "My shoulder's stiff, but doc says another week or two will take care of that. I'm glad too because this morning when I took my crew to the wharf somebody drove away in a real hurry. I know they were on the boat because my toolbox was out of place."

"Don't you lock up?" Baker asked secretly relieved that he wasn't the only one who made imprudent choices.

"Nah," Brad shook his head, "we got a watchman who's pretty reliable. He was sick last night and his replacement didn't show."

"So nobody saw anybody board your boat and nothing's missing. That's odd," Jake remarked. "You know Baker and I had a weird experience last night too. We always listen to that radio show, you know, the one where callers report bizarre happenings. Last night they talked about, a dog that ate a cellular phone, a statue crying and potatoes that resembled grandpa or some other relative. When we went down to work, there was a woman's face imprinted in the dough and . . ."

"Hi everyone," Lucy said favoring Brad with a head to toe elevator look, "Wow! Things have changed and for the better, I'd say. Brad you sure clean up good."

Brad laughed, "Thanks, I guess. Why don't you join us?"

"Sure wish I could," Lucy said, "but I'm waiting for a friend. She's gone to wash her hands."

"Lucy, I'm glad we ran into each other," Harv exclaimed pushing through the door. "We need to talk about your mother," his arm possessively circled Lucy's waist.

"What's wrong with Ellie?" Jake blurted.

"Nothing's wrong with mom. Sorry Harv, I didn't see you come in. Oh look, here's my friend. Valerie this is Baker, Brad, Harv, and this must be Jake," Lucy said pointing to each as she identified him. "Um, we have to go now Harv. Call me later, use my cell number please," she hustled Valerie out the door.

Harv looked perplexed, did he misread the signals? Hadn't she hung on his every word, stood way closer than necessary, assaulted him with the seductive French perfume she wore, gazed at him with those green eyes a guy could look into for - well, forever? He could not have been so wrong. Could he?

"Get with it stud muffin, the girl is smitten by your charms," Darcy said playfully nudging Harv. "Don't stand there looking like you swallowed one of Brad's fish raw. Didn't you see her friend's tears? Lucy is a sweet girl helping a friend. You sit next to Brad. That view alone ought to bring in the beach bunnies."

"What's up?" Harv asked, and perched on the extreme edge of the bench as far from Brad as possible.

Lucy drove Valerie to a secluded spot, parked beneath the old growth trees and waited for Valerie to speak. She didn't wait long before Valerie's story spewed forth like water from a breached levee.

"You know my father was frugal, but we lived well. Rather than wasting money on expensive toys, he plowed the profits into his business, and eventually held the deeds to six funeral homes. The company thrived and grew too large for one person to handle. Since I repeatedly rejected Dad's offer of a partnership he decided to accept an offer from a recent acquaintance." Valerie's voice broke and she angrily swatted at her tears. "I'm sorry Lucy. I haven't cried in a long time. Anger is a powerful catalyst to keep even my weepy eyes dry."

"Take your time Val," Lucy urged. Mom will understand when she hears Val's story.

"Then," Valerie sniffled, "Dad visited me at school and we had the talk we should have had years ago. He told me how much he loved me and that he knew he'd neglected me after mother died. We talked all night long. He was overjoyed when I said I'd join the company at the end of my pathology internship. He rushed home to cancel the partnership negotiations. Lucy, I swear he was happy, truly happy," Valerie said, her fists clenched so tight that blood welled from tiny wounds where short nails met palms.

Lucy gently loosened her friend's fingers, Valerie didn't appear to notice.

"Then I got a call from Daniel," Valerie spoke the name with revulsion, "dad's prospective business partner. He said if Father's reputation meant anything to me I'd better get home. I ask to speak to daddy and was told dad was too weak to come to the phone. Of course I rushed home. My father was dead, he'd poisoned himself. I fell apart."

"Valerie, why didn't you call me? You knew I'd come."

"I wanted to call you Lucy, but Daniel said not to. He urged me to cover up the suicide. He said we had to save daddy's reputation and the business he'd worked his whole life to build, he sounded so rational, and I was devastated. I could not think or do anything; Daniel hid Dad's suicide so that we got the insurance money." Valerie stopped speaking, her eyes focused on the blood on her hands.

Lucy reached into Valerie's handbag in search of a tissue.

"Lucy, I ask you, would a wealthy, successful man in his prime commit suicide when his only child had finally agreed to join him in the family business?" Valerie asked angrily. "Would he?"

Lucy gasped, "Valerie Tate, why do you have a picture of Dreadful Derwood in your purse?" She plucked a ratty photo from amidst the contents of Valerie's handbag. "And more importantly what are you doing standing beside that degenerate wearing a wedding dress. My god Val, is this a sick joke."

CHAPTER 10

Fresh sweet marjoram will be perfect in the poultry adaptation of the rabbit stew, Ellie decided peering down at the leeks, whole baby carrots, pearl onions, and plump mushrooms she'd sautéed. She placed the lids on both casseroles and carried them one by one to the aged refrigerator in the summer kitchen. There they'd rest and blend until it was time to pop them into the oven. Lucy could make the dumplings. She always produced fluffy, cloud-like mounds of flavor with little effort.

Where is that child? Ellie worried harvesting herbs from her ordered kitchen plot. It was light now and Lucy wasn't home. Anyway it was far too early to be picking herbs; she glared at the bounty in her basket cinnamon basil, chamomile, apple mint, Russian tarragon, I don't need any of these, where is my mind? Thinking of Lucy of course, she acknowledged crossly. What if she took Betty's car and they found *him*? Ellie's fertile imagination visualized her daughter as a victim of police brutality, handcuffed to a rusty iron bed and left to perish in a sinister, dank cell. Horrified she dashed to the garage, saw Betty's car and exhaled with relief. As she'd thought before her foray into insanity, Mother's car was gone. Cool that vivid imagination, and give your child credit for using at least half her brain. The sound of mother's powerful car broke the morning silence. When would she stop thinking of the automobile as her mother's?

"Jake will you come back with me or would you rather stay with the baker?" Brad asked, his voice so hushed that Jake knew that memories of the young man's lost family haunted him.

"That's Baker's lady's car pulling in. She's better company for him right now. You go on home. I'll be along shortly."

"Okay, but I promised my crew donuts," Brad said heading into the bakery.

"No!" Jake barked, "You go ahead. They'll be looking for a patsy and you're too damn convenient."

"Why would they suspect me? I've never been in trouble with the police."

"Just humor me. Let me get the donuts, and you get out of here," Jake muttered hurrying though the bakery door.

With the mental equivalent of a shrug, Brad edged into holiday Monday traffic. He wondered why the presence of Jake, a white man he'd known for a short time cheered him more than that of band members. The tribal elders tried, but their grief was as raw as his. Whatever the reason, he was grateful for the friendship he and Jake enjoyed. As mom always said, 'Don't question good fortune, accept it, and give thanks. Don't spit in God's eye.'

Slowing to turn into his driveway, he examined his home and the thick woods framing it. That house, a grey brick split-level was the subject of many noisy discussions. Momma always won the war though she occasionally ceded a battle. The eye-assaulting, lime green his dad had insisted on painting the shutters was a prime example of that principle in action, but mom had reigned victorious when she planted a profusion of brilliant red geraniums whose sole purpose was to clash with the gaudy shutters.

Brad recalled sharing his father's secretive mirth as they surveyed momma's handiwork. He alone among his siblings knew of his father's inability to distinguish red from purple, or black for that matter. Dad had asked for his help last year when momma wanted a scarlet sweater for Christmas. He'd never betrayed his dad's confidence and they'd enjoyed the joke on momma.

Brad's feet dragged as he approached the lime green door flanked by the red geraniums he'd planted that past spring.

"Sorry I took so long Brad," Jake dragged his bag from the trunk. "Would you believe Eric Platt had more questions? He kept jumping from one absurd hypothesis to another until I lost my temper and walked out." Jake wrinkled his nose comically, "In retrospect, probably not the smartest thing I ever did, but to hell with him."

"Calm down Jake. Come sit in the kitchen and tell me about it. I'll make coffee."

"What's wrong with Foster?" Jake asked, "Why's he so interested in that door? He's still not allowed upstairs is he?"

"Not really, but since the family's gone he gets lonely so I let him sleep in my room. When I'm not here he's taken to stretching out on the white bedspread in the guest room so I keep the door closed. But you're right, he's not himself."

"I can identify. I don't feel like myself either," Jake said scratching Foster's ears. "Is that coffee ready? It might help me relax. Damn Eric Platt, he and his deputies sent my blood pressure through the roof."

"Take it easy Jake."

"You don't understand Brad. They-suspect-us. Us!" Jake's voice rose as he interspersed each word with a rap of his fist on his palm.

"They're just trying to do their job and we know we aren't involved, so what's the big deal?"

"I guess you're right," Jake sighed, "but it burns my butt that while they waste time trying to incriminate us, the thief is spending Baker's money."

"I know, and I wish it were different, but I'm a half-breed and you're a new comer, so we're targets. Brad poured coffee into the gray earthen ware mugs his mother had loved.

"I think I'm almost too angry to drink coffee. Let me get my stuff out of the middle of the floor and then I'll tell you exactly what those asinine cops said. It's strange how being grilled by the cops even when you're innocent makes you sweat," Jake muttered as he climbed the seven carpeted stairs to the guest room. He dropped his bag near the door, but reconsidered when Foster stood by the closet door whining, a reprimand for my slovenly habits Jake wondered. "Alright old boy, I get the message. Stop nagging. I'm putting my suitcase away," Jake pushed Foster aside and reached for the closet door.

"Oh, oh, there's Mom," Lucy muttered, and she's not looking happy."

"Lucy, where have you been? I've been out of my mind with worry," Ellie masked her relief by scolding.

"Sorry Mom," the guilty 'only child' mumbled, eyes downcast, "but look who I found wandering around Darcy's."

"You stopped at Darcy's for a muffin and forgot how the telephone works? That must have been the magnum opus of all muffin-kind."

"Mom I can explain."

"And you will Lucille Amelia Wilson," Ellie threatened and then in saccharine voice addressed Valerie. "Honey, it's so wonderful to see you again." She gathered Valerie in a tight embrace, necessary, judging from the girl's worried expression, but Valerie flinched and Ellie quickly released her. "Lucy you haven't forgotten the parcel in the trunk, have you?" Ellie asked over Valerie's shoulder, her sharp glare belying the syrupy quality of her tone.

"Mom, let's save that for later. Val has a story that you and Aunt Betty need to hear and trust me, it relates to the package."

"What do you want me to hear?" Betty asked.

"Betty I don't believe you've met Lucy's college roommate Valerie Tate," Ellie said, good manners taking precedence over annoyance. "Valerie this is my oldest and dearest friend Betty Archer."

"Valerie, you're not the V. Tate who bought the funeral chapel out on the highway are you?"

"Yes I am. I'm surprised you guessed, even Lucy didn't twig to that."

"Fantastic!" Lucy enthused as the smallest seed of an inspired idea germinated in her fertile brain. "But for now I think we should go inside, sit down and talk." She pushed Valerie and Betty through the foyer into the spacious living room.

Ellie grasped her daughter's sleeve, "How is Valerie's presence relevant to the rapidly deteriorating package in the trunk?"

"You'll see. Come on. I don't want you to miss a single word Val has to say."

Ellie pasted on a smile, sailed past Lucy and directed Valerie and Betty to the comfortable, gaudy flowered settee her mother had loved and she hadn't the heart to jettison.

"I'll do a quick recap of what Val told me in the car," Lucy said circumventing her friend's inherent reserve.

"As Lucy so astutely observed," Valerie said taking up the story, "Daniel contrived a fraudulent ruse to conceal Dad's suicide, and I let him. I was in shock. I did not believe my father capable of suicide, and yet I was overwhelmed by guilt and shame. Daniel used that to manipulate and ultimately control me. He said we should marry and I went along because I felt indebted to him, and thought his companionship preferable to enduring my humiliation alone," Valerie toyed with the simple gold band that adorned her right hand.

Betty's gasp, an anguished expression illustrated her horror at a story so like her own. Her sad eyes held Valerie's, empathy impossible to verbalize flowed from her.

Valerie continued, "When I broached the subject of my inheritance Daniel hit me. No amount of pancake covered the bruises. After that I was too demoralized and frightened to question any decision Daniel made. I said I wanted to finish my degree, and was astounded when he agreed. He chose a university far enough away to make commuting impossible. He dropped me at the residence and I settled in. I was happier than I'd been since Father's death though I constantly zoned out or fell asleep in class. My faculty adviser insisted that I see a physician and..." Valerie's voice petered away to nothing.

"And? And what?" Lucy implored.

"The drug regimen Daniel said my family doctor ordered was actually a series of narcotics and amphetamines tailored to keep me dopey during the day and sleepless at night. I stopped taking the drugs and like magic, solutions to problems that had seemed insurmountable at home, presented themselves. Thankfully, Daniel never visited and being afraid to confront him I stayed away."

"Just like me," Betty murmured.

"Valerie your throat must be dry. Betty perhaps it would help Valerie cope with her situation if you told her a little about your life with Derwood," Ellie suggested. "Lucy, come with me to the kitchen," she dragged her reluctant daughter to her feet.

"Wait Mom, I think she's getting to the good part."

"Are Derwood and Daniel the same person?"

"Pray tell, oh super sleuth, what leads you to that perfectly accurate deduction?"

"The wedding photo you so cavalierly dumped on the sofa beside me was a slight clue," Ellie said filling the kettle.

"Bravo Mom," Lucy laughed clapping her hands. "Forget the tea. I think we all need something a little stronger. Open that foie gras I brought from Paris. Where's the corkscrew?"

"No you don't," Ellie objected gently lowering Lucy onto the rocking chair, with one slender hand on each arm she held her captive. "What were you thinking? Where does your brain vacation when you come home? First with the bakery thieves undoubtedly loitering about, you go out in the middle of the night alone and after stopping for muffins, you drag poor Valerie here with a tale you know will upset Betty, while you forget about the package in the trunk and you do all that without sleep."

"Take a breath mom, I slept on the flight over," Lucy artlessly lied. "I'm sorry Mom, but guess what I learned."

"Lucy! No guessing games."

"Okay, Derwood was alive after Aunt Betty ran out."

"How did you come to that conclusion?" Ellie asked packing the tea ball with Earl Grey, Betty's favorite.

"He cleaned himself up in Aunt Betty's en suite and left a mess. And there were two martini glasses in the study, so I think Derwood entertained someone after Aunt Betty left. It wasn't a happy meeting because there were blood stains on the hardwood. I found it," Lucy announced triumphantly waving the corkscrew, "and it's five o'clock somewhere. By the way, Derwood replaced Uncle Robert's entire art collection with fakes. I'll try to locate the originals, but I don't hold out much hope. Oh, I liberated Derwood's computer and all the checkbooks and stubs I could find. Michael is quite the computer hacker; he'll be happy to help."

"Jake has a financial background, perhaps he'd oversee the endeavor," Ellie suggested.

"I'll ask Michael. Anyway aren't you glad Aunt Betty didn't kill Dreadful Derwood!"

"That is wonderful news dear, can I assume you have evidence to prove it."

"Indeed I do. When I was escaping through the primal forest evading lions and tigers, whoops wrong story," Lucy giggled tiredly. "I tripped over a piece of the bed in the woods. Aunt Betty is not strong enough to throw a bed post that far and she hates poison ivy, therefore she didn't do it."

"I see and where is the bed piece now?" Ellie asked skepticism ripe in her voice as her mind flew back through time to envision Betty as pitcher for the local fastball team.

"Don't worry, it's well hidden. Didn't you hear me Mom? Aunt Betty did not do it."

"I know dear and while your evidence is compelling I suspect the police would find the odd problem with it. Before we go back I should show you what I found in Betty's jacket." Ellie pulled a large stained handkerchief from her trouser pocket. "I don't know how significant this is, she admits striking him so if it's his blood it doesn't mean anything, does it Lucy?" Ellie asked pleading for reassurance.

"It's nothing mom, the blood could be from anything, a hangnail for instance. We'd better get back before we miss anything. No wait, I almost forgot there was a glass in the open safe, an empty glass with a little gunk stuck in the bottom."

"The safe was open? It seems you've forgotten some important bits, but we'll discuss that later," Ellie mouthed, then for her guests benefit said loudly, "I've sent the recipes out to all the cooking class participants."

"The bastard, killing is too good for him." Betty gritted through clenched teeth. Ellie saw her usually placid pal hovering menacingly over Valerie, nearly dropped the tea tray.

"Lucy, bring the wine," Ellie shouted, "and hurry!"

Lucy forced herself between Valerie and Betty, plucked the photo of Val and Derwood from her aunt's clenched fist, plopped down between them and quipped, "You are both so lucky I lost those extra pounds. Okay now that you know Derwood/Daniel are one person, listen up because I do not want to repeat myself. Understand?" She planted her hands on her hips while she waited for their nods. "Mom, I know what I'm doing," she placed Valerie's hand in Betty's. "Both of you are victims. You were worked over by a pro, but I see a glimmer of light at the end of the tunnel. Let's hear the rest of Val's story and then decide what to do about Derwood or Daniel or whatever the bastard's real name was . . . is, I mean."

Betty relaxed her death grip on Valerie's hand, and caught both girls in an embrace.

Ellie's noisy exhalation prompted Valerie to pick up her narrative.

"I graduated, gathered my courage, rented a car, and drove home to an empty house with a sale sign on the lawn. I immediately contacted father's lawyer," she paused, "my lawyer I mean. Mr. Jacobs said Daniel had my power of attorney in hand and demanded to see Dad's will. I was the sole beneficiary and Daniel had instructions supposedly written by me indicating that he, my husband, was to take charge. Mr. Jacobs asked to see me, but Daniel said I'd tried to kill myself and he'd had no choice but to have me committed, for my own safety of course," Valerie grimaced and gulped her wine. "He said he was certain my mother committed suicide and that father's death had depressed and unbalanced me and I'd tried to kill myself. That bit of fiction set warning bells ringing in Mr. Jacobs' head, because he and my parents were long time friends and he had been strong for us during mother's long battle with cancer."

"Lucy, why don't you hand the snacks around, or would anyone prefer a hearty breakfast, bacon or ham, eggs, toast, coffee maybe?" Ellie fussed. Derwood's misuse of Betty was an atrocious betrayal, but Betty was a mature woman while Valerie, two years younger than Lucy had been a veritable infant when Derwood exploited her.

"She's not finished," Lucy objected refilling Valerie's empty wineglass."

"Mr. Jacobs's suspicion increased with every word out of Daniel's mouth. Later when he questioned the young partner he'd trusted with our stable and relatively simple account, he was appalled. Daniel had duped the inexperienced lawyer. Mr. Jacobs took charge of my account stopped Daniel's raid on the trust fund from Mother. He also stopped the sale of my empty house, and then he searched hospitals and sanatoriums for me without success. He hired a private investigator at his own expense, but with the erroneous information Daniel provided they couldn't locate me." Valerie nodded her appreciation when Lucy topped up her glass.

Val held Betty's hand and gazed into her eyes, "This will be hard for you to hear Mrs. Archer, but you have to know. The Investigator is in town right now, with two other women Daniel married and swindled. He wants our help. Maybe find a pattern that will help him locate Daniel's other victims, and maybe our money. I met the other wives last night," she grimaced, "that's why Lucy found me so distressed," Valerie hesitated while she searched for the least painful words. "Both wives are much older than you or I Mrs. Archer. Doris seems to be his first, she insists he never meant to hurt her and is sure he'll see the error of his ways and come back to her. Sue however wants him castrated, drawn and quartered and hung in the town square where he'd be dowsed with pails of hot diarrhea, ten times a day. Sorry," Valerie apologized, "but that's a direct quote. After I sold my house I trained as a funeral director, bought the funeral chapel just out of town, and here I am."

"It seems to me that you've coped and recovered extremely well," Ellie said.

"I guess I did, but I'm still frustrated and angry. I know Daniel poisoned my dad, but since he had the body cremated while I was grieving, I have no proof. But what really infuriates me is that he moved on to Mrs. Archer because I was too gutless to stop him. He's a ruthless bastard, and an unremorseful son of a bitch and I've wished him dead every day since I kicked the drugs." Valerie grinned. "Close your mouth Lucy. Living with Daniel taught to me to use the vocabulary you so wisely imparted." She grimaced, "Sorry Mrs. Wilson."

Ellie shuddered.

"Don't worry Val, Aunt Betty and even Mom know those words and as for me," Lucy giggled, "I guess not all my tutoring went to waste."

"Yes, I've found my spine. I'm not the inexperienced pawn you remember." Valerie said and they all smiled.

"I have no one to blame but myself. I did nothing. I cowered while *Daniel* robbed me of my values, my dignity, and my inheritance." Valerie slumped like a deflated balloon, her pale face hidden behind shaking hands.

"You're a child. And you are not to blame." Betty exclaimed. "It is I who should have seen through him. Even when I understood his nature, I didn't fight, I ran like a scared rabbit. If anyone other than *Derwood* is to blame, it's me."

Lucy leapt up as if jabbed in the bottom by a loose spring, "What the hell are you two on about? Stop! Are you crazy? Blaming yourselves for that bigamist bastard's betrayal? *Derwood* or *Daniel* is solely responsible and you know it. Stop the pity party and the damn snuffling. Turn all those wasted tears and tortured agony into righteous rage and let's get on with it."

"I am angry! I'm mad as hell, but anger and hatred will not quell the fear I have that he will victimize more vulnerable women," Valerie retorted.

"Don't worry child," Betty cooed, "*He* can't hurt anyone anymore. I killed *him*."

"For God's sake," Lucy shouted, "You did not kill him! I have the proof." Betty's eyes filled as she continued softly, "You didn't kill him, but that doesn't make him any less dead or us any less culpable. She sighed, "I do have an idea that with Valerie's help will solve our disposal problem."

Val listened, added a few prudent suggestions, and nodded agreement.

"Okay Foster, relax. I'll put my stuff in the closet." Jake laughed at the dog's comic rebuke while reaching for the latch. The door snapped open. Jake instinctively raised his arms to catch the slight figure hurtling toward him.

Foster's mournful howls reverberated through the house.

CHAPTER 11

"Jake, are you okay?" Brad yelled, taking the stairs two at a time. "Oh God Jake, who is that, is she all right?"

By Brad's slack jaw, stumbling speech, and stunned expression Jakes brief moment of wondering if he'd been manipulated fled. "Help me get her onto the bed," Jake spoke quietly and calmly. Brad stood as if rooted to the floor, "Damn it Brad, help me."

Jake's commanding tone reached through Brad's shock, he reached across the bed to ease Jakes burden. "I'll call for help."

Jake felt for a pulse, though certain she was dead. "Call the police, paramedics can't help her."

Jake hardly heard Brad try to explain the unexplainable to the Reservation Police. He saw only the woman's small face, disfigured by death, and fouled by clumped dough begging for justice since she'd been shown no mercy.

"What's that?" Brad asked, timidly fingering a white mass caught in her close-cropped hair.

"Don't touch it", Jake cautioned sharply, "its pastry. Our mystery of the face in the dough is solved." Profoundly sad, he asked for and was given a clean sheet."

"Do you know her?"

"Yes I know her," Jake said, envisioning the feisty woman he'd seen yesterday morning. "Her name is Rita Russell." Sirens blared as Jake pulled the starched white sheet over the district health inspector's face.

"What am I going to say, I don't know how she got in my closet?"

"Just tell the absolute truth, and pray," Jake advised. "And let the cops in before they break the damn door down."

Rita Russell's dedication to her job was inspiring though her feral persecution of Baker remained an enigma. She died in the bakery, her face forced into the dough and held until she smothered. Jake grimaced; Eric was right to impound the doughnuts. He waited for the cops, his mind racing; Rita must have interrupted the robbery. But why was she there and who put her body in Brad's closet? Who hates Brad enough to frame him for murder?

Captain Reese, a tall rugged man with the chiseled features of his Apache ancestors, paused to scan the room before he strode to the bed. With marked apprehension he uncovered her face, frowned, and carefully replaced the sheet. "We'll leave this for the crime scene investigators," He held the door and motioned Jake through, then firmly closed it. "What brings you to the reservation Mr. Carlton?"

"My house is being painted, and Brad's letting me use his guest room. Where is Brad?"

"Officer Orville is taking his statement. You know that woman?"

"She's Rita Russell, the district health inspector." Jake edged toward the stairway.

"And?" Captain Reese prompted, writing far more in his notebook than Jake's simple statement necessitated.

"She fell out of the closet and I caught her, that's all I know. Eric Platt is probably still at the bakery. You heard we were robbed?" Reese nodded. "I'd guess this death is connected."

"What do you mean?"

"Call Eric, he'll explain. I'm tired and I'm mean when I'm tired," Jake snarled, sidling down the steps. "We won't say anything more until we have legal representation," he shouted, shoving past Officer Orville. "You hear me Brad?"

Brad nodded silent assent, Foster growled and Jake glared as Captain Reese sent his deputy to the car to radio Eric Platt.

"Brad," Reese asked, "what do you know about the woman in Jake's bed?"

"Strictly speaking, it's my bed, and Jake has nothing to do with it."

"I know it's technically your bed," Reese growled, "But listen up! You two quit trying to jerk me around or I'll run you in. Understood?"

Jake spoke, "Rita Russell, had a vendetta against the baker, she was in yesterday morning. That's the last time I saw her before she fell out of the closet." But, he thought, I'm damn sure she was killed at the bakery when she interrupted the robber.

The hackles on the back of Foster's neck rose as Orville slammed the door. "The bakery was knocked over last night, and our friend here," he stabbed a meaty finger at Jake, "made a cast of an imprint they found in a pile of dough. Platt said he'll notify the big guys and hold the evidence for them." He snickered, "Hey Brad, I told you hangin' out with white guys was askin' for trouble."

"Shut up Orville!" Captain Reese commanded, and asked himself for the hundredth time why he'd hired a fool and not waited for a mature applicant. Nepotism was alive and well in the band; Orville was cousin to the chief.

"Are we suspects?" Brad asked quietly.

Orville crowed, "Can't say until you tell us everything ya' know."

"Shut up Orville," Reese ordered absently.

"Fine," Jake sighed, "Brad, call Ellie Wilson; ask her to get us a lawyer. Use that phone." Jake pointed and his authoritative manner subdued even Orville.

Ellie caught the phone on the first ring. "Slow down Brad I can't understand you," she said and then, eyebrows rising to meet her hairline listened. She sank into the worry chair and listened some more. "Do not say a word. Lawyers always say that on television so it must be valid. Don't worry dear; I'll get you an attorney right away."

Betty tugged the phone from Ellie's clenched fist. "Ellie you're as white as one of your garlic blossoms, what's wrong."

"Jake found a body at Brad's house and I almost asked him how they'd found Derwood."

"You don't need to worry about *him* Ellie, *he's* safe in the trunk, but I would have reacted the same way. It's a stretch to think of two dead bodies loose in our little town."

"Stretch or not, Jake found a woman's body and they need an attorney."

"I'll call Michelle Homes. She's moved back. She was at school with us." Ellie looked perplexed, Betty explained, "You remember the serious girl Zack played tricks on?"

In spite of the gravity of the situation Ellie grinned, "He plagued her for a whole semester."

"Well," Betty said, "She's a criminal lawyer now." Betty grimaced, "an ugly term, criminal lawyer, sounds like she's the crook, doesn't it?"

"The ditzy thing isn't going to make this situation better Betty, but thank you for trying."

"You know me too well; the ditz routine works on everybody else. They see my plump over forty self, assume I'm a fuzz brained idiot and before they discover I'm not I've bought their item at a great price." Betty laughed, "Teaches them not under value mature, fortyish woman." She dialed information.

Ellie said ironically, "It seems you've mislaid ten years Betty Archer, I am forty-nine, and you are several months older so either we convince Lucy she's twelve or you find those years."

"We'll work on Lucy." Betty sent up a brief prayer of thanks for Ellie's smile, jotted down a number, and placed the call. "Michelle, Betty Archer---no, I am not calling about *him*. Jake Carlton found a body in Brad Taltree's house." Betty asked, "Ellie do they know who she is?"

"Brad didn't say."

"Michelle, we don't know, but Ellie told Brad to say nothing until you arrived." Betty listened, "I'll be waiting." She replaced the handset on the ancient bakelite phone. "I'll go with Michelle I can help Brad and Jake deal with Eric."

"What if the police take them in before you and Michelle arrive?" Ellie fretted. "I'll go to the station. You call me when you get to Brad's house. I'll wake Lucy." Ellie climbed the stairs, Betty answered the phone.

"That was Valerie," Betty yelled. "Do you hear me Ellie? Val has to pick up the body Jake found. She can't meet Lucy! What are we going to do?"

"Calm down Aunt Betty, I will drive *Derwood* to the funeral home and wait until Val gets there," Lucy said. "Everything will work as planned. You take care of Jake and Brad. The phone woke me," she explained, "I heard and can't believe there's another dead body."

"The age thing just might work Betty, with Lucy's hair in braids like that she looks twelve."

Betty waved and kept waving until Ellie's car turned the corner. Suddenly exhausted, she made her way to the kitchen, and the worry chair. Alone for the first time since she'd found Derwood's body, Betty closed her eyes, rogue images stole the peace she sought, details played over and over as if the images were etched on her retina. She shuddered, and prayed to her guardian angel as she'd done since childhood, she asked for the calm she desperately needed. Tranquility flooded through her and she slept, head still bowed, hands still folded in supplication.

"Damn!" Lucy glanced at the speedometer. Old lead foot strikes again, and this time to quote mom, I've stepped dead center in the stinky stuff. She tramped heavily on the brake pedal when insistent blue lights flashed behind Aunt Betty's car. Do not panic, she told herself, Rick or Joe will give you the usual lecture, welcome you home and let you go.

Lucy gulped, "Hello Officer. I know most of the guys on the force, but not you," she batted her eyelashes and peered up at him, "I'd definitely remember you."

The distractingly gorgeous Brad look alike held out his hand, "License and registration ma'am!"

"Was I speeding? I'm really sorry Officer; you see this is my Aunt's car and I'm not familiar with it yet. Was I going too fast?" Lucy mimicked the scatterbrain act that worked for Betty.

"It's smart to drive a few miles under the speed limit when you're in a strange automobile," the officer advised and stepped behind the car.

Now it's panic time, Lucy tried to stop her hands shaking.

I knew I should have driven Derwood to the morgue, Ellie thought when she saw lead-foot Lucy stopped beside a black and white on the roadside. It took herculean effort to keep her foot off the brake. But she never gets a traffic ticket. Lucy had briefly considered the force as a career. Ellie sighed; fortunately Robert recognized and encouraged the artistic ability that led to her present career. But the guys on the force remembered Lucy's unstinting help as a volunteer. Lucy often brought her grandmother lost or abused women and children knowing grandma would feed, and care for them. Lucy held and comforted rape victims when woman officers weren't available. And she'd stood by mute, never an easy thing for her, during questioning when the force was chronically short of female staff. Ellie's face shone with motherly pride. Lucy, it was said, had been deputized more often than anyone else in the history of the county. She'll be fine without her mother's help and totally embarrassed with it. Ellie shook her head in disgust at the rambling of her undisciplined mind as she sailed past Huron Shores' police station.

Lucy watched the cop walk to the rear of her vehicle. She pushed open the door and sashayed out, gave her silky blond hair a sexy flip and presented her license.

"Always stay in the car ma'am. It tends to upset us when folks bound out like that," the officer cautioned, he smiled self-consciously and let his pistol slide back into the holster. "You'll want to tell your aunt that her tag expires next week."

"Thank you," Lucy said breathily. "She'd be awfully upset if she missed that."

"Wilson?" He asked. "Do you know Ellie Wilson, she runs a cooking class?"

"She's my mom," Lucy said enthusiastically, "we run the classes together. How do you know mom?"

He grinned, "I think she should tell you that story." He returned her license, "I'll let you go this time, but ease off on the gas." He swaggered toward the flashing lights, "See you Wednesday."

Lucy waved gaily until he rounded a bend. She laid her flushed face on the cool metal and groaned. Moments later, after the shaking stopped, she drove to where Valerie's mortuary, like a cliché, huddled beneath an ominous grey thundercloud. Lucy heaved a sigh and blessed the architect for putting the loading dock in back out of sight of the highway. She hit the switch of Valerie's remote, waited for the door to lift and eased into the loading bay.

The shrilling doorbell wrenched Betty from sleep. She rubbed cramped neck muscles and croaked, "Its open Michelle."

"Sorry I'm late. Mr. Aster dropped by with some papers work and I couldn't get rid of him. Apparently they're still at Brad Talltree's place. That is if Orville wasn't lying, and if," Michelle snarled, "he lying again I'll fry his ass in a hot skillet. Why Jeremy hired that incompetent bigot," she said disgustedly, "I'll never know. But get in, let's talk about your situation. Zack said he saw you at the clinic. Are you ready to talk restraining order, charges, and divorce?"

Betty studied her trembling hands, "I know what I have to do. I must eliminate him from my life if I'm ever to be happy again." She cringed as Derwood's bloody face, the face she'd battered flashed before her mind's eye.

"Whatever the catalyst," Michelle said, "You've made the right decision. I've seen too many abused women laid out on a cold slab, because they were mistresses of denial right to the bloody end of their lives." She paused and then added, "I've worried that one day I'd be called to identify your body."

"You'll never have to do that," Betty promised, gratified to see Brad's house ahead.

"This place has more cops than a donut shop." Michelle quipped. "We'd better go in before they get out the thumbscrews and rubber hoses."

"Good afternoon Mrs. Wilson. Did you bring cookies?" the desk sergeant asked hungrily.

"Sorry Rick, not this time. I'm looking for Jake Carlton and Brad Talltree. Are they here?"

"Are they supposed to be here?"

"I heard that they found a woman's body and I assumed Eric would bring them in for questioning."

"This town passes news faster than CNN," Rick declared patting his chin. "They aren't here yet, and you didn't hear that from me!"

"Do you know where they are? For cookies every week for a month," Ellie offered planning her annual Christmas cookie column.

"Ma'am, are you attempting to bribe an officer of the law?" He turned a small memo pad so that Ellie could read it, "That's a criminal offense you know."

"I would never wish my gratitude to our esteemed and valued police force to be misconstrued as graft." Ellie grinned, "What kind of cookies would I offer if I were to try a bribe, which of course I never would."

"Chocolate chip are still my favorite, those big gooey ones that melt in your hand and those chocolate caramel ones rolled in pecans are really good too, or maybe another multi-cookie taste test here at the station." Rick smacked his lips. "And of course, we would accept any offering as a well deserved tribute to our daring and valor, not a bribe," he hesitated unsure whether he should surrender further information. Hell, he thought, I've already said enough to earn a reprimand. "Um, I may have heard Baker's name and the word question come up in the same sentence, but you didn't hear that from me either."

"I see. And would this event I know nothing about be looming?"

"Sometime later this afternoon," Rick whispered eyeing his half eaten, mystery meat sandwich.

"Rick I won't keep you any longer. Speaking with you is always a pleasure I immediately forget. Oh, one more thing," Ellie tapped her head, "forgive my poor memory, has the victim been identified?"

He thumbed back a page and the informative memo pad inched across the desk.

Ellie gulped and dragged it closer.

Rick snapped upright, suddenly all cop, "Did you know her?"

"Not well, though I was in the bakery Sunday when she inspected. She was unpleasant to Baker, but vivacious and attractive. What a shame to see all that vitality wiped away."

"Yeah I know. I met her at a food fair. We dated until I figured out that all she wanted from me was help to close the bakery."

"How sad that her obsession caused her to miss a rewarding relationship with you," Ellie said taking little pleasure in the vivid, red blush that colored Rick's face.

"Thank you ma'am," he said ducking his flaming face below the desk to retrieve the pencil he'd deliberately dropped.

Ellie's cell phone buzzed, the text message said succinctly, 'proceed'.

"I'll see you later Rick," Ellie said and hurried to rescue her car from Eric Platt's reserved space.

Michelle knocked and shoved open the door leading to Brad's spacious kitchen. Uniformed and plain-clothed police from the reservation, town, and federal forces jockeyed for position. Officer Orville menaced Brad while Jake, cornered by Eric Platt, appeared aggravated and exhausted.

"What's the meaning of this?" Michelle demanded. Betty stomped over to place her body next to Fosters, woman and dog aggressive, and poised to defend Brad. "Have any of you officious thugs arrested Mr. Talltree or Mr. Carlton?" Michelle, hugely annoyed that her clients were being questioned without legal representation, (i.e. her) snarled, "I trust you've read them their rights and each has made his phone call?"

"Calm down, Ms. Homes, no one is arrested yet," Eric Platt said.

"Then you won't mind if I take my clients away," Michelle said. "Betty Archer tells me that Mr. Carlton hasn't slept in over twenty four hours. You boys know he's president of the Grey Power Chapter don't you? And Brad's a member of a visible minority. Enough said, I think."

Orville held Brad down, "So what?-that and a buck will get you a box of Cracker Jacks."

"Shut up Orville," Capitan Reese said mechanically.

Michelle snapped, "Keep your damn gorilla away from my client."

"You men are free to go," Reese said, "but don't leave town."

"I'll take them in my car," Eric Platt offered, his tone made his words an order.

"I'll be right behind you," Michelle promised.

"What in hell was that?" Lucy asked swearing to bolster her dwindling courage. It must be the wind rushing past this creaky, old building. What if this hill is more than a glacial moraine? What if it's a fairy mound and that eerie noise is the wail of a banshee, a harbinger of death to the hearer and all her family. "Get a grip," she admonished, you're not writing a spooky tale. If you were, you'd open this trunk and he'd leap out with blood soaked hands intent on squeezing the life from your swan-like, ivory neck, she giggled nervously. "Cut it out! The more you do now the less time you spend in this spooky place." I'm certainly better equipped to handle this than my mother; she shuddered and slowly turned the key. The trunk lid sprang open and Lucy saw the garish pumpkin face close one sleepy eye playfully.

Lucy slammed the lid and scurried out into the brilliant sunshine. She spied Ellie's car and a wave of relief washed over her. She stabbed the button and waved Ellie in before the large door raised enough to accommodate the Lincoln. Lucy put a shoulder to the door to force it open faster.

"Lucy stop, you'll hurt yourself," Ellie called through her open window.

"Mom you're late. I am definitely never being alone in this place again! Ever! I mean it mom, never!"

Ellie was surprised by her usually fearless pragmatic daughter's nervousness.

"Darn I should have backed in," Lucy howled.

"Never mind dear, we'll work it out. Is that wheeled cart for our use?" she gingerly opened the trunk. The orange smiley face beamed, indifferent to its odoriferous content. "Lucy, bring that cart. I could do this alone being Super Mom and all, but a little help from you will make it easier. Take that end. Be careful. Can you figure out how to lower the cart a bit?"

"Mom, stop calling it a cart like we're hauling groceries; damn it Mom, it's a gurney!"

Ellie thrust the gurney away and gathered Lucy's quaking body close. "Honey, you don't have to do this. There's no shame in experiencing fear. I love your strong stance and I love the way you always do what's right, but you are not infallible. Have you stopped to think of how long it's been since you've slept? Go on outside, I'll take care of this and then I'll take you home."

Lucy squared her shoulders, Oh yeah; I'm going to leave my aged, feeble mother to haul Dreadful Derwood around this haunted mausoleum. The odious place that has made brave little old me cringe like a coward." Lucy sighed nosily, "Thanks Mom. Don't just stand there lift that bag, tote that body, if we do it right we won't land in jail," Lucy sang more off key than usual.

Ellie laughed comforted by Lucy's return to near normalcy. "Honey, if I'm ever to have grandbabies 'promise me, oh promise me,'" she crooned, "You won't sing to my prospective son-in-law."

Lucy though a moment, "Okay I won't sing to him if we never mention my nerves of marshmallow again." Lucy tugged at the orange leaf bag. "If we get this end onto the gurney then we should be able to shift the other end," Lucy grunted, "I don't remember him being this stiff when we stuffed him in here. Rigor has set in and now he's twice the trouble."

"Push your end down while I lift mine up," Ellie ordered."

"It's not working. I'll have to get in and push from behind."

"I forbid it!" Ellie shrieked, "You will not get in that trunk with him! Lucy stop!"

Lucy stepped nimbly over the smiling orange bag, "Pull slowly while I lift, don't yank or you'll tear the bag."

"Alright it's half out. Now, Lucille Amelia Wilson get your slender behind out of that trunk."

Lucy complied and yanked Derwood's nether end onto the gurney, "Do you think this is what Val meant by broken rigor?" she asked innocently.

Ellie shuddered, "I neither know nor care to know." Ellie wheeled the ever smiling pumpkin bag into the spotless, white tiled preparation room. "I had no idea this sophisticated facility existed in our community, it looks like an operating theatre."

"Yeah, except the anesthetic equipment is missing."

"Lucy, gallows humor is inappropriate. Valerie is jeopardizing her livelihood to help us. She'll have to do copious quantities of paperwork. A thank you note will not suffice."

"What? You think we should bake a cake? We're illegally moving a murder victim and you think of thank you notes."

"Derwood was not a victim. He was a victimizer therefore this is more like erasing a nasty chapter from Betty's life."

"Housekeeping you mean, or editing?" Lucy snorted, "Are you, my prim and proper mother justifying homicide? Have my years of training at your sanctimonious knee been all for naught?"

Ellie chuckled, pinched Lucy's cheek, and drew her face close to her own. Owlishly she pontificated, "Occasionally one has to perform distasteful tasks to protect one's family, and those values were a major part of the training you so cavalierly dismiss as sanctimonious. You understand, don't you honey?"

"It was a joke mom, just a stupid, lame joke."

"Oh well then, let's get on with it. We must remove the bag. Even a vicious perverted tyrant deserves dignity in death."

"I'm not sure of that," Lucy grumbled," but if you insist." She opened drawers until she found scissors and masks, and then carefully cut the bag down the center. Derwood's eyes peered at her from his battered head. "Look Mom, Aunt Betty couldn't have done this. Mom, open your eyes. Don't shake your head removing the bag was your idea."

Ellie gagged, "Did our rough handling cause all that damage?"

"I don't think so. He got these," Lucy pointed to Derwood's face, "before death. If that's where Aunt Betty hit him," she pointed to abrasions surrounded by dark bruises on his forehead and near one ear, "then there should a bruise about here," she pointed to his shoulder, unbuttoned his blood encrusted shirt. "Yes, just as I thought, Aunt Betty hit him yes, but she didn't smash his nose, that was a fist. She didn't split his chin either that was done later, so who did us that favor?"

"Lucy, maybe we could be a little more sensitive?"

"Sorry, I'm trying to make sense of it. If Aunt Betty hit him with a piece of the bed like the one I found in the woods, she didn't do this," Lucy pointed to a deep gash high in the hair line," she's too short, unless she . . . ."

"Don't say it, and don't even think it. Betty would never hit anyone even *him* when he's down. No more guesswork aimed at her."

"I agree with you. These wounds were inflicted by a taller person."

"Is that the door? I hope its Valerie." Ellie held Lucy's arm in a vice like grip, "Valerie is that you?"

"Yes Mrs. Wilson, I'm back," Valerie confirmed pulling on a lab coat.

"I'm glad you're here, Lucy was a little nervous."

"I didn't think you were afraid of anything Lucy," Valerie said, "especially a corpse. Need I remind you that it's the living who do harm to their fellow man."

Lucy shrugged, "I know, it's this place that scares me." She shivered, "Can we get on with it. We've removed the plastic smiley face and made some guesses. Give us your expert assessment, and we see how wrong we were."

"Okay," Valerie looked down and winced, "I never wanted to see *him* again, but if you insist, shove over and turn on that very expensive, designed for this very purpose, light. We'll dispense with identification, weight, measurements, and physical description," she stated dispassionately. "Rigor mortis is fixed. The head is normocephalic and there is evidence of external trauma. The torso shows ante mortem ..."

"Val, we know you did that forensic pathology thingy and congratulations, but do you think you could dumb it down for mom and me?"

"Sure Lucy," Valerie responded preoccupied, "the torso shows antemortem."

"Valerie," Lucy threatened.

"Okay," Valerie sighed, "These wounds on his cheek, forehead and shoulder, possibly blunt force impacts are low force, nonfatal in nature and consequently could be the result of Mrs. Archer's blows, a supposition I draw based on an assumed significant survival period. That's the time from injury or onset of terminal illness to death. In layman's terms, the bruises look older, okay?" Valerie questioned. "His nose is broken, possibly by a fist, eye discoloration from same trauma, nonfatal,"

"Are you saying someone socked him in the nose?"

"Yes. There is a 2 ½ inch laceration in the hair line with fresh hemorrhage along the path, nonfatal. Superficial contusions are evident on the chin. Lucy, help me turn him over. Look here," she directed, carefully parting matted hair, "this deep scalp hemorrhage and a subgaleal hematoma beneath the wound may be associated with fracture of the skull or penetration of the cranium."

"English, please Val. Aunt Betty didn't do it, right?"

"In my opinion, it is unlikely Mrs. Archer killed him. As I said before, she probably is responsible for some of the grazes and more advanced bruising, but not these others."

"What about all those dark purple marks," Ellie asked peering through her fingers.

"That's Hypostasis…"

"Huh?" Lucy rudely interrupted.

"Also called Liver mortis, a discoloration of the skin caused by blood pooling in the veins and capillary beds, begins immediately after death with the cessation of circulation."

"Enough," Ellie blurted, "This is taking too long. You need to be on your way."

"You're right Mrs. Wilson. Lucy, help me with this utility box. We'll put Daniel in first. I can't bear to think of that poor homeless man under the bastard's weight."

"Yuck," Lucy shivered, "what is that all about?"

"This is no time for dubious humor. Valerie is ordered and perfectly logical in her reasoning," Ellie said.

"Uh huh," Lucy shuddered, "Lord preserve me from ordered logic."

"Valerie, we cannot thank you enough. You can't know what this means to us." Ellie held the younger woman in what Lucy called her fierce mother-bear hug, the bone crusher.

"I'll drop this lot by the crematorium," Valerie said as she and Lucy pushed the heavy cremation box housing Derwood and the John Doe into the funeral chapel's panel van.

Ellie retrieved the thick file of prepared paperwork while Valerie climbed into the driver's seat. Ellie whispered, "After you get rid of him and take the health inspector to the morgue. Come for dinner at eight, and we'll pretend this nightmare never happened"

"He's a big one," Valerie remarked as the utility box rolled along the crematorium conveyer belt.

"One size fits all," the attendant laughed.

CHAPTER 12

Ellie sliced plump, red tomatoes, allowing three slices per appetizer. She added a vibrant, green pesto made with fresh basil, olive oil, pine nuts, roasted garlic, and a little lemon juice, decorated each serving with tiny, perfect basil leaves and toasted pine nuts and placed them in the refrigerator. The bounty of a lavish summer garden would mingle over the next few hours into a light appetizer to accompany the substantial rabbit stew with dumplings main course. She collected the stew pans from the summer kitchen and slid them into the preheated oven, all the while wondering why she put up with the inconvenience of this old house. Her mother and grandmother squabbled over carefully sketched plans intended to fix a house designed for a bevy of servants. One catastrophe after another derailed each plan and nothing changed. Ellie complained every time she cooked at home, those women would laugh themselves silly if they saw her now. She, who had redecorated her home so often that when Charles, returning from a fishing trip, neglected to turn on a light, and tumbled 'ass over tea kettle' in his words, Ellie smiled. She'd raced to his side expecting irritation, but Charles lay prone and laughing. She'd righted and turned on the lamp. Gaping, he'd immediately apologized for being in the wrong house, and then laughed even louder. Not only had she redecorated and relocated their bedroom, she'd cut her long, auburn hair, very short and dyed it black.

Rodney watched Ellie through the screen door. He marveled that she prepared an elaborate meal for many, with little mess, while he could destroy a kitchen with a butter knife and a jar of jelly. He smiled, "A penny for your thoughts Ellie."

"Rodney, come in, I was remembering Charles falling over the loveseat."

Rodney chuckled, and recalled his brother's blissful face when he recounted the anecdote. "Charles said life with Ellie was never dull. He returned to a new home and a new woman. He said a wrenched knee was a minor inconvenience and life with Ellie a delight."

Ellie beamed, "What's in the bag?"

"I thought Kir Royal as an aperitif." Rodney replied. "I brought Crème de Cassis and I'll chill the champagne.

"Rodney!" Betty said happily, "It's good to see you again. Come help set the table," she linked her arm with his. "Let me tell you about Lucy's friend, Valerie. She bought the funeral home and . . .," she led him toward the dining room inconveniently located beyond the morning room.

"Hi Ellie," Baker poked his head into the kitchen, "I brought rolls and cheese biscuits."

"Lucy will smell those biscuits two floors away and come running." Ellie sighed, "I heard the police questioned you, how did that go?"

"Eric asked about my relationship with the health inspector. Relationship, did we have a relationship? He says Rita Russell was smothered in my dough. He's roped off the bakery with yellow tape, and the place is crawling with cops." Baker said disgustedly, "Darcy came by to pick up last night's pastries thinking she'd sell them at her place, but the police vetoed that. I guess my cinnamon buns are suspects too. But," he grinned mischievously, "I pinched your camera from the office. Where do you want it?"

"Thank you, I'm always forgetting the silly thing, put it on the desk."

"If you didn't forget it so often I'd think you were photographing my recipes."

"Never, you wound me," Ellie teased. "You are still available to be my mystery guest on Wednesday?"

"Hmmm, Wednesday might be tricky. Don't frown. I won't weasel out. I want to be your mystery guest, but if the cops let me open tomorrow or Wednesday I'll be pretty busy. Baker shook his head. "Ellie if you find out who killed Ms. Russell so I can get back to work, I'll give you my fritter and my biscuit recipe."

"I'm sure we can work something out." Ellie said suppressing a smile. She ran cold water through garden greens and put them in the spinner.

"Mom, Jake is coming up the walk and Rodney wants the stuff for the *aperitif*," Lucy interrupted. "Baker!" she squealed hugging and being hugged. "You're the best hugger in town. Did you bring biscuits?"

"You never change." Baker chuckled, "Let me open that champagne, that's no job for a mere girl."

"Lucy," Ellie called opening the door to Jake," bring Baker and the drink ingredients to the living room."

"Hurry Baker," Lucy whispered, "Jake found a body. I don't want to miss anything."

"It must have been terrible for you," Ellie said sympathetically, handing Jake's wine offering to Lucy. "Where is Brad? He's not alone in that house is he?"

"I kicked out my painters so Brad's staying with me instead of me with him. He'll be along soon." Jake checked his watch. "He had to meet his boat, but he's been waxing poetic about your taste testing dinners. He brags about being on the 'A' list." Jake sniffed, "I know this is my first, but if that delicious odor is what we're eating it will take an 'Act of God' to keep me away," he stammered, "that is, if I'm asked back."

"Surely Eric doesn't consider Brad a serious suspect." Ellie said, ignoring Jake's blatant request for future invitations.

Jake spread his arms wide. "He questioned Brad and me at the station. Unlike Orville, Eric's questioning was reasoned and unbiased. Orville wants only to railroad Brad, or failing that, me."

"Baker said Eric thinks Ms. Russell was murdered in the bakery so that should work in Brad's favor," Ellie postulated. "Have they settled on a motive?"

Baker snarled, "They suggested that I killed her so she wouldn't find the cat and close me down,"

"That's so stupid," Jake laughed. "If she found Rex we'd call the newspapers, I'd post the cat's history on the Internet. Cat lovers worldwide would rally to our cause. She'd be tarred, feathered, and run out of town on a rail. No they don't seriously suspect either of us." He scowled, "It's Brad they want for it. That idiot Orville believes Brad robbed the bakery, killed the health inspector, carted her body to his own house, and put her in the closet for me to find. Dumb just dumb!"

"Highly improbable; or conversely exceptionally resourceful of him," Rodney contributed as the doorbell rang again.

"Hello Mrs. Wilson, Mrs. Archer, Lucy, and everybody," Brad, with forced cheerfulness, greeted. "Mrs. Wilson, I wanted to bring salmon, but the police impounded my boat," he shrugged philosophically. "If they don't let us unload, the catch will rot in the hold, Lucy, I brought Peller Estates ice wine, to go with desert."

"Did they give you any idea when they'll release the boat?" Baker asked thinking of his stale inventory.

"I didn't talk to them, Stan, my skipper, warned me off. Orville was tearing my boat apart, when Stan called me. Stan says Orville is out to get me if he has to wreck my boat." Brad frowned, "Stan will call after Orville leaves."

"Lucy, the dumplings take thirty minutes to cook," Ellie reminded.

"On my way," Lucy said," and bowing low scooped up the forgotten photo.

Rodney's long fingers tightened around Lucy's wrist. "You need assistance with those dumplings and I'm your man," he towed his niece to the kitchen. He snatched the photo from her hand and peered closely, "The man is Derwood, but who is the child with him?"

"That's Valerie Tate when she married Daniel," Lucy began to explain.

Rodney's voice dripped disgust, "Betty explained that sorry situation, and now that I know Daniel and Derwood are the same unconscionable swine I understand his audacity." Lucy gaped, open mouthed, and Rodney explained. "He bragged about poisoning Robert and exploiting Betty's grief." Rodney paused, "Lucy I know you won't understand what I am about to say." Rodney shook his head, "Those of your generation are straight forward and cannot possibly understand the cunning of a lout of Derwood's ilk," he spoke with all the kindly condescension the older generation reserves for the young.

"Just spit it out Uncle, nothing you can say could possibly top Derwood killing Uncle Robert." Not an innocent like you, Lucy thought with all the hubris the younger generation habitually directs toward their elders.

"All right Lucy." Rodney described Derwood's long term extortion and their final encounter.

"You hit *him*?" Lucy said, grinning, "Marquis of Queensbury rules I trust?"

"No rules dear, he stood battered and bandaged in front of his open safe and I punched him in the nose."

"Bravo Uncle! Small enough pay-back for his abuse; the safe was open you say."

"Yes and crowded with documents, cash, and the goblet with my fingerprints and a residue of the poison he used to kill Robert."

"Why didn't you take the glass?"

"I did not think to take it; and when he gives it to the police; I will be charged."

"*He* can't give the cops the glass or hurt anyone ever again," Lucy blurted. "He's dead. We found him in Aunt Betty's bedroom. He wrecked the Renaissance bed, she hit him with a chunk of it, and thinks she killed him."

"Betty did not kill Derwood, I did," and stiff British upper lip firmly in place he said, "If I am imprisoned it is a small price to pay for her happiness,"

"You hit him in the study and we found him in the bedroom. Later somebody emptied the safe and killed him. Mom wants to believe it's God's will and all for the good of mankind."

"You found him in the bedroom? Then we must summon the police at once regardless of the consequences." Rodney held Lucy's hand, "While I do not often cook, and hesitate to question an accomplished chef, I doubt you need two pounds of butter in dumplings." He wiped the flour from her hands and held her close to his chest, "Dinner will wait, sit down and tell me what you have been holding back."

Lucy dropped onto a press back chair, and planted her elbows on the scarred table. "Thanks Uncle Rodney. There's no butter in my dumplings," she sighed, "and we cannot call the cops, because we disposed of the body and messed up the evidence that would have exonerated you and Aunt Betty," she nervously bounced to her feet, removed the floury butter from the bowl and assembled the dumplings. She told him everything; beginning with the answering machine and ending with Valerie driving to the crematorium, "there's no body, and nobody's going to jail."

"I am overwhelmed and a bit frightened by your resourcefulness." Rodney followed Lucy to the oven, and lifted the cast iron lids while she spooned dumpling batter onto the steaming stew. And though his shock remained palpable he inhaled appreciatively over each steaming casserole before replacing the tight fitting lids.

"Mom, Aunt Betty, Valerie, and I are going to clean up Betty's house tomorrow morning. Aunt Betty will call the police to report Derwood missing and the safe empty." Lucy checked the oven temperature, "You must promise to stay away and let us handle it."

"My dear, your devious mind amazes and to some degree, appalls me. Did it occur to you that someone may have seen one or all of us enter that house?"

"We each had a reason to be there. We are friends come to welcome Betty home, and to remind *him* that she is not alone."

"That seems a plausible explanation, but what of that glass in the safe?"

"I liberated it and hid it in a place only I know about. I don't know why I hid it, somehow it seemed appropriate."

Rodney gazed into her green eyes with his baby blues. "I've always said you were the most resourceful Wilson ever produced."

"Should we tell Aunt Betty the truth about Uncle Robert's death? Lucy asked in a small voice quite unlike her usual confident tone.

"Let's wait until she is stronger."

"Lucy," Ellie called, "how are the dumplings coming?"

"They're in the oven," Lucy replied and nudged Rodney toward the door. "You go enjoy yourself, and remember that you, the non-cook saved the dumplings" she grinned and followed him."

"Lucy did you assemble the salad?" Ellie asked.

"I'm about to do that. Gee, how's a girl to stay informed around here?" She groused for effect, and hurried to the kitchen. She'd called Harv earlier and he'd agreed to take the cherubs to her restoration expert in the city. Mimicking Humphrey Bogart, he'd said, 'Just put them in the trunk, baby. I'll do the job and get back to you.' Lucy imagined Harv as Bogart and her as Bergman, and enjoyed her Casablanca fantasy while she tore crisp greens into small pieces and watched for Harv. She smiled at Harv sporting a gray fedora, poised to tap on the window pane. "Shush," she warned index finger over pursed lips, "I'll be right out." She slipped through the kitchen door leaving it ajar, "I thought you'd forgotten."

"What, and miss a chance to see you, never!" Harv followed Lucy to the Lincoln. "Here let me get that for you," he said, gently belting the blanket wrapped cherubs into the passenger seat of his Porsche.

"Take them to the museum and give them to Martin Schneider-White. You may have to wait; he works in the restoration department in the basement. Give him this note," Lucy added pulling a small wrinkled envelope from the pocket of her black skirt. Harv took the note, but made no move to leave.

"Was there something else?"

"Would you do me the honor of accompanying me to the clambake tomorrow evening," he asked with courteousness so flawless that even the hypercritical Mrs. Wilson would have approved.

Lucy joked, "I'd love to, though Mom will make me carry a peanut butter sandwich. I'm allergic to any old innocent shellfish."

"Don't worry about that. My dad's allergic, too. Brad will supply salmon and trout. I suppose that means he'll be there." Harv grimaced recalling the look she'd given Brad at the diner.

"I suppose it does," Lucy replied, effecting a thoughtful dreamy expression. "I wonder if Brad will grill the salmon with cilantro and honey. He often prepares it that way for me."

"I didn't know you two were such good friends. Brad seems like an okay guy; maybe he could ask your friend Valerie to the clambake."

"They would make a cute couple; I'll suggest it. He's here now and Val's coming later."

"What's he doing here?"

"He's a regular at mom's column dinners. Where do you want me to meet you?"

"That's a rapid subject change and I'll pick you up right here and I'll bring you flowers. That should convince your mother that I'm a natural born gentleman."

"We'll work something out, but now I really have to go in," Lucy said. "I'm supposed to have the salad dressed and I haven't started on the vinaigrette."

"Wait a minute, would you come to the lighthouse dedication with me? My dad will be there and I know you two will hit it off, he's a reasonable man."

Lucy jerked her hand from Harv's, and said icily, "Are you implying that my mother is unreasonable?"

Harv blushed; "I'm sorry Lucy, but your mother is—," he sought the least offensive phrase.

His prolonged silence brought out Lucy's wicked imp. "I don't have all night Harvey Francis Benjamin Sterling Spencer Junior, come to think of it why, does any single individual need six names? Speak up."

"I, uh, my mother uh, thought it sounded classy?"

"Good answer," Lucy said.

Ellie's voice cut through the night. "Lucy where are you? Rodney, she's gone and she hasn't finished the salad."

"She's probably in the garden collecting parsley or lemons."

Lucy heard the sharp pop of a champagne cork. She hugged Harv enthusiastically. "Mom's radar is working perfectly. I forgive you for saying she's unreasonable 'cause she is, but only where you're concerned." Lucy sighed, "I would love to accompany you to the clambake and lighthouse dedication. I have to scoot before mom gets the shotgun and goes a huntin' Spencers. Call me. On my cell," she tucked her business card into his shirt pocket.

Harv set his fedora on her head and aped Bogart, "See you around kid."

Sporting the faded fedora, Lucy paused to admire her reflection in the window. The grey hat exactly matched her cashmere sweater. It's really quite retro; she thought and tiptoed into the kitchen. I wonder where he got it.

Ellie trembled and paled. My God, she thought, I can't stand it.

"Are you all right Ellie?" Rodney asked. "Lucy told me about your busy day, you must be exhausted. Come sit down," he led his sister-in-law into the hall. "Lucy and I will serve dinner."

"Rodney, it has to stop." Ellie grasped his sleeve, "She's falling victim to that wastrel."

"Come Ellie, we raised her well. She's too bright to be taken in by the likes of him."

"I hope you're right, but what if we can't dissuade her?"

Rodney grinned, "Then I'll have a go at him."

"It's so unfair of that horrid man and his rake of a son to invade our lives. He knows the misery his family caused mine and that boy is the image of his hedonistic male line.

"Ellie, calm yourself. Lucy hasn't met a man who held her interest for long. There is no reason to assume this young sprout is any different. If we fight her, we will lose. But if this relationship progresses like her others our secret can remain hidden. Meanwhile I've heard some uncomplimentary things about him, I'll talk to her. You go back to your guests."

Her voice knife-sharp Ellie asked, "What things?"

"Nothing concrete, just rumor and innuendo," Rodney evaded. "I'll talk to her Ellie, I promise."

Lucy leapt away from the doorway, "Hi Uncle Rodney! Is something wrong with mom?" she asked crushing garlic for the vinaigrette.

"She is concerned about your new young man. I've heard that Harvey Spencer's son is quite the budding Lothario."

"And," Lucy interrupted, "you've also heard that Ellie Wilson's daughter has never had a relationship that lasted more than three months."

"Yes I have also heard that," Rodney conceded.

"Uncle Rodney," Lucy pleaded, "please be happy for me."

"I've said my piece and I am pleased for you, but Lucy you must promise that if things become serious between you and the Spencer lad you will talk to me before things get," he searched for the correct word, gave up, and settled for, "heated. May I have your word?"

Lucy searched her uncle's face, saw an intractable firmness, and reluctantly acquiesced. But what are they hiding, she wondered?

"Lucy the hat is fetching, but since none of the other ladies are wearing hats, perhaps this is an inappropriate time to reintroduce a fashion trend." Rodney casually plucked the fedora from her head and tossed it onto the rocker. "Shall we serve the appetizer now?"

"The table looks fantastic," Lucy said, admiring the way the light of the red candles picked up the pale blues and whites in grandma's Wedgwood china. The Wilson heirloom silver glistened against white Irish linen. Napkins in bright red damask adorned each plate. Decanted red wine sparkled and danced in an antique carafe while red roses in shinning silver crowned the whole enchanting array. Lucy wondered if Ellie choose the colors as a final gesture to, or perhaps a salvo at Dreadful Derwood? Pallid bodies, white linen and white wine; red blood, red roses and red wine; yucky, really yucky Lucy thought.

"Ellie, the rabbit was marvelous. Everything was delightful as usual," Rodney complemented, enthusiastically cleaning up the last few crumbs of his raisin pie. "Is everyone ready for port?"

"I'll put coffee on and serve it in the living room," Lucy offered heading to the kitchen. The doorbell, one of the few modern conveniences her mother had installed, rang and she detoured to answer it.

"Michael, it's about time," Lucy said vigorously hugging her childhood friend. "We've saved you some of everything and remember the price is glowing, constructive critique, or enjoyment so blatant that appreciation is demonstrated. Come into the kitchen, your dinner is in the warming oven."

"No problem and Lucy you look great, as usual. Work agrees with you."

"You are a good liar. My poor head has barely touched a pillow since I landed. I feel like a dishrag."

Michael smacked his lips, "Then sit down, I'll help myself to dinner and a massive piece of raisin pie."

"Michael," Lucy said, "would you do something for me just because I asked without a lot of embarrassing questions?" Lucy her eyes downcast toyed with a button on his starched shirt.

"Uh," Michael croaked, "feminine wiles don't work on me, but in some perverse way they're flattering," he sputtered through laughter. "And I'd do almost anything for you. Does this favor involve something illegal? I really don't want the friends I'd make in jail."

"I'm serious," Lucy wailed. "I need your help, but you can't tell anyone," she warned, "promise?"

"I promise for an extra piece of pie," Michael said, solemnly placing his right hand over his heart. "Do we have to spit shake now?"

"Michael this is important."

"Sorry Mosquito," Michael apologized resurrecting a childhood moniker.

"Mickey darling," Lucy responded in kind.

"You win Lucy, I'll do it." He grimaced frowning, "What do you want?"

Lucy dumped Derwood's monogrammed computer bag onto the table. "I want you to hack into Derwood's computer, copy all the records, interpret them, and then I want you to try to make sense out of these," she pulled check stubs and bank statements from the open bag.

"How did you get your hands on that?" Michael asked awed. "I've tried, but he keeps them locked in his desk. And for the record, I'll do anything to stop him stripping Betty of everything she owns. How much time do I have? He's bound to miss this stuff."

"Let me worry about that. You work on the laptop first then the bank stuff. Mom said Jake would love to help, he was CFO of a multinational company," Lucy placed a colorful appetizer in front of him. "Michael?"

"Not another favor," he mumbled between mouthfuls of hors d'oeuvre.

"Derwood replaced all Uncle Robert's paintings with copies."

"Not all," Michael grinned. "I commissioned reproductions and made the switch when I realized he was selling the originals. Would you believe he complained to me when he peddled the fakes? He said he thought Robert had better taste."

"Michael, you are marvelous," Lucy exclaimed returning her friend's awed admiration.

"I know," he preened, "and what we get from the computer and bank information together with what I already have should be enough to let Betty clean up in the divorce. She told you she's going to divorce him, didn't she?" he asked nervously.

"Yes and its past time too."

"That's a relief, for a moment I was afraid she'd changed her mind, but on to happier subjects. Have you seen the bed? It's absolutely perfect. I wish you could have heard Betty when she told me you'd found it. She sounded like she did when Robert was alive. Lucy, you did a wonderful thing. What's wrong?"

"Derwood destroyed it."

"What do you mean destroyed? I was going to deliver the mattress this morning, but our guy is on holiday, and I couldn't reach Brad."

"Michael, listen to me. He cut it up with a chain saw. He destroyed it."

"That sorry son-of-a-bitch," Michael exclaimed, "I'll eat fast, and get to work on his computer."

"Quiet," Lucy whispered, "Val's coming."

"Sorry I'm late, Lucy. I told your mom I'd stay to," Valerie saw Michael, and paused, "clean up," she finished lamely.

"I don't think you've met Michael. He and Aunt Betty are partners in the antique store on Main Street. Valerie owns the funeral chapel out on the highway. Michael wanted to eat in the kitchen to be closer to the food, "Lucy pulled out a chair for Valerie, "I assume everything went like clockwork?"

"Yes I…" Valerie hesitated.

"With the health inspector's body, I mean," Lucy clarified.

"Ah, yes. The pathologist will autopsy her tomorrow."

"Rita Russell, that health inspector?" Michael asked. "Was she in an accident? Join me Valerie, and tell all"

"I've got to take the coffee out. Michael show Val where the food is and join us when you've finished."

She put the tray on the coffee table and listened. Rodney said, "Ellie if you force me to choose then the rabbit is my favorite, though the chicken merits a special ovation. Both won me over with their individual herby aromas before I had taken a bite."

"Do I have to choose one to be invited back?" Jake asked. "If I do, I prefer the rabbit. If I don't then both dishes tie for first place."

"Why don't you put detailed instructions for the rabbit in your column and include the changes for the chicken at the bottom," Baker suggested. "I liked the chicken best, though I'm outnumbered. How come no one ever rates my rolls?"

"I give your rolls a ten out of ten, you old glory hound," Betty teased. "Ellie both dishes were delicious, but like Baker, I preferred the chicken."

"Brad, that makes your vote the tie breaker," Ellie said smiling.

"I liked the rabbit best, but I wouldn't turn down the chicken, but Mrs. Wilson, why don't you write about adding locally caught fish to all our diets," Brad teased.

"We'll do fish in the spring Brad, I promise." Ellie laughed, "I will try all of Eloise' recipes."

"Mark me down for that fish test and I loved the rabbit and dumplings, but the chicken version was excellent and perhaps better suits the taste and budget of some of your readers," Michael said ambling into the room with Valerie on his arm.

"I prefer both," Valerie said with the enthusiasm of a food lover who doesn't cook.

"That's everybody so all that's left is to congratulate the cooks for a delightful dinner." Rodney led the applause that almost drowned the thunderous pounding on the front door and insistent doorbell.

"I'm coming," Ellie called flinging open the door. "Officer, what can I do for you? Wait one moment young man," she shrieked attempting to stall his headlong rush. "This is private property and I did not invite you in!"

"You are harboring a felon," Orville bellowed tramping into the living room.

"What do you mean felon? No one has been charged," Jake objected.

"Not that it's any of your business," Orville sneered, "but I found a wad of cash hidden on that boat of his."

"Lots of people keep money hidden in strange places Officer. Why my own father used to keep money in a tea can buried in the cellar," Betty said joining Baker, who'd planted himself in front of Brad.

"Stand out of the way lady," Orville ordered ignoring the baker. "I've heard enough from you. This time you ain't got no fancy lawyer. Get out of my way or I'll haul you in."

"It's all right, Mrs. Archer. I didn't do anything wrong," Brad gently moved Betty aside. "Please don't cry. I'd appreciate your calling Ms. Homes for me."

Betty addressed Brad while irritably dashing at tears, "I will accompany you to the station."

"No lady, you won't," Orville barked grabbing Brad's arm. "Nobody is comin' with us."

"Brad, we'll be right behind you," Jake, seconded by Rodney's quick agreement and Baker's terse nod, promised.

"Lucy, Michelle is dining with Zack this evening. Please call her," Betty ordered.

Brad smiled weakly at the women and nodded to the men; Orville dragged his arms behind him and clamped on handcuffs.

"You have the right to remain silent . . ," hovered in the air as Orville towing Brad, elbowed Ellie aside and pushed through the door.

Ellie sprawled on her deacon's bench; Jake helped her stand, "Did he hurt you?"

"I'm fine," Ellie assured all the concerned faces clustered around her. "Follow that cretin. I'm worried about Brad's safety."

"We'll call when we know what's happening," Jake promised, soon a second sharp slam of the door echoed the first.

"I could kill that moron," Betty said scathingly, realized what she said and shuddered.

"I can't believe he assaulted you right in front of us," Michael sighed, "Although I shouldn't be surprised. He's hassled me often enough. That's why I didn't go along. I'd only make things worse for Brad."

"Oh Michael," Betty groaned, "Did he harass you?"

"Michelle Homes is on her way to the station," Lucy said handing Michael a pie and the computer bag with duct tape over the monogram. "You should go now, you have important stuff to do."

"This is intolerable," Betty fumed as Michael hurried to his car.

"Aunt Betty, we don't have time for anger, tears or recrimination," Lucy lectured wishing she'd decked Orville. "Mom you and Aunt Betty rest. Valerie and I will clear up and wash the dishes. Then we'll figure out how to prove Brad's innocence."

"Ellie, you've been on your feet all day. I'll help the girls. I'll wash," Betty said, amused at the way the familiar old phrase slid off her tongue.

"I am tired, but before I rest I'll make fresh coffee. This has been a long full day, but I think they liked the stews, don't you?"

"They loved them," Betty replied, "I wouldn't be surprised if the new tasters beg for future invitations."

"Mom, do you want the tape recorder?" Lucy called from the dining room. "She keeps it running while her guests comment. That way when they say something clever she can quote it verbatim," she told Valerie.

"It can wait," Ellie said. "Betty tomorrow morning we clean up at your house and call the police. Though frankly after that ruffian Orville, I cannot guess what they'll do." She dropped into the rocking chair only to leap up again rubbing her backside. She gingerly picked up the mashed fedora with two fingers, and hung it on a wall peg, reminding herself that Charles too had owned such a hat. She picked up the camera Baker had returned, removed the chip, and absently inserted it into the card reader connected to her computer.

"Where did you take that picture?" Betty asked

"I did not take it!"

"No you didn't," Lucy agreed dumping a mass of cutlery into the steaming dishwater. "And I know," she added dramatically, "because this isn't your camera. Yours has your name engraved on it, and those tiny shoes are definitely not yours."

"Those look to be 4½'s and could be Miss Russell's," Betty said.

"Can you make the image larger?" Valerie asked. "Does that say Rex on the collar?"

"Yes and Rex is the bakery cat. That's Baker's mixer in the background," Ellie confirmed.

"Look at the time/date feature. If, as Jake suspects she died at the bakery, this picture was taken just before she was murdered," Lucy said.

"I'll make copies. Tomorrow we have to give it to Chief Platt. This could clear Brad."

"What if it doesn't?" Betty asked.

"Then we will find the killer," Ellie said, and find Derwood's killer while we're at it, she thought. Kill two birds with one stone, so to speak.

COOKING WITH ELLIE WILSON

Autumn, the time for our annual retreat back indoors is upon us. The grill is relegated to a corner in the garage and the picnic gear languishes in the basement. Cool nights prompt memories of hearty dinners, hot from the oven. Enticing aromas transport us back to the days when a pot of stew simmered on the back of the cook stove. Dumplings, everyone's favorites, often extended the meat and filled out the meal. Mmm, I can almost taste it. Today's recipe is a rabbit casserole my daughter Lucy developed while in France. I call it Lucy's Lapin.

Lucy's Lapin and Sage Dumplings
½ pound bacon
1 rabbit quartered
4 large carrots
4 small leeks
1 large onion
4 or 5 stalks celery
4 tablespoons flour
2 cups chicken stock OR 2 cups water and a bouillon cube
½ cup dry white wine
3 tablespoons chopped fresh sage OR 1½ tablespoon dry sage
Fresh ground black pepper
Salt to taste

1. Snip bacon into ½ inch pieces and fry in a high sided heavy skillet over medium high heat. Fry until the fat is released, add the rabbit quarters, brown on all sides.

2. Remove rabbit quarters to an oven safe casserole or Dutch oven. With a slotted spoon scoop the bacon over the rabbit, leaving the grease in the skillet.

3. Add coarsely chopped carrots, leeks, onion, and celery to the reserved fat. All vegetables should the same size, about an inch, sauté for ten minutes and add to the Dutch oven with the rabbit and bacon.

4. Sprinkle the flour over the contents in the Dutch oven. Add the chicken stock or two cups of water and a crumbled bouillon cube and the wine, sage and pepper. Stir well and bring to a boil, stirring often; season to taste.

5. Cover the casserole and place in preheated oven at 325° for about 1½ hours or until rabbit is tender.

To make the dumplings combine:
2 cups flour
4 teaspoons baking powder
½ tsp. salt
¾ cup milk
2 tablespoons chopped fresh sage

Drop generous tablespoons of dumpling mix into the hot stew. Put the tight lid on and bake without peeking, another 20 to 25 minutes or until dumplings are well risen and cooked through. Serves four

I do urge you all to try the robust rabbit version of this dish, as it received rave reviews but a few of my guests preferred the delightful chicken adaptation I developed for those readers who cannot locate or dislike rabbit.

<u>Luscious Chicken and Dumplings</u>

The ingredient list is much the same as for the rabbit stew with the following substitutions:
1½ cups whole baby carrots rather than sliced carrots.
1 cup pearl onions not chopped onions.
3 tablespoons chopped sweet marjoram OR 1½ tablespoon dry marjoram instead of sage (though sage is lovely too.)
And:
1 teaspoon dried thyme
1 cup small button mushrooms browned in butter

Steps 1 through 5 remain the same as in the lapin recipe. Add the thyme during step 5 and the browned mushrooms when you drop the dumplings into the stew.

For the dumplings substitute sweet marjoram for sage though once again sage is tasty. The oven dumplings are great because they are easy, light, and fluffy.

CHAPTER 13

His lips touched hers, tender, loving, caring. The kiss grew more passionate and his arms tightened around her; ardent, demanding. She felt his heart pounding as she molded her body to his.

He gazed deep into her eyes and finally reluctantly pushed her away. She felt abandoned, bereft as if her heart had been yanked, still beating, from her bosom.

"You know I love you, but we must go slowly. Let us get to know each other as friends first. I want you to be sure," he whispered urgently.

"I am sure," she insisted attaching herself to his chest like the proverbial limpet. I've waited all my life for you. I'm ready right now."

"No, I cannot."

"You don't love me; if you did, you wouldn't do this to me."

"I do love you; how can you doubt the depth of my feelings?"

"Then why? Why Harv? Why should we wait?" she asked with a frustration born of passion.

"Well frankly my dear," he whispered passionately, "your mother scares the lust right out of me."

"Lucy! Ellie shook her daughter gently. "Honey, wake up, you're having a nightmare."

Lucy groaned, "Yes Mother, I am now."

"Are you awake?"

"Humph," Lucy groaned.

"Oh, I see you set your alarm. Betty and I are going to Darcy's for breakfast. Honey, go back to sleep," Ellie pulled the blankets up around her daughter's shoulders before softly closing the door.

"The poor girl is exhausted." Betty collected her purse, "We could have left her a note instead of waking her."

"No, this way when she says we didn't invite her, I can say she didn't sound interested. I left her a note. She won't remember anyway," Ellie said, "Your car or mine?"

"Yours, I think. I'm not used to the car being mine again. Derwood didn't let me use it. He almost convinced me to let my license lapse. Some spark of sanity made me realize I couldn't function in business without my license." Betty giggled, "Ellie I'm free! I keep pinching myself to convince me that I'm not delusional." She buckled her seatbelt, "But Ellie in my heart of hearts, I don't believe it; I'm waiting for the other shoe to drop."

"You'll believe it when we've cleaned your room and dealt with the police," Ellie said, superstitiously crossing her fingers in the hope that what Betty felt was nervous tension, and not premonition. "I really should have dragged Lucy out of bed to come along. Should I call her now?"

"Stop dithering. Indecision doesn't suit you."

"I'll call her cell phone. She's had that darn thing surgically attached." Ellie stopped at the corner, hit speed dial and waited, only to hear Lucy say breathlessly, "Harv?"

"No Lucy," Ellie's tone was as frigid as the arctic winds that would soon freeze Huron Shores, "this is your mother."

"Oh, hi Mom, why are you calling? Where are you?"

"Darcy's, Betty was worried you'd sleep through your alarm. You did say you wanted to help with the cleanup."

"I'll come to the diner right away." Lucy stabbed the off button. Blast! Why do I feel guilty? Mom and I are going to have to have one of those infamous mother-daughter talks and this time I'll tell her the facts of life. Knuckling sleep from her eyes, she laughed, kicked back the covers and headed for the shower, planning what she'd wear on her date.

"Let's sit outside," Ellie suggested. "We should enjoy the last nice days of summer, soon the snow will fly."

"I may stay home this winter if everything goes as planned." Betty said, "Won't it be fun to cross country ski together again?" Then, like a sun bathed icicle, her cheerful smile melted.

"Betty Archer, stop wallowing! We are going to have a delightful chat, solve the entire world's problems, eat a fattening breakfast without guilt, and drink Darcy poor, sipping endless cups of coffee until Darcy tosses us out. There's Zack. Let's join him."

"You've always been a bossy broad," Betty giggled, throwing exuberant arms around her friend.

"Have you two been hitting the sauce early or won the lottery?" Zack questioned, one eyebrow risibly raised.

"Good morning to you too, Zackary, it's nice to see you out and about early. It looks like Darcy is short staffed. Zack, can I get you a coffee?"

"Some of Darcy's usual swill will be fine, thanks," Zack called to Ellie, already deep in conversation with Darcy. "It's great to see you back Betty. The guys get out of hand without you to keep them grounded."

"I'm sure Ellie does that. How have you been?"

"Fine, except that the new pills loose strange phantoms to roam free in my head. I'll tell you about it when Ellie gets back. She sees things in my dreams that I don't, and she makes me laugh."

"It's good to see your feeling better," Jake observed plopping down next to Zack. "Baker and I were worried about you the other night."

"How's Brad holding up?" Betty asked. "Sorry Zack, it's just that we're worried."

"Ms. Homes said Orville committed a raft of procedural infractions when he seized the boat and arrested Brad. She assured me he'll be released this morning. I'm just waiting for the call," Jake said gleefully. "Sorry to wreck your date with Michelle, Zack."

"We were finished eating and it wasn't a date, just two old friends sharing a meal." Zack replied nodding to Baker. "We went to school together, you know."

Baker slid his arm around Betty's shoulders and whispered, "About the other night when you were out walking, I saw Lucy in the study or I would have checked on you when I walked Zack home."

Betty's mind slipped away from the buzz of conversation around her. How could Baker see Lucy? Ellie and Lucy were viewing the refurbished lighthouse about the time Baker saw the woman. I was in the patrol car with Eric when he got the call about the burglary. The timing was wrong, so if Baker didn't see Lucy who was Derwood entertaining? Is another woman the reason our union was never consummated? Thank you Lord for that blessing, she sighed, confusion thy name is Betty.

"Hello Jake, hello Baker," Ellie juggled a tray full of coffee cups. "Coffee all round?" she grinned happily. "Our gang is together again."

"Zack wanted to tell you about his dreams," Betty interjected putting aside her troubling thoughts. "He wants you to interpret them."

"And me without my crystal ball," Ellie laughed. "But Zack, I'm afraid your dreams will have to wait. I forgot about our meeting with what's his name this morning. Hurry Betty or we'll be late."

Betty whined, "Lucy isn't here, and I haven't finished my coffee."

"Bring your coffee," Ellie ordered, pointing to where Valerie, trailed by two women, wound through parked cars. Ellie appropriated an empty table farthest from the men, "Lucy isn't here yet Valerie why don't you and your friends join us."

Val introduced Doris and Sue, Derwood's other wives. Doris was a worn looking blond, who held a brightly colored handkerchief to her constantly dripping eyes. She wore a floral print dress like those Ellie's grandmother had worn late in her long life; dark stockings and orthopedic shoes.

Sue, some years older, had with the obvious help of her beautician, ash blond hair held by a purple clip that matched her slacks and pale lilac blouse. She grabbed at the white sweater that slipped from her squared shoulders as her shaking finger found Betty's. "So you're the one the rotten bastard is working over now. Too bad we didn't find you sooner, but then you wouldn't have listened anyway. I sure as hell didn't."

"Where is my sweet man?" Doris whispered tearfully. "This is all an awful mistake."

"You stupid sap," Sue screeched punctuating each word with a fist to the table. "He ripped you off just like he did the rest of us. You were his practice run. Wake up you fool! Sorry," she apologized perfunctorily. "I've spent too much time with this whiner. She got her backbone ripped out by the dirty bugger or," she said thoughtfully, "maybe she's in on it with him, she's the only one legally married to *him*." Sue sat examining her idea like it was a thread, hard to see and difficult to grasp.

There's an idea, Ellie thought, maybe one or both of them are Derwood's accomplice. "It was interesting meeting you ladies, but we have a pressing engagement. Betty, you should have reminded me. Valerie, bring the ladies by my house tonight about eight? We'll have drinks and a private chat."

"Wait! I'm supposed to help you," Valerie said painfully grasping Ellie's arm.

"Lucy will be by to pick you up any minute," Ellie explained with a meaning filled look.

Trotting to keep up with Ellie's long strides, Betty protested, "What was that all about?"

"Call Lucy; tell her there's been a change of plans."

"No honey," Betty said juggling the phone and her rapidly cooling coffee, "it's Aunt Betty. Your mother wants you to swing by the diner to pick up Valerie right away . . . we'll see you at my house. We heard some things Ellie wants to mull before we meet Derwood's other wives tonight. Are you choking Lucy? All right dear, see you at my place."

"She thought you were Harv."

"Yes she did and what are we going to do about that situation?"

Ellie sighed, "I wish I knew. Rodney thinks we should batten down the hatches and wait out the storm, but I'm worried. I'm thinking of telling her everything."

"That may be premature since she's never had a long term relationship. I've seen her smitten one day and totally disillusioned the next, let's wait a bit longer."

"Times have changed Betty. What we called promiscuity, is normal behavior to today's women"

"Lucy is not into one night stands. That's part of the reason her relationships go sour. She runs if a guy comes on too strong. I often wonder if she isn't put off by my experience with Derwood."

"Well if it causes her to reject Harv, Derwood will have done some good," Ellie snapped. "Oh Betty, I'm sorry. I can't believe I said something so insensitive to you."

"Don't apologize. I understand your anxiety better than anyone. Why don't we talk about Sue and Doris? That's why we ran out of Darcy's before I finished my coffee isn't it?"

"I thought a private venue more appropriate in light of Sue's theories and her colorful turn of phrase, but they're quite the pair and taken together with Valerie, all similar in coloring, height and build," Ellie mused, turning onto Short Street.

"Pull over!" Betty shrieked. What is that filthy thing doing in my yard? Sam, get that off my lawn. Now!" Betty jumped from the car to yank at the for sale sign. "Sammy, get over here and get this abomination out of my sight. Look you've made a hole."

Sam Ranker struggled out of the porch swing and lumbered across the grass as fast as his bowed legs would carry him. "Betty! You're alive, I thought he killed you."

"What are you talking about?" Betty demanded.

"There's blood in a bedroom upstairs. I assumed it was yours," Sam explained.

"What were you doing in my house?"

Sam grinned like a Cheshire cat, "Derwood signed the listing last week. He gave me a key so I could measure. I got a couple want to see the house this afternoon." Sam continued as Betty fumed. Derwood's car stopped at the curb, "Here's Derwood now he'll straighten you out." Sam's Jaw dropped when Lucy, not Derwood climbed from behind the wheel.

Trembling Betty snarled, "*My* home is not for sale." She snatched up the sign and bashed it repeatedly onto the sidewalk scant inches from

Sammy's shiny shoes. "They don't call you Sleazy Sam for nothing, do they?"

"Mom," Lucy whispered, "Get her out of here and calm her down. Make sure she's got her story straight. I'll see what I can do inside."

"Oh my stars, you're right. She was not prepared for this." Ellie collected her scattered wits and rushed to separate the combatants. Sam backed into the street while he pompously explained the unbreakability of signed contracts.

Valerie opened the door. "I have some experience cleaning up crime scenes Lucy, but we better hurry."

"You girls better not go in there. Wait for the cops. I called them just before your aunt vandalized my sign."

"It's okay Mr. Ranker. Valerie is an experienced pathologist. She might notice something that will help Officer Platt."

"You gals will be in a lot of trouble," Ranker threatened, cradling his battered sign. "Ellie remember I warned them. Don't blame me when they come out puking."

Valerie wrinkled her nose, "This room is ghastly."

"Yeah, *he* turned her sanctuary into this *bordel*," Lucy threw her hands up in a Gallic gesture and spat out the French idiom that so aptly described the room with its red walls, lilac ceiling and oil stained Persian rug. "Ouch! Damn it! I've cut my toe," she scooped up a splintered cross.

"That cut is deep," Valerie said, "I'd better clean it up. Who knows what germs *Daniel* spread," she opened the door to Betty's en-suite and returned with sticky tape and gauze.

"That bathroom smells like my first year anatomy class. There's blood everywhere," Valerie dressed Lucy's toe. "It looks like the killer cleaned up in there."

"When do you collect *his* ashes?" Lucy asked, suddenly needing confirmation that *Derwood* was indeed ash and air pollution. She tugged Valerie toward the hall, "Shush, I hear the big feet and long arm of the law."

"Try to look sickened or disgusted," Valerie advised.

"Lucy, what are you doing here? Valerie Tate, you both know better than to mess up a crime scene. Did either of you touch anything?"

"Eric, Lucy cut her foot on a splinter and I bandaged it, I'm sorry I don't know where my mind was."

"Well no harm done I guess, your prints are on file. And Lucy we still have yours from your time with the auxiliary. I've often said you'd have my job and be Chief by now if you'd stayed with us," his quick eye scanned the room. "This town has gone crazy, a burglary, a murder, and now this bloody mess all in the same week."

"Chief Platt," Lucy said, grateful that he'd reminded her of his promotion, "Do you know what's happening with Brad?"

"You know Orville broke some regulations when he arrested Brad and assaulted Ellie while doing it, so it looks like he's stepped in it big this time." Eric shook his head, "That's more than I should have said. Now get out of here before I charge you with disturbing my peace."

Ellie held her ear to the window in back of Betty's house, but sounds were muffled, so she stopped listening and paced. Eric was spending too long questioning Betty. He'd needed only fifteen minutes to take Sammy's statement and five for hers. Sammy pompous, self important and bursting to share his knowledge set a speed record. Lucy and Valerie signed and left. Valerie to prepare a client who'd died peacefully in his own bed. Imagine that, a death in Huron Shore's that didn't involve treachery, chaos, or any of my friends, Ellie thought.

Why would anyone trim, rather butcher, these plants? Ellie wondered, frowning at a Grecian foxglove bed. Foxglove were Betty's favorite flower, and Robert had spent years planting, tending, isolating and finally harvesting seed in the hope of developing a special hybrid to name in his wife's honor. A path led through an immature stand of white pine planted to shelter the lavish shed where Robert had done his research. Derwood like a rabid animal left his noxious mark here too, Robert's once pristine lab was in total disarray. Pots, soil, tags, and tools were haphazardly tossed in a corner, but the missing foxglove was painstakingly pinned to ordered lines crisscrossing the ceiling. Neatly labeled, dustless bottles incongruous on a dusty shelf above the spotty sink caught Ellie's attention. Robert's voice seemed to echo, 'Grecian Foxglove, the herb Digitalis lanata provides the drugs digitoxin and digoxin, both used in orthodox medicine to regulate the heartbeat.' He'd always followed his lecture with a disclaimer that went something like, 'all foxglove species are poisonous and should be used by qualified personnel only' How strange I would swear I heard Robert's voice. Ellie selected a small, black notebook from the messy heap beside the vials and paged through it.

"Ellie," Betty called, "we can go now."

I'll need time to decipher *his* illegible script, Ellie thought, and tried to concentrate. "I'm in the shed Betty. I'll be right with you," she stuffed the notebook into her pocket, her mind leapt around like a mountain goat.

"Mom, don't wait up. We'll talk tomorrow," Lucy called hastily closing the door to side step the customary, 'isn't he coming to the door' query.

Harv, flowers in hand strode up the walk prepared to beard the lioness in her den. Dad suggested flowers without thorns in case they were rejected with force. Lucy flew toward him, every man's fantasy in an abbreviated red and white striped Basque fisherman's T-shirt, crisp, white clamdiggers cinched tight around an impossibly tiny waist and red straw sandals. He handed her a dozen red roses and after a scant moment's hesitation gave her the white ones as well, resolving to win her mother's approval another day.

Lucy wondered if the white roses were symbolic of surrender or a flag of truce. She sprinted back up the path, burst through the door calling, "Mom Harv brought us roses." She thrust both bunches at her mother and beat a hasty retreat before Ellie could lose her caustic tongue.

Harv helped Lucy into his car. He felt Ellie's eyes boring into his back. "Are we running late?" he asked as the engine roared. "I thought I was to meet your mother and the celebrated Uncle Rodney. I was sure he'd ask my intentions and tell me to have Cinderella home by twelve or be devoured by the big bad wolf or the three bears or something."

"A little sketchy on the fairy tales are we?" Lucy laughed. "We can work on that. I like the happy ever after parts best."

"I don't know much about those," Harv said, memories of his lonely childhood intruded on what he'd meant to be a lighthearted conversation.

"How's your father? Did I hear he has a heart problem?" Lucy remembered Ellie's remark and hid a smile, 'Heart trouble? Impossible, Spencer males do not have hearts.'

"As usual the gossips got it wrong. Dad had an allergic reaction. Cook put mussels in a pasta dish he fixed for me, but forgot to label the leftovers. Dad ate the pasta about midnight, and fortunately I was home to administer the epinephrine and get him to the clinic on time."

"I can sympathize," Lucy said, remembering eating scallops in a dish Derwood prepared. "I don't usually eat at an event like this. It was considerate of your father to provide the fish," she said wanting to know more of the mysterious Harvey Spencer Senior. Maybe the secret her mother and Uncle Rodney whispered about involved Mr. Spencer.

"He is considerate and thinks of everything. That's why he's successful in business."

Lucy forced her mind away from phrases like, robber barons, rapacious pirates, and larcenous swindlers, words her family used to describe Spencer men's business success. She saw Warden Ancestors spinning in their graves, and smiled as images of those relatives, all represented in water color, oil or photograph, swam in her mind's eye. All were armed with pitchforks and scythes and eager for the confrontation they'd been denied in life.

"Is that smile for me?" Harv asked. "Want to tell me what you're thinking?"

"I reserve all my smiles for you," she said saucily, and resolved to keep her imaginings to herself. She'd been grateful when grandpa told her an undoubtedly abridged version of the Warden-Spencer feud. He'd said the antagonism had to end and perhaps her generation would end it. I'm just following grandpa's wishes, she thought, and frowned when she remembered his closing remark. 'Let bygones be bygones and steer clear of Spencers. But, if you're ever forced to shake hands with a Spencer count your fingers afterward.'

"How was your dinner party last night?" Harv asked, thinking his date silent long enough. "Did you set Brad up with Valerie?"

"I didn't have a chance to talk to him. That rat Orville dragged him away in cuffs. Poor mom, her dinner party was more memorable then she planned."

"I heard about Brad. Scuttlebutt says he's a victim. The gossips say Brad's a great guy being framed," Harv said trying to be objective. "I hear your mother's dinner parties are memorable with or without entertainment," he said, "any chance I'll ever find out first hand?"

Lucy choked back the 'when hell freezes over' that sprang to her lips, coughed and smiled accepting Harv's hand to climb from the low slung car, but ducking his question. "There's Val alone as usual. She's so shy she'll stand there all night if I don't introduce her around. "Val, I thought we were meeting by the band shell?"

Valerie took a couple of careful steps, grabbed Lucy in around the neck, and running her words together said, "Just like the old days, Lucy Wilson sashays in with a great looking stud." She grinned and closed one heavily lashed, blue eye in a coquettish wink.

"Thanks, I think," Harv mumbled. Lucy's definition of shy was different than his.

Lucy disentangled herself from Val and sniffed. "Valerie Tate you've been drinking bourbon. Lucy plucked a plastic cup out of Valerie's loose grip. "Sorry about this Harv. She can drink three or four glasses of wine with no problem, but with liquor she has a total personality reversal, Lucy grimaced, "just before she throws up."

"Don't talk about me like I'm not here," Valerie sulked, "look what I got," she thumbed open a glossy calendar. "Take a gander at Mr. May and the Misters December."

Lucy tried to take the calendar, but Val clutched it to her chest, "Buy your own. These might be the only strong, virile firemen I get to hug.

"She'll be sick in a few minutes," Lucy predicted.

"I am not drunk, just a little happy. Don't I deserve a little happy, Ms. Lucy Ma'am?" Valerie slurred. "Look at this, Mister." She shoved the calendar open to October's under Lucy nose.

Harv snatched it away.

"Excuse us Harv, I have to take her care of her," Lucy said. "And don't let them sell out of those," she motioned to the crumpled calendar page covered by Harv's face, muscular chest, great legs, red roses and little else. "I may buy a gross." Lucy smirked. "I bet mom would like one," she teased, "Why don't you find Brad?"

Valerie stood strait; her posture would have pleased a drill sergeant. "Brad was talking to his lawyer. I didn't like to interrupt and when I leafed through the calendar I didn't know what to say. What is proper Lucy? Do I praise his great pectorals or tell him lilies are my favorite flower. And speaking of flowers Harv, I hope they de-thorned those roses?" Laughing raucously Valerie sank to the sand. "I don't feel so good," she whined.

"Come on kid, just like old times," Lucy yanked Valerie up, and led her to the toilet. They squeezed into a cramped cubicle. Lucy held Valerie's hair back as the alcohol extracted its revenge. Dealing with Derwood's carcass must have upset her more then she'd acknowledged. We could have had problems if she reaches the loquacious stage when she tells all. Lucy smiled wryly, that would be a disaster.

"I'm sorry Lucy. You're the best friend I ever had and I've let you down."

"Forget it. You've been through a lot," Lucy wiped Val's face with damp paper towel. "Do you feel better now?"

"I'm sorry. I knew you wanted to fix me up with Brad and I got scared . . . Daniel and I never did it. Do you understand? He only touched me to hit me. I'm ugly and repulsive!"

"There's nothing wrong with you," Lucy soothed." Derwood was a perverted predator, and a bastard who enjoyed wooing and destroying strong women. Val you heard Aunt Betty's story. You must have recognized his pattern. He's a victimizer and you met all his prerequisites," she forced Val's chin up. "You are interesting, intelligent, well educated, beautiful and as close to normal as any woman I know. Let all that show and you'll have to beat guys off with a stick." She gulped, that was a poor choice of words.

Lucy pushed Val from the tiny restroom, surprised to see two strange women bearing down on them. The dowdy one lagged behind waving timidly while the front runner shouted unintelligibly.

Val rolled her eyes and clutched her head in both hands, "I shouldn't have done that."

Lucy gestured to the women, "Are they friends of yours?"

"Sort of I guess," Valerie said, "they're Daniel's other wives. We're going to your mom's for an intimate chat." She stripped off her sneakers and lurched through the sand to intercept the wives.

"Walk Val; don't drive!" Lucy cautioned. A fine first date this is. I'll be lucky if Harv doesn't suddenly remember a sick friend he has to visit. He must regret inviting me to the lighthouse dedication, she thought gloomily.

"Hey Lucy, Brad said putting his arm around her waist, "Come on, I'll show you to the slave quarters. You came to help, I hope."

Her lips brushed his cheek. "Not today, I'm supposed to be on a date, though I seem to have misplaced him."

"Lucy?" Harv said his voice dry, and as luck would have it, close at hand.

Lucy swore under her breath. "Harv I was looking for you."

"I can see that."

"I was trying to co-opt Lucy for the food booth," Brad said. "I promised to grill fish. A novice cook can destroy fish," he added, though he doubted either Lucy or Harv heard him. They were busy making calf eyes at each other. "All the proceeds from the food and the calendar sales go to the families burnt out when the apartments caught fire. Harv, did you come to help?"

"I've volunteered him for the kissing booth and I'm his first and only customer," Lucy said grasping Harv's hand.

"I didn't know there was a kissing booth or I'd have offered my services," Jordan Platt, January in the infamous calendar and Eric Platt's only child, said.

"Jordan you're late. I was about to conscript Lucy and Harv for your job," Brad swatted Jordan playfully.

"Lucy's kidding about the kissing booth so stay where you are," Jeremy Reese snarled.

"Hey Brad, I hear they found a dead woman in your bedroom. Still can't get the live ones, huh?" Jordan taunted.

Only the hardhearted waves dared break the tense silence created by Jordan's attempt at humor. All activity within earshot stopped until Jeremy Reese drawled, "We can always trust you to see the sick side of everything, can't we Jordan?"

Jordan mumbled a garbled apology, and sulked.

"Brad, since that one," Jeremy said nodding at Jordan, "has finally arrived, you ought to go off with your friends and have some fun. You can trust me with the fish, scouts honor," he promised holding his hand palm outward. "Lucy I've a message for your mother."

"I'll be sure to find you later," Lucy promised, and hoped to salvage her first date. We only get one chance at a first date. She lingered watching Brad, slump shouldered, head to the calendar booth.

Harv took her hand, you're a good friend Lucy, "Brad has serious problems and I was out of line."

CHAPTER 14

Insert Ellie opened her door to a trio of unhappy women. "Welcome ladies," she said leading them into the parlor. "Please sit down. Could I get you a drink? Tea or perhaps wine?"

Each polite welcoming word Mrs. Wilson uttered resounded in Valerie's head like a ball-peen hammer wielded by an overzealous blacksmith. "Black coffee for me if it's not too much trouble," Valerie murmured stifling a moan.

"I don't suppose you have any decent scotch?" Sue snarled. "Just leave it," she ordered when Ellie produced Bakers Glenlivet. "Talking about that rat makes me thirsty."

"I'd take a little sherry, if it's not any trouble," Doris said, her voice barely audible. "It was ever so nice of Valerie to find our husband, and bring us to your pretty town, and it's ever so nice to be here too Mrs. Wilson." Doris wiped her dripping eyes with a large handkerchief.

"Do you buy those damn hankies by the gross?" Sue sneered, "so far I've seen puke yellow, seasick green, baby-shit brown and now putrid puce." Doris whimpered like a kicked puppy, Sue groaned aloud and emptied her glass in one gulp.

Doris clutched the proffered Sherry like a drowning sailor clutches a life raft. Ellie surreptitiously counted her finger and wondered if the tears were from grief or alcohol deprivation. Doris knocked back her fortified wine and handed Ellie the glass. Sad, hopeful eyes flicked from her hostess to the empty glass on to the bottle and back again. Ellie filled her glass and left the bottle close at hand.

Ellie waited for someone to mention Derwood/Daniel and when no one did decided to throw the cat or perhaps pit bull into their midst,

"Valerie tells us that you all knew Derwood by different names. Don't you find it extraordinary that he kept the same initials?"

"No," Sue scoffed," saved the lazy bastard a change of monogram."

Wow, I thought I was bitter; Valerie thought; though the elephant feet stomping in her head made thought difficult.

"I understand con men develop a method, try it, and if it works continue in the same vein. If we compare each of your unpleasant incidents perhaps we can figure out his next move and save future victims," Ellie suggested, asking the powers above to overlook her tiny white lie.

"Lady, you are the queen of understatement!" Sue snarled, "An unpleasant incident! Yeah right! An unpleasant incident is some slacker stealing your shopping cart. What that bastard did was ruin our lives. Am I right?" Sue glared daring anyone to disagree. "But you were dead right about catching him, and saving some other poor bitch." She paced as she snapped out the no frills version of her life. "Slob named Douglas Dale wins well-off husband's trust. Beloved husband dies," Sue let her hair hide her face.

Sympathy closed Ellie's throat and misted her eyes, profound sadness now overlaid Sue's angry voice.

"Beloved husband dies unexpectedly," Sue recovering her rage repeated. "Kind trusted friend becomes indispensable to devastated widow, marries widow, robs widow, and vanishes with all worldly goods. The end."

He hit Val after me and before Betty, but he honed his smarmy skills on her." She stabbed an accusing finger at Doris. "If she had any guts the rest of us might have been spared," she snagged the scotch bottle, sank deep into a comfortable chair, then with exaggerated care refilled her glass, and drained it in one gulp.

If looks were daggers Doris would have enough metal in her chest to get a job as a lightning rod, Betty thought. But how was a woman as street smart as Sue conned by Derwood? She must have been as lost when her husband passed as I was when Robert died. Maybe Derwood drugged her too. Wife number one's history might shed a little more light on things. "Doris, please tell us your story."

"A bit more sherry dear," Ellie offered.

Doris swallowed, attempted to dry her constantly running eyes, and emptied her glass in one gulp. She spoke so softly that Betty and Ellie had to lean forward to hear.

"Dillon was the first man who was ever nice to me. I'm not pretty or smart like you all," Doris said.

"Tell us something we don't know," Sue said scathingly, and slumped deflated when six angry eyes pierced her.

Doris ignored Sue, "When my daddy brought Dillon home, I was too shy to stay in the same room for ever so long. Dillon was ever so patient with me until he won my heart." She paused, dabbed ineffectually at her eyes, sighed deeply, looked with longing at her empty glass, and resumed her story, "My daddy was mad when I told him I was going to marry the man of my dreams. He was so angry he shook. He said Dillon only wanted my money. I didn't care and I told him so and he said I was an ugly fool and I would be sorry, but I'm not sorry and I never will be."

"He dumped you and took your money! What is wrong with you?"

"Sue, he didn't have to steal it. I would have gladly given him everything, but my daddy wouldn't let me. That's why daddy had to die. I'm sorry Sue. I still think I got the better part of the deal. He gave me the best years of my life," her little girl voice faded away.

"There is no reasoning with the village idiot."

"Now Sue, don't be mad at me. Dillon was ever so nice and nobody ever was nice to me before he came. Daddy never took me with him, and I was too scared to go by myself when he was gone." Doris' smile lit the room, "Sue takes me everywhere she goes and if it wasn't for Dillon, I wouldn't have met her."

"I could not have made you believe that could I?" Valerie asked, a note of wonder in her voice. "I'd hoped that we might convince her to join us in prosecuting *him*, but that's unlikely. I may as well take you ladies back to the hotel. Detective Warren has our information. He'll contact us if there are developments. With Doris' inadequate aid, she hauled Sue up, guided her around various pieces of furniture and into the foyer.

"Should I get that Mrs. Wilson?" Valerie inquired as the doorbell chimed, "we seem to be forming an effective block."

"Yes dear and please call me Ellie."

"Is this my lucky day or what?" The tall, lean, sharp nosed man asked. "Detective Warren of the Fraud Division," he announced holding up his identification. "All four together just like you said, Platt."

"You ladies don't mind staying a little longer, do you? In case I need more information after I chat with Mrs. Archer." His look encompassed Ellie and Betty and his arched eyebrow requested introductions.

"This is Betty Archer and Ellie Wilson," Eric volunteered, "you know the others."

"Are you people finished at my house?" Betty blurted. "I'm rather anxious to go home. There's so much to do."

"Not yet Mrs. Archer," Eric replied, emphasis heavy on Mrs.

Mrs. Archer? Betty wondered. Eric never called her Mrs. Was he advising caution?

"Ellie, do you have a room Detective Warren and I can use?"

"Certainly Chief Platt, come into the study. Would you like coffee or tea?"

"No thank you ma'am," Detective Warren declined. We don't want to inconvenience you more than necessary?"

Exhausted, Betty collapsed into the sofa; she massaged her temples to ease a throbbing headache. Detective Warren was openly skeptical when she couldn't answer his questions regarding her personal monies. She didn't know where to start to look for what? A ledger, did people still use those in the electronic age? Derwood had a laptop computer, but she didn't know where it was. After two hours of badgering questions she realized she sounded as stupid as she felt. She refused to answer more questions.

"Betty, drink this tea. I made it just the way you like it with lemon and honey. Eric, the coffee is ready," Ellie offered in response to the cup shape Eric mimed with his fingers. "Help yourself, while I see Detective Warren and the ladies out."

"Did I pass or do I have to retake that awful test?"

"Betts, if that was a test you definitely scored a solid C minus, but I wouldn't worry about it. The detective is trying to trace the money, a sizeable sum from what he's told me." Eric paused to do the math. "I could pay off my mortgage ten or fifteen times over with the missing funds. Warren says find the cash find Derwood." Eric elaborated, "Given Derwood's age and the duration of each relationship, Warren thinks there are more women he swindled. His partner's following up some leads. Don't worry Betts we'll get to the bottom of this."

"Thanks Eric," Betty mumbled staring at her clenched fists.

"You'll be happy to know she lived through the interrogation," Eric told Ellie. "I'll get out of your hair as soon as I drink the coffee you promised," he followed Ellie to the kitchen.

"What's wrong Eric? Is there a problem?"

"Yeah, the investigation is more or less out of my hands, I hate that, but as long as I behave, they'll keep me in the loop and I can, ya' know, help Betty. The guys spent the better part of the day at Betty's. They found blood in the study and on the stairs so nothing can be ruled out." Eric spooned sugar into his coffee and stirred vigorously. "They've issued a missing persons on Derwood; and Warren has us checking John

Does." He hesitated, shrugged, and continued, "They don't think Derwood left under his own steam." Eric bounced up to pace, "I can't give advice here Ellie, but if I could I'd tell those ladies to get a lawyer. I'm out on a limb here so you did not hear that from me."

"I'll talk to them." Ellie promised. "Uh Eric . . . . This is Rita Russell's camera." She proffered the digital so like her own. "I cannot say how I got it."

"I can figure it out," Eric gazed at the donut boxes on the counter. "I am Chief of Police, though nobody remembers my promotion." Eric screwed up his face to reflect comic dismay and Ellie giggled.

"There's just one photo depicting Rita's shoes and Rex the bakery cat, but it's the date and time that are telling. As near as I, a mere civilian, can figure she must have taken the picture shortly before she was murdered."

"You may be right, but it's getting late," Eric sighed, "I need to be off. We're understaffed, so everyone's clocking overtime. You don't suppose Lucy would reconsider do you? We need a female officer and she'd have no trouble qualifying."

"I don't think so. She's rather successful at what she does. Go home Eric. Things are often clearer once you've slept on them."

"Wish I could, but my son is at the clambake and I won't rest until he's home. I can't help thinking things might have been different if his mother had stayed. I think I'll take a run down to the beach and check things out."

"Lucy is there with the Spencer boy. Keep an eye on him. . . I mean them, will you Eric?"

"Betty, do you want more tea?" Ellie called, liberally spreading butter on a cheese biscuit she'd split and toasted. The only biscuit that escaped Lucy's midnight snack, breakfast, elevenses, lunch, mid afternoon tea and finally pre date jitters. Though why Lucy stressed herself over the likes of Harv Junior she failed to comprehend.

"I'm glad that's over," Betty sighed, and dropped wearily onto a chair at the old table that over the years had witnessed many heart to heart talks. "You wouldn't believe the questions that detective asked and the same things over and over again. I know I must keep up appearances, but I'm so tired, and those women make me profoundly sad."

"Forget that," Ellie ordered. "Did you notice you are odd woman out? I mentioned it this morning in the car. All *Derwood, Daniel, Douglas, Dillon's* other wives are tall, slender blonds. It's as if *he* had a tall blond obsession, why then did he choose you." She set the biscuit halves and a jar of strawberry preserves on the table and sat across from

Betty, "I wonder what carrot he used to trick a feisty woman like Sue. I think I'd pay to hear more details of her story, and Doris' too as far as that goes. If she's not as naïve and simple as she acts; we ought to nominate her for an Oscar. What do you think?"

"I was too busy wondering which of them Baker saw at my house to pay much attention to what they said."

"What do you mean? What did Baker see?"

Betty repeated Baker's words and added her own suspicions. "I was comparing Doris and Sue's coloring and carriage to Lucy's and wondering if Baker saw one of them."

"If it were one of them it was Doris, Ellie proclaimed. We know Sue wouldn't spit down his throat if his liver were on fire. However what if the four of you aren't the only women Derwood duped. What if Baker saw Derwood's next victim? You arrived home earlier than he expected."

"Maybe she was his girl friend. There's something I've never told you," Betty said refusing to meet Ellie's gaze. "I've thanked God on my knees every day that he didn't, but Derwood never, uh, I mean, we never, um."

Ellie held Betty's icy hands. "Spit it out."

Betty gulped and blurted' "Derwood never joined me in the marriage bed. At first I was hurt and confused, but after the abuse started I was glad." Tears streamed down Betty's face, "I was so stupid. I even asked him why he'd married me. He said he liked punching rich bitches, and hit me again."

Ellie swabbed Betty's mascara drenched tears, "You are neither stupid nor a fool. *He* took advantage of your grief, and violated your trust. Take a deep breath, count your blessings and we'll figure this thing out."

"I'm tired Ellie, I need wine and sleep."

Ellie heard the clink of glass on glass and cursed Derwood. Valerie smelled like a distillery, Sue downed Scotch like a Scotsman, and Doris gulped Sherry like it was going out of style. Betty, who pre Derwood rarely drank alcohol, routinely downed several glasses.

Ellie vetted one of the columns hit the send key, and went out to the porch swing to wait for Lucy. Swaying gently Ellie imagined the tall hollyhocks mom had tended with loving care reaching to enfold her in their warm embrace. She could almost feel her mother's arms and hear her voice softly say, 'Ellie you fool, burn that book, you know what happens to curious cats.'

"Sorry Mom," she said studying Derwood's purloined diary, "I have to know." He would use a simple code; he was clever and devious, but not a scholar. Derwood's scrawl was difficult, but not impossible to read.

The code was another matter; she reversed letters, tried significant dates, and then various combinations of the double D names he favored. Searching the star filled night sky for inspiration she tried the constellation names, but without result. The key had to be a series of words. She tried 'I-love-money, I-steal-art, greed-and-pain' and then, desperately 'I-cause-death,' all to no avail. What words would that son of a ...Ellie censored the word that completed the phrase. However the censored word brought to mind a phrase Betty had heard too often, Derwood's favorite insult, 'damn stupid loony bitch.' Ellie stripped the repeated letters and with DAMNSTUPILOYBCH as the key Derwood's diary read like a first grade primer.

Derwood listed the formulae, method, and exact amounts of the poisons administered to each victim with dates and times.

Often amended number sequences with dollar signs she presumed represented money embezzled from his victims shocked her.

She painstakingly transliterated the book though her brain balked. How could Derwood, filled with evil, look like a saint?

Derwood poisoned Robert! How could she tell Betty? She couldn't, but the police could. Ellie started for the phone, she could not give the poisonous document to the police. The pages were rife with reasons to kill Derwood. The spouse, or in this case spouses were preferred suspects. Ellie stretched to ease knotted muscles, and cursed. Damn you Derwood.

"You were right mother, I should have burned the book." She reread the last page. After I show Lucy and burn it. Betty never needs to know Derwood planned to kill her. "Lucy, come home darling. I need you." Profoundly saddened, Ellie waited for Lucy.

Soon her intelligent daughter would see past Harv's smarmy charm, good looks, and drop him, preferably off a cliff, Ellie smiled. In fact Harv was a handsome young man, who regrettably resembled his incorrigible, lascivious, profligate male ancestors. Gossip had it, that Harvey Senior wooed his third cousin's wife, married the woman, and adopted the child thus he'd acquired an heir without the bother usually associated with the process. Spencer Senior was an odious, deceitful rogue, and he'd raised Harv, like father like son. She frowned, Lucy looked lovely so fresh and perky. She'd hate that description, Ellie grinned. In reality Lucy's usual look was sophisticated chic. How unfortunate that she wasted herself on a Spencer.

Ellie parted stems and peeked through the closely packed hollyhocks. She'd been preoccupied and hadn't heard the ostentatious automobile pull up. Feeling like a ham actor in a third rate spy movie, she watched Harv fling open the door and arrogantly offer Lucy his arm. Thankfully Lucy wore slacks and was able to exit the low vehicle with dignity. They embraced, Ellie shuddered. Lucy snuggled close against Harv's chest her face upturned; her eyes gleamed in the moonlight, his hand danced ominously over her back.

My God I have to stop this! Unreasoned foreboding drove Ellie. She dashed inside, flicked a switch, and instantly the yard lit up like a runway. The halogen, anti-burglar system a slick salesman sold her mother, finally useful.

What can I say to make her understand how wrong this relationship is? Ellie asked her ancestor's portraits. Only Aunt Emily responded, her portrait slipped its sturdy hook and dropped to the floor. Ellie ignored Aunt Emily and opened the door. The spot lit couple slowly and reluctantly parted.

"Lucy, you're home? Just in time to join me in a nightcap. Mr. Spencer," she said, "We mustn't detain you. It's a long drive to the city." She checked her watch, "And it's very late."

"Not such a long trip, only an hour by air, but it's academic because I'm on holiday."

"Really, how unfortunate, Lucy is teaching a cooking class. It begins tomorrow."

"Great I've always wanted to learn to cook."

"Unfortunately the class is booked solid."

Lucy stood on tiptoe to noisily whisper in his ear, "Don't worry Harv; I'll give you private lessons."

Ellie said, "That won't be necessary Lucy, I seem to remember a cancellation. But we do need to prepare for the class and work on Brad's dilemma?"

Ellie gripped Lucy's right hand, Harv clung to her left; Ellie won.

Lucy mouthed, I'll be right back, "I now know how a wishbone feels," Lucy giggled, Ellie energetically shut the door. "Mom if you want grandchildren, I have to have at least one close encounter with the male kind," she teased. Lucy saw the situation as hilarious and hoped Harv would too. "Sometimes I wonder how I was ever conceived."

"Whatever do you mean Lucy?" Ellie's display of innocence was shattered by the clanging doorbell. "Who could that be calling so late?" Ellie asked. "Did your friend forget something?" she yawned, "Well, it's late; we should go to bed."

"I think I'll answer the door first," Lucy said wryly. "Captain Reese," she groaned, "I forgot to look for you. I'm so sorry."

"Don't give it another thought. Did you enjoy yourself?"

"I sure did. How were sales? The fish booth had a long line every time we came by. I almost offered to help, but this was our first real date and I..." she hesitated.

"Ah, it's like that is it?" Jeremy said. "I'd thought to cut in on your dance marathon, but a cigarette paper would've had trouble working its way between the two of you, so I reckoned an old guy like me was out of luck." He lowered his voice, "I told him about the time I took you and Brad out fishing, remember? It was hot and you gave up on the fish and went for a dip. You wore your first bikini with nothing much to keep it in place;" he chuckled, Lucy blushed. "Poor kid gave you his trunks to cover yourself, and by the time I got the towel he was wrinkled like a prune and cold as February ice. You two had as true a friendship as I've ever seen. Brad said he was going to marry you because you were the only girl who baited her own hook. But from the look on his face when he sold your friend Valerie a calendar, Harv can stop worrying . . . maybe." Reese gave her a little push, "Harv's waiting on the swing, go on get out, I need to talk to your momma. Send the guy off with something to remember. First dates ought to be memorable."

"How long will you be here?" Lucy asked though she meant, 'how long will you able to keep mom occupied?'

"The wife will soon send out the search party; so not too long. You get on out there before that lad gets discouraged."

"Thanks Cap. Captain Reese is here mom."

"Jeremy, what brings you out so late?"

"Sorry Harv, mom needed my help," she fibbed," but I'd rather take up where we left off. How did that go again?" She placed his hand on her waist and his arm around her neck. Folding her arms around him she asked, "Can you take it from there?"

"No problem."

"Has something more happened to Brad?" Ellie asked.

"Not that I know of and I would know. I've suspended Orville Wise. He was out of line and I've come to apologize. Jake, Baker, and Rodney told me he assaulted you. I hope you weren't hurt."

"Only my dignity; and I do not plan to file charges," she added, answering what he hadn't asked. "Why did you hire that one?"

"Pickings were slim, and band politics forced my hand. I shouldn't have let them push me. I did and been sorry ever since. Orville is sure Brads guilty, but Brad wouldn't kill anyone, and he sure as hell wouldn't rob Baker."

"I agree, but Orville's suspension will leave you shorthanded," Ellie said, handing Jeremy a beer. "Perhaps I can help." She spoke of Rita's camera and gave him a copy of the photo. "Betty says the shoes are Rita Russell's, and Betty knows shoes." Ellie mentioned Jake and Baker's discovery of an imprint in their dough. She told of their UFO sighting, and said the radio station logged the call. "That with the date-time on the picture should confirm the time." She described Baker's offer of his biscuit recipe in exchange for a speedy resolution to the health inspector's murder, and said if he'd help her she'd help him if she could.

He listened patiently; he'd been a cop too long to discount information from any source. Without promising anything he thanked her for the picture and the information.

"I'll share what I can, but Ellie, you be careful. A murderer will kill again to cover his tracks. I'd better go. You know it's nice to see Lucy with a local boy. I was afraid we'd lose her to one of those foreigners she's been dating. Title or no title, I didn't think much of that last guy. He was too darn slick."

"Uh," Ellie stuttered.

Lucy's shout saved her, "It is after one. Jeremy, you go on home right now. I'm sure your mother is worried silly," Lucy giggled, "I've waited years to do that."

"Out of the mouths of babes," Jeremy lamented, "You raise them, and then they start raising you." He smiled, "Cute isn't it Ellie? And she's right I better get home. My mother stopped worrying about me when my wife started. See you later Lucy. I'll try to remember more stories for your young man," he promised.

CHAPTER 15

Betty knelt, as she did each night to ask God's forgiveness for Robert, and for herself. She tossed and thought of Derwood's victims. Sue and Valerie's stories were not unlike hers, only Doris' differed. Doris hooked up with Derwood before her father died; the rest of us looked to him for support after a traumatic death. Was child like Doris Derwood's collaborator his or prey? Did Derwood perfect his strategy on the mentally challenged woman? He used Sue, Valerie and my grief to gain and abuse our trust. Valerie thinks Derwood somehow convinced her father to kill himself and leave her vulnerable, Betty sighed. She could use the same excuse; Robert's suicide broke her spirit and left her ripe to be duped, perhaps Sue felt guilt akin to her own. Doris was the variant that ruined *his* consistent model. And what did she mean by, 'that's why daddy had to die'?

Betty pictured each woman in the window as Baker saw them, they all fit. Did one of them take *his* computer and records the police wanted? No solutions, only questions. Betty sighed and spoke to the guardian angel she believed watched over her. She begged him for the release the enticing arms of Morpheus would bring. Her prayer was answered.

She wondered when Derwood replaced her doorbell with Gregorian Chants. *Dies Irae, illa,* day of wrath, that dreadful day that will reduce the world to embers, mournfully eerily echoed.

Two vaporous, six winged seraphim, obscure in shadowy darkness, grasped her arms drawing her downward.

Clad in gloom, Baker grappled with Derwood.

"Don't bother with him. He won't fall. He's dead, you know," Betty told the angels guiding her.

Baker raised his empty hand high above his head. A cloud drifted over his hand and when it passed Baker held the missing computer.

Derwood's sneering bloody face absorbed the baker's downward thrust. He absorbed the laptop and Baker, he grew and grew.

Betty closed her eyes. Derwood's apparition appeared on the inside of her eyelids, he beckoned, she followed, questioning; he leered and did not respond.

Corpulent with putrefaction he wrestled with a woman. Hands as large as leaf rakes tore at the poor creature's face ripping away one grotesque mask after another. He spun the woman toward him spitting out a stream of unintelligible gibberish.

"Who are you?" Betty asked the woman. With the aid of two enormous ebony angels, twins to those that once graced her prayer space she floated closer. "I've missed you since he sold you," she told the angels through blood red tears.

"Pay attention foolish female," her angel roared, flames shot from its genderless mouth. Betty shuddered when hooked horns sprang through the seraph's lustrous black hair Derwood's triumphant cry drew her attention. The woman's pitiful struggle ended, she turned pleading eyes to Betty hovering above.

"It's Lucy! I have to help her!" Betty frantically struggled against the seraphim's iron grip. "I can't come honey; I'm sorry," she sobbed, whirling she saw Lucy behind a rainbow.

Derwood held a Sixteenth Century Gothic candlestick resplendent with its aromatic beeswax candle to the sad heap of shattered, Renaissance bed remnants. "I'll light a candle for you darling," he promised, winking suggestively at a tattered ragamuffin clutching banded sheaves of large denomination bills in her small fists. Valerie as a child, Betty realized.

Sue, a wrinkled crone appeared, she snatched a cherub from the pyre. Betty turned away when Robert edged past the seraph to tug at her sleeve. He wielded a stalk of blood red, Grecian foxglove festooned from top to bottom with perfectly formed blooms.

"You perfected it darling," Betty cooed. "Watch out!" she screamed as a sulfurous, black cloud engulfed him. Wretched sinners reminiscent of those adorning Rodin's 'Gates of Hell' sang dirges from the darkened shroud of swirling mist.

"Why did you take him?" Betty begged of the seraphim that still restrained her.

"Because you've been a damn, stupid, loony bitch," her father's voice shrieked.

"No she isn't! You are a damn, stupid, loony bastard," Ellie screamed while she whipped Derwood with a bundle of withered foxglove stalks.

Ellie's lash tore the clothes from Derwood's bloated body. He bloomed with long bloody gashes, incensed Ellie screamed his victim's names with each rage driven slash. Chunks of flesh sloughed from off until his skeleton stood, arrogant and proud.

Lucy ducked the swinging flail; she caught putrid pieces of flying flesh and used smiley faced orange duct tape to artistically stick bloated flesh onto Derwood's bare bones. Ellie's foxglove stalk thickened into the decapitated bed post, she kept beating a steady rhythm, a tattoo like a drum roll ordering soldiers to battle.

Doris wept a sea of tears that slowly crept up Betty's body and over her head. She sucked in a last desperate gulp of air and screamed.

"Wake up; please wake up," Lucy hugged her aunt's trembling body. "Auntie Darling, it's just a dream."

Betty sobbed, "You shouldn't use that tape."

"Aunt Betty, wake up!"

Betty wiped her eyes with the corner of the sheet and shuddered, "I had a nightmare. I couldn't wake up."

"I'll stay with you a while. Tell me about your dream," Lucy coaxed attempting to warm Betty's icy body with her own. Betty shivered violently each time she uttered Derwood's name, but when she spoke of Uncle Robert her voice held profound sadness. Betty's soft voice lulled Lucy into dreamland.

Careful not to wake Lucy, Betty slipped from beneath the covers. Lucy was beautiful, kind and thoughtful. Betty smiled, dressed, and quietly slipped from the room.

She climbed into her car, 'my car,' she thought. I'll get cheese biscuits as a proper thank you for Lucy. I'll be Baker's first customer, she predicted. Heat from the rising sun evaporated all vestiges of her dark dream. She parked in front of the door in the empty lot, frowned when a Mercedes parked next to her. She'd hoped to question Baker about the woman silhouetted in her window. Betty hurried into the bakery, placed her pastry order and coffee in hand, sheltered behind a leafy Ficus Benjamina.

A male voice enthusiastically said, "Lucy . . . ."

Betty held her breath and listened. Is that the infamous Harv? Must be, she thought peeking through Ficus leaves, because the other man is Harvey Spencer Senior and after all these years he's hardly changed. A little heavier maybe, but still too handsome, the old rake doesn't have the decency to run to fat or go bald.

The maligned Sr. Spencer and his son carried their trays to a table behind her tree.

"Dad, do you remember that skinny blond kid who hung around with Brad Talltree?" Harv asked and continued when his father nodded. "I met her again in Amsterdam of all places, and Dad she's changed."

"Hmm," Harvey Sr. murmured noncommittally.

"Dad, don't give me that look," Harv scolded. "She's hot and gosh dad, you must remember what hot is. Wipe that disgusted look off your face. I know I've said that before, but Dad this is it. Lucy's the one."

"Harv, do you realize you used hot and gosh in the same sentence? It's either love or you've regressed to seventeen."

"Don't tease Dad, I'm serious. She's gorgeous, elegant, brilliant, talented, capable, independent and . . ."

"Walks on water," Harvey Sr. teased.

"Dad listen, I think I love her. She's got it all," Harv grimaced, "in fact she has too much. She's got the mother from hell. That woman protects Lucy like a bear defends her cub from bloodthirsty hunters or in this case one hunter, me."

"Why does the girl's mother disapprove of you?"

"How the heck would I know? Lucy doesn't understand her mother's behavior either, but thinks its funny and her mother will get over it," Harv threw up his hands, "When she gets to know me. I have my doubts, but I'm trying. I'm even taking her cooking class. Lucy is helping. Did I mention Lucy is a gourmet cook?"

"Lucy is it?" Harvey Sr. hid a smile. "When will I meet this paragon of virtue?"

"You'll meet her at the Lighthouse Dedication though I imagine you'll be busy with the contributors, so I'd like to invite her to go fishing with us. You'll love her. She's fun, athletic, beautiful, and she baits her own hook and takes the fish off like one of the guys."

"Like one of the guys? Harv is there something you want to tell me?" Harvey asked laughing.

Ah Dad, you know what I mean. She's perfect."

"You're gushing and blushing like a teenager with his first crush. If I read you right her mother is the blot on this paragon of perfection." Harvey Sr. frowned, feigning deep thought. "Lucy sees a *bon vivant* while her mother sees a predator?" Harvey lost the battle, and laughed loud and long. "Makes you feel like a gauche teenager instead the Good Time Charlie the rest of town sees."

"It's not funny dad, and you're not helping. I've found the perfect life partner."

Betty listened spellbound. Harv detailed Lucy's virtues. Anxious to relate all that she'd heard, Betty ran to her car, and sped to tell Ellie.

Lucy carried her coffee into her mother's garden. She'd heard Aunt Betty leave. It's nice to see the sunrise every once in a long while, she thought, heading into the garage as the sun breached the horizon.

With an excitement that never diminished Lucy tugged the vinyl cover off what grandpa called her 'Red Roan.' She methodically checked the tire tread and air pressure. If she closed her eyes she could picture grandpa, like a magician, whisking grandma's quilt away, revealing her heart's desire. The smells she associated with Grandpa, Irish Spring soap and Dunhill pipe tobacco, still cling to the walls in the old garage. Eager to thank him, she'd flung herself at him, knocking him down. Grandpa's laughed so loud grandma and mom came running. Mom's despairing 'oh dad,' and grandma's, 'if she gets hurt old man, it will be on your head,' echoed in her memories

I loved that moment, grandpa soothing mom while grandma scolded and threatened. She carefully added brake fluid and drained the oil, replaced the filter, from the stock shelved near her bike. She added oil remembering grandpa's warning against leaving the engine vulnerable to condensation, and corrosion. He'd insisted she learn to maintain her motorbike. Someday she'd thank him, he'd said, and she did. She checked the drive chain tension, measuring its travel midway between the front and rear sprockets. Good, she heard grandpa say. You taught me well gramps, she thought. Sharing his knowledge was valuable, but their time together was his real gift to her. She shot lithium grease down the throttle and clutch cables ensuring that they moved freely. She disconnected the battery from its battery tender on the shelf and slipped it into position taking care not to mix the terminal cables. She touched the tiny dent grandpa had insisted they leave in the rear fender. A reminder of the folly of carelessness, he'd said. She'd never told Grandpa Brad's recklessness damaged the bike.

Jeremy Reese happened by in time to patch up the worst of Brad's wounds. He loaded her mangled bike into his pickup, and brought them to the Warden house. Lucy explained how Brad risked his life charging up the hill to snatch her and the bike from the brink of certain annihilation. Jeremy's incredulous expression, and his muttered, uh huh his only comment.

Peering over his bifocals grandpa looked them over, nodded, and suggested that grandma could probably be persuaded to prepare a poultice that might diminish the bruises Brad incurred during the daring rescue. He'd sent her for one of his shirts so Brad's mother wouldn't be alarmed by tatters.

Grandpa and Jeremy had treated Brad like a hero, and told everyone in the entire town how fourteen year old Brad risked life and limb to save Lucy. They'd embellished on her story detailing how the boy was battered and bruised while the girl looked no rattier than usual. Raised eyebrows, speculation, and outright disbelief were widespread that season.

That was the summer Brad and I learned there were fates worse than grounding, and that lies were inconvenient and expensive. Lucy filled the gas tank, wheeled the bike out into the yard, and engaged the kick stand. Aside from the ribbing, an entire summer's allowance plus every cent she earned at the bakery hadn't covered the cost of the repairs. Brad contributed his allowance and all he earned unloading fish, but it wasn't enough. Grandpa loaned her the rest. When they tried to repay him, Lucy's grin split her face; he said if our government could forgive debts, he could too.

Lucy climbed onto the bike, bounced to test the suspension, smiled contentedly, and started the bike; she advanced the throttle and revved the engine.

"Turn that thing off," Ellie yelled, "Coffee is ready, and Lucy," she modulated her voice when the engine stilled, "please don't get on that thing without a helmet again. Wash your hands," Ellie gave her a vintage tin of degreaser. "Oh," Ellie said sadly, as if describing the national debt, "You've broken a nail. You stop biting your nails only to break them toying with that awful machine. I'm happy you stopped biting your nails, what was your motivation?"

"Guys like long nails. Ever think you don't have grandkids because of my ugly hands?" Lucy scrubbed at the offending grease.

"Lucy if a man can't see all your beauty, sincerity, great personality, and . . . ."

"Personality you say. Ouch, that's the kiss of death," Lucy remembered 'great personality' was used to describe each dud Ellie presented as marriage material.

"Quick wit," Ellie continued ignoring Lucy's comment, "a figure women diet for, hair so naturally blond that Marilyn would have purchased it."

Lucy mumbled, "And probably did,"

"Then he doesn't deserve you," Ellie finished.

"Mom, did you have something to tell me?"

"I want you to look at something." Ellie fumbled behind ancient cookbooks shelved in a Stickley bookcase.

Lucy watched curiously, a portion of her mind saw the cabinet doors with their prominent maker's signature stored in the attic, and longed to see it whole again.

Ellie found Derwood's journal and her translation, "Read the journal and my notes. I'll get your coffee." Ellie prepared the espresso, forcing steam through the dark-roast granules.

"*He* was an unconscionable bastard and I'll kiss whoever whacked *him*." Lucy paged back to the details of Uncle Robert's murder. "Uncle Rodney confronted Derwood the night Aunt Betty came home. He said Derwood admitted killing Uncle Robert. *He* kept the poisoned glass with Uncle Rodney's prints are on it, in the safe. I agreed to keep that to myself, but since you know," Lucy grimaced.

"I don't tell you things I've promised to keep secret either." Ellie set an aromatic demitasse before her daughter. "This incriminating glass, Rodney took it right?"

"No he didn't, but on impulse I did. I hid it in the copse behind Aunt Betty's house, in an old tree. I put the bedpost with it."

"You hid them in a tree?" Ellie asked, thinking of Lucy's tomboy days when she spent more time in trees than on the ground. "The police have been all over Betty's property by now. What if they search the woods? We have to get the glass and the bedpost we must destroy them. Or we could wash the glass and put it with the set." She scowled remembering the antique, rippled glass Derwood stripped from Betty's china cabinet and replaced with Plexiglas. "The bedpost we'll wipe clean and leave there. I don't want anyone punished for Derwood's death."

"Don't worry, I have a plan. Now let me tell you about Aunt Betty's dream, it relates to that," she pointed at the notebook

Once again the scarred old kitchen table stood mute witness to abysmal disclosure. Ellie rehashed what she'd learned from Derwood's journal, and welcomed Lucy's remarks.

"He poisoned Uncle Robert, planned to kill Aunt Betty and murdered that woman's husband."

"Sue," Ellie said.

"*He* poisoned Val's dad too?" Lucy paced, "Valerie will have to be told. She'll be relieved to have her suspicions confirmed, but do we tell Aunt Betty? She thinks she failed by not recognizing Uncle Robert's depression, we have to tell her there was nothing to notice, then she can bury Uncle Robert, metaphorically I mean. I say we tell her right away. After her dream last night," Lucy draining the last sip of espresso," "we have to. And in light of Detective Warren's suspicions, I'll tell her that I took Derwood's computer." Lucy flipped through the encoded notebook, and wished for a cigarette.

"No!" Ellie insisted. "Betty can't know about the computer. She cannot lie. Her nightmare tells us how heavily this affair is weighing on her. Promise me you'll keep the computer secret for awhile."

Lucy nodded agreement, though keeping promises was problematic lately.

"Betty will be questioned again. What she doesn't know she cannot tell." Ellie accepted Lucy's grudging agreement. "I wish I knew who Baker saw that night."

"Aunt Betty said he thought he saw me, he didn't. Someone was with Derwood. Baker saw her and I found two martini glasses in the study. I backed into the full one and it shattered. I didn't want to waste time cleaning it up so I left it. I wonder what the police will make of that."

"Eric said there was a struggle, and mentioned blood stains in the study. If I were a betting woman, I'd wager the unmentioned broken glass is playing a major part in his investigation."

"Mom," Lucy said, "You met those other women, do you think one of them killed Derwood?"

"I don't know Lucy. Sue is angry enough and Doris might not be the innocent she seems." Ellie lapsed into a thoughtful silence.

"Whoever he pushed off a cliff," Lucy pondered. "Judging by this," she traced a sloppy sketch, "He had a female accomplice."

Ellie's eyes followed Lucy's finger. She had considered the squiggles a product of Derwood's demented mind, dismissed them.

"See, male and female smiley-faced, stick people standing on top of a cliff and a male figure sprawled on the ground below. These Xes in place of eyes show the one at the bottom is dead, and the sad smile is appropriate. Look, he's drawn in trajectory lines to indicate the falls trajectory."

Ellie covered her face with both hands, "That's why daddy had to die." Lucy's explanation put Doris' words into context and explained the complacent acceptance she'd shown when relating her story.

Lucy sighed, "So the dead stick figure is daddy and those smiling at the top are Derwood and Doris?"

"Yes and I'm sorry I didn't take Doris seriously. I heard her, but I let it slide on by."

"If she is mentally challenged she isn't responsible," Lucy said, studying each page of Derwood's childish drawings. "He was definitely not an artist."

"Lucy, did Valerie talk to you about her, uh, relations with Derwood?" Ellie questioned. "I only ask," she rushed on, "because Betty told me that she and Derwood never…uh, joined."

"Strange you should ask," Lucy said concealing a grin. "Val said he didn't do 'the nasty' with her either. She's thankful now, but at the time it did a job on her confidence. I wonder if *he* did all his wives that favor. Maybe Val knows." Lucy stared enthralled by the last page of the notebook. She jumped up like scalded cat, all color drained from her face, she leaned against the wall and slid to the floor.

Ellie rushed to help; she pushed Lucy's head between her knees. "I'm sorry Lucy; I forget how young and inexperienced you are."

"I didn't faint, I'm in shock" Lucy's voice uncharacteristically quavered. Ellie held an icepack to her nape. Lucy waved Derwood's journal. "If *he* wasn't dead I'd kill the bastard myself!" She shoved the noxious journal under Ellie's nose.

"I can't make head or tail out of his scribbles." Ellie said seating Lucy at the table.

"I can," Lucy snarled. "He hatched a Machiavellian scheme to repay you for taking Aunt Betty to the clinic." Hands palsied with anger, Lucy struggled to hold the book steady. "This figure on the gallows with short, curly hair, sad face, and tears has to be you, and the little plumpish one at your feet with X's for eyes is Aunt Betty. But I can't figure out what these dashes underneath the figures signify." Lucy's forehead puckered in concentration.

"That's a game, honey. Don't you remember playing hangman as a child? One starts with an empty gallows, I'll show you," Ellie said retrieving paper and pencils from her desk. "One person thinks of a word or phrase and represents it with dashes under the gibbet," she made six dashes then a space and a final three dashes. "This is a phrase. You guess a letter."

"This is really sick," Lucy said. Ellie frowned, "Okay I'll play how about a Q?"

"There is no Q, so I draw a head at the end of the noose, and with each incorrect guess I add a body part, the torso, arms, legs and sometimes hands, feet, eyes and so forth, one body part for each wrong letter. When the entire body is represented you are the hanged man and you lose. If you fill the spaces with the letters correctly, you prevent the hanging and win."

"This is for kids?" Lucy scoffed, "whose sick mind thought this a game for kids?"

"It's actually a lot of fun. However, this puzzle is difficult because we lack input from the drawer."

"Right," Lucy said grabbing the pencil. "Let's get started. It looks to be two words. The first has six letters and the last three. What would he use to murder Aunt Betty and implicate you? We need to keep that question in mind."

The clock, Michael's birthday gift to Ellie, noisily ticked away the minutes.

"I'm never going to figure this damn thing out. I'm not good at puzzles. I might be hungry, since all I came up with is cherry pie and pickle jar, unlikely murder weapons."

"I've got it," Ellie croaked. "The diabolical, demonic, nefarious, heinous, vicious, foul, immoral ---" Ellie stuttered, "fiend."

"I agree, but tell me the answer before I start pulling my hair out?"

"Herbal Tea!" Ellie shouted. "He meant to poison Betty with the tea I blend for her."

Lucy filled in the blanks on her page, "You're definitely the brain in this family." She trembled, "I wonder if he poisoned the tea before he died. And did he also poison her supply at the store."

Ellie was half out the door when Lucy caught her, "We must warn Michael."

Lucy steered her toward the rocking chair. "Relax Mom; Michael drinks your herbal tea only to please you." Ellie's looked hurt and Lucy rephrased Michaels, 'it tastes like dirt' comment to, "he says it tastes a little odd, but I know he serves it to good customers from time to time. I'll warn him just in case it is contaminated."

CHAPTER 16

Lucy pulled her helmet over her pony tail, waved gaily to Ellie who anxiously proffered the car keys, revved the bikes engine, flew down the drive, and out into the street. Sultry summer air, speed and the powerful vibrations of the bike were an exhilarating combination. She sped around slow moving cars to ride up the center line between the traffic. A sharp, horn blast from a grey Mercedes, reminded her that splitting lanes was illegal here. She cut in front of the Mercedes and slowed to a safer speed. Her thoughts turned to contaminated tea and who could analyze it without embarrassing questions? She sped up, Michael might serve the brew to a customer.

Speeding into a small, neat parking lot adjacent to the large Victorian that housed 'The Olde Antique Shoppe', Lucy skidded to stop at a prim, little gate in the white picket fence encircling the house. She knocked the gate open with her front tire, bumped up the single step, roared over the grass, and stopped inches from the back entrance. She killed the engine, kicked down the side stand and crashed through the door. Ransacking the shop's tiny kitchen cum storage room, she ripped tins bottles, and plastic bags from cupboards and shelves stacking them haphazardly on a table of questionable provenance. Each dark bottle containing inexplicable goop, each unlabeled bag of anonymous herbal mixture, and each reused coffee can holding a substance other than reliable, old Joe accelerated her desperation. "Michael get in here."

Michael bellowed, "I was with a customer and you scared her away!" He stalked into the workroom his arms tightly folded in his older and infinitely more responsible, cousin will now lecture mode. "What are you doing? You ruined my gate, ripped up my grass, and poor Mrs. Bicknell nearly fainted. She had to toddle off in search of soothing tea."

"I did not," Lucy said ripping open containers, plastic bags, and old coffee cans.

"If you've come for coffee, I'll get it; you needn't tear the place to pieces."

A single word in his rant made it through to Lucy. She grasped Michael's arm, "Tell me you didn't serve mom's herbal tea to customers."

"That would be a lie," Michael said calmly.

Lucy crouched to search the lowest shelf "Where is it?"

"Stop," Michael ordered, "If you don't stop vandalizing my store, I'll have to evict you." He stared down his newly remolded nose; hooked a chair with one foot and unceremoniously shoved Lucy at it. "Take a deep breath, and tell Michael what's troubling you."

"Where the hell is that herbal tea mom mixed for Betty?" Lucy struggled to rise, "Why can't you label things like normal people?"

"You mean this little box conveniently marked, Ellie's Herbal Tea?" he asked plucking an old tea caddy from atop the jam cupboard. "Are you sick? You must be to drink this concoction. If its iron you need swallow a few six penny nails, they taste better."

Lucy forced a smile. "Sit here Mikey and listen," she told him a about Derwood's notebook and Ellie's transcription.

Michael spent a moment matching Lucy's disclosures with what he knew. "I never believed Robert killed himself. I should have killed *him* when I had the chance."

"What happened?"

"Last week Derwood called. He said Betty wanted her Sixteenth Century walnut trunk with the caryatids sold. I knew he was lying, I told him it needed a coat of wax to get the best price, and I'd do it at the store. I figured I'd delay until Betty returned, but he insisted I take it that day. He grabbed one end and backed down the stairs, he slipped, I braced myself and held on. Had I let go of the trunk it would have landed on Derwood's head, killing him, and smashing an ugly antique. See two birds with one stone."

Lucy patted his hand, "Michael, you're not like him. You have a conscience."

"You're right, but if *he* were here now I'd strangle *him*. He stole Robert from Betty and—and from me."

Lucy took his white knuckled hands in hers. "I know you loved Robert, he was your surrogate father," she expressed empathy gained only through experience.

Michael covered her hands with his. "You've always understood."

Michael, Lucy thought, was too sensitive for his own good, but he was also a pragmatist and man of action.

"Enough of this, I can't rewrite history. Derwood killed Robert and we can't even guess how many others." Michael snarled, and paced. "He planned to kill Betty and frame Ellie. He has to be caught. Give that book to the cops."

"Michael, if I have a secret I'd tell you if you promised never to repeat it." He nodded and Lucy surged ahead. "Listen to what I'm not going to say and know that I will not elaborate. Derwood will never hurt Betty or anyone else again . . . ever."

"You can't possibly," Michael scoffed, reconsidered, and said, "like that tonic your mother calls tea?"

"No! He might have poisoned the tea. That's why I have to find it."

"How will you know?" Michael asked peeling the lid from the caddy and sniffing. "Yuk, what does Ellie put in this stuff?"

Lucy mugged a witchy face. "Eye of newt, wing of bat, fetid breath of viper and your little dog, too; double, double toil and trouble; fire burn and cauldron bubble," she quoted adding a cackle or two.

"I don't have a little dog."

"And now we know why."

"Lucy dahling, how can you quote from William Shakespeare's, Macbeth and tastelessly follow with a line from the Wizard of Oz? You muddied the classics - for shame."

"So I took a little literary license, that's not a crime, but you might think what I did this morning, is."

Michael sighed, "What did you do Lucy?"

"When Mom and I talked about her tea blend, I may have mentioned that you think it tastes like dirt. She felt bad, and I embroidered a tiny bit, I said you saved it for your best customers. She will improve it and, guess who gets to test new batches?" Michael shuddered, Lucy giggled. "Got you!"

"You're a wicked brat, but I'm glad you're here. I've run every password crack program on Derwood's computer. Nothing works and it's going to take time I don't have; unless you talk Betty into working at the store."

"Work could help get her mind off Derwood's dirty deeds." Lucy's smile became a grin, "I wonder if the lazy bastard used the same pass word for his computer and journal? Mom cracked the journals code; try DAMNSTUPILOYBCH.

Michael jotted the alpha series Lucy dictated on a handy bag and read it back. "What does that stand for? I can see damn and conceivably stupid, but where did the rest come from?"

"What was Derwood's favorite insult to Aunt Betty?"

"Damn, stupid, loony, bitch," Michael snarled. "I should have guessed."

Ellie rocked and reviewed tonight's scheduled cooking class, the first of four. Her mind wandered to Betty. How could she inform her without crushing her? Betty bustled into the kitchen loaded down with bakery boxes. Ellie asked, "Did you think you where feeding an army?"

"Of course not, but Lucy doesn't eat enough for a growing girl, so I got three dozen cheese biscuits, apple fritters and some other things. Baker needs to recoup his losses." Betty chirped like a sparrow discovering a cache of seed.

"I need to talk to you."

"Me first," Betty busied her nervous hands artfully arranging pastries on a tiered cake plate. "Sit down, eat, and listen." She repeated much of Harv and Harvey Senior's conversation, omitting only Harv's remarks about Ellie. "I would have recognized Harvey Sr. anywhere Ellie. He looks good," when Ellie frowned, Betty hastily continued, "for a loathsome old rake."

"So Harv, Huron Shores' own Don Juan, is two timing Lucy. A rotten apple never falls far from the tree. Spencer males do not understand words like fidelity or commitment." Ellie rubbed her hands together in glee. "This is perfect. Now, help me figure out how to tell Lucy and not hurt her."

"Ellie you weren't listening," Betty asked. "How can I say this without having you blow like Mount Saint Helen?"

"I heard you Betty, and I'm a reasonable woman, so just say it."

"Okay, reasonable woman, Harv was telling his father about Lucy. He used the word love more than once and babbled like a kid."

"Don't be ridiculous, Betty, he's a cad. The whole town agrees."

"Ellie, he said, 'life partner'. And when did you start believing the town gossip? We need to be realistic. Harv is genuinely smitten, and Lucy is talking wedding. Your opposition to Harv makes him more attractive to Lucy, like Eve and the apple."

"You make sense, I'll think about it," Ellie lied, dismissing Harv's dubious infatuation for Lucy. She had to tell Betty about Derwood' diary. "Betty, we have to talk about Robert's death." She pulled her translation and Derwood's journal from behind the cookbooks.

Betty cringed, "Tell me," she whispered. Ellie put the book and papers on the table, Betty read Ellie's translation and studied the journals pages fouled with Derwood's distinctive script.

Her voice gentle and compassionate, Ellie began to speak.

"Hey girl, what're you up to? Ain't nobody home. Ah, it's just you," Betty's aged gardener said, "Ms. Archer ain't here. Got any notion where she's at? Her old man run me off, but dammit, the good-for-nothing didn't hire me and Ms. Archer told me not to listen, she paid me even if he didn't let me do my job. I kept an eye and when he weren't here I snuck in to do stuff." The old man iterated his clandestine accomplishments, and paused for breath.

Lucy spoke rapidly, hoping to have her say before he got his second wind. "Aunt Betty is staying with Mom for a while. You can phone her there Mr. Parker, I'll write down the number for you," she scribbled on the back of one of her cards. "I've come to pick up some of her clothing."

"You know Sammy Ranker? He peddles houses. He said the bugger runned out on Ms. Archer. And if you excuse me saying, it ain't no loss. He weren't good enough to clean her outhouse. Look at what he done to Mister Robert's foxglove? I called him out. Got bruises to prove it, fool kept chopping; I'd a stood my ground, but the dope would a chopped my foot right off. Numskull don't know nothing 'bout flowers."

Lucy used Betty's key and edged inside, "You can reach Aunt Betty at our place or the store."

"Ain't got no time today, fixing to clean Mister Robert's workroom. Slob made a right fine mess of it, he did," he shuffled off. "A right shame what that dimwit done to our flowers."

"Ain't that the truth?" Lucy agreed, relieved to be talking to his back.

Lucy located the herbal tea, and tucked it into her backpack. Resisting the urge to revisit Derwood's study and Betty's bedroom, she tiptoed to her bike, pushed it to the end of the street, ready to speed home.

"Damn!" Lucy watched Sammy Ranker run toward her like a puppy runs to the food dish.

"When can I show that house?" he demanded gesturing at the Archer home. "I've got a signed, exclusive contract on that place. In real estate you strike while the iron's hot. I can't keep my people on a string forever. I need to talk to Derwood. He'll put your Betty in her place. Where is he anyway?"

"Mr. Ranker, if you can't find him with your awe inspiring knowledge of the local populace, how could I?"

Sammy either ignored or didn't recognize sarcasm, "I heard there's a bunch of Derwood's ex-wives sniffing around. He emptied his bank accounts and skipped town. If you ask me he didn't have a choice? Those darn women hounding him; and Betty running off all the time, you ask me, it serves her right if he left her"

"Nobody asked you," Lucy snapped. "You can contact Aunt Betty's lawyers about the house, and get out of my way." If there's any justice he'll be rundown by a truck carrying a load of pig manure. The bike rumbled to life, she pivoted; he had a choice, jump or be run down. He jumped.

Lucy raced the mile to Valerie's funeral home fuming and wondering how to protect Aunt Betty with gossips like Ranker loose. The bike slid on the coarse gravel of Val's drive, she corrected and roared to the loading dock.

"Who's there?" Valerie glanced away from the body she was preparing when Lucy pushed through the swinging doors. "You can't be in here. Put on a lab coat and don't touch anything."

"Fine hello that is," Lucy scrubbed at the grease spots on her cutoffs. "Can you take a break Val?"

"Say hello to Frank Rupert," Valerie prompted. "He's enrolled in your cooking class. Frank, meet Lucy Wilson. I'll be back in ten."

"Hello Frank," Lucy held out her hand, Frank glanced down, Lucy's eyes followed his "I'll wait outside," she said and backed out fast.

Valerie hid a smile and peeled off her gloves, and followed Lucy. "I'm sorry about the beach party."

"Forget it Val. Taking care of each other is what we do. You need to sit down. Mom found the bastard's diary, broke the code and" Lucy detailed the murders and Derwood's plan for Ellie's herbal tea.

Valerie listened without interruption, and was quiet long after Lucy stopped talking. "I knew dad didn't kill himself."

"You were right," Lucy said.

Val beamed like she'd been given a gift. "You gathered all the adulterated tea?" Val asked. Lucy said she had. "I want to know if it is poisoned."

"Me too," Lucy said.

"Good because I know a chemist I can trust," Val said. "With a list the known components the poison can be easily isolated." She paused, "That book gives all of us a motive for murder. You have to destroy it."

"Mom has plans for it," Lucy evaded. "You don't need to worry. I have to work on the health inspector's murder. The police are focused on Brad, and not the real killer."

"There is more bad news for Brad. I had coffee with the diener at the hospital this morning."

"Who's Dee-nur and why is he in the hospital?"

"Not who, what, a diener assists with autopsies and this diener works in the hospital morgue. If you stop interrupting I'll tell you."

"Okay talk," Lucy said

"Preliminary autopsy findings; Ms. Russell had a severely compressed carotid artery." Lucy grimaced and crossed her eyes, "Fine, I'll keep it simple. The killer might have caught her around the neck in a choke hold, not unlike the shime-waza maneuver practiced in judo. Conversely, he or she may have jammed Ms. Russell's hyperextended neck against Baker's table compressing the artery, but that's all guesswork at this point. She lost consciousness within ten to fifteen seconds, but that didn't kill her. She died an asphyxial death due to obstruction of the airways. To put it simply, she smothered. Those findings are supported by facial edema, cyanosis, and petechial hemorrhage."

"That last is about as transparent as mud," Lucy said.

"Petechial hemorrhage is," Valerie began.

"I think I get the drift. How does that affect Brad?"

"You're always rushing me," Val whined. "I hadn't come to the good part yet," Lucy glared, "there was bruising, etcetera consistent with a struggle, but the interesting thing was what they found on the body. Can you guess?"

"Valerie!" Lucy threatened.

"Fine, they found *Oncorhynchus tshawytscha* scales on the body."

"That'd be the Chinook King Salmon. Brad is a commercial fisherman. There are fish scales all over his house. Ms. Russell's body was hidden in Brad's closet. Jake caught her and they moved her to the bed, of course she had fish scales on her."

"Be that as it may, the police are certain that evidence will convince a jury. They will question him again," Valerie predicted."

"Another nail in his coffin, you mean. How can they harass him when they haven't confirmed or refuted his alibi? I'll tell him. It's better if he's prepared."

"I already called him," Val said sheepishly. "I thought I might redeem myself if he saw me drunk last night."

"He didn't."

"I didn't know and he seems such a nice guy. Anyway, I offered Brad and Jake a place to hide out. My house."

"Jake's to chaperon is he?" Valerie's blushed. "You know Sammy Ranker could gossip a week on that tidbit. He was ranting today about grasping wives while extolling Derwood's virtue."

"I bought my house from him. Even if he is gossiping about me, I love the house." Val hugged Lucy. "Thanks for telling me about dad."

"You helped us. It's the least I can do."

"I owe you Lucy. I'll talk to Phil about the tea, and get back to you. I have to get back before Frank sends a search party."

"Give me a couple of bags. I'll separate the tea and stop bugging you.

Valerie handed Lucy a cardboard box," Not so fast girlfriend. You have to take this."

"What is it?" Lucy asked, prying up the clear tape.

Valerie lifted Lucy's hand and smoothed the tape, "Derwood."

"I have friends searching for a specific type of home on the Costa Brava or was it the Costa del Sol in Spain," Betty said. "The point is they are fussy and haven't found an agent who could stand them. While this isn't exactly in Lucy's line, she found my elusive bed, so finding them a suitable house should be a snap for her. The commission is generous, but comes with strings." Betty searched for the kindest way to describe the old man's young bride. A poster child for augmented, dimwitted, trophy wives everywhere, while accurate, seemed harsh. "The third wife lacks sophistication and um, almost everything, but sex appeal. She wants someone dedicated to her needs and her needs only. Lucy planned to spend a month with us so she might not want to cut her vacation short. She probably won't be interested."

"Betty, you're doing the ditsy thing again; but anything that will get her away from Harv is fine with me."

"I'll miss her; I wish there were another way."

"I will too, but we can muddle through without Lucy."

"How could you possibly muddle through without me? I'm shattered," fortunately Lucy heard only the last few words.

"Lucy no good comes of eavesdropping."

Lucy caught her mother and her aunt in a tight hug, "You may be able to get along without me, but I don't know what I'd do without you. What's wrong?"

"Everything is fine honey," Ellie said. "Look, Betty brought cheese biscuits."

"What have you got in the box?" Betty picked up the carton of ashes.

"Uh, nothing," Lucy stuttered.

"Sweetie, people don't carry around empty boxes." Ellie took the box from Betty and shook it. "It's not very heavy."

"It's Derwood," Lucy blurted. "Valerie doesn't want him."

"Neither do I!" Betty rasped, "He let me believe Robert committed suicide." She smiled, "However I know of a farm with a huge, liquid manure tank. That'd be righteous justice."

"Aunt Betty I am shocked by your callousness." Lucy giggled, "Can we dump him now, or do we wait until dark?"

"No," Ellie objected, "Have you forgotten the vagrant?" Ellie grinned evilly, "If it were possible we'd separate Mr. Doe's ashes from Derwood then dump the degenerate in the pit. The farm is miles away, but the abattoir is close and has an open lagoon. Tonight after class we'll dump *him* with the rest of the offal and if we are discovered we'll tell the truth. "Lucy gasped and Betty protested, "We'll say we're a performing a cleansing ritual."

They laughed until tears ran down their faces and laughter as everyone knows, heals.

CHAPTER 17

Ellie's equipment heavy handcart tracked over the newly mopped floor. She smiled an apology at Tom, the high school custodian. Tom nodded and patiently mopped over cart tracks.

"You're early Brad. You'll get extra credit for that," Ellie happily surrendered her cumbersome cart to his able hands.

"It was too late to go home after Chief Platt finished grilling me," Brad sighed, "I figured you could use a hand. Who's taking the class?"

Ellie let his reference to Eric slide and replied. "Pretty much the same crowd as the spring class. Harv Spencer enrolled late and will likely drop out when he finds cooking is hands on. Robby Brown, the tinsmith who set up shop on Main Street is new as is Mac McGregor."

"How did you meet McGregor?"

"He stopped me for expired tags and when I told him about the class, he asked to join.

"Did he give you the ticket?"

"Yes he did, but we can't fault a man for doing his job."

"Most people do," Mac McGregor said; he held a plastic milk crate loaded with baking supplies. "Good evening Mrs. Wilson."

"Hello Mac, have you met Brad Talltree?"

"We've met," Brad said tersely.

"We have," Mac agreed, "but not socially."

Brad and Mac postured, taking each other's measure like two pugnacious fighting cocks.

"Rodney!" Ellie shrilled, thankful for her brother-in-law's timely arrival. "Say hello to Brad and meet Mac."

Rodney shook Mac's hand and greeted Brad. McGregor was similar to Harv in height and build. Mac was rugged, honest, and healthy, while

Harv, in Rodney's opinion, was too slick. "Ah, you gave Ellie the ticket."

"I'm sorry to say I did." Mac hung his head in mock shame. "But she complimented me for doing my job."

"She would," Rodney laughed heartily. "Ellie, perhaps now you will allow me to handle renewals."

"Lucy, you're late," Ellie called. "Isn't it fortunate that Brad was here to help?" Ellie's voice held a critical bite, but Lucy learned innuendo avoidance from a true master, grandpa, and ignored her.

The remainder of Ellie's students followed Lucy, "I dropped bread crumbs, and led the guys right in," Lucy joked. "What now?"

"Partner everyone up and assign stations. Our late registrant will work with me, while you circulate and help when needed."

Lucy nodded though working with Ellie might send Harv running. She washed her hands; demonstrated work space layout using Mac's supplies and directed each pair to their allotted space. "One more thing before we start. Tom," she waved at the custodian, "will clean the floor, but you will leave the counters walls and ceilings clean. We'll have coffee and a question period while your goodies are baking. You'll try Mrs. Wilson's pie and compare with your own. Have I covered everything?"

"Yes, Lucy you've been your usual efficient, enthusiastic self. Now is everyone ready?" Ellie's raised voice commanded attention. "Good, let's bake. We will prepare the filling for your pies, proceed to pastry, and while your pies bake, make date squares. Both raisons and dates are available when tender fruits are prohibitively expensive. Please ask questions or for help anytime," she met each pair of attentive eyes to establish rapport.

Old Fashioned Raisin Pie
1 cup seeded raisins
1 ½ cups water
Cook together until raisins are tender plumped. Add
¾ cup white sugar
1 tablespoon molasses
1 tablespoon vinegar
Mix 4 tablespoons flour with
1 tablespoon melted butter
(Blending flour with butter prevents clumping)
 Add to raisin mixture.

"Measure and wash Sultana raisins, (remove any seeds or stems) into a medium sized pot with 1 1/2 cups water. Bring to a boil, stirring often. Reduce heat; simmer until raisins are plump approximately five minutes." Ellie watched her students jostle for stove space. "Lucy we are short students, perhaps we should call Zack."

"He had a problem getting past the road work so Harv and Michael stopped to help him. I hear them now."

"It's my fault we're late, Teach," Zack said, "Where do you want us?"

"Zack you work with Michael. Harv you'll work up front with me. Lucy show Zack and Michael their station, and pay special attention to our new students, Robby and Mac. Come along Mr. Spencer."

Ellie demonstrated method and coached Harv without the aid of sarcasm. Lucy moved from one pair of fledgling cooks to the next, while wondering when Ellie would use her razor sharp tongue on Harv.

"Now that you've added the flour and butter, sugar, molasses and vinegar and thickened your fillings, set them aside to cool while we make pastry." Ellie commanded, waiting while veteran students checked recipes and set out ingredients. First time participants dutifully followed suit.

Pie Pastry
3 1/2 cups flour
½ pound lard or shortening (1 cup)
¼ teaspoon baking powder
1 teaspoon salt
1 teaspoon white vinegar
Coldest water available.

"There are as many recipes for pie crust as there are cooks. All use flour, salt, liquid, and fat such as lard, shortening, butter, or oil. Our recipe is simple and reliable.
Sift the flour, salt, and baking powder together into your bowl," she paused giving new students time to catch up. "Harv pay attention, Lucy is just fine," she murmured, glaring at Lucy whispering to Rodney, while Mac looked lost. "Add half pound lard to your dry ingredients. If you want to use shortening the recipe and method are the same though the crust shrinks a little more. I prefer lard." She smiled, while Jake guiltily pushed a block of shortening into his backpack and borrowed lard from Michael. "With a pastry blender quickly work the fat into your flour mixture against the side of the bowl. Turn the bowl as you work, like this," she demonstrated. "Gather a handful of your pastry, squeeze

gently, and then rub your thumb across it. If the pastry breaks apart in little globules the size of large peas, you've worked it enough. That's exactly right Mr. Spencer. Hold yours up for everyone to see," Ellie said, genuinely surprised.

"Mix the vinegar and 1/2 cup of cold water, make an impression in the center of the dry ingredients, and stir quickly with our hand, your pastry should be soft and slightly sticky. Now separate your dough into two equal portions, liberally sprinkle flour over your work surface and roll," she used a substantial rolling pin to demonstrated rolling techniques. "Start from the center gentlemen. Make your circles about an inch and a half larger than your pie tin, gently fold in half and fit the circle into your pan." She demonstrated. "Harv, I think you've got it. Roll the remaining portion for a top crust."

"They're doing well, aren't they, Mom?" Lucy watched because she knew greenhorn bakers could turn defenseless food into an inedible mess in moments.

"They're fine, and as usual quiet, but they'll loosen up once they've had a success." Ellie returned to the front of the class. She put a pie together and fluted the edges, cut steam vents and said, "Here we have a perfect pie ready for oven or freezer. Now when people say 'as easy as pie,' what will you say? Think on it while you finish your pies."

When all pies were in preheated ovens they moved on to the evening's second project.

<u>Date Squares (Grandmas Woods recipe)</u>
1 lb. dates, chopped, cover with
¾ cups water, add a
Pinch salt,
Bring to a boil turn down the heat and simmer slowly until the dates are soft, 10 to 15 minutes.
Add:
½ cup white sugar
Stir until sugar is dissolved. This mixture should be spreading consistency, if it is too thick add a little more water, until desired consistency. Add
½ tsp. vanilla.
Stir well and cool.

Crumb mixture:
1 ½ cups white flour
2 ½ cups oatmeal (not instant, regular or old fashioned large flake if you can find it.)

1 cup brown sugar
1 teaspoon salt
1 teaspoon baking soda
1 cup butter (softened)

Mix first 5 ingredients together add butter and rub gently together with hands until coarse crumbs are formed. DO NOT over mix.

Put half of crumb mixture into the bottom of an ungreased 8 X 8" if you like a thick square, or a 9 X 13" pan if you favor the thinner style, Pat down gently but firmly. Drop dates by tablespoonful evenly over base, spread. Top with remaining crumbs. Bake in a 350 degree oven for 30 minutes. Remove from oven and cool completely. Cut into squares and enjoy thoroughly.

Store in an air tight container in a cool place.

Freezes well.

"Lucy, pay attention, Mr. McGregor is abusing his crumbs."

Everyone laughed but Harv, he glowered when Lucy put her arms around Mac, took his floury hands and demonstrated the gentle crumb method.

"That's better," Lucy said, "I think you've got it." She moved on and Harv stopped grinding his teeth.

"Harv," Ellie admonished, "you are making a crumb base not a sidewalk. Brad stop patting, it's a crumble base not a cutting board."

"Drop spoonfuls of date mixture over the base and spread evenly. Put the remaining crumbs on top, and pop your square into the oven."

"Ellie," Zack winked roguishly, "My crumbs are lifting, can Lucy hold my hand?"

"There's a clown in every group," Ellie said, taking pity on Harv, and putting her aversion to the Spencer clan on hold. "Harv, I can't believe you've never baked before."

"It's because you're an excellent teacher Mrs. Wilson," Harv said, and hoped he was growing on Ellie.

"Mom it's coffee time."

"It is, and you get to pour."

"Maybe Harv can answer that pie question now. Come on Harv what's the answer?" Zack badgered, mischievously.

"We speak of mathematics." Harv said imitating his father's boardroom manner. "The generally accepted value of pi is 3.14159, though it would require approximately 133 years without breaks to recite the 6.4 billion known digits in pi."

"Correct." Ellie applauded. "Now let's have coffee."

"Mrs. Wilson, I really enjoyed the hands on part of tonight's class," Mac said.

Harv and Brad glared at him like a tiger at prey.

Ellie hoped his remark wasn't as ingenuous as it seemed. He was handsome, articulate, employed, and age appropriate, an excellent match for Lucy when she saw through Harv Spencer. "Thank you Mac, we hope you will be comfortable in the kitchen when you complete this course."

"Mrs. Wilson, why is this raisin pie you made for us to taste rectangular?" Robby the tinsmith, asked helping himself to a second piece.

"So one pie would feed everyone," Ellie replied and proceeded to answer a myriad of questions about canned fruit and fillings, frozen fruit, apple varieties, etcetera.

Rodney motioned Lucy to where he stood apart from the chattering group. "Finish what you were trying to tell me about that blighter's notes."

Lucy whispered, "Mom has concrete proof that Derwood murdered Uncle Robert."

"Lucy, check the ovens please," Ellie said. "Rodney come have your coffee."

Lucy absent mindedly took pies and pans of sweet-smelling date square from the ovens and decided she'd better move the glass and bedpost tonight. The old tree was too risky now that Hank the gardener was back at work.

"I need to talk to you." Harv's husky whisper weakened Lucy's resolve, and her knees.

"Sorry you got stuck working with Mom, but I warned you."

"That's all right. I think she's warming to me."

"Like me, she's a victim of your charm," Lucy said.

Harv's eyes suggested things Lucy hoped Ellie hadn't seen. "Talk fast," she sighed. "Mom is headed this way, but if you help with clean up we can be alone."

Ellie surged through her students like the Miami Dolphin's all time leading rusher, Larry Csonka going in for a Super Bowl touchdown. "Brad has offered," she panted, "to help with the clean up in my place Lucy. I'll go home if you don't mind."

"Sure mom that's fine, but Harv has offered to help. We wouldn't want Brad to stress his shoulder."

"Many hands make light work," Brad insisted, and grabbed a broom.

"Harv, give us a moment please," Lucy said. "Maybe you could walk mom out to her car?"

"I'll take care of that," Jake said. "Ellie can teach me how to juggle two flawless, hot from the oven baked items. Baker said he'd provide coffee if I shared, you're invited too Ellie."

"Have fun mom," Lucy called, "but be home by midnight." Lucy winked at Jake. "Harv, I really need to talk with Brad alone."

Harv scowled, moved out of earshot, and vigorously wiped counters.

Lucy lowered her voice, "Brad, you know I love you, you're like a brother to me. Only this morning I was thinking about the summer we crashed the bike."

"I haven't forgotten. I still owe you for taking the blame. You may consider that ancient history, but I don't."

"You don't owe me, but if you feel you do; look in on mom when I'm not here and we'll be square."

"I already do that." Brad set his jaw, "When things don't work out with Mr. Moneybags, I'll be waiting. I'll go, but Lucy I mean what I say."

"Brad old friend, take Val up on her offer of a room," Lucy urged hugging him tight. "She likes you and I know you. You're attracted to her too. Tell you what, let's go fishing Friday evening," she suggested, anxiously watching as Harv repeatedly wipe the same foot of counter. "I'll sneak a bottle of wine from mom's cellar and we'll talk like we used to. I'll meet you at the pier about four. What do you say?"

"Sounds about right to me," Brad grimaced, "I'll go if that's what you really want."

"That is what I really want." Lucy gave him a quick peck on the cheek and shoved him toward the door.

"Alone at last," Lucy sighed, "oops, sorry Harv. Tom, I put a plate of goodies in the staff room with your name on it. We'll be another ten minutes or so."

The custodian, a man who wasted few words, nodded agreement, abandoned his mop bucket, and ambled off to find the food.

"What did you want to talk about? We may have a few minutes." Lucy said, scrutinizing the classrooms multiple entrances.

Unconsciously mimicking her scrutiny Harv said, "Why don't you answer your cell phone?" And why did Mr. Schneider-White almost faint when he opened your bundle of cupids? I thought I was going to have to administer CPR."

"I'm sorry about the phone. I forgot to charge it. Now then, put the extra pans in the cupboard. Tom wants to mop up."

"Lucy, don't change the subject. What is so unusual about those cherubs? I'll straighten up while you explain."

"It's a little complicated."

"I'm all ears."

"Okay, remember when we met in Amsterdam, I told you I'd located a Renaissance bed for my aunt." Harv nodded, "I told you why the bed was important to her. Well her husband Derwood," Lucy wrinkled her nose in distaste, "destroyed the bed and when I saw the remains, I wanted to salvage something for Aunt Betty so I took the cherubs. In light of Derwood's bigamy, fraud, and disappearance, the house is a crime scene, if they knew I'd removed evidence I'll be in trouble. But that's not why Martin Schneider-White was upset. He saw a Seventeenth Century artifact deliberately vandalized and he loathes vandalism."

"So you're telling me that I aided and abetted in the destruction of a crime scene?" Harv asked solemnly.

"I'm afraid you did, but unknowingly," she stressed the last word.

"Lucy, life with you will never be dull." Harv grinned, and reached for her, "I like that."

"You folks done in here," Tom drawled, "I wanna finish and go home."

"Yes Tom, we're finished. Thanks for your patience."

"Yup," Tom said.

Are they all in league to keep us apart, Lucy wondered, and led Harv out.

Ellie sat on the porch sipping a steaming cup of Baker's excellent coffee. Baker tasted Jake's pie, enthusiastically approved it, and moved on to the date square. Talk turned to Brad's ordeal and Eric's handling of it.

"I bet the cops are fingerprinting my money right now, and when they get the results they'll round up everybody in town and throw us all in the hoosegow," Baker groused.

"Brad?" Ellie questioned a shadowy figure striding across the darkened parking lot.

"Yeah it's me. I thought I might get a cup of coffee since Harv is helping Lucy."

"Alone?" Ellie asked.

"Lucy, I know we have another cooking class tomorrow and the Lighthouse Dedication Saturday, but how about catching a movie Friday?"

"Oh Harv, I'd love to, but I'm going fishing with Brad."

Harv frowned "There's nothing between you two is there?"

"Mr. Spencer, I do believe you're jealous."

"I'd resent anyone that steals time I might spend with you."

"You have nothing to worry about. Brad and I are friends. Do you want to talk or do you have something else in mind?"

"I could think of a thing or two." Harv enfolded Lucy's obliging body in his arms. "You have the sexiest, most kissable lips I've ever encountered," he murmured as headlights silhouetted them.

Lucy stifled a giggle. "That'll be mom. Can you put up with this? She does it from love you know."

Harv led Lucy across the grass to where Ellie waited. "I can, but we'll have to be tricky if we're ever to be alone together. I'll put a ladder up to your window an hour or so before the lighthouse dedication. You arrange for an early bit of darkness and we'll sneak out. You must have inherited some of that magic your mother uses to keep us from touching."

"Harv, you're on dangerous ground. He who mocks the prophetess mother shall suffer the curse of ten thousand warts."

"I'll take the risk. Could I chance a quick kiss without being turned into a . . . ?"

"I wouldn't say that if I were you." Lucy smothered her laughter.

"Mom, you didn't have to come back. I have my bike and anyway Harv would bring me home."

"Yes dear, I know."

The thief waited in the darkened automobile. It was a lucky accident that put him at Darcy's dump nursing a hangover. If he hadn't eased his throbbing head against the cool table and closed his eyes, he wouldn't have recognized that quiet hum.

No problem, he'd take care of the loose end, and be home free. Her car couldn't be traced to him. A sweet irony, he laughed enjoying his cleverness. Here comes the cripple free for the picking . . . off.

Running rapidly through the gears, he stamped on the accelerator and surged ahead. God, he loved that old deer in the headlights look. Damn he swore, who knew the gimp could move that fast. Clutching the steering wheel he braced for impact he sideswiped a new shiny SUV ramming it into a Ford Fairlanes' glittering metal body.

The thief glanced in the rear view mirror, and laid rubber peeling around the corner, he cut the engine, coasted into Library Lane, and slammed the shift into park. He shot out of the car and into a nearby thicket.

Voices rang through the still night. All the busybodies were out. Good, the thief gloated, witnesses, lots of witnesses to identify her car. That's fair; every damn thing that had gone wrong is all her fault.

Puffing up the final hill, he stripped off plastic gloves; the television glowed in the window of his house. He climbed over the sill into his room, donned pajamas, rubbed his eyes, and stumbled toward the living room. His Dad; his irrefutable alibi.

CHAPTER 18

The crumpled ruin of Zack's chair was caught between two cars, like a mouse in a trap.

"Some bugger hit Zack!" Baker jumped the railing, and sprinted across the lot to the smashed vehicles. "We need more light!"

Hazard lights flashing frenzied anxiety, Jake backed into the street aiming his headlights at the hit-and-run scene.

"I saw Zack try to wheel between these cars. He's got to be under here." Baker reached into the dark space under the SUV.

"Here, take this." Jake threw himself to the tarmac and shoved a flashlight at Baker. "I think I see him. We have to get this thing off him. He could be alive."

"Do not disturb anything," a woman's voice commanded.

"Who's that?" Baker demanded.

"Michelle, Michelle Homes; come around, he's here."

Jake and Baker rushed to where Michelle huddled between the first vehicle and the curb, Zack's head cradled in her lap. His silence, closed eyes and ashen face brought Baker to his knees

"Is he alive?

"Yes," Michelle responded. "I've called 911," she tossed her daily planner at Jake. "Write this down," she dictated a plate number. "It's probably stolen, but the police might get him before he dumps it."

Baker tucked Jake's car blanket around the part of Zack's body not trapped under the Sports Utility Vehicle.

"Stop that, I'm not dead," Zack mumbled.

"Probably in no hurry to get out of there, either," Baker joked nervously. "Trust you to be hit by a drunk and land in the lap of a beautiful Florence Nightingale savvy enough to get the plate number."

Zack snorted as police cars, fire engines, tow trucks and an ambulance illuminated them in a confusion of multi-colored lights.

The medical crew strapped Zack to a backboard. Firemen directed the tow truck driver who expertly lifted the confining SUV and Zack was released.

True to form, Zack quarreled with the paramedics.

"Zack," Baker barked, "you're getting into that ambulance if I have to put you there myself. You can try to fight us off, but strapped to that board you're no match for Jake and me."

"And me!" Michelle said grimly. "Take him." She told the ambulance crew, "Shut up Zack, we'll follow."

"I'll go, but you're making a fuss over nothing. Be careful with my chair," Zack yelled as the ambulance doors snapped shut.

"Was he talking about this?" asked a burly fireman pulling a flattened mass of titanium tubing out of the SUV's grill."

Ellie awoke from the heavy slumber she been thoroughly enjoying to fumble for the phone with a sleep deadened hand. After picking it off the floor twice she mumbled a greeting.

"Ellie, this is Jake. I'm sorry to wake you so early, but I knew you'd want to know Zack was stuck by a hit and run driver last night."

"What hospital is he in?" Ellie leapt from her bed groping for clothing.

"He wouldn't stay in the hospital; he's here at the bakery."

"I'm on my way," Ellie struggled into the jeans and sweat shirt she usually wore to garden. Remembering Betty's fatigue she let her sleep, then tip toed down the stairs avoiding the squeakers as she had in her youth.

"Lucy, why are you sitting in the dark?" Ellie asked flipping on the five brilliant overhead lights.

"I *was* meditating," Lucy lied, worrying better described her thoughts. Who killed Derwood? Why am I stuck with his ashes? Brad's jealousy and unbrotherly interest in her; add Rita Russel, the bakery robbery and she had enough to keep anybody awake. But what kept her awake was that the glass and bedpost were gone from her tree. Her letters to her dad were still there, but all of the incriminating stuff was gone.

Ellie leaned a hastily scribbled note against the vase of vibrant, red roses. "Zack had an accident. He refused to stay in hospital. He's at the bakery. I'm going to see if I can talk him into going home."

"I'll come along," Lucy said unfolding from a yoga half lotus position, and threw on a tattered jean jacket she'd rescued from the rag bag.

"Jake, what happened?" Ellie demanded bursting into the mix room.

"Somebody deliberately ran Zack down," Jake said. "Michelle's with him. They're reliving their misspent youth."

"Did anyone recognize the car?"

"No Ellie, but Michelle got the license number and thinks the driver was male."

"The police are still measuring, I saw the cars. I can't believe he's not injured."

"Why don't you go see for yourself?" Jake gently pushed Ellie towards the stairs.

"It's a miracle he survived," Ellie heard Baker say as she and Lucy entered the coffee shop. "His chair's that pile of scrap metal on the counter. We're taking up a collection to replace it. It's a custom titanium sports chair and cost big bucks," Baker explained steering clear of the word disabled because Zack was the least disabled guy he knew. "Zack was planning to enter the upcoming games, so dig deep."

Ellie motioned Lucy to the outdoor table where Zack happily regaled the early morning group with details of his accident.

"Hello Zack. Did I chase away your entourage?" Ellie asked scrutinizing him for injury.

"Nah, they ran when Sammy Ranker graced me with his presence. Michelle has an early appointment.

"I'll get coffee," Ellie offered seeing Zack's empty cup.

"Sure that'll look great. Lazy Lucy makes feeble, ancient," Lucy paused when Ellie scowled, "though still dynamic and attractive mother climb mountainous steps at local eatery."

"She's got you there Ellie," Zack said. "Ranker would enjoy dissing our local celebrity."

Ellie laughed, "Since Lucy's paying we'll have coffee and breakfast."

"Thank you," Zack said, "I'll have coffee, two cheese biscuits heated 45 seconds, double butter and a cranberry muffin, for starters."

Lucy turned her pockets inside out, "Uh, I seem to have forgotten my wallet, can you lend me some money mom."

"Ah ha the old forgotten wallet ploy," Ellie said. "Takes you back doesn't it? You and Mandy filled your van with cheap little urchins; take them to the drive-in movie where they graciously allowed you to buy their popcorn and sodas."

"Grandpa always paid Zack back," Lucy said, fleeing into the bakery.

"I hope this crowd left a cheese biscuit for me," Lucy moaned, joining the long queue. "Rex old boy, how have you been?" She stooped to greet the bakery's mascot or mas-cat as Baker called him. "You must be fifteen years old, but you're as frisky as a kitten," she told the huge cat happily stropping against her bare legs.

"Foster! Come back!" Brad shouted, the dog darted from his truck, skirted the line of customers, and dashed into the bakery.

Rex's growl rapidly developed into a guttural howl and every hair stood on end. His erect red and white banded tail fluffed out like a fuzzy barber's pole. He arched his back, baring spiky fangs and hissed. Razor sharp talons raked empty space very close to the denim clad legs standing behind Lucy.

Lucy scooped Rex into her arms just as Foster; his short claws scrabbling for purchase on the hardwood skidded to a stop. Lucy held Rex tight while she lunged for Foster's collar. The snarling dog's strong jaws snapped on empty air inches from those same denim clad legs.

Brad forced his way through the crowd and clipped a leash on his wayward canine. "I don't know what got into Foster, he never leaves my truck without permission, and he loves cats."

"Yeah, they taste like chicken," Jordan Platt, the owner of the denim clad legs, sneered.

Brad glowered at Jordan, thanked Lucy, and dragged his dog back to his pickup sorry that Foster had missed Jordan. Why, he wondered do I assume Jordan Platt and not Rex was Foster's target?

"You should shoot that damn animal," Jordan shouted.

Brad tucked Foster into the cab, climbed in, rolled up the window, and carefully pulled into the beach traffic.

"Damn drunken Indian, better keep that wolf under control or I'll sue his ass!"

Finding no satisfaction in berating an absent opponent, Jordan redirected his spite. "Damn cat's nuts. Baker should shoot it before somebody gets hurts. I've got the afternoon off, I'll do it."

"What's going on?" Baker queried eager to quell any fracas that disturbed the tranquility of his establishment.

"Your crazy cat tried to scratch me!"

"Rex scratched you? That's hard to believe. Are you sure he wasn't playing?"

"Lucy, you saw the damn thing attack me, tell him.

Ellie heard the fracas and rushed to defend the cat. She plucked Rex from Lucy's grasp. "Lucy dear deal with him," she glared at Jordan, "and get Zack's breakfast, while I take our feline friend to his quarters."

Fine Mother, I'll deal with him, but you're not going to like my methods, Lucy thought.

Jordan threw his arm over Lucy's shoulder, and crooned, "Tell the nice baker exactly what happened, Lucy dear.

"Jordan, take your arm off my shoulder," Lucy purred, "or I'll break it off and beat you to death with the bloody stump." She shoved him onto a stool, "Pay attention, and I'll educate your sorry ass. Rex is a placid cat and Foster a Siberian husky, a breed of dog not wolf. The males look masculine like you, but unlike you, they are never coarse or uncouth." She calmly placed her order.

"Coffee is on me this morning," Baker yelled over customer applause and Jake's hearty, "Bravo!"

"We," Ellie whispered to the old cat, "will go while the going is good." She carried Rex to his bed in the storeroom, "He needs a time out," she said smiling at Baker, the regulars who often heard Baker expound on that useless disciplinary tool for cats or children, laughed

"You are an unhappy boy; want to tell me what's wrong?" Ellie asked, waited, and grinned. "If Jordan hears me he'll euthanize both of us," She stroked Rex who purred and snuggled deep in his bed. "You have a bee in your fur, and I wonder why." Rex stared into Ellie's eyes as if transmitting his thoughts to her. She smoothed his luxurious fur. "I'll be back, you think of a way to help us lesser creatures read your mind." Rex sighed and covered his eyes with his tail.

"Hurry, Mom, Zack's weak from hunger."

"Lucy I swear Rex has something to say, and is annoyed by my lack my understanding."

"Uh okay, if you say so," Lucy said skeptically, while she emptied Ellie's wallet into the coffee can labeled 'Zack's New Wheel Chair Fund'. "Did you notice Zack when Jordan badgered Brad? I was afraid he'd faint."

"Somebody wants him dead; perhaps he finally accepted that fact."

"He'll need to talk about it, Lucy said, but he won't talk if I'm here." She settled the tray in front of Zack. "Did you think we'd been abducted by aliens, or run off with some hunky guys?"

"Why run off with another guy with me to fulfill your every whim." Zack' laugh was forced, "The thought never crossed my mind. What was the fuss about?"

"Foster went after Rex, but Jordan thought the cat and dog were after him," Lucy explained. "I tried to smooth it over, but Jordan, the moron called Brad a drunken Indian and I lost my temper. I see Baker needs my help." Lucy rose from the table with the easy grace of youth and fled.

Ellie sat across from Zack. "If you need to talk I'm a good listener."

"Ellie, can I trust you to keep something under your hat?"

"Yes."

"I'm scared Ellie," Zack murmured, "Can you believe that? Me scared? I wasn't as scared in Vietnam as when that car missed me and swerved to try again. I threw myself between the vehicles and clawed my way under the SUV, thank God those things are higher than cars." He flashed his torn fingernails before closing his fist.

Ellie sipped coffee, nibbled an apple fritter, worried, and listened.

"But what scares hell out of me is, I thought I was hallucinating and he nearly got me. I knew the new meds caused hallucinations and crazy dreams, but the car was real and tried to kill me. Zack scrubbed his face with his hands. "Damnitall Ellie. I don't know what's real anymore. He gulped coffee and sighed, "what if the other thing I thought was drug induced is real too?"

"Why don't you tell me about it? Maybe we can work it out together."

"Aw hell Ellie, you've got enough on your plate, without my neurosis."

"Zack," Ellie glared, "Am I your friend?"

"I hope so."

Ellie slapped the table sharply, "Well friend, in my life friends help friends."

"I knew that, but it's good to hear you say it." He shuddered, "I'm so damn confused I can't tell my ass from a tea kettle. The only thing I am sure of is I'm not sure of anything.

Baker approached, Ellie said quickly, "Somebody tried to run over you, that's as real as it gets! Come to dinner at seven tomorrow, and we will talk it out. Can I buy you a coffee, Baker?"

"No, but I wouldn't say no to that dinner invitation."

"Baker you are always welcome at my table."

"How are you feeling Zack? Jake asked sitting next to Baker.

"I'm fine, but I hear my chair is ruined," Zack replied turning talk back to last night's narrow escape.

"Mom, I'm going to take these goodies to Aunt Betty before she goes to the shop, Lucy said. "No need to rush home, I'll set the bread for tonight's class."

"Thank you Lucy, I don't know what I'd do without you."

Lucy greeted Tom, who used a few of his hoarded words to ask what was on tonight's menu.

"We're making bread, it is such a long process I came early to get it started. Want to help?"

"Yup," Tom said, succinct, as usual.

"Okay," Lucy said, "fill the biggest kettle, we need boiling water," she finished measuring honey, salt, shortening and milk powder into huge crockery bowls before the tight-lipped custodian spoke again.

"Um, I saw you at the clambake with the Spencer kid. I seen him around town pretty often when he's home. I know him pretty good."

"Uh huh," Lucy replied, wondering what Tom was getting at. She snapped her fingers as the answer came to her, "Are you spying for mom too?"

"No, I don't spy for nobody. But I never see Spencer without some woman on his arm. That fellow sees more action than a platoon of marines. I don't want a nice kid like you hurt." His face red, Tom muttered, "I got to do my own work now," he backed toward the door.

"Wait Tom, I appreciate your concern." Lucy hugged him, "Thanks."

"I came to help. Hello, Tom," Harv said to Tom's hastily retreating back. "I don't think he likes me." Harv grinned, "Do you have to hug all the guys?"

"That's Tom's way, and yes I do have to hug all the guys." Lucy giggled. "Pour two cups boiling water," she pointed at the steaming kettle, "in to each bowl while I stir. Hey, pay attention; you almost poured that on my hand." Harv poured carefully, but glanced around between pours. "What are you looking for?"

"I'm here alone with you and your mother hasn't come out of the woodwork." He put his free arm around her waist. "Do you want me to kiss that hand better?"

Lucy heard Ellie's running footsteps, "Hi Mom!"

"Harv, what a delightful surprise," Ellie fibbed. "Honey you worked all day, take a break? Harv can help me. You don't mind, do you, Mr. October?"

"I could use a break," Lucy saw panic in Harv's eyes and said *sotto voce*, "I won't be gone long. I promise"

He'll be fine. Lucy poured a cup of Tom's industrial strength coffee, and thought of Ellie's reaction to the firefighter's calendar. The calendar was open, as luck would have it, to October. Ellie saw Harv, Mr. October, her hazel eyes glowed. She glanced at the perfectly placed roses in the pinup and flashed to the bouquet on the table. Blushing as only redheads could, she voiced each derogatory term reserved exclusively for Spencer males, added a few exclusive to Harv, like immodest, shameless and exhibitionist. Lucy chuckled, she'd casually flipped to December, and read Baker and Jake's witty caption. Baker wearing a diaper and sash and Jake clad in an ultra short, gladiator-style toga armed with a scythe and hourglass said, 'We appear last, because, after the eye has been assaulted by the inferior physiques of lesser males our generous flesh is restful to both eye and mind.' Mom laughed until tears ruined her mascara. Lucy joined her, and treasured the laughter they'd shared

She refilled her coffee cup and idly caressed the letters in her pocket. Who took the glass and bedpost from her tree, if the cops found it, why did they leave the letters? She glanced at her watch, and ran to his rescue Harv.

Never Fail White Bread
In a large bowl put:
4 tablespoon honey
4 tablespoon lard or shortening
½ cup dry milk powder
2 teaspoons salt
2 cups boiling water
Set aside to cool
In the small bowl put;
1/4 cup lukewarm water
1 teaspoon white sugar

Stir to dissolve the sugar then sprinkle 1 pkgs. dried yeast (or 1 dessert spoon of yeast granules) over the water. Let that stand for 10 minutes. Add 1 cup cold water to the mixture in the large bowl.

If that does not bring the temperature down to lukewarm, wait until it cools.

Add the yeast mixture to the large bowl. Stir.

Add 5 cups bread flour or all purpose flour.

Beat vigorously with a spoon. Turn out on a generously floured board. Knead for 10 minutes adding more flour as needed until the dough does not stick to your hands. 2 or 3 more cups flour could be needed.

Wash and grease the large bowl. Put the dough in the bowl and turn it once so that the greased side is up.

Cover with a clean tea towel and let rise in a draft-free area until doubled in bulk (2 hours).

Punch dough down and let rest for 10 minutes. Divide into 3 equal portions. Roll each portion into a rectangle with a rolling pin until it is 1 inch thick. Roll up jelly-roll style tucking the ends under. Place into greased bread pan, seam side down.

Cover and let rise again until double in bulk. (About 1 hour)

Bake in 375 degrees F oven for 40 minutes or until loaves sounds hollow when tapped on the top. Remove from oven, brush tops with butter, remove from pans, and cool on wire rack. Enjoy.

"Your small bowl holds lukewarm water, sugar and 1 package dried yeast. Remember if the water is too hot you kill the yeast. If you forget the sugar, you starve it. Add one cup of cold water to the large bowl bringing the temperature to lukewarm. This is important. The yeast is still at risk. If your mixture is too hot, wait. Harv will demonstrate from here," Ellie smiled at Harv, who beamed.

Just what happened while I slurped coffee? Lucy wondered.

"Now for the fun part, add half of the flour and beat vigorously with a spoon. A good way to release tension," Ellie suggested, watched them and laughed, "I didn't know you all were that strung out."

Lucy wandered around cleaning up spills, told them to add the remaining flour, and continue mixing.

"Now, Ellie said, "dump one cup of flour on your work surface and spread it around. I meant on the table Rodney."

Rodney, used to being her straight man smiled sheepishly.

"Dump your dough onto the floured surface. Gather it into a mass and using the heels of your hands push down firmly. Rotate one quarter turn and push again and repeat. Add more flour until the dough doesn't stick to your surface or your hands. Knead ten to fifteen minutes. If you tire think of your ex-wife and the guy she lives with. If that doesn't get you moving, remember your truck, the one she got in the settlement, and he drives," Ellie teased. "Stan, who are you that angry with?"

"Orville! I'm pretending this is his neck," Brad's skipper said and grinned.

"Me too," others echoed.

I would not want to be Orville, Ellie thought. "Stop kneading and test the dough by running your thumb lightly over it. If small bubbles appear you have completed your mission. Now grease the large bowl turn the dough once to grease the top. Cover with your baking sheets and keep out of drafts." Ellie pointed to the counter near the ovens. "It will rise, doubling in size over the next two hours and then we'll punch it down, rest it for ten minutes, shape it, and let it raise another hour in greased loaf pans. We started early and will be ending late. It'll be a four-plus hour class. While your dough is rising, Lucy will demonstrate several ways to use bread dough. Harv you get to sit beside me and watch."

"I could help Lucy," Harv said tossing his dough into the bowl. "I could turn her pages."

"Thank you Harv, but she's quite experienced at this," Ellie took his hand. "You listen and learn."

Lucy winked at Harv. "You can shape your dough into three boring loaves or be creative and make split-top, dinner, clover leaf or cheese stuffed rolls, butter fans, even hotdog or hamburger buns. Choose what suits your meal plan. A hamburger is ecstatic when surrounded by a homemade bun." Lucy snickered and so did the class. "But, you say, I spent all day making bread and have no dinner, dessert or breakfast. Relax you've got that covered. Take one third of your rested dough and roll it into a rectangle measuring about twelve by fourteen inches. Liberally spread with butter, sprinkle on a half cup of brown sugar and a cup of washed and dried raisins. Add a few chopped walnuts or pecans if you like and dust the lot with powdered cinnamon. Then starting with a long side, tightly roll, cut the roll lengthwise, and knead lightly into the original roll. Pinch the edges together to seal. Now a decision, do you make coffee cake or sticky buns?"

"Since you can't agree, I'll decide. First a fragrant coffee cake; put the roll pinched side down on a greased cookie sheet, curve it until it almost meets. With a sharp knife or scissors slash across the top every inch or so. Cover and let rise for an hour, brush with an egg wash and then bake at 375°, when cool, dribble icing over the top. Mom say to make icing with sugar, butter, a little vanilla, and milk, but Betty Crocker makes one I like, and will save time. That's mom's fave, but for me, take a round cake pan, spread four tablespoons of butter on the bottom, add a good handful, about a half cup brown sugar and some walnut pieces. Cut the roll into slices of equal thickness, small pan—thicker, larger pan—thinner, your choice."

Ellie uncovered each sponge and punched the dough, then replaced the covers. Looks of doubt were endemic. Ellie sat down.

Lucy continued, "Place slices close together in your prepared pan. Cover and let rise again, bake at 375F. When baked turn it onto a plate, wait a minute or two, and carefully lift the pan." Lucy turned the page on her flip chart. "Now for the main course, a substantial pizza crust. Again, use approximately a third of your sponge. That's what you've made, a sponge. You can roll it out or use your hands to shape it. Directions, with pictures are in your package."

"Your usual superb job Lucy," Ellie said, "Okay gentleman, your hour is up. Check your dough."

All eyes turned like a synchronized dance routine.

"You ruined it!" Rodney accused.

"No, it needed to rest for ten minute, before we continue. Gentlemen, grease your pans, collect your dough, and shape when the flag drops," Ellie dropped a blue checked dish towel. Harv's dough fluttered to the table top. "If you need help, watch my star pupil shape a perfect loaf, twelve clover leaf rolls, and Lucy's favorite sticky buns. Lucy will be delighted to assist you. During the second rising, we'll make a quick bread with beer and herbs. Then later, as your breads bake, we'll drink coffee and discuss the wonders of bread machines."

Ellie sat while Lucy gave advice and made decisions for the undecided. What fool said men make quick decisions?

Lucy Dropped a kiss on her mother's head, "You're tired, I'll do the quick bread." Lucy boisterously mimicked the stereotypical drill sergeant. "Listen up, the easy life is over. You're mine now. March to your stations. Come on ladies, double time it."

"Eric said she'd make a great cop, but I'd say Master Sergeant or pirate," Zack quipped.

"She could order me around anytime," Mac said quietly.

"Measure the first eight ingredients into a bowl. They are flour, baking powder, sugar, salt, mustard powder, grated cheddar cheese, fried bacon, and a handful of your favorite fresh herbs, *chopped*. A small handful," Lucy amended, comparing Harv's version of a handful to her own. "I like a combination of basil, oregano, and flat leaf parsley, a couple of pinches of garlic powder. Wait" Lucy shouted. Don't get your little selves all bent out of shape."

"I know garlic wasn't on the list, stop nagging, and use mine, and for the adventurous among us, mom brought extra herbs. I see parsley is very popular today." After the garlic powder and herbs made the round, Lucy said, "Now you throw in that beer. I use a heavier Mexican brand. Uh, Uncle Rodney, you must open the bottle first. Combine the ingredients, but do not beat. Dump your batter into a greased loaf pan, and voilà," she said with a flourish, "an oven ready quick bread in under ten minutes. Bake one hour. Eat it warm with a stew or soup or toasted next morning."

"I think it'll take them a few more minutes to catch up and get their loaves baking," Ellie said, "Your ten minutes may have been a little optimistic."

"Harv kept up," Lucy said, pointing to where Harv diligently scoured the table.

"He did at that," Ellie admitted, "and you made it look so easy they might even try it at home. Lucy, you did well, very professional, perhaps a little too hands with our Mr. Spencer, but over all good."

Lucy giggled, "You're a gas, mom. Hold on, here comes the gang, finished and ready for the bread machine talk? I'll pour, you uncover the samples."

They discussed the pros and cons of bread machines until the timer buzzed, "Time to put your yeast bread in the oven."

Conversation was lively. Brad asked about Zack's health and talk turned to the previous night's incident. Mac said the police found the suspect vehicle in the library parking lot, traced it to a woman in the city who'd loaned it to the health inspector, Rita Russell. The owner was on vacation and didn't know anything.

Stan was silent and obviously had something on his mind. Ellie, certain it concerned Brad, quietly asked what bothered him.

"Mrs. Wilson I have a problem." Stan had a fog horn voice that carried, "I shared my raisin pie with my sister and may have bragged a bit. Somehow I talked myself into supplying the main course for our annual family dinner, a week from Sunday. Could you suggest an easy, really impressive recipe to feed thirty hearty eaters?"

Ellie sighed gustily," Was part of your brag criticism of your sister's baking."

"Well shoe leather and pastry might have slipped out," Stan admitted.

"You forgot my opening advice?"

"You talked about raisins and dates and fruits in winter," Stan said amid nods of agreement.

"Did I forget the most important part of my opening?" Ellie asked chagrined. "I'm sorry everyone. I'll give an abbreviated version now. It goes like this: In this class you will learn slicing, dicing, stewing, baking etcetera, but you will not learn enough to criticize your wife, mother, granny, or any woman who's spent a lifetime over the stove cooking. Since my oversight contributed to Stan's dilemma, what do you say we help him out? Tuesday we'll make a savory pastry with chicken filling. If each of us makes an extra pie for Stan we can solve his little problem."

"I'll pay for everything," Stan said enthusiastically.

Sensing accord, Ellie listed the ingredients and said she'd supply whole wheat flour and aluminum pie plates for Stan's pies.

"I salivate at the thought of the chicken pie, my mother's recipe," Rodney boasted, "though I would have liked to make the raisin spice cake."

"We may have time for that too," Ellie said.

"I hope we do. I was going to ask Betty to share mine," Rodney muttered.

"Good idea!" Jake whispered. "She needs a decent man."

Ellie heard both comments. She'd have to remind Rodney that only they knew Derwood was dead, the town thought him missing, but alive.

When the bread was baked, and tops buttered, Ellie provided boxes to facilitate handling, the men reluctantly headed home.

Lucy said, "You look tired mom, I'll finish up, go home."

"Thank you Lucy, I'll see you at home." Ellie said, "Zack, wait for me. I want to hear Baker comment on Jake's bread and coffee cake." Ellie caught up with her favorite pupil. "I also wanted to thank you for making the class fun and for taking my ribbing. Give me one of those hot boxes."

Zack slowed to wheel along beside Ellie. "If you need an escort I'm always at your service. I wondered if my shenanigans were wearing thin."

"We enjoy your jokes. You're a keen observer and never offensive," Zack bumped the borrowed chair over a rough patch of road.

"Well this keen observer thinks Harv Spencer has the hots for our lovely Lucy. And the way she looks at him I'd say you'll have that grandbaby real soon."

"Bite your tongue. Lucy is too young to make such a momentous decision."

"Ah Ellie, isn't she thirty. How old were you when she was born, seventeen or was it sixteen?"

"Lucy is twenty-nine and it was a different time. Let's talk about you. Tell me what's bothering you."

Keeping pace with Ellie, Zack said, "Last night scared the hell out of me. I really hoped what I saw was a drug induced dream, but my gut says it was real. I saw . . .," finger to lips he said, "Hush."

Ellie held her breath and listened. Only her footsteps, his wheels, and the sighing of Lake Huron disturbed the silence. Yet the hair on the back of her neck bristled and in spite of the warm night air, goose bumps erupted on her arms. Following Zack's pointing finger she peered into the dense shrubbery.

Zack laughed nervously, "I thought we were being followed, but it seems I'm just paranoid."

"If it's paranoia, it's contagious. Let's go. I don't like this." Ellie buttoned her cardigan.

"How is Betty getting along," Zack said, a little too loud. "Does she know when or if Derwood's coming back?"

"She's well and tending the store. She seems relieved that he's gone, but the uncertainty is eating at her. You know Derwood was not a straightforward man," Ellie chose each word with care. "You were at the clinic, you saw how he hurt her and he'd done it before. Betty would like to divorce him and get on with her life."

"Ellie, tell her—if there's anything I can do" Zack licked dry lips, and began again, "tell her I'm a damn good listener."

"She knows that, but I'll remind her for you." Ellie said. "We have arrived at your castle Sir Knight," Ellie giggled. "This is my first time escorting a handsome man to his door? I rather enjoyed it, where do you want the bread?"

"The counter will do until it cools. Can I get you something to drink?"

"Not tonight thanks, I'm going to skip the bakery and mosey on home."

"Oh, no you don't. It's black as the devils heart out there. I'll call Harold's cab, he needs the business and I insist so don't argue."

"If you're worried Lucy will pick me up. She should be finished," Ellie dialed and waited, "She's doing the cleanup again. I bet Harv stayed to help."

"I'd make book on that," Zack chortled. He cocked his head to listen, "Problems solved, that's her bike, I can hear it a mile away."

"Yes," Ellie agreed. "I try to dissuade her, but she loves the awful thing. Every season she gets nostalgic when she greases, or whatever she does to that nuisance. I'll see you tomorrow, don't come out."

"I'll see you to your chariot my lady," Zack said gallantly, hitting the big red release button adjacent the door.

"Mom, you forgot to give me your keys or I would have brought the car, but look, Harv came to give you a lift."

"Give me your extra hard hat. I'll ride with you dear."

"Are you sure?" Lucy eyed her mother's neat sweater set and matching skirt.

"Mrs. Wilson, if you don't trust my driving I'll ride with Lucy and you can take my car."

"Your offer is most generous Mr. Spencer, but I was very fond of uh, motorbikes in my youth," she lied jamming the helmet onto her head with a wince as the visor caught her nose. She fumbled with the strap until a giggling Lucy came to her rescue.

"Mom you cannot ride sidesaddle. Straddle the seat, tuck your skirt around your legs, sit straight and for mercy's sake, don't lean into the turns," she instructed wishing grandpa could share the moment.

"I'll follow them home," Harv whispered to a guffawing Zack.

"Wait Ellie, I'll get my camera," Zack yelled laughing so hard tears streamed down his cheeks.

CHAPTER 19

"Look Mom, this says we can flatten our abs in just two weeks." Lucy pointed to a glossy magazine protruding from one of the overstuffed bags threatening to cascade from their cart. "Is that why you bought it?"

"No dear, there's a nice drapery idea I might use if I ever remodel Mother's house."

"You are going to change grandma's house?"

"Don't get excited, I'm said I'm thinking," Ellie sighed, "Mom and grandma hated the inconvenient layout in the ancestral home, so why is changing it, at least to my mind, a betrayal?"

"I have no idea," Lucy shrugged. "When you're ready, we'll do it together. The antiques you would toss, I love. Where do we go next?"

"Burke's on the Highway has standing rib roasts on sale, stop there and then we're finished. Zack, Baker, and Darcy are coming to dinner tonight."

Lucy rolled her eyes. "You could feed the entire Marine core with what we've already bought," she sighed, "but we can't miss a sale." She tapped her nails on the steering wheel. "Did Zack say what's bothering him?"

"No, we were interrupted. That's Ruby's car. Pull over."

"If she drives she can change a tire. It's a basic skill. And why would I help her when I don't like her."

"Lucy if she knew what she was doing she'd raise the trunk, not the hood. Not everyone had a grandpa like dad to teach them. Turn around. We have time to help her," Ellie giggled, remember a good deed a day keeps the uh, something or other away."

"I'll phone the garage."

"Lucy, she earns minimum wage working at the bakery."

"All right," Lucy said grudgingly, she made a flawless illegal U-turn.

"Ruby can we help you?"

"Could you call the garage?"

"I'll loan you a wrench. You can change it."

Ruby looked at the flat tire like a candy striper at brain surgery. "We better call the garage."

"Sure, no problem," Lucy agreed grabbing her cell phone.

Ellie glared at Lucy. "I'll help you change it Ruby."

Lucy heaved a sigh that was heard from Sauble Beach to Moscow, teeth clenched she said, "Stand aside mom. I teach Ruby how to change a damn tire."

Ruby clapped her tiny hands, "Wow, would you? That'd be great!"

"Close the hood and open the trunk. I'll show you where the spare, jack and lug wrench usually hide. Changing a tire doesn't require a lot of strength. Mom, give Ruby your keys to get that four way wrench Uncle Rodney gave you last Christmas."

Lucy pushed aside a sloppily folded blanket, and lifted the matting over the spare. "Mom, look at this!" she gingerly opened Rita Russell's flat black wallet."

Ruby returned with the wrench. "This was in your trunk," she flashed the wallet and driver's license in Ruby's face.

"I've never seen that before!" Ruby said vehemently.

"You know it's Rita Russell's." Lucy said and waited.

Ruby paled, swayed, and clutched at Ellie.

"Put her in your car before she passes out," Lucy ordered, and wished she'd waited until the tire was changed to show Ruby the wallet.

"You poor thing," Ellie soothed steering Ruby to the Lincoln. She nudged the dazed girl into the passenger seat and tucked a rainbow colored, afghan around her. "Sit here, I'll help Lucy, and we'll take the wallet to the authorities."

"Mrs. Wilson, I'm scared, I don't know how her wallet got in my trunk."

"Have you loaned your car to anyone lately?"

"I never let anyone drive it but I think someone took it joyriding the night of the rave, because the driver's seat was pushed as far back as it goes." Ruby blurted, "You believe me don't you?"

Ellie ducked the question, "Sit still and collect your thoughts while I help Lucy."

Lucy wiped grease from her hands, "She killed Rita Russel and drove her body to Brad's in this trunk. She did it!" Lucy slammed the trunk.

"No she did not. She is too short to have smothered Rita in the dough and too weak to carry a dead weight any distance. The wallet was a shock to her, but she knows, or thinks she knows who killed Rita."

Unless she's playing us like a three dollar fiddle, Lucy thought. "She could she be acting?"

"I'm certain she isn't."

Lucy lowered the car, and tightened the lugs, "I'll throw the flat tire and tools into her back seat, that way no more possible evidence will be destroyed. Call the police. "They can take it from here."

"We cannot just abandon her."

Lucy scowled. "Why not, she's nothing to us."

"She has no one. Her divorced mother died, father had a new wife and family. Child services took her, and she moved from one foster home to another until she was sixteen." Ellie shook her head disgustedly, "Her father shows up on her birthday with an extravagant gift, like this car and disappears for another year. Baker gave her a job and arranged lodging. He told me all this in confidence," Ellie paused and then repeated, "She has no one."

Lucy sighed, another sob story, another sucker—me. "Remind me get her a four way wrench."

Ellie said, "You drive her car and I'll follow."

"No one drives her car but her."

"She's lost all of her sass Lucy; she'll do anything we recommend. On second thought, I'll drive her car. Since you changed her tire, she may feel obligated and talk to you. You could offer to help her get an attorney."

"I'd rather have Doc Holliday gambler, and doctor of dentistry, pull a tooth." Lucy grumbled, "I'll drive the sniveling twit, but you call the lawyer."

"Be sensitive and sympathetic Lucy," Ellie cautioned, "remember what she knows could help Brad."

Lucy stalked to the town car, "Buck up," she commanded, shoving a handful of man-sized tissues at Ruby, "and pull yourself together. You're no good to anybody, blubbering like a fool. The cops will grill you, so unless you want an all expense paid vacation at the women's pen up north, get your story straight." She watched Ruby's pasty face mottle with anger and her tears instantly dry up.

"That idiot used my car," Ruby snarled. "My plan was foolproof and if he'd stuck to it those two stupid, old men would have caught him red-handed. He would've got his for what he did to me."

Lucy bit back a sharp retort at Ruby's characterization of Baker and Jake. *The ungrateful bitch needs a wakeup call, but I can't give it until I know who earned that hostility.* "What did he do to you?"

"He held me down and wouldn't stop. His friends—my friends, egged him on. I begged them for help, but they'd been drinking and smoking up and they laughed while he did—what he did." Ruby sniffled, "They started asking me out for one thing, and when I refused it was the same scene all over again. I hate them all, but I hate him most. He said if I told, he'd say I was charging and I'd go to jail. Nobody would have believed me, but you believe me don't you Lucy?"

While Ruby sobbed, Lucy's mind was off and running. *Is any part of that story true? Did she really plan the robbery to punish the infamous he? And who the hell is he? Madre de Dios, could he be Derwood?* Lucy pulled to the shoulder.

A small wave from Ellie as she sailed past signaled her understanding.

"You see what he's done? He made it look like I killed Rita Russell and put her in Brad Talltree's house, but I was at the beach." Ruby swiped her tears with trembling hands, "What am I gonna do?"

Lucy's phone signaled a text message. It read, M H in place. "First you stop whining. Mom got you a lawyer, Michelle Homes. She'll be waiting for us at the police station. Tell her the truth and do exactly what she says."

"You still don't understand. I can't tell anyone. He'll kill me!"

"If you don't tell, you'll be railroaded and take Brad with you and I won't allow that."

"Nobody will believe Brad robbed Baker or killed Rita, he's a good guy." Ruby muttered, "What if I say I did it all alone?"

"You just said you were at the rave. How many people saw you?"

"I really messed up," Ruby whimpered, her squeaky little girl voice rife with self-pity.

"Tell the truth and mom will stand by you, so will Baker." Lucy pulled into traffic. "Think about what to tell Ms. Homes. I'll drive slow."

"He said the bakery heist was too dangerous so he didn't do it, but I know he did and he killed Rita Russell, too. He said he didn't have the money, but he'd get it from his personal bank. Then he took me to Derwood Day's place. The door was open, so we didn't break and enter or anything like that."

She's trying to convince me, her new best friend, that she didn't break in. There goes another theory. Derwood wasn't the he to whom Ruby referred, Lucy admitted, albeit reluctantly. "How you got in isn't important, continue we'll sort the details later."

"Okay, we saw the safe open and full of money, he said we'd take it and Derwood would never know, but Derwood heard us, he came down stairs carrying a stick." Ruby shuddered, "Somebody beat him up, and he was pissed. He came at us, but Jordan dropped the cash, grabbed the stick out of his hand, Derwood ran back upstairs, stupid Jordan chased him."

"Jordan? Are you talking about Jordan Plat, Eric Platt's son?"

"Uh huh," Ruby whispered.

"Where were you when all this was happening?"

"Derwood knocked me flat. When I got up, Jordan hit me hard. I fell down and stayed down."

"What happened next?"

"There was a crash and a crack like when a bat breaks. I took off, I didn't realize I had the bag Jordan put the stuff from the safe in," Ruby's voice changed from sincere to crafty. "I was so scared I just ran back to the beach, I said I was sick and went home. That's it, honest Lucy, I never did anything wrong."

Lucy worked to keep the contempt she felt from showing, she slowed the car to a crawl as they neared the police station. "What happened to the bag?"

"I threw it under a porch. I don't remember which one."

"Why didn't you keep it?"

"Duh," Ruby sneered, "Ya wouldn't take a duty free bag to the rave, would ya?"

Lucy ground her teeth; she thinks I'm the village idiot. She's just dumb enough to think she's smart, and I'm just dumb enough to get talked into helping this twit. Lucy pulled into the police station and parked behind Ruby's car to keep the liar from running. "There's Michelle Homes, Take her advice, don't talk too much, and you'll be okay."

Michelle introduced herself, told Lucy to go, and led Ruby into the police station.

Feather duster in hand, Betty flitted about her storeroom, checking to see what stock might be moved into the showroom, she lifted a dust sheet and squealed gleefully. "My trunk, I thought *he* sold you." "Michael, bless him, saved you." She ran her hand lovingly over the glossy caryatids, and wondered if anyone was ever as slim as the carved figures.

She found an Eighteenth Century Schmieg Kotzian table in the back and added it to the window that Michael's friend designed, instantly cluttering what had been perfect. She wondered if George could be persuaded to repair the wreckage Derwood made of her home. A taxi stopped in front of the shop, Doris climbed out, hesitated, then rushed headlong for Betty's door.

"Mrs. Archer, Sue says she's taking me back to the home, but before I go we're all going to eat together in a restaurant," she blurted as if frightened that some part of her message would escape before she told it.

"Thank you, Doris, that sounds lovely," Betty said assuming Ellie had accepted the invitation and set a date.

"Mrs. Archer?"

"Call me Betty."

"Can we talk about our husband?"

I'd rather eat shit, Betty thought, but sighed and led Doris to the workroom. "If someone comes in I'll have to tend to them."

"I know 'bout work. Once a week I work in the craft shop at Shady Acres so I know work comes first." Doris examined her shoes, "Ms. Betty, I can't talk to Sue about Dillon, she gets so mad, but I gotta talk to somebody. I'm ever so sad."

Betty smiled at the pathetic figure seated before her, "I'll listen."

Words flew from Doris' mouth like bubbles from a fountain, "I know what happened to my daddy was bad and I surely wish I could take it back. Dillon said daddy was a champion diver and if I gave him a little push it'd give daddy a chance to show off, but it didn't. He fell ever so fast, just like a rock. Dillon said it was an accident and he told me to tell the story I told you before. He made me say it over and over till I got it right. He said I better say what he said or he'd come back and kill me. I only started to think when Valerie told me what he did to her. I tried to tell Sue, but she won't listen, so I came to talk to you." She carefully accepted the steaming tea cup Betty proffered.

"I lied about wanting him back; I don't! I know what married people do and we never did that. Delia, my friend at Shady Acres says that's not normal and I believe her. I never told the truth to anybody but her and that's not all; if my daddy didn't get me a place at Shady Acres and pay, I'd be a street lady. Dillon is a bad man taking my daddy and my money, and Delia said he stomped on my love, too. I knew I could tell you, Mrs. Betty. I know you can keep a secret because I heard that bowlegged man saying you made Dillon go away. He don't know diddly squat. What do you think I should do? I know lying is a sin just like Delia says, but if I tell the truth he'll kill me just like he said."

Doris relayed her entire life story and Betty decided the woman harbored as much bitterness and anger as the rest of Derwood's victim-wives, and could be Baker's woman in the window.

Hands folded in her lap, Doris waited patiently. She wore a large medallion depicting Saint Agnes, the patron saint of children, holding a palm leaf and a lamb. Betty asked, "Are you Catholic?" Doris cradling the medallion on her broad palm nodded. "Would you like to go to church with me? If you tell God all that you've told me, and ask His forgiveness, you can forget Dillon ever existed."

"I don't know about that. I been praying I'd get my money back before I get kicked out of Shady Acres, but God don't hear me."

"Maybe if you go to his house and speak to him personally he'll hear you and help you." That's one prayer I will answer, Betty vowed. Doris will not be on the street while I have two nickels to rub together.

"Thank you Mrs. Archer," Doris said reverently, "I know you're busy, but you got a real good idea there. You're ever so smart. I'll go talk to Him right now." Having said all she came to say Doris charged out the door and into her waiting taxi.

Betty sank onto a low Louis XVI chair. I was right to pity her. What she's lived with all these years makes me detest *him* even more, and I didn't think that was possible. I'll have to tell Ellie that Doris knows it was wrong to push her father off the cliff, and is angry enough at Derwood to kill him. She, like Sue fit Baker's description of the woman in the window. Betty held her aching head in her hands.

The doorbell chimed.

"Who was that woman getting into the cab?" Lucy called above the chiming bells. "What's wrong Aunty? I'll get you tea or toast or something. Aunty, please don't cry," Betty threw her head back and laughter gushed forth like Old Faithful on its best day. Lucy thought Betty her aunt in the throes of a full scale mental breakdown clutched her aunt's plumpish body tight to her own.

Betty gasped, "Lucy you're breaking my ribs."

"I should get a doctor or a nurse or the paramedics. I know I'll call mom!" Lucy raced for the telephone.

"Lucy, come back. That was Doris. Calm down and I'll tell you a tale that will reassure you that we did the right thing when we uh . . . disposed of *him*."

Lucy's eyebrows met her hairline as she listened, "What if Doris tells the priest she killed her father?"

Priests never divulge the secrets of the confessional. Let's face it he didn't know Derwood, and he won't likely believe her story. Would you?"

"I don't know if he will or won't, and it doesn't matter if he can't tell. But I want to know why mom hates Harv," Lucy rushed on, "I might love him. I've never felt like this before and I think he feels the same, but I love mom and I want her to like Harv," Lucy hesitated, all or nothing, she thought and took the plunge, "Aunt Betty I want Harv. He is the one. It's for real. Please tell me why Mom hates him so that I can fix it."

"Lucy you know there's bad blood between your family and the Spencers."

"Yeah a Spencer swindled a Wood Warden in Aunt Emily's time, but that's ancient history, there must be something newer than that!"

"You know Ellie and I have been inseparable since childhood. I cannot break her confidence any more than I could break yours," Betty said searching Lucy's face. "You know I love you, but when I fled from Derwood's brutality I couldn't eat or sleep. I had a prescription and knew if I took all the pills at once I'd drift off and never wake up. I had them in my hand when your mother pounded on my door. She'd left her conference in New Orleans and flown to Portugal where I was hiding. The voice of an angel demanded I open the damn door or she'd break it down." Betty laughed at the memory. "When I finally acquiesced, she flushed the pills and threatened to hit me with the rock she'd used to damage my door if I tried suicide again. Every time I touch the damaged door I think of Ellie and what friendship really means. Anyway, she stayed with me until I could face the world again even though her sudden disappearance hurt her career." Betty giggled, "She was the principal speaker, and to this day she has never mentioned the incident. That kind of loyalty happens once in a lifetime, and is why I can't tell you what you want to know."

"I understand, but I've just got to know why mom hates Harv."

"I'll talk to Ellie," Betty said. "Now go home; I work here you know."

"I'm chastened and gone," Lucy said closing the door. "I love you," she mouthed, her face distorted against the window.

Giggling Betty picked up her duster and hauled out a small ladder to organize the shelves in the storeroom. Strange, she thought, Michael is a neat freak but these shelves look like a tornado hit them.

The bells on the door chimed again, Betty sighed and climbed down.

"Mrs. Archer?" Harv called.

"Sorry Harv, you just missed Lucy."

"That's okay. I saw a pair of combs in your window I thought Lucy might like. What do you think?" he asked avoiding the actual purpose of his visit.

"She'll love them. They're tortoise shell, very old and quite rare." Betty led the way to the display window.

Harv examined the combs, "Would she wear these?"

"Oh yes she would, she often wears her hair in an upsweep style." Betty watched amused as Harv turned the combs over and over in his manicured hands. "Shall I gift wrap them for you?"

"Yes," he said quietly, "and then maybe you can tell me why Mrs. Wilson hates me."

"What makes you think she doesn't like you?" Betty asked evading his question

"Every time Lucy and I get close she turns up to drag Lucy away. She has a radar system NORAD needs. I feel like a leper."

"Just be yourself and give Ellie time. Ask Spence, your father should know how the feud between the families started. I'm sorry Harv. I know that's not what you hoped to hear." Betty handed him a beautifully wrapped box.

"Thanks Mrs. Archer. I will ask dad. Will I see you at the lighthouse dedication?"

"Yes, I'm looking forward to it."

"I'll see you then," he said closing the door quietly.

"Hello Sue, come into the kitchen. I do my best thinking in here." Ellie pointed to a press back chair and placed a mug on the old table across from her own. She added a plate of the pineapple cheese loaf she'd been perfecting for her column.

"When a woman invites you to sit in her kitchen she's offering friendship or else she wants you close to the door to ease you out," Sue laughed heartily. "Or," she sobered, "there's bad news. This is fine coffee Mrs. Wilson, thank you. Like I was saying you don't know me well enough to be offering friendship, and I haven't been here long enough to wear out my welcome so what's the bad news?"

"Please call me Ellie, and you are partly right, I have news that concerns your first husband's death." She told of the potentially toxic foxglove Derwood had collected, related the story of Robert's supposed suicide, and ended with, "so there's reason to believe he had a hand in your husband's death too."

Sue took several deep breaths, "After his stroke Abby, my husband, began to improve. He regained the use of his arm and was on the road to recovery." Sue clutched her cup, gulped the scalding liquid, and stared into the past, "Sudden death after optimism beats a body down like nothing else can. You know if you'd done things different, if you checked on him one more time, been less selfish," tears made streaks in carefully applied makeup, "and inside you die."

Ellie held Sue's hand and patiently waited.

At length Sue shuddered, dried her eyes, and continued, "When my friends back home hear Douglas is a bigamist and a thief, well," she sighed, "it doesn't matter because Doris is an innocent so money runs out I'll make a home for both us. Sue tightened her hold on Ellie's hand, "You know you have to tell the cops."

"I have guesswork, innuendo and supposition, but no evidence to take to the police," Ellie lied, and true to her red roots, blushed.

"We have to go to the cops! Douglas has to be stopped!" Sue slammed her fist to the table, coffee sloshed; she reached to steady the cups, snagged the table cloth, and upended both cups.

Ellie bundled up the cloth. "If you say you're sorry once more, I'll make you do the weeks laundry," she said after Sue had offered to wash the cloth, hang it out, and clean the entire kitchen. "Accidents happen, that's why we call them accidents and not on-purposes."

Her rigid back to the table Sue scrubbed the tablecloth. "We've got to stop him! Whatever proof you have, you gotta give it to the cops."

"You know him. Do you think he left evidence to implicate himself? What he left is designed to hurt all of us, and you have suffered enough."

"He's a filthy rotten . . ." Sue spat out an impressive string of derogatory adjectives, some new to Ellie who wondered if Abby had been a sailor.

At length Sue apologized, "Sorry, I learned to curse at the rehab center, but there aren't words profane enough to describe Douglas. He fed me drugs until I was addicted. It was hell fighting the drugs, so if I kill him and go to hell, it won't be a new experience."

"Stop scrubbing that thing and sit down," Ellie ordered. "If you kill him you will be caught, and he will have ruined another good woman. I cannot allow that!"

"I was a good Baptist once, but now I want him castrated and . . . ."

"We'd all like to see him emasculated," Ellie rushed to prevent the colorful list she knew was coming, "but if we give those fraud police all the financial evidence we can gather maybe we can gut him that way. I cannot believe he paid taxes on the money he stole. I hear government agents cross the river Styx to catch tax evaders." Sue smiled, Ellie was pleased.

Swallowing a profanity Sue said, "By G. . . gosh you might have something there. We'll hit him right in the pants bulge—the wallet I mean; the other was never good for anything. But, I've taken enough of your time."

Ellie looked up from her watch, "Would you like to stay for dinner?"

"I know you're only asking to be polite, but a home cooked meal with adult conversation is irresistible." Sue sat back down, "Now, can I help, or are you one of those women who cook alone?"

Ellie pointed to a framed photograph, "Years ago I taught young mothers to feed their families nutritious meals economically. We couldn't afford to rent a kitchen, so I used my own. We had tons of fun, and still hold a reunion every two years. This summer, much to Lucy's chagrin, I'm leading a cooking class for men, and it's a hoot. The guys rarely diet and never blanch when I mention cream or butter or the dreaded L word." At Sue's puzzled expression, she laughed, "lard, I mean." Ellie's giggle turned to a look of horror when she spied the raw roast on the counter, "You may change your mind about dinner, that should be half cooked by now."

Sue shrugged, "No problem, we have time to whip up something nice. She opened the refrigerator, "I see chicken."

"The chicken is for the chicken in whole wheat crust pies for my next class, but if we double the recipe I could be a whole day ahead. Lucy will love that."

"Won't the pies get soggy?"

"No, and that's the best part, the chicken pie can be frozen baked or unbaked."

"Sounds good," shoot I forgot the booze," Sue ran to the porch, "I left my peace offering outside." She grinned, "After drinking all your scotch last night I thought I'd better bring a replacement. I noticed Betty Archer and Doris put an end to the Sherry too, brought a bottle."

"Thank you Sue, but you didn't have to do that. I understood. Derwood drove all his wives to drink."

"Well," Sue grinned sheepishly, "I didn't understand, but now I know my Abby died by his hand, not neglect from me." Her smile lit the room, "I like this town in spite of Sam Ranker's gossip. I got to get Doris away from him before he wears her down." She brushed her shoulder as if pushing the problem of Doris and Sammy off. "What can I do to help?"

CHICKEN PIE WITH WHOLE WHEAT PASTRY
2.2 pounds chicken breasts or a whole chicken

1 lemon, pricked all over with a skewer
1 chicken bouillon cube
1 generous teaspoon dried tarragon or 3 sprigs fresh
1 bay leaf
1 tbsp salt
Boxed chicken stock to cover (I use my own stock, or Swanson, or Kitchen Basics sodium reduced chicken stock)
¾ cup white wine
3 leeks
4 celery stalks cut in 1/2 inch pieces
4 large carrots diced or 2 cups baby carrots
8 shallots, peeled and quartered
1 cup sliced mushrooms
4 tbsps butter
½ cup cream
6 tbsps. Flour all purpose or arrowroot
3 cups reserved chicken stock
Salt and pepper

In a large pot put the chicken, lemon, bouillon cube, tarragon, bay leaf, and salt cover with chicken stock. Bring to a full boil, reduce heat, and simmer for 30 minutes or until chicken is tender.

Slice leeks in half lengthwise, hold under cold running water until clean, discard dark green tops. Slice into ½ inch pieces, set aside. Cut carrots lengthwise then into ¼ inch slices, set aside. Cut celery into ½ inch pieces.

When cooked, remove chicken from stock cool and cut into bite size pieces, set aside

Add carrots and celery to stock, bring to a boil, reduce heat and cook ten minutes.

In a large skillet sauté shallots in 3 tablespoons butter until transparent, add the mushrooms and cook a further 3 min. remove from heat.

Strain the vegetables into a colander, **save the stock**. Discard the lemon and bay leaf.

Add drained vegetables to the skillet, cook 2 minutes, add leeks, cook 3 minutes mix well, being careful not break the vegetables. Add the chicken pieces to the skillet.

Mix flour and cream to make a paste. Whisk in 1 ½ cups of the reserved stock. Add to the skillet, stir; add another 1 ½ cups of reserved stock, cook and stir until mixture thickens. Add salt and pepper to taste. Cool.

WHOLE WHEAT PASTRY
3 ½ cups white flour
3 cups whole wheat flour
1 pound lard or shortening
¼ teaspoon baking powder
1 tablespoon white vinegar
2 teaspoons salt
1 cup coldest water available

Sift white flour, baking powder and salt into large bowl add the whole wheat flour, and stir well. Work the lard into the flour using a pastry blender or your hands (or a large processor) until the mixture holds its shape when squeezed together in your hand. Mix the vinegar with the water. Make a well in the middle of the flour mixture, add 1/4 cup of the water swirl with a fork or your hand until it has absorbed as much as it can, remove to the table, repeat until all the flour is used up. (You may need more water or less depending on the moisture in the flour.) Knead gently until it holds together. Wrap in plastic wrap.

ASSEMBLING THE PIE
Roll part of the pastry into the size to fit your dish and overlap the edges ½ inch. Fill with enough cooled chicken mixture to mound slightly, cover with top crust (cut slits to vent steam) Fold the ½ inch overlap over the top and crimp to seal the edges Brush with beaten egg. Bake in a 400 F for 20 minutes. Brush with egg again. Reduce heat to 375. Bake for 45 min. more or until browned and done.

Ellie handed Sue the recipe and an apron imprinted with 'Welcome to Ellie's kitchen'. "I'll start the chicken breasts cooking then we can gather the herbs and vegetables from the garden."

"I'll get the veggies and herbs while you make the pastry." Sue said happily, "I dearly miss the home Douglas sold, but I miss my garden more."

Ellie nodded, "There's a basket and shears by the side door and a sun hat on the hook above."

She watched Sue move among the verdant plants combining an economy of motion with obvious plant knowledge. She's like a different person, Ellie thought, and wished she could tell her Derwood/Douglas was dead, because if Sue knew *he* was dead, and how he died all that well earned bitterness would fade like sun washed snow.

While she prepared the pastry Ellie planned; if Sue stayed in Huron Shores they could room with Valerie. Valerie wouldn't be alone and Sue could tend her neglected gardens. Darcy always needed help at the diner. Ellie wrapped the pastry in plastic wrap and set it aside to rest. I have solved all of their problems. She giggled, Betty's right, I am a busybody. If Sue's as good in the kitchen as in the garden she could help with the classes and free Lucy to enjoy her vacations.

Sue entered beaming, "Your garden's a treasure trove. Heritage plants up the wazoo and great new ones too." Dropping her harvest in the sink she said, "I want to live out there. I love the Dahlias; red was Abner's favorite color. When I get a place of my own, I'll be haunting you for cuttings and seeds," She peered into the simmering pot. "Is that a whole lemon?"

"Yes, the lemon adds a subtle flavor and color, there's a bouillon cube, tarragon, a bay leaf and homemade chicken stock, layers of flavor, as they say on T.V."

"The veggies are fresh enough to yell bloody murder," Sue laughed, plunging them into the deep sink.

That woman needs a garden for therapy, Ellie decided, slicing the vegetables as Sue washed them.

"I picked extra miniature tomatoes and zucchini. I thought I might make Abner's favorite appetizer," Sue blushed, who the heck was she to change Ellie's meal plan?

"Show me," Ellie said racing for pen and paper. "I'll write while you prepare. I love new recipes."

Ellie filched a pear shaped tomato, "Mmm, it looks delicious."

Sue slapped Ellie's hand, "Wait until the vegetables absorb the dressing." She proffered the vinaigrette cruet, Ellie tasted and approved. "You're as nervous as a long tailed cat under a rocking chair. That's the umpteenth time you've checked that window."

"My daughter Lucy is late; I worry when she rides that unstable motorbike."

"I had a scooter when we had our place in Florida. Sue sighed, "Douglas sold that too. Lucy sounds like my kind of girl though."

"Don't encourage her."

"There's nothing wrong with independent youngsters," Sue declared with the child rearing assertiveness of the childless.

"Uh huh."

"After my behavior the other night, I better be presentable when I meet her." Sue pressed wayward strands of hair and fled to the washroom.

Lucy dropped her helmet on the table, "It smells like chicken. What happened to the beef roast?"

Ellie explained, Lucy shrugged, "We need the pies for tomorrow so we're ahead of the game, what can I do?"

"Relax and listen to why I think Sue is blameless." Ellie explained Sue's explosive reaction when told Derwood murdered Abner, and her insistence on police involvement.

Lucy repeated Betty's impressions of Doris, "So Doris is back on the list?"

Springy footsteps signaled Sue's return, "I'm not putting you out of a job, am I?"

Lucy shook her head, "It's nice to meet you." She grinned, "I've heard about you all over town."

"Notorious am I?"

"The words I heard were, short tempered; patience of an angel; hard drinking, handsome woman

"Sounds about right," Sue grinned, and vigorously stirred the vegetables. "Could we make an individual pie for Doris? She won't go out alone. I don't know why since she's the only one still cares about the bas, uh jerk."

"She's terrified," Lucy said, and repeated Betty's story.

Sue exploded, "Why didn't the damn fool tell me?" she grinned, "Kind of answered my own question," she said wryly. "Hey Lucy, that's a great bike you got there."

Ellie harrumphed, and added the cubed chicken to the over-stirred vegetables.

"It sure is; my grandpa knew his bikes." Lucy watched Ellie and Sue work. "You have a champion helper mom, so I'm off to play Barbies."

Sue watched Lucy climb the stairs, "Did I miss something? She did say Barbie dolls?"

Ellie chuckled, "That's code for fishing with Brad. She thought she fooled us, and Dad insisted we play along. That's why Warden Wilson Women go gray early. Oh dear, I forgot dessert."

"That loaf cake I gobbled up would have been perfect."

"I have more of the pineapple cheese loaves. Mixing, or rather not over mixing loaf cakes was Monday's lesson before Stan bragged about his baking prowess while criticizing his sisters. Hence he will supply the main dish for his family reunion. So the class will make savory pies and donate them to Stan's cause."

They laughed together like old friends.

"What if I cut thick squares of loaf cake, hollow the center and fill it with ice cream, then top each with a slice of pineapple and a wedge of cheddar. Maybe add a sauce."

"Make that a hard sauce and it'd be perfect," Sue agreed sliding Doris' pies into the oven.

"Those pies need about an hour to cook and then should cool for fifteen minutes before serving. That gives us ample time to enjoy a glass of sherry. Come into the living room and rest your feet before you take Doris her dinner."

"I'll bring some wine back with me. Do you have a specific brand in mind?"

"Something white I think, you choose."

"Tell me more about you're lovely daughter."

CHAPTER 20

Following a long established pattern Lucy crept down the cellar stairs, added a bottle of wine to her basket, and retrieved granddad's fishing rods. Her vest hung on a hook over a pink Barbie case filled with hooks, lures, line and sinkers and not the minute clothing it was which it was designed. Lucy donned her vest, and left through the cellar door.

Ellie motioned Sue to the window. "Lucy and her friend, Brad Talltree found an old wooden boat when they were children. Over a period of a couple of weeks they repaired it and set out for a grand adventure on Lake Huron. A storm blew in and the old rim they used as an anchor didn't hold. After a night of worry I foolishly forbade my tomboy daughter from ever fishing again, hence the sneaking out ritual."

Sue brushed away a tear. "Makes me wish my man and I'd had a few kids. I envy you Ellie, she's a lovely girl."

"If you turn your head you may reconsider the lovely part," they watched Lucy strap a wicker hamper to the bike. Her long hair in pigtails, wearing patched denim shorts and a ratty plaid shirt over her bathing suit.

Sue sighed wistfully, "She looks awesome to me, exactly the kind of kid Abner and I dreamed of."

The oven timer rang. Ellie packed cutlery, plates, napkins and an appetizer in a small cooler with thin slices of loaf cake and cheese. She put the hot chicken pies in a separate box in a carrier bag.

Sue smiled, "This spread will please Doris; she loves picnics."

Ellie added a bright luncheon cloth and after a pause a carafe of her mother's favorite cordial.

Sue grinned, "That ought to keep Doris happy and ease my conscience."

Lucy buckled her helmet, started the bike, revved the engine, listened to the mechanical symphony beneath her, and escaped. Only the bouncing rucksack, a nasty reminder that Derwood, thanks to the unidentified drifter would get a fine send-off. She favored flushing *him* but as outvoted.

Her mind racing Lucy pulled from the macadam onto an overgrown trail. If Chief Platt hadn't kicked me out I'd know how long I have to find the duty free bag. If Ruby tells Eric the truth, Lucy snorted, like that would happen, Eric knows who killed Rita Russell and robbed Baker. If Ruby lied I'll kill her before Jordan gets his chance. I've searched under so many spider infested decks I could spin a web. If I find the embezzled money it's worthwhile, if not I can always strangle Ruby.

Lucy threw her bike into a slide to avoid a downed cedar tree, accelerated to clear a small hummock and land the jump neatly.

If Jordan murdered Rita Russell, did he kill Derwood or did lying Ruby kill them both? Unlikely, Ruby, while devious isn't murderous, or is she? No, Baker would have recognized her if she were the woman in the window.

The boggy trail led through a half remembered marsh, Lucy slowed to a crawl.

What had Val said about Derwood's body? Non fatal laceration in the hair line, and when they flipped him she mentioned a deep scalp hemorrhage and possible skull fracture. According to Ruby, Jordan took a wooden stick from Derwood and chased him up the stairs.

Lucy lifted her sneaker clad feet and splashed through a narrow stream. Was Jordan's the fatal blow? I won't mention Ruby's dubious revelations until I find the bag, if it exists. The marsh ended; Lucy sped to the dock and slid to a stop next to a gleaming craft, its luster eclipsed only by Brad's smile.

Lucy caressed the varnished mahogany hull and red leather upholstery, "She's a beauty, is she a '46 or '47?"

"She's a 1947 twenty foot Chris Craft Custom Runabout, one of the last of the vintage runabouts made with double hatches over the engine compartment." Brad pulled open one of the hatches. "She's got a rebuilt, 6-cylinder 158 horse power engine."

"I bet she's a real workhorse. You had her hardware re-chromed? How's her bottom?"

Brad leered, "Original and tight just like yours."

Lucy ignored him, "Can I be captain?"

"Of course not, that would be inappropriate."

"How come you always get to be captain?" Lucy whined as she always had.

"Because I'm still the boy and girls can't be captains," he answered as he always had. They chuckled and Brad said they should get going before the fish were all caught.

Lucy saluted, "Ready when you are Captain," she raised the anchor. "Did you remember the bait?"

"We're going fishing, what kind of captain forgets the bait? Did you bring lunch?"

"Uh huh," Lucy waited for the serenity being on the water usually brought. "Hand me that box from my pack and head for deep water please?"

"You can't be hungry; we haven't been afloat for fifteen minutes."

"I promised to do a job for Valerie, and since you're captain, you get to say the prayer."

Brad said wryly, "You know Lucy this is weird even for us. Who was that?"

"Remember the old gentleman they found on the beach?" Brad nodded, "Nobody really knew him, but he told Baker he wanted his ashes spread over the lake he loved," Lucy improvised; any version of the truth was problematic for Brad until he was cleared.

"I'm all for fulfilling the old guy's wishes. Too bad we don't know his name."

"There's not much interest in putting a name to a vagabond. You say the prayer while I spread."

"May you find the reward you earned in God's hand." Brad filled the empty box with water and they watched it disappear.

"That was nice," Lucy said, "thanks."

Brad nodded, "What do you want to catch?"

"Chinook, I'm going to start with a J-Plug."

"Salmon it is," Brad agreed. "They're biting at 40 to 100 feet and I've heard guys are having good luck with Magnum Dream Weavers and Silver Streaks."

Lines in the water they sat in companionable silence. Brad corrected the slow moving boat.

"Brad, what do you make of Foster's behavior this morning? He was scary, and Rex acted strange too. Rex and Foster are usually friendly for a dog and cat."

"I don't believe Foster was after Rex, I think he wanted Jordan. Foster hates Platt as much as I do. Animals are intuitive; Rex likely knows Jordan is no damn good."

Lucy reeled in her line, and ignoring Brad's suggestion, attached a Bomber lure. If Eric Platt's son killed Rita Russel, and Rex saw it, the cat's aberrant behavior was explained. Foster could have smelled Jordan when he put the health inspector's body in Brad's closet. Lucy mechanically fed out some line. Was it a stretch to think animals understood evil?

"You're quiet."

Lucy saw the sappy lovesick expression she feared splashed over Brad's face.

"Can I ask you a serious question?" She nodded, "I've loved you since we were kids. I want you to marry me even if you don't feel exactly what I feel. We're best friends and that's a good foundation to build a life on. Lucy Warden Wilson will you marry me?"

Lucy fitted her rod into a holder and locked it down, while she searched for a way to say no without losing her lifelong friend. Unable to stall any longer and satisfied that a leviathan wouldn't dash off with her pole, she wound her arms around Brad's neck and shifted onto his lap. She planted an ardent kiss on his lips and held it long past the prudent point. "Was that what you anticipated?"

"Uh...let's try it again to be sure."

"Ah Brad, be honest. Kissing each other is pleasant, but the spark just isn't there. There's no magic and I need the magic. Lucy grinned evilly, "Besides my biological clock is ticking."

"Does Spencer have the magic to still that clock?"

Lucy nodded.

Brad leered, "Okay I get your point. I admit I didn't get the rise I'd expected." He unlocked her rod and tenderly placed it in her hands, "But I want you to know the friendship we share is a kind of magic." His smile held sadness that quickly turned to mischievousness, "Besides you promised you'd marry me."

"I never did!" He nodded and kept nodding until Lucy demanded, "When did I promise that?"

"You never remember the enchanted moments," he pouted. "Remember that night we were marooned out here? We fell asleep in each others arms."

"I remember the part where we nearly froze to death."

Brad tsked, "You never remember the tender moments. You said we had to get married because we slept together and that's how it is today, so I should start saving." Brad sighed, "Here I've been pining all these years awaiting your whim, and now you throw me over for Spencer. I'm shattered."

Lucy giggled delightedly, "You actually read all those racy, romance novels I gave you? That is a direct steal. And I was eleven so you were nine. Right?"

"Ten and a couple of months."

"And you'd hold me to that promise? Stop laughing you're scaring the fish. Here I am trying to be sensitive and you know how good I am at that," they laughed heartily, "and there you are being so damned . . . male."

Brad sobered, "Make no mistake. I do love you." I'll always love you, and I'll be here when Spencer breaks your heart, he thought sadly. "I'm deadly serious Lucy, call anytime and I'll come."

"I do love you, Brad. I do."

He gazed into her eyes, saw tears, and was content to wait. "If you say love me like a brother, you are so overboard." He grinned, "Now that you've crushed my spirit, my hopes, and broken my heart I'll admit meeting Valerie has me questioning my vow of celibacy."

"Celibacy," Lucy snorted and kissed his cheek, "Seriously Brad, nothing could come between us, but let's make a pact. If we're single or single again when we're thirty five we'll marry each other and have a bunch of beautiful kids." She spit in her hand and waited.

"Wow a spit shake, that's serious stuff," he spit in his hand and shook hers. "It's a deal and this time no welshing. Hey Mosquito! Pay attention, you got a strike. Play him. I'll get the gaff."

"I am playing him, Big Chief Got No Tact." Lucy snapped taking a cautious hand from her rod to slap him.

"Play him, play him, play him!" Brad shouted. "Don't let him break water!"

"I'm bringing him alongside. You get him!"

"He's a beauty, you want him?"

"I caught him; he's mine," Lucy echoed a phrase from their past.

Lines back in the water, Lucy asked, "How are you getting on at Val's?"

"I rarely see her," he grinned. "And if I did try anything, well, Jake takes chaperoning seriously. I think he does a bed check every night. I'm kidding, but he does pop in really often."

"It's probably a generational thing. Harv and I never touch that mom doesn't turn up. I don't know why she doesn't like him he's handsome, employed, he has a trust fund and money in the bank." Lucy smirked, "And best of all he's got a great . . . personality."

"Lucy, Spencer has dated and dumped every eligible woman, and some that weren't so available within five hundred miles. Maybe Ellie objects to that. I do!"

Lucy grinned, "Warden Wilson Women live to hate dastardly, devious Spencer men; that I know. But since Harv is neither devious nor dastardly I'll break the tradition." She tugged her line, "So that takes care of me. How about you? When are you moving back home?"

"Who knows? Eric keeps looking for evidence the crime scene guys missed. You should have seen him when they found salmon scales in my house. Like a kid on Christmas. We're moving to Jake's as soon as the paints dry, but I'm hoping my alibi will clear me so I can go home."

"You have an alibi? We're best friends and you leave me in the dark." She curled her fingers around his throat, "Who is it?"

"I got one! Get the gaff!" Brad skillfully wielded his springy noodle, coaxing the fish alongside.

"He's huge and he's a she," Lucy carefully extracted the hook. "Keep or release?"

"Release, unless you want her."

"I don't like to keep the ladies," Lucy gently freed the fish. "Damn, too bad we didn't weigh her. Now there's no proof that yours is bigger than mine."

"Nah ah, mine's much bigger," they remembered times when such talk delighted them, and laughed like little kids.

"You want food?" Lucy asked, "I brought pâté, brie, grapes, and French bread. Don't make that face. I brought Baker's biscuits and chicken pies for you. Open the wine?"

"You took this from your grandpa's cellar didn't you?"

"What makes you think I didn't buy it? I am of age."

"It's a French Grand Cru, and the dust is a dead giveaway."

"Are you going to pour or just criticize? Let's drink a toast to the fish and the sunset while you tell me who your alibi is and why you didn't tell me before."

Brad raised his glass, "Here's to Harvey Spencer Senior," he enjoyed Lucy's slack jawed amazement.

Lucy snarled, "You have three seconds to explain."

"After the chamber of Commerce meeting we went to the pub for drinks," he paused. "Okay, okay," he pried her fingers from his throat. "After the funerals," unshed tears roughened his voice, Lucy squeezed his hand, "Mr. Spencer asked how he could help. I wasn't ready to do anything then, but later when the banks turned me down for being too Indian and the Band for being too white, I called Mr. Spencer. He arrived with a contract and a bucket of cash. Enough money for boat and gear, it's paid off now, and I'm buying another boat. He's financing it."

"I am so proud of you Brad, but why didn't you tell me?" Pride kept you from asking me for help, Lucy thought.

"Some of the laws are restrictive where fishing quotas, financing and Indian rights are concerned, so Mr. Spencer wanted to have his lawyers check first. I told Eric, but he claims he can't find Mr. Spencer.

Anyway he'll be back tomorrow. Chief Platt will have to find another patsy."

"He'll be at the lighthouse dedication tomorrow, so you'll be off the hook. And speaking of the dedication, did you ask Val?"

"I got nice ribbon leeches. Want to move closer to shore for pan fish?"

"I never could resist a man with his own leeches; did you ask her? Tell me now, or feel the wrath of Lucy."

Brad laughed and caught both Lucy's fists in one hand. "I asked and she agreed." He dropped anchor, and opened the container of leeches, "To prove I'm a good sport, you pick first."

"Hey, you weren't lying, these are great leeches, I'm going to use a slip-bobber rig," Lucy threaded an annelid onto a number six hook.

Brad mumbled agreement between mouthfuls of Ellie's chicken pies. "I hope this is the recipe we'll be making Monday."

"It is. I got a bite. "Lucy reached for the net.

"A nice little yellow perch, about half a pound I'd say," Brad tossed it into the live well.

"You'd probably catch one too if you stopped stuffing your face and put your line in the water."

"Yup, you're right," he refilled their glasses. "Ruby Thurston called me earlier today."

"Why the hell did *she* call you?"

"She said you found Rita Russell's wallet in her trunk. The cops impounded her car. Ms. Homes got her released, but she thinks they'll hang the murder on her."

Lucy landed another perch. "I know all that. I asked why Ruby called you."

"We have a history, and if she says she's innocent, she is. She wouldn't lie to me."

"Why the hell not! She lies to everybody else."

"Something awful happened to her years ago and I sort of helped her out."

Lucy filled his glass, "If you're referring to the rape, she told me."

"Jordan Platt had forced himself on her. When I happened along Ruby was begging and crying and that bastard was pulling up his shorts and choosing which of his friends was next." Brad fiddled with the wicker basket, "The kid wasn't more than thirteen. She didn't have a chance. I lost it. I hit Jordan and kept hitting him until his friends pulled me off, and then I hit them until they bled. I knew if he got away with it, you or Ruthie could be next." Lucy thought Brad sounded as if he regretted letting Jordan live. "I took Ruby to old Doc Rowe. He did what he could, but when I told him who the rapist was, he said to forget it. The word of a foster kid and a half-breed wouldn't stand against a cop's kid. We knew Doc was right." Brad thrust a leech onto his hook. "Doc gave Ruby some pamphlets, and sent her to the free clinic, she didn't want to go and I didn't insist. She asked me not to tell anybody, and I didn't. I waited for the cops to arrest me, but they never came. Brad laughed, "Jordan said ten guys from the city jumped them. Chief Platt's still looking for the gang."

Lucy waited until Brad stopped shaking, "Seeing Jordan daily must be hell for Ruby. No wonder she set him up."

"Set him up for what?"

"Ruby didn't tell you she planned the robbery so Baker would catch Jordan red handed. I wonder if she killed Ms. Russell too.

"No way," Brad insisted. "She isn't strong enough to smother Ms. Russell, but Jordan is. And besides I know Ruby, she'd plant a few dollars and keep the rest. I pity her, but I'm not an idiot."

"You're right on all counts," Lucy said. "Pay attention! You got a bite," she handled the net, "Fish must be hungry to bite that mashed bloodsucker."

"When this comes out Eric Platt is going to be one hurt white man."

"Yeah I hate it too Brad, but Eric is an honest cop, he'll do the right thing."

Brad snorted, "You've got more faith in the system than I do."

Lucy ignored him, "What if Ruby confronts Jordan, gets him to confess, and tapes it, would that stand up in court?"

"I don't know about the legalities, but it sounds like entrapment to me, and damn dangerous too. Lucy, if he killed Rita what's to stop him killing her?"

"I always thought it a shame that you didn't finish law school."

Brad shrugged, "That was my mother's dream."

"I know." Lucy sighed, "Hand me my lucky hat and let's fish. You hogged all the good leeches again."

"Stop crabbing. I left a biggie for you!" Brad dropped his line into the water and stretched, "I'll eat up the rest of this pie so it won't be wasted. I'll finish the pâté and runny cheese on Baker's biscuits."

"Did you eat at all this week?"

"I'm a growing boy. Peel me a grape while I open the chardonnay chilling in the fish well."

"Peel you grapes?" Lucy sputtered, "You are not Julius Caesar."

Brad smiled. As long as they fished and kibitzed together they'd be fine.

Refreshed after a leisurely bubble bath, Ellie sipped a cup of herbal tea, a new and improved batch of the blend denigrated by Lucy. She was pleased by Lucy's table setting and the low centerpiece she'd made with the roses left from Harv's bouquet.

Baker, laden with boxes, backed through the kitchen door. "I brought cheese biscuits for Lucy, fritters for you and Betty and some wine," he slid his packages onto the countertop. "Brad's gone fishing and Jake and I weren't invited, so being great detectives we deduced he's with Lucy, since your slave is AWOL. I came to help?"

"You can uncork the wine. I had a new helper today," she told him about Sue. "She's joining us for dinner."

"Good because the real reason I came early is so you can explain why Lucy turned Ruby in to the cops."

"She didn't. We stopped to fix Ruby's flat tire and found Miss Russell's wallet in the Ruby's trunk. At her request we drove Ruby to the police station." Baker still fumed, "Calm down, she did not kill Rita Russell; she did however orchestrate the robbery."

"I don't want to believe that," Baker said quietly, "I know it's possible, but I, well she hasn't had an easy life."

Ellie sighed; it was neither the time nor place to educate Baker about his help.

Darcy pushed Zack's borrowed wheelchair over the raised door sill, "Smells great in here." She moved chairs aside, "This old fool is hurting, and has given me the privilege of pushing him around."

Sue followed and put the chairs back in place.

"Don't make it a big deal or I'll run over your foot," Zack threatened." I heard the cops nabbed Ruby."

"She's being questioned," Ellie said hastily. "Would you serve drinks in the living room while I get the dinner out of the oven, Baker? Go on Sue, you've helped enough."

"I'll take care of the ladies and the drinks—that's man's work," Baker said with a wink.

"I'll take a soft drink," Zack said, "I'm driving."

"No you don't," Ellie whispered blocking his chair. "Tell me what's bothering you." She regretted her words when Zack's brash manner evaporated. "Yesterday at the bakery you said you thought you saw something that might hurt a friend, you were confused and worried that what you saw could be dangerous to those you told. Is that right?"

"Basically, and if anyone impugns your memory tell them to get stuffed."

"Please, no jokes. Do you think the hit-and-run was tied to what you saw?"

Zack nodded.

"Please tell me."

When he spoke Zack's voice was a raspy whisper, "The night Baker was robbed I'd just started on my new medication. I wasn't sleeping well so I went down to the bakery a little earlier than usual. I saw Ruby Thurston's car out back, so I rolled down the hill for a closer look. I saw a man take a small body out of that old freezer by the back door and put it into Ruby's trunk. I thought I was still caught in a drug induced nightmare so I went back home."

"But it wasn't?"

"No," Zack said sadly, "It was Jordan Platt, and now I know it was Rita's body he moved. Later, still unsure I went back to the bakery." He shrugged, "Jake showed me the imprint in the dough and I began to wonder, but I wasn't sure so I kept quiet. Now I think Jordan knows I saw him, maybe tried to kill me; that's about it."

"We can't keep this to ourselves Zack." He shook his head wildly. "You know we can't. What if he tries again?" Ellie shuddered, "Remember the noise we heard in the bushes?"

"Ellie, there's no real proof, but if they find his hair or fibers from his clothes in Ruby's trunk, Eric will have to look closer. Give it a few days."

"Ruby and Jordan are friends. His hair or fingerprints in her car mean nothing. You have to tell."

"Yeah Ellie, I'll just do that," Zack snapped. "I'll wheel right up to my friend and say, hey Eric, the other night while I was drugged to the teeth I saw your kid move the health inspector's body, and I'm pretty sure he tried to run me down; you might want to look into that. Yeah, that should do it," he clapped his hand over his mouth. "I'm sorry Ellie, I've been over it a thousand times, and it's a still a lose-lose situation for Eric."

"You're right, but that help you. You're in danger; you cannot be on the street alone until this is resolved." She grinned, "But for tonight we'll enjoy our dinner and keep you safe."

The meal progressed with typical friendly conversation, and Ellie was pleased to see Zack's buoyant personality come back. He patted his stomach and said he couldn't eat another bite, but would enjoy a digestive since he'd not had a sip of wine. Baker served him in the living room, while Ellie fetched the coffee. Soon after, Darcy hired Sue and scheduled her to work the busy Sunday after church rush, so they should go.

Ellie pulled Baker aside. "I'm worried about Zack Maybe you should go home with him and see that he locks his doors."

Baker listened to Ellie's not so subtle warning. "No problem, I walked over, I'll ask him for a lift, and make sure he's never out without Jake or me."

Ellie shooed her guests out amid protests that they should help with the clean up. After they had piled into Zack's van and gone. She packed plates, and cutlery into the dishwasher, put the tablecloth and napkins aside for laundry and gathered and washed the crystal.

She settled into the kitchen rocker with a glass of Sherry, worried about Zack. He was correct about Eric being in a lose-lose situation, but with Jordan on the loose, so was Zack.

"Ellie, are you awake?" Betty asked gently.

"I was just resting my eyes. Are you hungry?

"Michael and Jake brought Chinese takeout, but I'd love some tea. How was the party?"

Ellie related what she knew of Ruby's dilemma and added Zack's story, in the hope Betty could help find a solution to the Catch-22 Zack was mired in.

Wet to the knees, Lucy stomped into the kitchen and deposited her catch in the sink. "You ought to see Brad's boat, she's a real beauty." She patted the fish affectionately, "I got a nice salmon, a couple of walleye and two perch. Don't worry, we cleaned and scaled them. Why the long faces?"

"Zack is worried." Ellie repeated Zack's scary tale.

"That doesn't surprise me, Jordan's a bastard. Ruby planned the bakery burglary to get even with him. She has good reasons to hate him," Lucy clamped her lips tight.

"Are you going to tell us the rest or are we to guess," Ellie asked.

Lucy sighed, another promise down the tube. "Apparently when Ruby was only thirteen Jordan raped her." Betty groaned, Ellie slapped the table, and Lucy decided to omit the part about Jordan and Ruby breaking into Betty's house, confronting Derwood, and emptying the safe. "But what really pisses, uh angers me is, she experienced Jordan's violence first hand yet wanted Baker and Jake catch him in the act. The self-centered bitch didn't care if Baker and Jake were hurt." Lucy quoted her maternal grandmother, "She's a waste of skin."

"Lucy, she didn't know Jordan killed Rita."

"Did the nitwit think it was the shoemaker's elves? She must have figured it out when the shop was full of cops. But she didn't bother to clear Brad, who incidentally saved her sorry ass. If Brad hadn't beaten

Jordan and his buddies off she would have been gang raped. Aunt Betty close your mouth, it's all true."

"It's not that I doubt you dear, but with Sammy Ranker spreading rumors faster than farmers spread fertilizer, how could we not know? And," Betty worried," how can we help Eric, his boy is the apple of his eye."

Yeah he's an apple all right, Lucy thought, a rotten apple. "Unless Ruby tells the truth we can't prove anything, and unless it's to save her own skin that ain't gonna happen."

"Lucy, Ruby is also a victim, and we should warn her about Jordan."

"I understand that mom, but let's wait until we have proof," Lucy's eyes glazed and her mind slid to her scheme to trap Jordan. "I can't think anymore. Goodnight."

Betty put her cup in the sink, "We have an early hair appointment tomorrow. Let's put our worries on hold until after the lighthouse dedication."

They climbed the stairs hand in hand.

Betty said, "Goodnight girl."

"Goodnight friend," Ellie said completing their nightly ritual.

CHAPTER 21

Saturday morning Ellie woke to a multihued sunrise, dragged herself to the shower, shivered under the icy spray until life seemed worth the effort, dressed, and make-up applied, followed the pungent aroma of Kenyan coffee to the kitchen. She dropped into the worry chair to update her notes with all she knew about the awful events rife in Huron Shores.

She sipped coffee and wrote: Zack saw Jordan move Ms. Russell's body. Jordan probably drove the car that hit Zack. Ellie thought for a moment, a witness who admitted delusion as a side effect of medication was not reliable. However Zack would not be safe until he told the police, but he's a grown man and the decision is his.

She turned the page to record her guest's reaction to Sue's appetizer. Flipped to a fresh page and wrote; did Doris kill Derwood? She allegedly pushed her father off a cliff, and. Betty thought her angry enough, but Sue said she was afraid and never went out alone.

That should be with my Derwood notes. I keep mixing the murders. Why? She thumbed back to an earlier entry concerning the bedpost and glass Lucy hid in her post office tree. Where are those items now?

In her notes, Derwood's unexplained injuries was followed by, who other than Betty whacked Derwood? Next, she'd written extensive notes pertaining to Derwood's code book and there was little more to say on that sorry subject. Note to self, she wrote and underlined twice, remind Lucy to ask Valerie about the tea.

Who did Baker see in the window; Sue, Doris or Derwood's next victim?

She flicked Derwood's pages aside to record Ruby's role in the burglary. Ruby set Jordan up, probable motive; revenge. But Rita Russell stumbled upon him and Jordan allegedly killed her.

Ellie leaned her head back and closed her eyes, the pencil slipped beneath the chair's overstuffed cushion. She grabbed for it and got instead the blood spattered hankie Baker loaned Betty the night of Derwood's murder. She dashed to the washing machine, flung the blood spattered cotton in, added half a bottle of bleach, and went back to her notes. Buy Baker a dozen handkerchiefs for his birthday, she wrote and again underlined heavily. The timer she'd set buzzed, saved by the bell, she muttered and went to wake Betty and Lucy.

There was a note taped to Lucy's door, TIRED - **NEED** SLEEP! WILL, sketch was scribbled through, DRAW ON BEACH.

Ellie pocketed the note to add it to her collection and headed to Betty's room. No one was late to Evelyn's salon, because the town's finest hairdresser gave them a tongue lashing and sent them home unwaved and unmanicured. Mazy, the manicurist lectured her regularly for neglecting the important things in life, like finger and toenails. "Rise and shine!" she chirped. "Thirty-three minutes to salon time."

Betty grunted, swung her legs over the side of the bed, and stumbled to the shower.

Evelyn gave Betty to Mazy's tender care and ushered Ellie to the sink. "Jane my new stylist will do your hair today. Evelyn ran her knotted, arthritic fingers through Ellie's short hair. "I was lucky to get Jane. She moved up from the city, married a local boy ya know."

"Hi, I'm Jane, "I'll be your personal stylist today." Jane arranged and rearranged Ellie's curly auburn locks. The ultra chic stylist offered suggestions, Ellie agreed, and her *own* personal stylist shampooed and rinsed. Jane's monologue required no customer participation, and moments later she led Ellie to a secluded room. "I hope you don't mind being back here. Evelyn said you wouldn't. We're just so busy with the lighthouse dedication and it's quieter, don't you think?" Jane nattered on dispelling the preferred quiet.

"I don't like sitting in the front window with a wet head," Ellie said.

"Me neither." Jane, scissors clipping asked, "Do you know Derwood Day, the guy everybody's talking about?" Ellie nodded. "Well my husband, Dave, we just got back from our honeymoon," she said blushing. "Where was I? Oh yeah, Dave said Sammy Ranker the real estate guy is talking Day's wives down all over town. Ranker says all four wives are druggies, and hanging around like tax collectors with a hot tip. He says they're all bitchy, money grubbers, and they forced Day to grab his cash and run, and that's a quote." She pulled the hair down framing Ellie's face to check for length.

Ellie drew a calming breath and opened her mouth, but Jane was unstoppable.

"Ranker says his current wife was always running off to a gigolo in Paris, and left her poor husband to tend the store and that big house and garden, too. But Evelyn says Mrs. Archer is a sweetie, and Day was lucky to get her. Dave says Derwood never did a lick of work in the garden because they had old Hank do the yard. Then Derwood ran Hank off and nothing got done. Dave, my husband, does landscaping, and he says Hank knows plants better than anybody alive. Hank told Dave that Derwood Day is a lazy, thieving wife beater, so I don't know what to believe, but we do hair for three wives, and they're real nice, so I figure Day's the problem, and Dave agrees. How do you like the length?" she asked and to Ellie's amazement awaited a response.

"A little shorter in the back I think."

"Sure Ms. Wilson. Anyway Ranker was in here this morning to put up some sales flyers, but when Evelyn heard what he was saying she tossed him out. You like the cut though don't you?"

"Yes the cut is lovely. What did Sammy say to upset Evelyn?"

"He said all those women were after Mr. Day for alimony. Evelyn just laughed, but then he said Day told him they were all into kinky sex, and started to describe it. Evelyn threw him out and not hard enough if you ask me. Evelyn says Ranker and Day are pond scum. Dave told me what Ranker said about the sex." Jane blushed again, "Sammy said Ms. Archer was the worst and Day had to sell his house and run or be corrupted. Dave says Ranker's like a blue bottle maggot, happiest when wallowing in shit – oops sorry, but that's what Dave said. Mrs. Wilson, are you having an allergic reaction? Should I call a doctor? Your face is real bright red." Jane scurried toward the door, "I'll get you a glass of water. Are you diabetic? I'll get juice."

"I'm fine," Ellie mumbled while she got her anger in check. Derwood not only abused and embezzled the women, he also trashed their reputations. If fate was kind *he* writhed on the devil's trident.

"As long as you're sure," Jane dithered, when Ellie's flush faded, she continued, "soak your hands in this." She presented a small bowl of viscous, grayish liquid. "Mazy says you have problem cuticles."

"Did Dave tell you anything else Ranker said?"

"Boy did he ever. Ranker said all those wives probably got together and knocked Day off. Like you know, took him for a ride or something. Ranker says Day's most likely fish food now. Evelyn says they likely didn't, but if they did, the town owes them a favor. Ranker says Ms.

Archer's first husband was a saint, and she drove him into an early grave with her demands -- if you know what I mean," Jane Blushed again. "My husband says it's all trash talk. He says he'll believe a nice guy like Hank over a sleazebag like Ranker any day. Do you want rollers or blow dry?"

"A blow dry," Ellie said absently. Let's give her a few facts to strengthen her skepticism. "Sammy Ranker is a malicious gossip. I've known Betty Archer all my life. She is my best friend. I will tell you the truth."

Unwilling to miss a word, the stylist snapped the dryer to low.

Ellie enlightened her, "Derwood Day is a lying, thieving bigamist. He abused and embezzled from all the women he illegally married. Not satisfied to steal millions from Doris he raided her trust account leaving her destitute, in fact she is about to be evicted from her home. He turned Sue into a drug addict." Ellie left Valerie's sad tale untold. "Furthermore there were no perverted sexual acts; in fact Derwood Day failed to fulfill his conjugal responsibilities."

Jane broke her stunned silence with an apology, and then the noisy dryer barred further conversation.

"Betty you look seductive yet demure. Turn around. Charming! Crepe chemise in soft peach becomes you, the keyhole neckline and matching pumps are perfect. You are a portrait of grace and elegance."

Betty crossed her eyes and stuck out her tongue, "Thanks Ellie. You look pretty good yourself. I wish I could wear that three quarter length, and the Wilson pearls are a nice touch with that Brandenburg neckline. I love that the lace is repeated in the side gussets, but if you don't stop pacing you'll tear out the seams or break an ankle." She gasped, "Are those actually Jimmy Choo's? You found a knock off? Or did Lucy buy them for you?"

"They are really Jimmy Choo's," Ellie giggled, "and I bought them myself."

"Not to get too personal Ellie, but did you also spring for a boob job?"

"I have not had a lift, boob, or other . . . *friend,*" Ellie deadpanned, "Remember my motto! What failed to form I fill with foam."

"Thank God!" Betty sighed theatrically, "I don't have to hear gory details or see surgery scars." On the fifth pass she caught Ellie's skirt, "Relax, Lucy will be here. Remember she's going with handsome Harv Spencer." Betty fanned her face and sighed heavily.

"You're a card Betty, but she's on her dirty bike. What if she's hurt or accosted by a crazed motorcycle gang?" Ellie's frenzied pacing increased. "Those lawless scoundrels travel in packs. Like that hoard that descend on Baker every Sunday."

"It's a dirt bike Ellie, and my lawyer is one of those Sunday riders." The Gold Wings they ride are high end Honda products and cost more than your car. You, my ignorant friend, mean Harley Davidson motorcycles and need I remind you that both Charles and Rodney rode Harleys in their youth."

Ellie laughed, "I remember you perched on the back of Rodney's bike until your father found out."

"Oh my goodness," Betty exclaimed, "look at her;"

Lucy kicked her grubby sneakers under the foyer bench, smoothed torn jeans with dirty hands and long hair covered in spider webs raced for the stairs.

"Lucy, hurry. Brad will be here any minute."

"Brad is taking Val," Lucy called over the gleaming oak banister, "as you know, I'm going with Harv. Aunt Betty, entertain Harv and make *her* behave."

Betty giggled, pushed Ellie aside, and opened the door, "Harv, come in. I'm to entertain you until Lucy is ready." Impishly she said, "I could answer your earlier question." His tan faded alarmingly, "Relax, I'm joking." He exhaled loudly, and Betty suggested a drink.

I feel like a sixteen year old on his first date Harv thought, "Thanks, Scotch over ice."

Ellie charged in to smoothly claim the drink. (A move, Betty thought, the Miami Dolphins could use.) "Mr. Spencer is driving."

Harv resembled a kitten surrounded by pit bulls, Betty patted his hand and spoke of Charles' death on the lake. The evening, she said, was difficult for Ellie and Lucy. "I'll watch Ellie; if you watch Lucy?"

"That will not be a problem."

Listening from the hall, Ellie whispered, "The Spencers are infesting our lives again. I wish you could tell me how to stop them." Above Gertrude Wood Warden's portrait a black cloud formed, her eyes turned toward Aunt Emily's portrait. Great, great aunt Emily's painted lips curved upward while a dusky halo formed above her auburn tresses; in her right hand a gelding knife appeared. Ellie shivered, I should have kept him on the porch. Trembling, she climbed the stairs.

"Come in, mom. Wow, white suits you. You look incredible!" Lucy grinned. "What's wrong? Harv's not tied up in the basement, is he?"

"We haven't imprisoned a Spencer in the wine cellar since Aunt Emily's time." Her voice softened, "My darling you are so beautiful," and to herself she added the requisite, sadly it's wasted on a degenerate

Spencer. "Wait here, you should be seen by your date descending the stairs," she silently added the Spencer addendum.

"They could be sisters," Betty gushed.

Rodney swiped at his eyes, "Ellie is as lovely as when she and Charles married."

"She is beautiful," Jake said and straightened his tie.

Betty nudged Harv, "Shouldn't you comment?"

"She's beautiful; eyes you could drown in, hair like spun gold, and legs right up to her . . . ."

Betty clamped her hand over Harv's mouth.

Aunt Emily's portrait crashed to the hall floor, a moment later Gertrude Wood Warden's followed.

Lucy raced down the stairs grasped Harv's arm and rushed him out the door.

"Oh Rodney," Betty sighed, "The grounds are positively medieval, and the food smells so good."

Zack wheeled to a stop next to Harv and Lucy," Smell doesn't count. It'll be rubber chicken and watered drinks as usual."

"It better not be," Harv laughed, "Dad said if the food wasn't first rate Mrs. Wilson would not be pleased. He's followed your career, you being a home town girl, uh, woman."

"Ah, the senior reprobate makes an entrance," Ellie mumbled.

Harv handled the introductions, "This is Mrs. Wilson, Mrs. Archer," he moved down the line until he came to Lucy. He placed her hand in his father's, "And this is Lucy Wilson."

The love in his eyes melted a chunk of the ice around Ellie's heart and the overflow almost made it to her eyes.

Harvey Senior also noted his son's lovesick expression, "Harv tells me you are the perfect woman," his hand closed over Lucy's and Ellie glared. "He forgot to mention how captivatingly beautiful you are."

Ellie plucked Lucy's hand from the manicured paw of the senior reprobate and placed it in that of the junior. "Is that Valerie over there looking lost? Perhaps you should rescue her." Lucy spied Valerie and excused herself; Ellie dragged Betty to the washroom.

Michelle caught Ellie's elbow, "We need to talk! You put me in a precarious position. I'm Brad's lawyer; Ms. Thurston's case could be a conflict," she paused for thought, "unless they plan to plead together."

"Brad is innocent when his mysterious alibi appears he'll be cleared and your conflict problem solved."

"Who is his alibi?"

"I do not know, but Lucy said tonight will see him vindicated. I'm sure Ruby told you Jordan Platt burglarized the bakery."

Michelle's jaw dropped, "She certainly did not, but if that's true, I will insist Eric be removed."

"Oh dear," Betty moaned, "Is that necessary?"

"It's not only necessary, it is essential!"

Baker's lady friend rushed in, "If someone doesn't claim those handsome men waiting outside the door I'll round them up and put them in my corral."

"Thanks for the offer," Betty said, "We'll rope them in before they end up with a strange brand." She giggled and tugged Ellie and Michelle out the door. "No more gloomy business talk, this is a party."

"We were so worried we sent in the rescue squad," Zack joked.

Rodney nodded, and proprietarily tucked Betty's hand in the crook of his arm.

Jake pronounced, "I simply suffer from separation anxiety."

Harvey Senior approached. "Sorry Jake, you're doomed to suffer a while longer if Mrs. Wilson will honor me with this dance."

I'd rather eat dirt, Ellie thought. "I'd be delighted, but I promised my date the first dance," she lied.

"Later then," Harvey promised.

"Come on Michelle, let's cut a rug." Zack wheeled his chair toward the sparsely populated dance floor.

"Betty?" Rodney asked.

Harvey Senior watched with brooding eyes until Jake and Ellie rounded the floor. He tapped Jake's shoulder, caught Ellie in his arms, and murmured, "We must talk! Our children have been given a precious gift. We don't have the right deny them happiness."

"Harvey old chap, you don't mind if I cut-in do you?" Rodney swung Ellie away from the senior Spencer. "I saw your terrified expression, and know when to rescue a damsel in distress. Why is that cad bent on dancing with you?" he saw Harvey stride purposefully toward them. "I'll pass you to Baker. Spencer won't cut in on a new partner."

"Thank you," Ellie breathed.

"You're a popular lady tonight." Baker sniffed audibly, "Must be the perfume."

Harvey watched as Ellie and Baker spun by. He spoke to the band and waited for the waltz to end.

The throbbing beat of a steamy Argentine tango filled the night with its sultry, dangerous beat.

Harvey strode to Ellie, his smoldering eyes claimed ownership. He raised his left arm, sardonically presented a slightly upturned palm. She gingerly placed her hand on his, he closed his fingers, pulled her body against his, and planted his hand high on her back to prevent escape. He ignored her panicked expression. The traditional dance embrace complete, he confidently led her through the opening steps. Sensuously they executed the demanding glides and sudden pauses of the dance. They swayed as one until the dance of sublimated sexuality drew to a close. Right knee bent left leg behind, her back dramatically arched, Ellie felt powerless and embarrassed. Harvey's cologne jumbled her thoughts as his lips lightly brushed her hair. "We will talk," he promised. He held her long after the last chords died, then helped her stand and added, "Soon Ellie—very soon."

The crowd's appreciative applause added to Ellie's chagrin. Shouts of encore and Harvey's mocking grin followed her from the dance floor. She shoved past the inevitable line and into the restroom. Angry at herself for allowing the reprobate to involve her in an exhibition of chauvinistic male dominance, and honesty forced her to admit, her enjoyment of the dance.

Betty pushed through the door hard on Ellie's heels. "I couldn't get anyone to cut in. I'm so sorry, but nobody else can tango. I thought of trying to stop the band, but that would have drawn more attention." She grinned impishly, "But Honey you were a beautiful sight with all that leg wrapped around that gorgeous man. The priest was right about the tango, it is very close to sex on the dance floor." Ellie gasped, "Oh Ellie, I have a big mouth I'm sorry."

"If that conceited lout tries anything like that again there will be another Spencer bound and gagged in the wine cellar, I inherited more than this damn red hair from Aunt Emily. How I wish she'd used the gelding knife and ended the line of degenerates.

"I didn't know my mother could dance so—perfectly" Lucy muttered. "Who am I kidding? That was an erotic performance."

"My dad doesn't usually participate in lust, uh; I meant affection on the dance floor. Maybe they've buried the hatchet."

"If my mother buried a hatchet it would be in your father's head."

"I don't know Lucy, that looked like a prelude to make-up or make-out to me. Want to try it?"

Lucy grinned, "Not in front of our parents." She saw the glare Uncle Rodney sent Mr. Spencer's way and sighed, "Doesn't look like Uncle Rodney enjoyed the tango. He has blood in his eye." She eased through the fox-trotting couples to intercept Rodney before he reached the senior Spencer. "Aunt Betty is frantic to find you. She's waiting by the band," she lied.

"Mr. Spencer, come with me." Lucy tugged his sleeve.

"I would love to know you better Lucy, but if I return with my clothing disheveled my son will challenge me to pistols at ten paces, and only his will be loaded."

Lucy brushed at his sleeve, "I'm sorry, but you have to tell Chief Platt that you and Brad were together when Rita Russell was murdered." She dragged Spence to the bar where Eric vigilantly watched Brad.

Harvey noted Eric's unblinking stare and understood.

"Chief Platt," Lucy touched his arm, "Mr. Spencer can clear Brad."

Eric listened attentively though his eyes never left his quarry. "You'll have to sign a statement. We'll have to verify it. There were witnesses?"

"We were at Sandy's Bar on Dugal Street, stayed way past closing; the waitress was anxious to lock up, she'll remember."

Lucy stood on tiptoe to whisper in Eric's ear, "Ruby knows the killer. Lean on her."

The worry lines in Eric's face deepened. "I was wrong about you, Brad." He said and trudged wearily to the door.

"I wouldn't have done that to him for anyone but you, Brad."

Brad frowned, "I didn't want it this way either Mosquito, but he has to know." He handed her a wad of tissue, "You look like a raccoon. Better clean up. Wouldn't want Mr. Clock Stopper to see you all leaky eyed."

Spence saw the chemistry between Brad and Lucy. Harv better man up if he wants to win the race for Ellie's daughter.

"Thanks for your help, Mr. Spencer."

"It was nothing," Harvey said, "call me Spence. Is that your date struggling with Ranker? She needs rescuing."

"You're right, but I have to see that Lucy's okay first."

"I'll wait for Lucy, you save your girl." Harvey smiled when Brad swung Val out of Sammy Ranker's sweaty grasp. The girl's smile was as bright as signed contract.

"Jake, have you seen my daughter?" asked Ellie.

"She dragged Harvey Senior outside—maybe to warn him away from you. Anyway when they returned they spoke to Eric then Brad. Eric left right after that."

"She could have saved me from that blatant exhibition of domineering machismo," Ellie snarled.

Jake jumped back, "I hope I never bring out that side of your nature."

"I'm sorry Jake. I shouldn't take my anger out on you." Her bowed head did nothing to hide the blush that started at her décolletage and slowly crept to her hairline.

"Forget it. Let's dance. If I'm lucky we'll circle the floor before he," he nodded toward Spencer Sr., "cuts in."

"If you don't mind I'd like to sit this one out."

"All right, but only one song, then we dance. How about I get us a drink?"

Ellie nodded and Jake fought his way to the bar.

"Jeremy, how nice to see you again so soon," Ellie welcomed Jeremy Reese.

"I've been trying to corner you," Jeremy grinned. "Did you see Lucy grab Spencer Senior? She looked like she was going to take a round out of him. Is she protecting her mama or is it Brad she's looking after?" He sat beside Ellie, "Then they talked to Eric Platt and Platt left. I wonder what happened."

"Lucy said Brad's alibi would clear him tonight."

"It's past time; Brad's an intelligent kid, and a woodsman. He's hunted these woods since he was five years old; if he hid a body it would never be found. And he's too smart to rob the bakery and stash the loot on his own boat. The kid was accepted to university on a full scholarship, he's smart. It's true he wants to expand, but he's got the financing arranged with Spencer there." Jeremy motioned to Harvey loitering outside the ladies room. "Ah Ellie, my mouth ran away with my brain, sorry."

"Don't apologize, I wholeheartedly agree." They watched the dancers in companionable silence.

"There's Lucy." Jeremy pointed. "Looks like Harvey Senior asked her to dance. She's almost as proficient as her mother."

"Where's your wife tonight, Jeremy?"

"Our youngest has mumps, but she insisted I come anyway. Look, Brad just cut-in; he and Lucy make a great couple. I wish they'd get on with it and marry. It's obvious they're meant for each other."

"I fear my daughter is infatuated with Harv Spencer," Ellie said sadly.

"He's old enough to be her father!"

"Not Harvey, Harv and though Harv is dancing with that woman in red his eyes never leave Lucy."

"I see what you mean; I was hoping that was a passing fancy. I thought Lucy and Brad would get together, he's dated a lot of women, but he carries a major torch for Lucy."

"I'm disappointed too. I was sure their friendship would mature into something more."

"Yeah, I'd hoped to be godfather and I know my wife has been stocking baby clothes, you know, to fill in for Eloise. Brad misses his whole family, but he was closest to his mother."

"Brad is with Valerie Tate, Lucy's friend from university and a lovely girl. Maybe they'll get together."

Jeremy sighed, "It won't be the same."

"Good evening Jeremy," Jake said pleasantly. "I've come to claim my date."

The event coordinator grasped Harv's arm. "Lead the way in to dinner right now," he whispered frantically. "The wait staff is threatening to quit."

Harvey Senior smiled indulgently and offered Ellie his arm.

Ellie clutched Jake's arm like it was a lifeline and Spence a circling shark.

Betty set her hand on the arm Ellie rejected. "Are you enjoying your Wooton desk Spence? It's a wonderful old oak piece," Betty continued for the benefit of those accompanying them. "It's adorned with gilt incised carvings. The William Wooton Company only made a few patent secretary desks in the Rockefeller style. Lucy found it in Indianapolis where it was originally made in 1874. She has a talent for finding rare things and a way with the customs of people that I envy."

"My son is expert at finding rare things too; Lucy is a treasure beyond price," Harvey said. "She looks familiar, I wonder if I've encountered her somewhere before."

"She's the image of her father," Rodney said dismissively, "and she works in Europe. Perhaps you saw her there."

Betty smiled, "That must be it."

"Betty, I believe your party is seated here," Harvey held the chair, while Rodney glowered.

"Cheeky devil," Rodney muttered

Jeremy, Jake, Ellie, Zack, and Michelle joined them.

"Baker, you're over here with us," Zack called waving an emblazoned place card. "Do I need all this silverware for rubber chicken?"

"The big ones for combing your hair," Baker said and demonstrated.

"Don't encourage him." Michelle threatened, "Zack you promised to behave."

"What do you suppose is going on up there?" Zack asked with his customary lack of tact. "It looks like two gals fighting over the same cowpoke."

"Looks like one too many bodies for the chairs," Jeremy said. "Who's the scarlet woman glaring at Lucy? Boy she's madder than a wet hen."

"Harvey Senior is mad and I'd say the girl in red is on his shit list," Zack said happily.

"Language, language," Michelle chastised.

"Damn, did you see that? The slu... hussy elbowed Lucy aside. I'll fetch her." Jeremy shoved his chair back. "Lucy can sit in my wife's place."

Rodney held Ellie down, "Jeremy does not need help."

Jake grinned, "Looks like they've reached a compromise, and the woman in red will join us."

The object of their scrutiny flounced up and plopped onto the empty chair between Jeremy and Betty. "I'm Cecile," she snapped.

Jeremy introduced himself and continued around the table ending with, "and this is Lucy's mother, Ellie Wilson."

Betty swore icicles formed on the centerpiece.

"How do you do," Ellie chose to ignore Cecile's icy glare. "Harv said you arranged this incredible gathering. Was the lamb on spits your idea too?"

Cecile snarled, "Lamb on a spit is my fiancé's favorite food."

"What a lovely ring," Betty enthused in an effort to cover the woman's obnoxiousness.

"Harvey is known to have exquisite taste."

"Oh how nice, perhaps Harv will have siblings," Betty's ditzy act was at full strength.

"I am engaged to Harvey Spencer, Junior."

"Oh dear," Betty asked, "Does he know?"

Cecile glared.

Betty glanced anxiously at Ellie.

"You don't suppose he's forgotten?" Ellie voiced the least offensive of her thoughts, "That is an important thing to forget."

"He's just sowing wild oats with that bimbo."

Ellie's eyes blazed, "Do not insult my daughter." She caught Harv with a look that, had it corporeal presence, would kill him. Her gaze softened into eyes of profound sadness when they met Lucy's.

Lucy gasped and whispered, "I think Mom just put a curse on you."

Anger barely controlled, Harv stalked across the room, he leaned over Ellie, "I'm sorry I didn't tell you and Lucy about *her*," he jerked his thumb toward Cecile. "But when I saw Lucy running through the airport I was a goner. Then when her case opened and her lingerie spread over the Amsterdam airport floor and she laughed instead of crying, she had me heart and soul. I fell in love like never before." His rueful smile, so like Lucy's tugged at Ellie's heart. "I'll tell her about Cecile tonight," Harv glared warningly at Cecile and introduced her as his father's executive assistant and his former fiancé.

Betty caught his coattail and with an impish grin pulled his head close to hers, "Maybe if you take the ring back it will help her remember."

"The ring means nothing to me," Harv said scornfully, "and neither does she."

Rodney snarled, "There's entirely too much of his father in that one."

Zack, to ease the tension, quipped, "Finally the food, a guy could have starved to death waiting."

"You and your stomach, I swear that's all you think about," Michelle teased.

Cecile aligned the cutlery, rose gracefully, and left the hall.

"Tell Lucy to watch her back," Jeremy Reese muttered," I don't trust that woman."

"Was it something I said?" Zack asked innocently, they all laughed politely.

Ellie's eyes met Bettys across the sparking white cloth. "Another Spencer victim," she mouthed.

Lucy listened to one long winded orator after another. "Harv, I'm going to wash my hands, I'll wait for you by the band shell."

"Wait," Harv whispered and rose to follow. His father's hand stopped him.

"She'll be fine; pay attention to our long winded mayor."

Michael hastily dropped the cigarette he'd been enjoying and covered it with his foot, "Lucy what the heck went on," he pointed inside. "It took both Val and I to keep Brad from rushing to your rescue."

"Thanks for that," Lucy giggled, "it was just a mix up with the seating."

"Sure and that's why Harv charged over to talk to Ellie. I don't think so. Anyway what are you doing with the Spencer scion? He's a great buddy for guys, but poison to women. He's way out of your league."

"Hey, what do you mean out of my league?"

"I mean he goes for women like the one almost wearing the red dress, the *demimondaine* type. He's not good enough for you."

"You've been refining your French again. Let me see, if I remember, a *demimondaine* is a woman who lost her standing in society because of an indiscretion," Lucy grinned, "But gets to keeps her wealthy lovers; really Mikey darling who is your tutor?"

"Lucy I'm not joking, that guy sniffs after a woman until he gets her, then he's history."

"Michael sweetie, I love you for being concerned, but you're wrong about Harv, he isn't like that and I have to visit the lady's room."

Michael sighed; she's twenty nine years old and still dumb as a stick.

CHAPTER 22

Every few seconds Harv checked his watch and glanced at the door. Spence caught his eye, nodded and flicked his gaze from the younger version of himself to the exit. Harv took off like a thoroughbred out of the gate at the Kentucky Derby.

The mayor droned on and on while Spence' thoughts wandered. Has Harv found a filly to go the distance? He usually led the field with maidens and a few mares hot on his heels, but this is a different race, the track is fast and the stud colt may be lagging. Thank God Cecile floundered. She'd have gelded my boy before he was successful in the breeding shed.

Harv will need a steady hand to bring the Wilson girl to the finish especially with Brad, a definite stayer, in the field. Still my son's little filly is a good choice. Her dam, Ellie Warden-Wilson, comes from an old moneyed family and Charles Wilson? Well, it never hurts to have a little English bloodstock in the stable. Harv had top line breeding, he could attest to that, so there was no reason to believe that their progeny would be anything other than outstanding. The fact that Harv loved Lucy was an added bonus.

Harvey's wandering gaze landed on Ellie's table just as all the women stood and, like a swarm of multi colored butterflies flew to the powder room. His eyebrows shot up when three or four minutes later, all the males discreetly followed. The mayor's speech was uninspired, but the Warden Wilson table's mass migration was ludicrous. Both Rodney and Jake were major contributors to the lighthouse restoration fund, strange that they'd leave before the official dedication.

"She's not in the ladies room and Harv is not in the men's room," Ellie worried. "Where do you think that boy took her?"

"Ellie," Jake said calmly, "they're not children."

"I know," Ellie sighed. "That's what worries me."

"Mrs. Wilson, she went up Park Street with Spencer. He was stuck to her, and I'd say didn't have talkin' in mind," Tom blurted. "They're in the Smyth's yard. You take back-up; Spencer's got hands on all eight arms."

Harvey Sr. fought the urge to yawn, lost the fight, and since the mayor was in election mode, told his fellow sufferers he needed air and escaped to investigate the mass exodus. Cecile was the probable cause, she left early, but how far did she go? I'd fire her if she wasn't so good at her job.

"Tom have you seen my son. I expect he's with Lucy Wilson."

Clearing his throat to deposit a gob of spit near the Senior Spencer's shiny, Italian leather shoe, Tom pointed to Park Street.

"There's a light in the Smyth's yard," Jake said.

"I wouldn't think they'd need a flashlight for what their up to," Zack quipped, and earned a playful, albeit sharp jab from Michelle.

Ellie led the procession over the Smyth's manicured grass.

"I see them, they're by the deck." Baker stabbed a long finger at vaguely silhouetted figures.

Harvey Senior, unseen in darkness, stole across the grass toward Ellie's *cortege*.

"I'll thrash that lecherous Don Juan if he's taken liberties with my niece," Rodney threatened.

Betty placed a restraining hand on his arm, "Lucy would never chance grass stains on that dress; it's a Paris original."

Across the yard were two dark shadows, one prone the other hunched on hands and knees. "Oh no," Ellie breathed when the flashlights each person carried to enhance the lighthouse's anticipated glow, turned to light the Smyth's new deck.

Harv, jacket in hand and tie askew knelt with his arms and head under the decking. Suddenly highlighted he thumped his head against a concrete support cursed, and blinked owlishly in the glare.

The flashlight wielders reflexively turned to illuminate a breach in the deck's siding which was at that moment occupied by a shapely bottom clad in very brief, lacy, black panties.

"I'd know that fanny anywhere!" Ellie leapt to shield her overexposed child.

Harv draped his jacket over Lucy's exposed derriere. "Lucy," he said wryly, "Your mother's here."

He could have pulled her dress down to preserve her modesty, but he didn't touch those scantily clad buttocks, instead he used his jacket,

Ellie thought. The Spencer boy displayed class and decorum, perhaps the Spencer blood has thinned, or his debauched father failed to corrupt him, she reluctantly, tentatively hypothesized.

Harvey Senior charged into the light bellowing, "Harv, what the hell is going on here? Help that poor girl up out of there right now!"

"Mr. Spencer, Harv's manners are impeccable. When my daughter sets her mind on something no mere male, Spencer or otherwise will stop her. Your son appears to be a gentleman. Perhaps you haven't devoted enough time to his corruption." Ellie thought of Aunt Emily and shuddered. She just defended a Spencer male, adopted, but a blood Spencer male. Aunt Emily is not amused.

"I raised him to be a gentleman," Spence retorted. The ludicrous situation turned anger to sardonic amusement.

Betty giggled girlishly.

Rodney cursed softly.

Harv helped Lucy wriggle from the confined space beneath the deck; wrapped his tuxedo jacket around her to conceal the object of their nighttime sortie.

Lucy blinked in wide-eyed innocence. "What are you all doing here?"

"Young lady explain," Ellie ordered. "Harv has conducted himself with commendable *savoir-faire*, while your behavior is abominable."

"Mom, I was rescuing a kitten. The poor little guy scuttled under there on three paws. You would have done the same thing."

"She's always been an animal lover, it's a trait she inherited from me," Betty said illogically.

Jeremy Reese guffawed. Betty's comment and the absurdity of the situation revived memories of Lucy and Brad's childhood exploits and their subsequent fabrications.

"Why didn't you crawl in there to get the animal?" Harvey Senior demanded. "Lucy could have been injured. Frankly son, I'm ashamed of the conduct Mrs. Wilson finds laudable."

"Dad, I have the Spencer chest and shoulders. See a problem?" Harv tried and failed to keep a face straight face. "Anyway the kitten ran away just before you got here. I did get scratched," he showed the hand he'd caught on a protruding nail while shielding Lucy's curvaceous form.

Lucy led Jake into the shadows, they whispered intently. Lucy gave him a bulky bag that he quickly tucked inside his jacket.

Ellie observed, but did not comment.

"Let's go, we don't want to hold up the ceremonies," Baker said and led the way.

"Some good has come out of this," Betty chirped gaily, "We all know our batteries work." Zack guffawed, Betty ignored him, "Ellie, you go ahead. I'll help Lucy straighten up. Maybe even convince her to put her shoes on."

"I will help you," Rodney said valiantly.

Betty made little shooing motions with her hands, Rodney fled gratefully.

"Honey," Betty said, "where are those darling GUCCI's?"

"Here," Harv proffered the gold studded, strappy black sandals.

"Thank you Harv," Betty beamed, "losing nine hundred dollar GUCCI shoes would break any woman's heart."

Harv bent to fasten the light gold buckles; his hand lingered on Lucy's ankle.

The darkness hid Lucy's blush. "Promise you won't tell mom what I paid for these."

"Have I ever told?" Betty said. "Now take your hands out of Harv's pockets and give him his jacket."

"What's this?" Lucy asked.

"Open it honey; your beau picked it up at my store," Betty brushed sand and grass from Lucy's gown.

"The combs are beautiful, I love tortoise shell."

"Stop squirming," Betty ordered combing cob webs from Lucy's silky blond hair.

"But shouldn't I thank him?" Lucy asked edging away.

"You can thank him later." Betty swept Lucy's hair into a French twist, and secured it with the combs. "Lovely! Now hurry it's almost midnight."

"Did we miss anything?" Lucy asked.

"No they've just started," Jeremy replied.

"This is the fulfillment of a dream." Ellie said tearfully, while old memories overwhelmed her.

Harv slipped away and Lucy and Ellie held each other tight. Rodney's body screened them from prying eyes.

"Charles would be pleased to see the lighthouse restored. He disliked seeing our historic relics deteriorate." Rodney smiled sadly. "Don't cry Ellie darling, let us remember the good times, and rejoice."

"I am happy Rodney," Ellie whispered. "Lucy your father loved ceremony. However," she said," Charles would have limited the mayor's speech to five minutes."

From the podium Harv watched Lucy with her family. He yearned for a love like Ellie had for Charles, an enduring love that outlasted death. (Fortunately Harv was ignorant of Aunt Emily and Gertrude Wood Warden's hatred for his family that also endured after death.) The ceremony ended and from his elevated position Harv saw Sammy Ranker bulling his way through the crowd. He jumped off the platform. "Rodney, Ranker's almost on you. You should go."

Betty whispered to Lucy, "No Lucy, you stay and enjoy the evening. We'll see Ellie home. Don't waste this delightful evening. Life is short." She caught Harv and Lucy in a hug. "Have fun children. Let's go Ellie." She hurriedly opened the car door, shoved Ellie in and jumped in beside her. Jake slammed the door. "Look! Spencer Senior, Harv, and Lucy are forming a blocking line. It's like Ranker is a cornerback about to be crunched and Harvey Senior is a lineman blocking down on the defense, but look at Lucy! She's going for the chop block and Harv is the tight end, big and fast with great hands," Betty enthused.

Ellie tried to decipher Betty's observations, but football was Greek to her. "Betty, Lucy is the image of her grandmother."

"I know, honey." Betty murmured, "Let's not buy trouble."

Moments later Betty bid Rodney goodnight, Ellie offered Jake a nightcap that he declined. "I'm anxious to see if the papers Lucy found under the deck are Derwood's accounts. If they are we might find the money he embezzled."

"That would be good news, Jake. Thank for all your work, and for putting up with my foolishness," Ellie said. "You must think me an idiot.'

"Quite the contrary, I think you good as wife and mother and that Charles still lives in your heart. I can wait until there's room for me."

Ellie kissed his cheek, "You are a good man Jake Carlton."

Jake grinned, "That doesn't mean I'll stop chasing you, Ellie Warden Wilson." He held her tight for a moment. "Come on Rodney, I'll drop you off."

Betty put the two portraits she'd pick off the hall floor on the Stickley table, led Ellie to the sofa, filled sherry glasses, and sat next to her.

"That was quite a spectacle my under dressed daughter put on with her fanny exposed, and poor Harv trying to cover her spotlighted derriere while Spence reprimanded him. That was a spectacle only your errant niece could pull and escape virtually unscathed. How does she do it?"

"I don't know, but it was hilarious, all those flashlights highlighting her scanty panties. I'm thankful she wasn't wearing a thong, but what amused me," Betty smirked, "was you defending the Spencer scion."

Betty threw her arms around Ellie, "Me and my big mouth. Cry honey, tears always help."

"Oh Betty, what would I do without you?" Ellie sighed, "Lucy looked exactly like her father in the moon light. I tell myself I should be over it, but then everything rushes back." Heart wrenching sobs ripped from her throat, "I thought I'd locked it away, but tonight it was as if it happened yesterday. Maybe it was a mistake to come home."

Betty repeated the advice Ellie gave her after Derwood's violence. "This is your home and with the help of your friends and family you'll get through it. And when things are too much for you, we'll take long exhausting vacations like we used to when Derwood abused me."

"I am a selfish fool. I weep over events long past and you who lost Robert, and endured *Derwood,* comfort me."

"I'm your friend and what happens to you happens to me," Betty said. "If those words have a familiar ring it's because they're yours. Tomorrow after church we'll visit Robert's grave. I want you to see what I've done with it. No, I won't tell," Betty said, "You have to see it for yourself."

Ellie smiled and moved on, "Did you see the duty free bag Lucy surreptitiously passed to Jake?"

Betty nodded.

"I'd like to know what she thought important enough to crawl under that deck in a Dior original."

"It could be the duty free bag I dropped at the foot of the stairs with my luggage, it's missing."

"If it is your bag, how did it get under the Smyth's deck and how did Lucy know where to look for it?" Ellie refilled their glasses. "Jake said it held interesting papers that could help you, but I was too self absorbed to listen."

Betty did her best Sherlock Holmes, "We shall interview all of them in the morning. Do you want more sherry?"

"No, I hear our beds calling."

They climbed the stairs, two friends as close as sisters. Ellie stopped abruptly, "What did you mean the Spencers and Lucy were making a block, Ranker was back in a corner and Harv had a tight end and fast hands?"

Betty said enthusiastically, "I've been thinking about that and I wasn't quite accurate. What I meant was, the role of the offense is to protect, and of course the defense destroys. So Sammy Ranker was more like a linebacker trying to destroy the quarterback, that'd be you Ellie. Harvey Senior acted as a lineman blocking or a guard."

"Oh, that's all right then," Ellie said, "But what I'm worried about are Harv's fast hands and tight end?"

"You're a card, Ellie. Listen and I'll explain once more. Harv was like a tight end that blocks and protects, is fast and has great hands. Lucy was a wide receiver running a pattern to draw the defense away from the offense."

"That's ridiculous, Lucy couldn't run in those heels, and what would she receive anyway?"

Stifling laughter, Betty lectured, "Listen very, very carefully, I'll try to make it simpler for you. You might have been a running back and Lucy could have been the quarterback. If that was the case, the blockers protect both backs and then the quarterback, that's Lucy remember, runs a fake to distract the linebacker. Do you understand now?"

"I don't think so," Ellie admitted, albeit reluctantly.

"Last try," Betty sighed, "Sammy Ranker was a linebacker, just like Dick Butkus of the Chicago Bears. Dick loved to hurt and annihilate for the meanness integral in the game, so either way Ranker is a Butkus style linebacker. Is that clear?"

"Sort of, I guess. You're saying Ranker is nasty and mean and I agree, but Betty, its Harv's tight end and fast hands that concern me."

Betty threw her hands in the air, "I give up." She laughed heartily.

"What's so darn funny?"

"I'll explain it when you are old enough to understand. See you in the morning girl friend."

"I've always loved this beach at night," Lucy said wistfully. "I used to sneak out while Grandpa and Grandma slept to sit and to dream."

"Was I part of those dreams?" Harv asked his breath sensuous and warm on her neck.

"Not unless you lived in Lake Huron, were large and scaly. I was ten or eleven and my dreams centered on fishing and my dad emerging from the water to carry me home in his adoring arms."

"I'd love to carry you home and I am kind of large, so I cover two out of three on your list." Sweeping her from her feet he carried her to the nearest bench, and withdrew his arms. Raw emotion raced across his face and Lucy felt a foreboding chill.

He took her hands in his. "There is something I have to say, and I should have said before, but . . ."

"There's always a 'but.'" Lucy sighed, "Just spit it out."

"I was engaged when I met you."

Lucy ran to the water's edge, "You could have told me before I made a fool of myself."

Harv picked up her abandoned shoes, tucked then into his jacket pockets and tried to explain. "It was over for me for a long time. I just went along hoping I was wrong about Cecile's game playing." Harv stepped in front of Lucy, "Then I saw you running through the airport in Amsterdam and."

"Why?" Lucy demanded, "Why didn't you tell me you were engaged."

"I was afraid I'd lose you."

"Did you love her?"

"No, but I thought I did. I was lonely, Cecile was there. I thought anyone was better than no one. Then I met you and knew how wrong I'd been."

"Cecile is the woman in the red dress, right?'

"Yes."

"She's very beautiful. Are you sure you're over her?'

'Look at me,' he murmured, "I haven't thought of anything but you since we met. I love you."

"We've only known each other a short time, are you sure?"

"Lucy you've taken over my life. I'm like a kid with his first crush, but . . ."

"Not another but?" Lucy fought the urged to lose herself in his golden-green eyes.

"Baby, I want you, but, there's that word again." A boyish smile lit up his face. "But, I want more. Don't get me wrong I'd like to lay you down in the sand and love you like no one ever has. However," he qualified, "what was I going to say? I can't think straight with you so close." He cleared his throat, and extended his arms to put some distance between their bodies. "I want our forever to hold more than physical satisfaction. I want a partner; a soul mate and a friendship like you have with Brad."

"The kind of relationship my mom and daddy had."

"Yes that kind, so let's take it slow," he distractedly dug his toes in the sand. "I've learned the hard way that . . ."

Lucy pulled his face down to hers and closed his mouth with one kiss and then another and another. They stood bodies entwined; one heart beat indistinguishable from the other.

"You're not making this easy, darling." He threw his jacket to the sand and pulled her down beside him. "Soon you'll go back to Paris and dad is sending me to the Far East for a month, so I want you to have this," he tugged a heavy, embossed signet ring from his finger. "I swear no other woman will breech the threshold of my heart, or my bedroom," he promised folding her fingers over the ring.

Lucy opened her hand to examine his love token. "Are you sure?"

"I'll take a blood oath if it will convince you. Look into my eyes and into my heart where you will live forever."

"I believe you because I feel the same about you." Lucy placed a ring in his hand, "This was my father's ring, I wear it next to my heart, and I give it to you as a token of everlasting love," she unwittingly uttered the exact words her father and said to Ellie. "I've waited my whole life for you."

Harv groaned, "Much more of this and I'll renege on that taking it slow thing."

"I know what you mean."

"Come on baby, let's walk. I want to know everything about you."

'Want to go skinny dipping. It might cool us down."

"Not a good idea, but we could wade with all our clothes in place." Harv rolled up his trouser legs and strolled to the water's edge.

"Don't forget those lovely patent shoes," Lucy mimicked Betty's ditzy manner, "That would be heartbreak akin to psoriasis." She ran into the shallow water where Harv waited. "One more tiny, little, innocent kiss and then I promise we'll talk."

They spoke of childhood dreams, plans for the future, likes and dislikes and the hours flew by unnoticed.

"Isn't the sunrise beautiful?"

"Hmm," Harv said tilting her face up, "it's nice, but not half as lovely as you."

"This has been one of the most memorable nights of my life."

"Only one of, when were the others?"

"I'll never tell." Lucy splashed water at Harv and ran onto the smooth sand. "I'll race you to the car."

"You cheated," Harv yelled, "You got a head start."

"I'll show you what a gracious winner I can be," she whispered against the ticklish spot on his neck.

He tightened his embrace, "I'll be happy to lose to you any day," he smothered her lips with hungry kisses.

"Good morning children, the coffee's ready," Betty called from the shadowy depths of the porch swing.

Lucy tittered, rolled her eyes and they roared with laughter.

"Lucy, I'd better go. If your aunt sees the condition of my suit, she'll get the wrong idea."

"*Au revoir. Je t'aime!*" Lucy touched his lips with hers.

He returned her kiss and chuckled, "Baby, I don't do the French real good, but I love when you talk sexy."

"Go home before Aunt Betty gets the garden hose."

Lucy watched as Harv strode into the newly awakened dawn.

"Your mother was right he does have a tight end," Betty giggled.

Lucy, familiar with her aunt's knowledge of and propensity to liken life's events to football maneuvers, and her mother's misinterpretation of any sports analogy said, "Yeah a girls gotta love a tight end."

CHAPTER 23

"Ellie," Betty said, "I'm glad you're with me; sadly two of the town's worst gossips attend my church. Father Hoyle speaks on the evils of gossip twice a month. His sermons are funny," Betty qualified, "if you're not the subject. Father says something like 'One of our parishioners has caused grievous harm by spreading rumors.' Sammy Ranker glares at Mrs. Hooper certain the priest means her, she returns his glare as sure Sammy is Father Hoyle's target. The next sermon invariably quotes Robert Burns words; 'O, wad some Power the giftie gie us to see oursels as others see us! It wad frae monie a blunder free us.' Of course the gossips think he means someone else. Isn't that strange?"

"It's not strange at all; they both thrive on other people's misery. I think they were lawyers or serial killers in a past life." Ellie ducked behind one of the large columns flanking the church doors. "Hurry, here comes Mrs. Hooper. If she catches me in her sanctimonious clutches I'll be here all day."

"That's true, when that lady sees a prospective convert she clamps on like Staffordshire terrier to a mailman." Betty towed Ellie out of her hiding place, "We'd better find a pew before she sets those pious dentures in your jugular," Betty suppressed a giggle, sobered, genuflected, and led Ellie to the Archer pew. She nodded sedate greetings to friends and acquaintances, but Mrs. Hooper's censuring glower sent her into a fit of giggles.

"Okay if we join you?" Sue pried Doris' hand off her arm and shoved her into the pew.

"Mrs. Betty," Doris said, "I told Sue what you said about talking to God in His house, and she said you were ever so right. I don't feel hardly scared now, so I think God heard me."

"I'll explain later," Betty mouthed at Ellie whose eyebrows met her hair line.

The serenity of the service enveloped them and brought peace to their souls, but Ellie's serenity fled with the final words of the dismissal. Mrs. Hooper, white dress billowing around her shrunken body, bore down on Ellie like a yacht approaching the finish line at the annual regatta.

"Ellie Warden, I'm delighted you've returned to the one true faith," Mrs. Hooper exclaimed. "It was wrong of Charles to steal you from us," she had her skeletal hand clamped on Ellie's forearm.

In spite of Ellie's unspoken plea, Betty fled. She's a big girl, Betty rationalized, and she can cope with one little, old lady. Doris and Sue can run interference while I, coward that I am, wait outside.

"Mrs. Archer, Chief Platt wants to talk to you down town," Sergeant Rick offered Betty his arm and rushed her to one of the three black and whites parked at the curb.

"I came with Ellie. She'll wonder where I've gone," Betty tried to catch Doris' eye. Doris it seemed didn't like Mrs. Hooper's repetitive diatribe either.

"I'll make sure Mrs. Wilson knows, but Chief Platt wants you at the station right now. Somebody posted a nasty version of your experiences with Mr. Day on the Internet," Rick explained glaring at Sammy Ranker, who was being detained by Father Hoyle. "The wire service picked it up and reporters staked out your place." He shook his head disgustedly, "The pests got the Wilson place, the mortuary and the hotel covered too."

"I can't come until I tell Ellie."

Rick beckoned to Mac, "Tell only Mrs. Wilson where Mrs. Archer is."

Mac Nodded.

"Are you arresting me?"

"Hell no! It's like I said, the Chief wants you to hide out at the station until we get rid of the reporters."

Doris watched slack jawed, "I'll tell Sue. She won't yell in God's house. Sue is ever so smart; she'll know how to save Mrs. Betty." She bolted into church. "Sue," she whispered, "A policeman took Mrs. Betty away in his car."

"I'm a Baptist," Sue announced loudly," but I've been thinking of joining the Catholic Church."

Mrs. Hooper dropped Ellie like a lost cause, and latched onto Sue. Her face shone like she was face to face with the spirit of the Mother Theresa. "What a wonderful surprise," she trilled interest wholly absorbed by the opportunity Sue's proclamation presented. "I heard what that awful Mr. Day did to you all. I'm sure you crave the solace one can find only in the true church."

Ellie cast Sue a grateful smile, and hustled Doris out the door.

"Ruby pay attention," Lucy said for the third time. "This recorder is voice activated you turn it on and forget it."

"What if the tape runs out?"

"It's a ninety minute tape, it won't run out."

"You won't let me down will you, Lucy? He knows I haven't told anybody, and he won't believe I wrote it all down either." Ruby shuddered remembering Jordan's threats, "He'll hurt me if he suspects anything."

"You won't be alone," Lucy promised, "I'll be right outside your window."

"Yeah and what are you gonna do when he gets rough?"

"I won't be alone Ruby, I'll bring somebody strong that we can trust."

"If you're really sure I'll try it," Ruby agreed, but without confidence in the plan.

Lucy cajoled and assured, Ruby balked and resisted until Lucy tried a new tactic. "I'm putting myself at risk to get you off the hook, Ruby. If you're too pathetic to save yourself say so and we'll forget the whole damn thing."

"Don't get mad, Lucy. I'm really scared."

"I understand, but remember the evidence he left in your car? Either he confesses on tape or you take the fall."

"Hey Ruby, do you still work here?" Sammy Ranker yelled waving a two year old coupon for a free coffee.

"I gotta work." Ruby stood tall. "I'll set it up for tomorrow night." Her shoulders slumped, "You won't forget will you?"

Lucy sighed and repeated; "Leave your address and the time on our answering machine, and I'll be there." Her cell phone would have expedited the project, but it was lost in the sand on Huron's Shore. "Leave a detailed message Ruby."

"I got it the first time. I'm not stupid, you know."

Uh huh, Lucy thought.

"Why the long face," Harv asked, "you lose something?'

"What are you doing here?" Lucy asked, not surprised that his worn jeans and tight T-shirt clad body made her quiver.

"Looking for you; I found your phone in my jacket. I dropped it through the mail slot at your house. I came to try the cheese biscuits you love." He inhaled deeply, his chest expanded; using all of her willpower Lucy did not throw herself into his arms. "Also my mother's in town and I'd like you to meet her."

"Oh Harv, I'd love too," Lucy gushed, and wondered when she, a sophisticated woman became a gusher.

"Great, I'll pick you up at five. How's about one of those hugs you're so free with?"

Lucy acquiesced happily. She leaned against the bakery sighing dreamily, shook herself, and repeated the sophisticated woman thing, and thought of cheese biscuits, the cure for all life's afflictions, even lust. She paused in the doorway. Sammy Ranker regaled the clientele with his version of the morning's post Mass events.

"I told Eric I saw Hank, the Archers' old gardener, hauling out everything that wasn't nailed down. That Betty Archer's stealing all Derwood's stuff. I saw that redheaded sergeant drag her off in handcuffs right there in front of the church. Platt didn't arrest her soon enough, if ask me."

Lucy raged, "Mr. Ranker, since no one asked you, shut the hell up. Derwood Day brought nothing, but shame to Uncle Robert and Aunt Betty's home, and for your information, not that you deserve any information, you spiteful, malicious, acrimonious, vicious little man, Derwood Day is a lying, thieving, bigamist, but he isn't half the two faced hypocrite you are." She stalked to her bike and roared away.

Sergeant Rick Green, fair-skinned face out shining his flaming red hair attempted to block Ellie's assault on his Chiefs office.

Ellie ducked under Rick's outstretched arms, and shrieked, "How dare you arrest Betty! Was she represented when you used the rubber hose? What cell is she in?" She drew a quick breath, "You are a fair weather friend."

"Quiet," Eric commanded. "Rick, get back to your desk. Close the door, and keep everybody out." He faced Ellie, "Honoria Warden Wilson, I am an officer of the law. There can be no friendships where duty is concerned." Eric's sad smile stripped the sting from his words.

Ellie stalked to and fro, she ignored Eric's attempt at *détente*. "That won't wash with me. Betty has been our friend since we were infants." Ellie slapped his desk. "You may abandon a friend when she hits a patch of trouble, but I do not!"

"If I don't do my job you'll be the first to complain. I haven't forgotten the interview I innocently gave you."

"I don't want to talk ancient history," Ellie retorted.

In quick succession, Eric lost control of his temper, saw the absurdity in the situation, and laughed aloud.

Ellie expanded like a broody hen, "I see nothing amusing."

The office door flew open, struck the wall and Rodney Wilson, hair on end, shirttail trailing, sans tie and socks strode through. "Release Elizabeth Archer immediately," he shouted, "I killed the treacherous bugger!"

Eric stared dumfounded while Ellie sputtered.

Rodney drew breath and intoned, "Derwood was an unrepentant black-mailing villain unfit to clean Betty's lavatory!"

Was there ever a more unlikely murderer, Ellie wondered, and wished Betty could see her valiant knight in action.

"Calm down, Rodney. Another word and I'll cuff ya." Rodney, not fond of cold steel, shut his mouth. "Sit in that chair," Eric pointed. "I'm a tolerant man. I've been bawled at, insulted, and accused. I'm up to here with it," he indicated a spot a foot above his head. "Now Rodney, you tell it again in a civilized way or I'll put you in a cell until you calm down." Eric pointed at the door, "Get out Ellie!"

"Don't go Ellie, please," Rodney begged.

Ellie searched her purse, "I need to call Michelle. Rodney don't you say a word until she gets here." She ran to the pay phone.

"Summon a stenographer to record my statement. I'll sign it and then I insist you release Betty."

"I'll take your statement myself."

Rodney detailed Derwood's extortion. He described each of Betty's injuries in graphic detail. His melodious voice trembled when he told of her plea that he help her get away before any one saw her shame. "Her shame?" he repeated sadly. "I failed her over and over again. I paid what Derwood asked and still he beat and robbed her. I make no apology. My only regret is not killing him sooner. Betty suffered because of my inertia." Vindicated in his own eyes, Rodney exuded unkempt dignity. "I do not require an attorney; I am prepared to take my punishment."

Eric selected a piece of paper from the stack on the left side of his desk, placed it in the exact center of his pristine blotter, picked up a ballpoint pen, shook it and said, "Start from the beginning, what happened when you got to the house, where was Derwood when you got there and where you left him. Include the time as near as you can remember."

Ellie had not closed the door tight, and she'd heard enough. "No Rodney, no more talk until Michele arrives." She held his gaze, and thought of a gladiator set to die for his ladylove. She headed for the door, "Remember Rodney, not another word!"

Sound erupted from the foyer as Rick tried to restrain a whirlwind named Lucy. "Damn it Lucy, cut it out or I'll throw you in the can."

"If you do you'll never get another gooey, luscious, deep, dark, chocolate, chunk macadamia nut cookie from my mother," Lucy ducked under his arm and ran to Eric's office. "Put away the thumbscrews, Michelle will be here any minute." Lucy peered under the desk, "Where the hell is my Aunt," she spied Rodney. "What in blazes are you doing here?"

"I have confessed to Derwood's murder, now Eric must discharge Betty."

"Damn that was brave, and really stupid," She kissed his forehead. "Can't be helped now, just don't sign anything."

Eric's temper snapped as did his pen. Black ink spurted and, ran over his hand and down his arm to his cuff. "Ellie, Lucy, get the hell out of my office."

"Oh, Hi Chief Platt," Lucy smiled innocently, "I didn't see you there, sorry to show up uninvited. Mom, is Aunt Betty okay?"

"Mac, get these females out of my office. If they give you trouble, arrest them," Eric commanded. Mac chased Lucy around a chair; Ellie blocked him when she could. Eric sighed heavily, a scene strait out of a Keystone Cops movie. "Mac, if Lucy won't leave under her own steam, carry her, but watch your back," he muttered.

Ellie told Rodney that he'd said more than enough.

Lucy saw the sweat on Eric's brow and allowed Mac to catch her, "Remember Uncle, don't sign anything."

Ellie shouted, "Recant Rodney, recant!" and followed Lucy.

"Better come quietly Mom, the cells color will clash with your hair."

"Ladies," Mac panted, "Mrs. Archer is in the break room."

Ellie broke Roger Bannister's four minute mile sprinting down the hall.

"What in the world are you doing here?"

"We heard Eric arrested you. We're the breakout squad, but that's not necessary, because Uncle Rodney confessed to killing Dreadful Derwood. I ask you," Lucy demanded, "is that ludicrous or what?"

Ellie shushed her affronted child when she saw Betty pale.

Betty gasped, "What do you mean arrested."

Ellie pulled a chair close and explained.

"Okay Rodney," Eric said, "Let's start again. What made you believe I arrested Betty?"

"Your men picked her up at church. I heard she was manhandled into a police car by one of your henchmen. What else was I to believe?"

"Rick, get back in here!" Eric yelled, paused to wait, and then demanded, "Who brought Mrs. Archer in?"

"I did, Chief. She was coming out of church when we arrived so I drove her here. She called her lawyer and I put her in the break room and served coffee, even gave her the brownies my mother packed with my lunch."

"That will be all, Rick." Eric sighed turning back to Rodney. "Still think she was treated roughly? She may feel tortured if she drank Rick's coffee or ate his mother's brownies, but she was not manhandled. I had her brought in because there are reporters hanging around town like vultures waiting to feed on her. Now why do you think Derwood is dead, and didn't just run off with the cash?"

"I uh, well; the truth is I don't know. I deduced that something was radically wrong when he didn't return to sell Betty's house and when I heard you were arrested Betty I . . ." Rodney stalled.

"And you thought Betty killed him," Eric said, "right? So tell me, what did you two do with the body?"

"I did nothing and Betty certainly would not harm him. I admit going to the house when he called demanding more money. I arrived to find him sporting several contusions. He was vile and I lost my temper. I punched him in the nose, but he was alive when I left, and Betty was not there."

"If that's the truth you'll have no objections to us inspecting your vehicle."

"What has my automobile to do with anything?" Rodney asked. "Oh I see, you think I moved Derwood's body. If I were dimwitted enough to kill him and use my vehicle to move him why would I then charge in here to confess and thus implicate Betty, the person I want exonerated? If there's reasoned logic in that theory, will you explain it to me?"

Chief Platt cleared his throat and Rodney recognized the low growl that meant back off 'cause a blow up was a comin'.

"I meant no harm."

"What the hell is going on in my town? Has everyone gone nuts? Rita Russell killed and her body planted in Brad's home, Zack run down by the dead woman's car, Baker burglarized and Ruby too scared or brainless to tell the truth, Derwood gone missing with the cash of not one, but four women he married bigamously and now you suggest he's murdered, not missing. And all without a shred of proof or a sensible story," Eric roared.

"I did not intend to trivialize your investigation, I simply wanted to..."

"You've had your say, now you listen. What I don't need is my friends adding confusion to an already messed up case. Do you know what kind of flack I'm getting? I look like a yokel to the brass." Eric snorted, "I ain't Sherlock Holmes, but I ain't Barney Fife either so stop trying to manipulate me."

"Eric, I apologize."

"Rodney," Eric muttered exhausted. "Go home and take Betty with you. I've had enough of the lot of you. An innocent woman is dead, Baker was robbed, Derwood is missing, and you bother me with crap, go away." Eric trudged around his desk, pointed at the door, pushed Rodney into the corridor, and slammed the door.

He opened Rita Russell's autopsy report. She was held face down in Baker's dough until she smothered. Who in this sleepy little paradise could do such a thing? And who hated Brad enough to frame him? Eric propped his size twelve's on an open drawer and wished he'd retired when he'd done his twenty years.

The bakery murder and burglary were not his problem anymore, but Derwood Day's disappearance was. The embezzled money, while connected, was the Feds problem. How was Ruby involved? She was scared and lying her ass off. His son admitted he often borrowed Ruby's car without her knowledge. Jordan said Ruby was stupid and wouldn't know the truth if it slapped her in the face. Eric dragged himself to his feet and brushed his hand over his shoulder, as if he could, by that gesture leave the job behind.

Betty shoved a sandwich bag at Ellie, "Put these brownies in your handbag. Rick's mom made them from scratch. I don't want to hurt Rick's feelings, but I think she forgot a few ingredients." Betty fidgeted, "I hope Eric lets Rodney go home soon, this place is depressing."

"Vomit yellow and dung brown are colors probably chosen to make criminals long for a nice battleship gray cell."

"I was lunching with Zack and he was paying," Michelle whined, "You know how rare that is, and I didn't even get dessert. Now what is so damn important?"

"Rodney confessed to Derwood's murder to save Betty," Ellie hastily explained. "He didn't kill Derwood, but he's thinks Betty did and needs a champion. He's her Galahad."

"Derwood's dead! They found his body? What's wrong with you people? I moved home for a less hectic life." She shrugged, "Do not feel obligated to keep me in clients! I'd better go shut him up, Lucy you come along, I may need backup."

"Uh, I'd rather stay here, Eric is a little pis, uh, miffed with us."

Michelle exhaled. "You know, when this is over, you all owe me big time, my fee will be hefty so be prepared. First you people call me to represent Brad, and don't mention his unimpeachable alibi. Next its Ruby's turn, but, since Lucy told her not to talk to anybody she won't talk to me." Michelle paced, "Lucy interrupts my meal to tell me Betty's arrested. I arrive and I'm representing Rodney if, that is, he actually requires an attorney." Michelle touched each woman's shoulder, "I never want to hear this mess mentioned outside of this room, because if any of these shenanigans reach the city I'll be the butt of real lawyer jokes, the ones we tell each other."

Betty stifled a giggle and slipped a hand into Ellie's purse. "Michelle I know that people who miss dessert have low blood sugar and are cranky. Why don't you try these brownies?"

"Thanks Betty, that's very kind," Michelle said and turned to find Rodney filling the doorway "I see you're not shackled, that's a good thing. Tell me everything you said."

CHAPTER 24

Much later, after Michelle lectured each of them separately, and scorched collectively, Rodney offered Betty sanctuary and asked Michelle for a lift, "It seems the police need to inspect my vehicle."

"How did they manage that? Michelle snarled, Rodney said he'd ask for it because he had nothing to hide.

"You have been a foolish, foolish man," Michelle said, "Get in the car, you two infants, before you use up my whole Sunday."

Ellie and Lucy watched until Michelle and her passengers rounded the corner. "Give me your cell phone," Ellie demanded. She angrily keyed in a well-remembered number. "Mr. Samuel Ranker, this is Mrs. Ellie Honoria Warden Wilson. Do not speak!" she barked. "I have heard enough of your vicious fabrications. Now you will listen to me. If you allow the name of even one of the women Derwood Day exploited to pass over your forked tongue again, I shall expose every underhanded real estate transaction you've been party to. "She drew a quick breath, "Quiet! Do not speak, and stop sniveling. I will expose your lifetime of petty crime to the reporters, who thanks to you, infest my property. Do you understand me?" she waited. "Yes you may speak."

Lucy grinned and hoped her state of the art phone didn't melt.

"Your apology is noted, but not accepted," Ellie hit the off key.

"What did he say?"

"He said he's truly sorry for spreading the rumors, but the vile website is Mrs. Hooper's."

"Toss my phone in back until its cool enough to handle," Lucy teased. "He's lying. When her son Patrick bought her a laptop, she, certain it was the devil's work, doused it in Holy water. Patrick posted pictures on Facebook, so we know she didn't post that stuff."

"Of course she didn't, she's anti progress; she turns on her television only to watch reruns of Lawrence Welk. She even picketed the Library when they installed computers. The children are afraid to use them when she's around."

Lucy giggled, "Why are there flowers in the backseat?"

"Betty and I were to visit Uncle Robert's grave today. Do you mind if we make a detour?"

"I always visit him at least once when I'm home." Lucy said turning toward the ancient, Catholic cemetery. "I miss Uncle Robert. He was my best teacher. I learned more from him than any art class."

"You ran to him each time you drew a new wild flower, weed, or insect. I worried that you disturbed his work, but in his fusty way he said, 'Ellie Wilson, would you punish me by keeping that inquisitive mind, my inspiration, and Charles' beloved child from me?' He was a special man. Betty and I often imitated his stodgy speech pattern. He caught us and he let us struggle to apologize for at least five minutes, then he laughed until he cried. Derwood has so much to burn for."

Lucy parked beside a tall red cedar. "I'll place the flowers, you pray." She fell to her knees, "Look Aunt Betty added daddy's name to Uncle Robert's stone," Lucy's eye's filled and tears rolled down her cheeks.

"Visiting Robert's grave gave Betty strength when life with *Derwood* became unbearable. She has given us a generous gift." Ellie knelt to pray. Lucy replaced the wilted foxglove with fresh, and hands folded, joined her mother in prayer. Several quiet moments later Ellie said, "It's time to go home. I have columns due and you can check my spelling," Lucy chuckled and Ellie smiled. Lucy rarely cried, she grieved in her own way. When Charles died she spent countless hours on the lake shore talking to him and building totems to tie his soul to hers. She wrote Charles long agonizing letters that she hid in the old hollow tree. Perhaps Betty's unselfish act would end Lucy's grieving. "Home dear, those columns will not write themselves."

"I'll drive," Lucy said, and drove the short distance by rote; her mind busy sorting emotions she thought buried long years ago. "Damn, are those reporters infesting our porch?"

"Reporters," Ellie said disgustedly, "yes I'm afraid they are."

"Some of the vultures are in our garage. I'll run a few over and make it look like an accident."

"Not a good idea, they're doing their job." Ellie pushed her way to the door.

"Ellie, talk to me. Give me all the dirt," coaxed the stringer from the rag euphemistically called the Daily Slime.

Lucy bellowed, "Get out of my garage," she revved the engine. "Mom has a bizarre affinity to you bunch of lowlifes, but I don't. Get out and take that camera shit with you," her foot to the accelerator, journalists screeched and jumped to safety, Lucy stopped millimeters from the garage wall. "I'm going to kill Ranker," she mumbled, the overhead door smashed against the asphalt. "You still got Grandpa's shotgun?"

"Lucy control yourself," Ellie said and tried to reason with the reporters, "What you read on the Internet is all nonsense. It was posted by Sammy Ranker a mendacious gossip, and if you print any of those lies, the ladies will sue you and the papers you represent," she smiled, gave them Ranker's address and phone number, wished them a pleasant afternoon, and while they watched, dialed 911 to report trespassers. "You see honey, one need never be uncouth."

Lucy groused loud and clear, "I still think the shotgun would work better."

Ellie closed and locked the door.

"Hurry Lucy," Ellie commanded, "We have to bake. If Michelle tastes Rick's mother's brownies her fees will double. Dinner is at the Plaza and starts at seven. I hope that's not too early for you."

"Harv wants me to meet his mother, and she has a new husband she wants Harv and Mr. Spencer to meet. How weird is that?"

"Lucy, the ladies went to a lot of trouble and expense to book a private room, try to be on time." Ellie giggled, "But get all the gory details, I've often wondered what kind of woman not only escaped the grasping Spencer Empire, but left with a fat alimony check, and seven houses."

"Is that a prurient interest or natural nosiness?" Lucy asked. Visions of Ellie dancing in the arms of Harvey Senior came to mind.

"I have no interest in the Senior Spencer's love life. I'm simply curious about the woman who got the degenerate to the altar. A normal curiosity, wouldn't you agree?"

"Uh huh" Lucy agreed, "I've wondered that myself, and I promise to notice every detail, but you know it takes two to tango."

"Don't be absurd," Ellie said, and changed the subject. "Where did you leave your bike?"

"It's at the police station. Aunt Betty said the dinner with the wives is casual, so after I meet Harv's mom I'll pick it up and come directly to the restaurant."

"Honey, you look lovely, good enough to eat, as dad would say, or too good to stick gum on as Aunt Gracie still says. Did you buy that dress in Hong Kong?"

"Yes, the saleslady said the green silk matched my eyes and the dragon and phoenix motif is lucky," Lucy pirouetted batting her eyelashes. "What do you think?"

"I agree with the salesclerk, though the dress back might be a tiny bit higher and the side slit a whole lot lower, but the shoes and bag match perfectly."

She'd have me in an abaya, a head scarf, and burka if she could, Lucy thought, especially around Harv. "What do we hope to get from this dinner with the ladies other than good grub," she asked emulating her mother's penchant for quick subject changes.

"I'd like answers for some nagging questions, for instance which woman did Baker see in the window the night Derwood died, and who killed *him*?"

"Who do you think it was, Sue or Doris?"

"I can't imagine either of them murdering *him*; but then I like them too much to be impartial."

"We know that Uncle Rodney didn't kill him and Aunt Betty didn't do it either. What if the woman Baker saw is a red herring, and not connected with his death?"

"Lucy, what are you thinking?"

"Ranker was yapping about Hank stealing Derwood's stuff. If Hank feels confident enough to clean the shed, then he—," The ringing doorbell broke her concentration. "Hello Harv, I've missed you."

Harv spoke over Lucy's head, "Good afternoon Mrs. Wilson, I brought you daisies. I hope you like them."

"Thank you Harv, Lucy's father often brought me daisies."

"I know I'm early Lucy, but mother arrived early and I want to be there to stomp out the fires she lights under dad."

Ellie waved them off, Harv's concern for his adopted father surprised her. She put the daisies, her favorite flower in water.

Ellie thought, Mom had grown every variety of daisies known to man. Then one memorable night, for reasons known only to herself, she dug up, and burnt every daisy cultivar, and never planted another. I will plant a few in the back of the garden, maybe mother's spirit won't notice.

"I hope that bottle is not for mother, she has a problem with alcohol."

"I'm sorry Harv. I didn't know. I've lived in Europe too long I guess."

"Baby, don't apologize, dad will enjoy your gift."

"Tell me about her, are there any topics I should avoid?"

"She hates references to age, especially hers and her new husband's. I call her Crystal because she insists. She doesn't admit having a thirty year old son."

"I can't imagine anyone not wanting to brag about you."

"She tells everyone she's thirty," Harv snapped, "Does that answer your question?"

"Harv," Lucy exclaimed, "I'm sorry I upset you. At my house there aren't too many taboo subjects." If, she thought drolly, you omitted the Spencer clan, and grandma and Aunt Emily's response to them.

"Do not apologize. I shouldn't take my anger out on you," he drove past huge maples, around a sparkling fountain where carved fish spit water at laughing cherubs, and parked under the portico of a, grey stone edifice. "Just be yourself. I love you and she will too. But you know her opinion is irrelevant to me." He raised Lucy's hand to his lips and planted a hot kiss on her palm.

Lucy sighed; this taking it slowly thing could be difficult.

"Do you like the house?"

"It's big, but rather austere and cheerless."

Harv frowned as if seeing it for the first time. "It was left to me by my paternal grandmother and it's caused more fights than it's worth. Crystal wanted it, but it's tied to the Spencer firstborn." He grinned impishly, "Sort of feudal don't you think?" He led her up the stairs, "Ready to face the music?"

Lucy said she was ready, but was she?

"That outfit suits you."

"You don't look half bad yourself," Lucy murmured, nuzzling the ticklish spot on his neck. He kissed her. Hot damn! There have been three or four great kisses in all of history, Anthony and Cleopatra, Romeo and Juliet, Bogart and Bergman and now, she sighed, Wilson and Spencer.

The door emblazoned with the Spencer crest was opened by Cecile wearing a figure enhancing red suit, her hair perfectly coifed, she was beautiful; brittle, and when she saw Lucy, totally infuriated.

Harv snarled, "What the hell are you doing here?"

"Crystal asked me here to meet Lance." Cecile took Harv's arm, Lucy she ignored. "And I had to make reservations for our . . ."

Harv freed himself from Cecile, "I'm not going anywhere with you!" He put his arm around Lucy's waist, "Welcome to my home, sweetheart."

Cecile's smirk sent a shiver down Lucy's spine.

"Lucy, is it?" Cecile said with saccharine sweetness. "That's a lovely dress. It was stylish twenty or so years ago, did you get it at the thrift shop?"

"'Cecile, is it?" Lucy said. "Actually I bought the dress in Paris last month. Unlike you, I wasn't around for the first run."

"Baby doll," Harv said, "The dress heightens your amazing green eyes, but then everything you wear looks great."

Lucy snuggled close in Harv's arms. Cecile's dark eyes narrowed to slits, she gagged audibly, and snarled, "Excuse me, while I puke."

With her nemesis gone Lucy put her purse on a French Empire table with carved griffin legs. "This foyer is amazing."

"Like you," Harv breathed into her hair.

"Family portraits are great, but who has been ostracized?" Lucy asked noting a patch of darker wall paper.

"Harv, my sweet darling is that you?" echoed shrilly from an adjoining room.

"That'd be my mother's dulcet tones," Have whispered. "Sure you're ready for this?"

Lucy nodded, but a glance into the ornate hall mirror sent cold fingers down her spine. She saw Cecile's hate filled face with its promise of vengeance mirrored over and over in the beveled edge.

Clad in a faux leopard miniskirt, tight low cut sweater and snakeskin boots, Crystal with the help of an arsenal of scalpels, implants, and peels, resembled a prepubescent country singer. Two of grandma Wood Warden's less caustic axioms crossed Lucy's mind 'mutton dressed as lamb' and 'cradle robbing hussy.' She stifled a giggle, if Crystal were the kind of woman who appealed to the Senior Spencer, my elegant mother hasn't a chance, and I can stop worrying about being my own grandma.

"Mother, uh, Crystal, Lance this is Lucy Wilson."

Crystal unsuccessfully hid her reaction, but whether to Harv's use of mother or to Lucy was anybody's guess. Lance smiled.

"Wilson," Crystal slurred, "You're not related to Rodney or Charles are you?"

"Yes I am," Lucy said.

Crystal slurred, "Yah, that figures," she gazed blearily at Lance, "Weird bunch of foreigners think their shit don't stink."

"Charles Wilson, my father, was a distinguished gentleman. Uncle Rodney continues the tradition. How unfortunate that you do not approve," Lucy said. Damn. I sound like mom, she thought, and shivered.

"I don't mean nothin' honey. Come here, let me look at you. You remind me of somebody."

"'I'm told I favor my father," Lucy said, "Is this your," she swallowed twice, once to avoid saying boy toy and once more to avoid swallowing her tongue, "husband?"

"He sure is." Crystal waved her glass, "Lanceypoo, pour me another." Lance poured from a huge thermos. Crystal's pinched face reflected thought. "We must'a met before. I never forget a face," she slurred, and emptied her glass.

"Don't let it tax your mini mind Crystal," Harvey Senior drawled. "Lucy bears a striking resemblance to her mother. I'm sure you saw Mrs. Wilson's picture in the paper." He chuckled, "Though that's unlikely as it's a food column, and your knowledge of the kitchen is nebulous at best." He kissed Lucy's cheek. "I apologize for Crystal, she's not known for her tact. Welcome to our home. I trust you enjoyed last evening."

"Thank you." Lucy smiled at Harv who returned her seductive smile, "I had a wonderful time."

"Have you met Lance?" Harvey Senior asked. "Harv has the dubious distinction of having a stepfather several years his junior. Crystal, what does your toddler have in the thermos? Kool-Aid? No, I suppose not," he took the flask, sniffed, and frowned. "Crystal, why are you here in this condition?"

"Is it a bloody crime to want to see my son?" Crystal slurred. "Don't be mad at me, Harvey honey; I thought you might give Lance job." She hugged Lance and covered his blushing cheeks with noisy kisses. "He's very skilled."

"There's no place in my firm for your—husband. How old are you junior?"

"I'm..."

"Don't answer him Lance; it's none of his business."

"You are embarrassing our guest. Stop or get out."

"You're a hard man, Harvey Spencer," Crocodile tears trickled down Crystal's nose and off her chin. She pushed Lance aside, "You can't throw me out of my son's house."

A bell rang, and Harv tugged Lucy toward the dining room. His parents couldn't be civil for five minutes.

Crystal gazed at the table myopically, "Where's Cecile? I asked her to join us."

"She is an employee, I uninvited her."

"She's engaged to my son. That makes her more than your hired help, Spencer lover."

"Crystal, we were never lovers!"

"Mother, Cecile is a non-issue," Harv searched for a subject change, "Dad where's Gran's picture?"

"I sent Mother's portrait out for cleaning."

"Cleaning," Crystal laughed shrilly, "That's the first time the old biddy and cleaning are in the same sentence."

"Shut up, Crystal," Harvey Senior said mechanically.

Harv sighed and tried again, "Is that an original?" Harv pointed to a small oil painting on the sideboard.

"Klinsten says it's genuine but without provenance, the price was right so I bought it on speck. What's your opinion, Lucy?"

Lucy stalled, "I'd have to examine it more closely. The short loaded brush strokes of bright colors in immediate juxtaposition, used by the artist to represent effects and changes in light look right. You said no provenance?" The French Impressionist piece is Uncle Robert's missing painting, or a perfect copy, she thought.

"No provenance, Klinsten said the seller lost it. I bought it because I like it."

"Liking a piece is what's important," Lucy dithered. "The artist, if it's a fake is good enough to fool the experts, and is as talented, if not as creative as the master. But don't quote me."

"Take a guess," Harvey Senior ordered, "is it real or not?

"I don't know," Lucy, now certain it was Uncle Robert's, lied. "You need an expert's opinion."

Crystal listing like a yacht in a gale, sneered, "Lucy, how is your old man?"

"My father died in a boating accident when I was a child Mrs. Spencer."

"Crystal, I warned you," Harvey Senior held the door until Crystal stumbled through. Lance still smiling apologetically followed.

"I'm sorry." Harv whispered, "She always promises to stay sober but she never does."

"I understand," Lucy whispered back.

The slam of the massive front door was followed by Harvey Senior's return and the removal of place settings. "I don't know about you but I need a drink. Lucy?"

Cook entered carrying an enormous tray, "Tea will be fine," Lucy said, Cook beamed.

With the unholy trio, Crystal, Lance, and Cecile gone, father and son relaxed.

"Lucy?" Harv asked. "Don't you like the food?"

"I was thinking about your dad's art purchase," she lied. "The cucumber sandwiches are delicious."

"Try the scones," Spence suggested. "We've strawberry jam and Devonshire cream or maybe you'd prefer the trifle, it's one of cook's best dishes."

"Thank you, Mr. Spencer." He's nervous, Lucy thought, I wonder why.

"Call me Harvey!"

"Yes sir."

"Dad is having a birthday brunch next Saturday, would you like to come?"

"I'd love to. I'm indulging myself with a little longer vacation this year."

"I'm glad," Harv responded. "Lucy, when is your birthday?"

"It's the week after next and I'll be a grand old lady of twenty nine."

"Dad's much, much, much older," Harv teased. "More like fifty hard years and a few easy ones, right dad?"

"We don't need to advertise that fact, do we son?"

"My mom turned fifty this year and it was a major birthday for her. She changed her schedule, and moved back home. She wants to slow down."

"That sounds like a wise thing to do. Maybe I'll follow her example." Spence smiled. "My son could take over the business abroad and I could semi-retire."

Lucy enthused, "Good idea, then I'll ask mom to include you in her taste test dinner parties."

Harvey smiled, "I might run that idea by your mother very slowly if I were you."

"Look at the time," Harv exclaimed, "We have to go, Dad. Lucy has a dinner party with the ladies tonight." And I want us to walk on the beach while I try to explain my weird parents, he thought.

Lucy spent ten minutes thanking cook for the tea and Mr. Spencer for the Saturday invitation.

"Ms. Betty, we were ever so worried about you," Doris blurted her anxious face radiant to see her ally walk free. "I was ever so sad when that cop took you away. The bowlegged man wanted to hear too, but Father Hoyle said he had unclean thoughts and talked to him for ever so long. I tried to hear, but then that other cop said me and Sue had to go with him. He took us to a new hotel and all our stuff was already there." She sat pondering the amazing mystery of the relocated luggage.

"Here's Ellie now," Betty announced, hoping Ellie could unravel Doris' ramblings.

Ellie apologized and said Lucy would be along soon, and wondered how Sue booked the whole room during the busy season.

Sue explained, "I started working for Darcy, she arranged everything. It's great to have friends with pull."

"Valerie and Sue ordered all the food for everybody," Doris said.

"I hope you all don't mind. Darcy recommended the house specialty, and I thought family style would let us talk freely, no servers to interrupt," Sue whispered when the last platter reached the table.

Betty grinned, "Sounds great to me, after the day I've had I'm ready for some quiet,"

Valerie leaned close and whispered in Ellie's ear, "The herbal tea my friend analyzed was poisoned. You were right, it was a plant distillation."

Lucy greeted everyone, awkwardly stowed an unwieldy bundle under her chair, and turned to Val, "What were you saying about the tea?"

"It was poisoned with an extraction derived from Grecian foxglove."

"*He* would have used Robert's work to murder me and blame Ellie, *he* destroyed everything *he* touched," Betty lamented. "I owe a debt to whoever killed *him*."

Lucy heard Betty's soft murmur, she switched places with Ellie, "Aunt Betty, *he* didn't destroy everything. Look," she revealed a cherub's perfect, unblemished smile. "I rescued both your angels and before you get all blubbery, I love that you added daddy's name to Uncle Robert's headstone. I could never thank you enough for that."

She tapped on her glass, "Okay ladies it's time to open the mystery box." She waved her hands in the air over a large box like Houdini over a chained casket, "My friend Vickie sent the answer to all this misery."

Everyone spoke at once, Lucy waited for quiet. "Chocolate," she said, "Caramel, and most importantly, Truffles," she uncovered boxes of Luscious Kiss Candies' chocolate goodies, and for the piece de resistance placed a bag of gleaming caramel popcorn in front of each woman. Doris spotted, 'This bag was prepared especially for Doris' as her name was on the bag and she squealed with delight. Lucy continued, "I told Vickie about our victory dinner, and she wanted to help us celebrate."

Sue was the first to taste; Lucy waited for the reaction she knew would come, "OH MY GOSH, tell me where I can get a lifetime supply of these." Mischievously she declared, "Our man problems are over ladies, these are better than an orgasm." The room resounded with laughter.

Doris laughed with the rest and then said, "Sue, you got a good idea there, but I got a better one. We could put these goodies in the gift shop at Shady Meadows."

"A wonderful idea," Lucy said, "Vickie will be pleased."

Doris grinned happily, "Then all the ladies at the home can have an orgasm just like Sue." Laughter rang.

"Isn't this a good party?" Doris asked excitedly. "Just wait till I tell Delia. She'll be ever so jealous."

"You know what burns my as...uh, backside?" Sue asked rhetorically. "*He* will never be out of our lives! Whenever I get comfortable I check my bank balance, and everything *he* did to us rushes back. Now you say he was gonna murder Betty and plant the blame on you Ellie; and I know for sure we gotta get him. I'm from the west, a length of rope and a big tree is all we need for bastards like him."

Doris whined, "Why do we always have to talk about *him*? You're ruining the party, and making me ever so sad."

"I won't talk about him anymore." Sue promised, "Why don't you tell Ellie how much you enjoyed the chicken pies?"

"I liked them a lot. I want to make them at Shady Acres. Delia and me get to help cook every second Sunday. I know our cook will like them ever so much too."

"What a fine home you have Doris. I'll give you the recipe and some frozen pies to share with your friends. I have lots in the freezer." Ellie was taken aback when the child-like woman's eyes fill with tears.

"It's a really good place. I'm ever so happy there, but I have to go soon. Daddy only paid until January; then I'll be a street lady 'cause my house is gone just like Valerie's and Sue's."

"We won't let that happen to you." Valerie promised. "I'll call Shady Acres management and tell them I'll take over your expenses," she awkwardly patted Doris' quaking shoulders.

"See Sue, I told you *he* wasn't all bad. Look how many friends I have now. And that's all 'cause of him too."

"I'd also like to contribute," Betty said.

"We'd be honored to help, wouldn't we Lucy?"

Lucy agreed wholeheartedly.

Sue excused herself ostensibly to ask that the hot drinks be served, but the tears spilled down her face. Amazed to see the stout hearted woman weep, Ellie followed.

"What's wrong Sue?"

"Ellie, Doris hit the nail smack dab on the head. We are blessed to know all of you, but when Douglas finds out, he'll be back to spoil it. He'll manage to take the money before it reaches Shady Acres. He's like a disease we can't shake."

"Together we'll thwart him. You are no longer alone, and now we have ammunition to fight him, and remember the police want him too."

"I want to believe you, but when I laid it all out and begged the cops for help, they didn't believe me. Only when the cops saw how young and pretty Val is, and how many we were, did they believe us and fall over each other to help." Sue said bitterly. "When there was just me, they treated me like I was too old and too stupid. How could a batty old recovered drug addict be believed?

I kept the books and did the taxes for our business, and for our church, but the cop's saw a menopausal woman, and saw stupid hysterical, and senile. Ya know Ellie, being robbed and abused by Douglas hurts real bad, but when the cops treat ya rotten it hurts worse."

"Dry those tears." Lucy who had been curious, and eaves dropped said, "If not for you three brave women Derwood would be sniffing after his next victim, Aunt Betty dead, and mom in jail. You are all champions. Come back to the party, Jake and Michael are here, and you're going to love what they have to say."

Michael spoke first, "We traced a lot of your funds using Derwood's computer and the papers Lucy found under the Smyth's deck. Jake has taken the liberty of placing Doris' portion in an unbreakable trust that he will administer, if there are no objections."

"I'd like Mrs. Archibald to perform a yearly audit," Jake quietly interjected.

"I'd be happy to," Sue replied and in words Doris would understand told her she didn't have to leave Shady Acres because Michael and Jake found her money and gave it back. She told her Mr. Michael and Mr. Jake would make sure nobody could ever steal her money again.

Doris beamed, "Ms. Betty you were ever so right. God does hear our prayers in church. He even sent the angel of mercy to tell us. The Archangel Michael is the angel of righteousness, satisfaction, and repentance," Doris recited in a practiced singsong. "I never should have forgotten about you," she looked Michael in the eye," But where are your wings?" she asked with an innocence that contradicted her impressive knowledge of angels.

"We never wear them down here," Michael joked before he realized her question was in earnest. His panicked expression brought welcome laughter.

"I see," Doris said solemnly. She turned to Jake, "Are you an angel too?" she asked in her heart rendering child-like manner.

"No, I'm not an angel," Jake said, his voice full of compassion, "I'm just a man who wants to see that you are never hurt again."

"Then God did send you. I know because I asked God to let me stay at Shady Acres and here you are."

Jake cleared his throat and changed the subject while he still maintained a little composure. "Sue, was your husband an oil man?"

"Yes, he was."

"I think I met him years ago, a tall slim fellow called Abner Arnold Archibald as I recall. I'm sort of a collector of old or unusual names, so when I read your husband's name, I recognized it. We've recovered most of the cash generated when Derwood sold off your hard assets and leases. Unfortunately he let everything go at bargain basement prices and I'm sorry to say there's nothing we can do about that."

"I'm just happy I'm not destitute and the bastard is," Sue paused, "I hope," her wary eyes were bright with unshed tears.

"You want a hanky, Sue?" Doris offered a chartreuse handkerchief.

"Ladies," Jake raised his voice over their laughter, "everything we've said tonight must be kept secret. I see no reason to include the authorities; each of you has paid enough. I have papers for each of you to sign to make it all legal. Don't waste your time worrying; because we are smarter than Derwood-Douglas-Dillon-Daniel and he cannot touch your funds."

"You are wonderful," Valerie said. "It's almost too good to be true."

"It's true," Michael assured her.

"I can't believe it. I won't have to sell my home." Betty's smile made the bright overhead lights appear dim.

"Michael, tell her," Lucy ordered.

Betty beamed, "I know already. I found my lovely chest in the back room at the store."

"Aunt Betty, Michael's a genius. He saved most of Uncle Robert's art collection. Tell her Michael!"

"I didn't do it alone. Actually my friend, George was the master mind, and by the way he hates what Derwood did to your house, and wants to help fix your decor. You will love his designs."

Lucy kicked him none too gently.

"Ouch, that hurt. Why can't you wear sneakers like you used to?"

"Tell her everything," Lucy ordered.

Michael sighed heavily, "George uncovered one of Derwood's early thefts. He replaced your genuine pieces with clever reproductions. He's a gifted copyist; and has duped experts, so fooling the *cretin* wasn't a problem. *Derwood* sold the copies cheap, so the buyers got a bargain. We didn't save the French Impressionist piece, but since its sale alerted George to Derwood's thieving, it was worth the sacrifice. George hid your art at his place; he'll hang it for you when you're ready."

Betty embraced the young man who was like a son to her, "Robert would be so proud of you."

Michael cleared his throat, "All the real brains in this room belong to Jake. He cut through Derwood's financial maneuverings like a hot knife through butter. I don't understand most of what *he* did, shell companies, offshore and numbered accounts, currency trading and all sorts of complicated stuff. I'll let Jake explain."

"Thanks, but I've said enough. I'll meet privately with each of you to discuss your funds and address the questions you undoubtedly have."

A loud ominous knocking shattered the joy Jake and Michael's news created. Val trudged to the door and hesitantly opened it.

"Good," Officer Warren of the police fraud division announced, "You're all here, I won't intrude on your party for long. I've been reassigned, but your cases will stay open."

Betty said, "We appreciate your efforts on our behalf, if you have time stay for dessert?"

Sue rolled her eyes, and with massive restraint, held her tongue.

Officer Warren sat next to Jake and when he had Jake's undivided attention closed one eye in a prolonged wink.

Ellie caught the gesture and her respect for the fraud squad skyrocketed. I'll tell Sue. Warren knows the money is recovered, but chooses to ignore it. That might restore her faith in the police a little, and ease her mind.

"Look at the time," Doris announced. "I have to wake up ever so early. Sue is driving me to Shady Acres tomorrow." She whispered, "Sue gets awful lost if I don't read the map for her."

Hugs and promises to stay in touch were exchanged. The women Dreadful Derwood used and abused were happy at last.

"Mom, wake up! Ranker said Hank was stealing Derwood's stuff, Lucy whispered, "Hank can't get in the house so Ranker meant the shed."

Ellie opened one eye, "Of course he did. Hank likes things tidy. Go back to bed honey, you need your sleep."

"Maybe you're right, goodnight Mom."

"Night," Ellie mumbled.

CHAPTER 25

The sun barely peaked over the horizon when Ellie climbed up the stairs.

"Don't squirm Lucy," Ellie ordered. "We are going to talk; you will endeavor to explain how you knew about the bag you so elegantly recovered during the lighthouse dedication."

"Mother, sarcasm is not your *forte*," Lucy mumbled her head buried beneath a mountain of pillows. "Is that Kenyan coffee I smell?"

Ellie shifted from Lucy's legs to the edge of the bed, holding the fragrant mug inches from the hand that groped its way from beneath the blankets. "First we talk, and then if you deserve it, you get coffee."

"Why don't I drink the coffee first? Let's think of caffeine as a lubricant for the gray cells, to jump start my engine, so to speak."

"I'm aware of your need for caffeine, dear."

Lucy groaned, stuffed pillows against the headboard, and made a show of plumping them. "What was the question?"

"The duty free bag, how did you know about that bag and why didn't you tell me?"

Lunging Lucy grabbed the mug, "Ruby said she didn't know what was in it or which deck she tossed it under. I didn't trust her then and I don't now. She knew exactly where it was, but she let me crawl under every spider infested porch in Huron Shores rather than tell me, and mom, there were snakes."

Ellie shuddered, snakes and nightmare synonymous to her. "How did that bag holding the contents of Betty's safe fall into Ruby's hands?"

"It's kind of complicated."

"Lucy!"

"Ruby said Jordan told her he didn't rob the bakery and suggested they get money from Derwood."

"Why would Derwood give Jordan money?"

"Jordan has dirt on him."

"So they visited Derwood, and Ruby somehow got the bag, but why hide it under a porch?"

"She's crafty, she probably saw an opportunity to keep the money and blame Jordan."

"All right," Ellie mused, "knowing Ruby, that's feasible. Now, why don't you explain why you chose Saturday night to retrieve that bag?" Ellie grinned, "And should you ever do it again you'll find a pair of Aunt Emily's pantaloons in her trunk in the attic."

Lucy giggled, "I'll do that next time, but I thought we could grab the bag and get back before anyone knew we'd gone," she gulped coffee and sighed." Is it my fault the Smyth's picked that afternoon to put skirting on their deck? Harv couldn't reach the darn thing; and if Ruby knew Derwood's papers were worth more than the cash, she'd be on it like scum on a frog. I had to get it before Ruby. You understand, don't you?"

"Only too well, now stop dancing around and answer my other question."

"Uh, what question was that?"

Ellie shook her head, "Lucy! Why didn't you tell me?"

"I wanted to protect you and Aunt Betty. I'm sure Jordan killed the health inspector, and burglarized the bakery. Ruby said Jordan raped her; Brad intervened, and that's why Jordan tried to frame Brad. We're fairly certain Jordan ran Zack down too, so we can safely assume he's dangerous."

"Get dressed, I'll wake Betty. She needs to know."

"I don't think so, mom. She's still brittle. Derwood didn't just wreck her life, he did a job on her confidence too."

Ellie smiled wistfully, "She was her old self at the dance. I even liked her football analogies, although I didn't understand a word. Ellie dithered, "I'm not good at keeping things from Betty."

"You know her. She'd have to tell Eric, and what real proof do we have? Ruby's word?" Lucy demanded. "We know that's worthless; Zack says his medicine makes him dopey so that won't wash. We can't mention the duty free bag or Derwood's safe without getting Jake and Michel in trouble. I'm pretty sure they bent some laws to find the cash?" Lucy tucked her blankets under her chin, "I need another day. If I can't find real evidence against Jordan we'll give Eric what we have and let him take it from there."

"I suppose a day won't hurt," Ellie said, "but one day only."

Lucy emptied her cup in one gulp, "Let me tell you about Crystal, she was wearing a mini skirt and cowboy boots."

"Lucy, do not judge people by their attire."

"Ah mom, she makes Harv call her Crystal and she looked like a tricked out cheerleader who took a wrong turn thirty years ago."

The wrong turn she took, Ellie thought; was marrying not one but two lascivious Spencer males. That would warp anyone.

"She has a dangly bellybutton ring with hearts and doves. Oh and she's a dipsomaniac too."

So they drove the poor woman to drink too, why am I not surprised, Ellie thought, but didn't interrupt Lucy's flow.

"She was zonked, zapped, plastered, soused, loaded, three sheets to the wind."

"Lucy!"

"I mean," Lucy said more kindly, "She's an alcoholic. She was a little tipsy when we arrived, and loaded when Mr. Spencer threw her out."

"Harv must have been embarrassed," the mother in Ellie commiserated, but her catty side wanted to know more.

"I almost forgot the best part. She married a boy toy, years younger than Harv. Can't you hear grandma?" Lucy mimicked Gertrude Wood Warden, "Marrying money does not take the trash out of the woman. It simply places her in a doublewide with velour curtains, indoor plumbing, and a car port."

Ellie laughed, took Lucy's cup, and opened the door, "Dad said you spent too much time with mother, I should have listened. Get dressed, we have things to discuss."

Minutes later, Lucy tiptoed down the stairs, left a note by the phone, and scurried out the summer kitchen door. She pushed her bike a block up the street before kicking the engine over. She had things she wanted to do, and being grilled by Ellie wasn't among them. What mom doesn't know can't hurt her. She needed to see Uncle Rodney, the only other person who knew about the glass and bedpost.

"Lucy, what a delightful surprise," Rodney said. "Would you like coffee?"

"That'd be super," Lucy kissed his cheek. Morris, Rodney's omnipotent butler appeared with a coffee pot, and two cups and saucers on a silver server. "Uncle, remember when we talked about the wineglass Derwood used to blackmail you?"

Rodney raised his eyebrows in a how could I forget gesture.

Lucy blurted. "It's gone and so is the bedpost."

"I know, I retrieved your treasures from your lightning blasted tree."

"'You knew? Did you read my letters to daddy?'"

"Yes, we were all concerned about you. I'm sorry we infringed on your privacy, but we..."

"It's okay. I knew as I matured, it was you or Uncle Robert who opened them. It was a comfort to me and a loving thing to do. Now what about the missing evidence?" She sipped delicious coffee and waited.

"I thought it prudent to remove the evidence when the police broadened their search to include the copse."

"Good thinking, but how did you manage it?"

"I should have called you."

"Yeah a call would have saved me a few nightmares, but spill, how did you do it?"

"It was quite simple really. I've been walking Mrs. Wicket's dog since she fell and broke her ankle, poor thing. I took plastic bags to scoop the poop as I always do. I feel it's important to be responsible for the animal's waste, but I digress. I usually walk him in the park, but he needed a longer run and perhaps a small degree of freedom from the leash. He's rather a large animal, an Airedale terrier and..."

"Uncle," Lucy moaned, "the tree, remember?"

"I am getting to that. A young policeman accosted me, but strangely when I shook my bag of dog soil while I boisterously complained of careless dog owners leaving feces for fastidious people to clear away, he lost interest."

"What about the bedpost? It would have stuck out of the bag."

"My dear I cannot take full credit," Rodney laughed, "I tossed that chunk of wood into Fiddler's field; Bowser fetched it, chewed merrily until it was unrecognizable, and ran off down the street with the evidence firmly clamped in his teeth."

Lucy grinned, "I may have underestimated you Uncle, you're not just crafty, you're sneaky too."

"Thank you my dear, lately that seems to be a common error," he pictured Derwood's astounded face glaring at him from the study floor.

"Uncle Rodney, if they don't find evidence in your car, the police could search your house, so what you did with the glass."

"Don't fret, I stuck it in the dishwasher on that sterilizing cycle, and put it with my own goblets."

"And the bedpost?"

Rodney laughed. "It is Bowser's favorite chewy toy and bears little resemblance to its former self."

"Okay, one more question."

"And what might that be?" Rodney asked amused by his niece's seriousness.

"Last week at mom's rabbit stew tasting; did you say Derwood had bandages on his face?"

"Let me think. When I arrived he had the effrontery to offer me a Martini that was actually a Gibson."

"Did you drink it?"

"Need you ask? I drink only with friends."

"Did he drink his?"

"He did."

"So the full glass I broke was yours." Lucy asked, "What about the bandage? Did he have one?"

"Yes, a large, stained bandage high on his forehead and another by his ear, though I don't recall which side. Is it important?"

"No I was just wondering. There is one more thing though."

"Another, one more thing Lucy?"

"Do you remember when we talked before dinner?"

"Yes dear, of course I remember. I may be older, but I'm keeping senility at bay."

"Remember you asked me to promise to tell you if things got serious between Harv and me?"

"Yes," Rodney said uneasily.

"Well they have."

"What exactly do you mean? Have you ah—acted on this seriousness or are you considering acting on it?" he asked uncomfortably.

"Umm, I want—but Harv wants to take things slow, really get to know each other as friends first, so I guess the answer is no."

"You guess, or the answer is no?"

"We haven't done what you mean yet, so no."

Rodney breathed, "I agree with the Spencer boy. Friendship is extremely important and one does not become friends overnight. Sometimes real friendships take years. When are you going back to Europe?"

"Too soon as usual; and Uncle don't worry; I know what I'm doing." Lucy kissed his flushed cheek.

Rodney, his hands shaking, dialed the phone before his slammed front door stopped vibrating.

Ellie navigated the gravel road to the Reservation with care. Visiting Brad's home sparked memories of Brad, blind with grief, struggling to understand how he would survive the death of his entire family. Jeremy, like a knight of old took Brad under his sheltering cloak, arranged funerals, fended off well meaning friends, kept silent vigil with Brad, and then late one night, took him to the bakery where Baker plied him with sweets, and Jake, a stranger to Brad though not to Jeremy engaged the grief stricken youngster in conversation. Later they cried together and Jake offered sanctuary in his home for a night or two and their bond of friendship endured.

Ellie felt sad when she thought of Eloise, Brad's mother. Eloise called to suggest she feature authentic American Indian cooking in her column and she'd been thrilled with the suggestion, as was Lucy, who loved fried bread and fat back.

She and Eloise became friends, Eloise shared the location of a coveted patch of stump mushrooms her Polish mother had called putt-pinkies. Her sudden death left Ellie empty and longing to comfort Brad, Eloise's child.

She parked in Brad's driveway and wound her way toward the bush in back of the house, changed her mind and found the stone pile where Brad kept a spare key. Entering the kitchen she fended off Foster's licks of adoration and washed and put away the breakfast dishes.

Ellie opened the hall door, Foster streaked past to frolic up the stairs. I can't leave the dog loose in the house while Brad's out she rationalized, darting after the animal. "Foster come back here," the dog nosed open a door. This is the room she thought, indulgently rubbing the large animal's head as he climbed onto the neatly made bed. We'll need to help Brad clean up the fingerprint powder. I'll have to ask Eric how we get that stuff off, she peeked into the empty closet; "Come along Foster, there's nothing here, and you aren't allowed upstairs when Brad's away."

Back in the kitchen she filled Foster's kibble dish and water bowl, "How about some mushroom hunting with me?" She led the way along the well worn path to the bush. Foster bounded ahead barking at birds and Ellie wondered why Lucy called him old. She gathered her courage and jumped the storm widened ditch, landed short, and went slip sliding down the greasy bank. Saplings slid through her grasping fingers until her foot lodged against a rotted cedar stump meager inches from the muddy stream. Foster ran back and forth above her whining and barking his concern. "It's all right Foster, only my butt and dignity are hurt." She scrambled up the bank clutching a soiled fabric scrap. She cleared debris to reveal a zippered, bright pink bag, laboriously stitched by an unskilled hand. Ellie gingerly rubbed her backside and wondered if it had once held shoes. In her mind's eye she saw the Health Inspector's photo of Rex and the tiny shoes Betty said were size four. Were they Rita Russell's? Would a fashion conscious woman like Rita use such a bag, and why would her shoe bag be in this ditch? Why not with her body?

Jeremy, drawn by Foster's barks slid to a stop, "Ellie someone reported a strange car at Brad's. I came right over.' He frowned, "Strange place for a mud bath?"

"I do not routinely bathe in the woods," Ellie said. "I did Brad's dishes, and now Foster and I are hunting mushroom."

"They don't grow under water," Jeremy said smiling. "That's a pretty fancy mushroom bag you got there."

"It sort of found me when I slid into the ditch. It might be the health inspector's shoe bag. There's a name by the zipper," Ellie squinted at the tiny embroidered stitches. "I can't read it without my glasses."

"You're right, it's a shoe bag. I know because I'm a great detective, and because it says shoes, right here by Ruby's name." He unzipped the bag. Several crumpled bills fell out. Jeremy caught them before they hit the ground. "Do you know a Ruby Thurston?"

"Yes, I know her."

"Is there more?"

"She works at the bakery." Ellie explained, "Lucy and I helped her change a tire, and found Rita's Russell's wallet in her trunk. Eric questioned and released her. If we believe Ruby, she's not involved in the murder, but if that's Baker's money," Ellie shook her head. "Lucy says Ruby planned the robbery, but she's so young, I can't believe it."

"Kids twelve and under are committing crimes these days, and until someone is caught and convicted Brad is guilty. In this town an Indian is guilty until he proves he's not guilty."

"That's true, perhaps the next generation will change that," Ellie said sadly. "Jeremy, do you want to pick or hold the basket?" she greedily eyed a mushroom laden stump.

"That's woman's work," he teased, "besides I'm on duty. Maybe I should arrest you to justify my trip out here."

"Ah, then you can lead the cooking class, write my column and take flack from Lucy while I lounge in a lovely, quiet cell with three square meals a day." She curtseyed, and held out her hands, "Cuffs please."

"I held onto hope for Lucy and Brad getting together, but I guess that's out now."

"You're right she's smitten with Harv Spencer." Ellie couldn't stop the grimace.

"Too bad, Brad and Lucy are perfect together."

"I agree, but in spite of all their escapades, nothing more than a friendship developed for Lucy."

"Yeah I know. But Brad fell ass over tea kettle for her when they were kids and he hasn't changed."

"I thought they'd marry, which shows how little parents know about their children," Ellie sighed. "By the way Jeremy, was the head over heels reference accurate? I never believed the tale you dreamed up for them and that darn motor bike," She imitated her grandmother's thin shriek, "You young scallywag."

Jeremy was still guffawing when he drove off with Ruby's pink shoe bag.

"Gentlemen, you have been very efficient tonight, you should be proud of yourselves. Look at all those magnificent chicken pies baking in the ovens!" Ellie praised. "That means we have time to make the raisin spice cakes. I see everybody has their ingredients measured and ready, so proceed to the stoves."

Sue appeared, "Lucy said she had an errand to run, I offered to be her stand in."

"Thanks," Ellie whispered and then loudly added, "Sue will be delighted to help anyone who experiences a problem. Put the firmly packed brown sugar in your pot, add the raisins, water, shortening, and spices. When the mixture comes to a boil reduce the heat and maintain a gentle simmer for five minutes, stir occasionally."

Ellie moved from one student to the next, guiding inexperienced hands. "While you are waiting, sift the flour, soda, salt, and baking powder together into your bowl and then scurry back to the stoves to stir."

When the mixtures neared completion, Sue asked, "Will we put the pots into cold water to hurry the cooling?"

"That's a good idea," Ellie said distractedly.

"Is something wrong?" Zack asked his voice pitched low.

"No, I was just wondering where my Lucy went. It's not like her to miss a class or a chance to make time with Harv."

Zack grinned, "I think you mean spend time with Harv."

"Now we will grease and flour the loaf pans. Why do we flour the pan, you all cleverly wonder? The obvious answer is so you can see any spots you may have missed with the grease, but the flour also absorbs excess grease if you grease the pan too heavily. Empty out the extra flour by gently tapping your pan. I meant the outside of your pan, Rodney."

"Everyone is ready to combine their wet and dry mixtures."

"Thanks Sue, let's do that and stir well. Then pour the combined mixture into the pans and pop your cakes into the preheated 350 degree oven for approximately an hour."

"And all done in a timely fashion too," Sue praised the group. "The coffee, sample pies, and cakes are ready. Hurry guys, it's taste and question time."

"That was a great class. These chicken pies are the best I've ever tasted," Brad enthused reaching for another piece. "I wish I hadn't agreed to give Stan my extras."

"Should we ice that spice cake?" Mac asked.

"You can but it's good without," Ellie replied absently, her mind on Lucy. She's up to something, I'm worried.

Zack asked if he could use dried cherries or cranberries instead of raisins, and cinnamon in place of allspice. When Ellie didn't answer Sue said he could, but if he used cherries and cinnamon he would have a different cake. Happy conversation flowed around Ellie while she fretted. Jordan extorted money from Derwood; did *he* open the safe to pay Jordan off? Did they argue, and did Ruby take the opportunity to grab the bag and run? What did Jordan have on Derwood, but more importantly where was Lucy? "Has anyone seen Lucy?"

"I saw her drive by about fifteen minutes ago," Harv said.

"Mrs. Wilson," Brad said, "why don't you go on home and see if she's there. Harv and I will clean up and drop the stuff at your place."

"Thank you Brad, I'll leave you a key in case I'm not there." Ellie's voice trailed away as she scurried down the hall.

Harv yelled, "Wait, you forgot the key!"

"I've got a key," Brad said and at Harv's raised eyebrow added, "I look after the place when she's away."

"I can't believe she doesn't know where Lucy is; I thought they were held together by a mental umbilical cord that transmits Lucy's every move."

"Maybe that's why she's worried." Brad said, thinking of the escapades she hatched and the trouble they got into. Her latest idea to trap Jordan was both dumb and dangerous.

Lucy crouched beneath Ruby's window and fretted. Was the tape recorder well enough hidden? Trust Jordan to be early and the class run late on this of all nights.

Ruby's voice surged through the open window, "You moron, you robbed the bakery, put all the money on Brad's boat, killed the health inspector and to top it all off, you use my car to move her body. And you left her wallet in my trunk!" Ruby stalked about her tiny bed-sitter, "You brainless moron, you're as smart as bear bait. I'm headed for jail while you're covering your ass. If you're smart you'll get lost and stay lost until your father railroads some sap, probably me."

"Hey watch your mouth Ruby; my dad's an honest cop. I didn't do it."

Lucy risked a quick peek. Jordan, his back to the window, hulked over Ruby.

"Yeah right Jordan, you're a moron, and you killed Rita."

"Watch your mouth Ruby, if I killed her, what's to keep me from killing you?"

"Because I'm smart Jordan Platt, I wrote it all down. Starting with you stealing from the old ladies when you *kindly* carried their groceries, then lists the drugs you at sold school. I even wrote how you bragged your stash had police protection. It's all there, how you stole cars for joyrides and wrecked them," Lucy held her breath, this was the big one, "I tell how you killed Derwood and stole the stuff from his safe, and how you murdered Rita Russell, the health inspector, and robbed the bakery. Anything happens to me; it goes to the cops and not town cops either."

Lucy's jaw dropped. How did Jordan pull that stuff and not get caught?

"Ruby," Jordan coaxed.

"I said don't touch me," Ruby spat. "Just tell me how you got rid of Derwood's body?"

"I didn't kill him, I fell over him, and the hunk of wood hit the floor and cracked. He was so scared," Jordan laughed nervously, "he fainted. Honest to God," Jordan crossed his heart, "Derwood was breathing when I left. Ruby, that's the truth."

"Yeah right, that's a good one Jordan, when you tell the truth; we'll need umbrellas 'cause pigs will fly."

"You've gotta believe me. I didn't kill him." The open hand Jordan extended in entreaty, clenched and dropped to his side. "Don't say I robbed the safe! And don't shit me Ruby, you took the stuff."

"I didn't take anything," Ruby lied. "But Baker saw Lucy Wilson at Derwood's that night, I bet she took it."

You rotten, lying tramp, Lucy fumed. You know this tape is going to the police and you accuse me. I should have let you rot in jail.

"Lucy Warden Wilson?" Jordan jeered. "No way! That stuck up bitch didn't do it, you did!" He hulked over Ruby, "You got a lotta guts calling me a liar when you shoot the shit like a pro. Anyhow I'm not lying about killing Derwood." Jordan's voice got soft and husky, "I wouldn't lie to you Ruby, you mean too much to me."

"Jordan you'd lie to God. Cut the crap. Level with me, maybe I can help."

"Maybe?" he sneered. "You will damn well help. You set me up. You knew that bitch would look for the cat. Hell, she paid you to spy for her. Lucky for me I was early or Baker and Jake would've caught me red-handed."

"Never mind that now, tell me what happened so that I don't say anything that'll get you caught."

"You mean get us caught?"

"I mean what I said, stop stalling, how'd you do it."

"Remember Ruby," he shook his fist in her face, "I got experience now, double cross me and I'll kill you,"

"You don't scare me Jordan Platt! I got my book for insurance. You need me healthy, and don't you forget it! Tell me!"

Jordan gloried in the details of Rita Russell's death, described his aborted attempt to frame Brad with Baker's stolen money and his clever disposal of the body in Brad's closet He said Zack saw him put the body in her trunk. He described his ingenious use of Rita's car to bump Zack off. "Get it Ruby? Bump him off," scornful laughter filled the room and like a crazed entity granted independence, flew out the window. "After I waste the gimp, I'll get Ellie Wilson for wrecking my second try, like the gimp would buy all that caring crap."

"Don't be stupid; killing Mrs. Wilson is too risky."

You'll kill my mother over my dead body - or yours, Lucy promised.

Ruby feigned confusion "I still don't get why you tried to frame Brad."

"That was pure genius," Jordan smirked. "Too bad Jake found her, I would have paid money to see the half-breed's face when she fell out of the closet. Did I tell you I almost put her in his bed? I figured that's the only way he'd get a woman there," Jordan laughed raucously.

I'd have jumped into his bed in a heartbeat, if he'd ask me, Ruby thought.

CHAPTER 26

Harv's eyes swept the counters, "I think we're done in here."

Brad agreed, "Looks good to me."

"I'll run the stuff over to Lucy's." Harv checked his Rolex against the school clock, "is dad picking you up here?"

"Yeah," Brad stacked most of the load on his cart, better not overload the city guy, he thought, and led the way. "Man those are fancy wheels."

"Yeah she's a Porsche 911 Turbo, with a displacement of 219.7 cubic inches and she redlines at 6600 rpm. She's got a six speed manual transmission and maxes out at 189 MPH."

Brad looked in the backseat, "Not much room for a baby seat in there."

Harvey Senior pulled up before Harv stopped laughing, "Ready Brad?"

"All ready to go sir."

Harv dropped a box of Ellie's utensils on the ground and jumped in his car. A string of curses followed the dull thunk of a dead battery.

Brad rescued the fallen box, "Don't sweat it man, I'm sure your dad has jumper cables."

"You don't understand," Harv yelled slamming the car door. He shoved his cell phone under Brad's nose. "Lucy needs me."

Brad hurled the box and himself into Spencer Senior's backseat Harv leapt into the front.

"Drive, Dad!"

Brad sighed and gave directions. "She's at Ruby Thurston's place, trapping the killer."

Ellie crept over uneven ground; and crouched next to Lucy. Lucy took her mother's shaking finger from under her nose and placed on Ellie's lips then pointed it to the window. Together they watched the farce unfold.

"What about the money?" Ruby demanded. "Did you leave all of it on Brad's boat? That was stupid Jordan, you should a kept some of it."

"Who says I didn't?"

"Are you admitting you kept some of the bakery money Jordan Platt?"

"I might have kept a few bucks."

"Yeah, that's what I figured. Even you aren't stupid enough to throw it all away. Where'd you hide it?"

Jordan shook his fist in Ruby's face, "Listen bitch, that better be the last time you call me stupid." His pacing brought him close to the window, Lucy and Ellie ducked low and held their breath. "I've done all the talking, now you're gonna tell me where you hid Derwood's stuff. Don't try the innocent act on me," he snarled. "Where's the cash you took from the safe?" He thrust his face into hers, "If I go down Ruby you'll be coming with me, and speaking of going down," he leered and reached for her, "how about it?"

Ruby leapt away, his groping hand whacked the dresser, dislodging the diary and exposing the tape recorder. Jordan lunged for the book; Ruby snatched it out of his groping hand.

"You can read it later. Take it with you, I've outgrown it. By the way," she backed out of his reach, "I threw the bag under the Smyth's deck. Where'd you put the bakery take?"

"Let's just say it's under daddy's protection."

Ellie shifted to rub a knotted muscle in her calf.

"What the hell was that?" Jordan snarled.

"What's the matter? You got nerve problems?" Ruby casually tossed a sweater over the tape recorder.

"You sneaky bitch, you're taping me." Jordan tossed the sweater aside, and flung the machine onto the floor. Jordan's powerful hands closed around Ruby's throat.

"Damn," Lucy swore and grabbed Ellie's cardigan. "Wait mom, he's too strong for us."

Ellie crashed through the door, propelled herself onto Jordan's broad back, her blunt nails raked his contorted face. "Let her go," Ellie gasped.

Jordan shrugged and shook trying to rid himself of Ellie without releasing Ruby. Ruby's hands clawed ineffectually at the fingers crushing her slender neck. Jordan dashed Ruby from side to side like a pit bull mauling a Pekinese.

Lucy launched herself into the melee, bending back Jordan's fingers, breaking his hold.

"Let her go," Ellie screeched.

"You asked for it, bitch," Jordan roared flinging Ruby aside. He grabbed a handful of Ellie's hair.

"Leave my mother alone," Lucy screamed and kicked Jordan in the groin, her rigid fingers jabbed at his eyes.

Ellie bared her teeth like a vixen in defense of her kid and she sank them into Jordan's neck.

Jordan snarled and grabbed Lucy's blouse. He dragged her along as he lurched backward into the wall. Ellie's head impacted the wall with a stomach-turning crunch; she slid off Jordan's back.

Though she knew she couldn't win against Jordan; the sound of Ellie's head hitting the wall gave Lucy the impetus to try.

"What's going on here?" Harv bellowed, and charged through the open door just as Jordan's fist met Lucy's right eye. She fell, Harv stepped over her and rushed Jordan, he punched and kept pummeling until Jordan dropped.

Brad took Lucy into his arms, planted a kiss on her swelling eye, and yelled, "I told you, you can't let a guy get close, we practiced. How the hell could you forget and why the hell didn't you call me?"

"I think you have something that belongs to me," Harv growled. "Lucy baby, are you okay?"

"I almost had him," Lucy mumbled cautiously shaking her head to clear her vision.

Harvey Senior knelt over Ellie who opened her eyes and smiled before she remembered and struggled to rise. "Lucy?"

"She's fine. Stay still, you always had more guts than brains," Harvey Senior murmured. Her courage dredged up memories he didn't want unearthed. "Brad, find something to tie that fool up," he ordered jerking his head at Jordan.

"Use these," Ruby rasped, proffering several black stockings.

Brad knotted the nylons around the wrists and ankles of the police chief's only child. "Are you all right Ruby?"

"I think so," Ruby whispered.

"Mom!" Lucy called scrambling from the safety of Harv's arms to brusquely push the Senior Spencer away. "Mom, oh God Mom, your head is bleeding. We have to get you to the hospital."

"Nonsense," Ellie protested. "An ice pack is all I need, just help me up."

"Lean on me," Harvey Senior ordered.

"Sit down Lucy," Harv urged. "You're going to have quite a shiner."

Harvey Senior tightened his arms around Ellie, "Lucy is in good hands, but she's right, you need a hospital. Head wounds are nothing to fool with."

"I'm fine," Ellie insisted though she was forced to lean heavily on Spence.

Jordan seized his opportunity, and with bound hands grabbed the damning evidence.

"Stop him," Lucy screamed.

Harvey Senior wrenched the tape from Jordan's grasp. "No you don't lad, the ladies seem to think this is important."

"Ladies?" Jordan sneered. "Ain't no ladies here, just two bitches and a whore."

"That was an inappropriate thing to say young man." Harvey Senior jerked Jordan Platt to his feet to deliver a punitive slap, but Ruby stepped between them and with anger behind her fist delivered the knockout punch. "Not sporting, but necessary I think." Spence said, a broad satisfied smile crept across his face. "I'll call the big guys. Jordan's father shouldn't have to deal with this mess."

"We need to copy the tape first. Harv and I can go to our place to copy it," Lucy said.

"No dear, you always have a problem with mother's antiquated machine, I'll do it. Brad will drive."

"Let's leave all the young muscle in place," Harvey Senior said. "I'll take you home Ellie."

Tape in hand, Ellie walked unsteadily toward her car leaving the Senior Spencer to trail along behind.

"Mom, please let Mr. Spencer drive."

Ellie whirled to defend her driving abilities, stumbled, and only Harvey Senior's protective arm kept her upright. "Perhaps a little vertigo," she said. "Thank you Mr. Spencer, I am fine. Lucy, please loosen Jordan's bonds, his extremities have turned purple. We want him in good health when the police arrive."

"I'll take care of that," Brad offered, "just as soon as you're in Mr. Spencer's car."

"I am perfectly capable of walking on my own," Ellie insisted though she held tight to Harvey Senior's arm.

"Ellie, you are a foolish woman! You'd risk further injury rather than accept my help."

"Yes, I believe I would," Ellie spat.

Shaking his head, Harvey held the door to his Mercedes, and let her enter unaided. He slid behind the wheel and with an uncharacteristic show of temper, slammed the door. "You were a lot of things Ellie Warden," he allowed catching her eye, "but until now you were never a fool."

"A fool accurately describes the Ellie Warden you knew, but she is gone, you see Mrs. Charles Wilson."

"Your husband is long dead, Ellie."

"I loved Charles with every fiber of my being and I still do. For me his death happened yesterday."

A conversation stopper if ever there was one, Harvey reckoned lapsing into a silence that lasted for the duration of the drive.

"Wait, I'll help you out," Harvey ordered pulling up as close to the Warden front door as possible.

Ellie ignored his outstretched hand and stiffly marched up the walkway rifling through her purse for the house key.

"Your door's open," Harvey noted.

Ellie's vision blurred; she misjudged the height of her familiar stoop, and stumbled. Spence swept her into his arms, and carried her to the gaudy flowered sofa. "I've had enough of your phony reassurances," he snapped. "Stay put while I check the house for intruders."

'That's not necessary, I'm sure I left the door open when I went to rescue Lucy."

"Fine, then I'll get something to clean that cut. Don't move."

The pounding in her head eased, Ellie dosed. She awoke to Harvey gently cleansing her wounded head.

"Where do you keep the antiseptic cream?" he asked his face too close to hers for her comfort. She pointed up the stairs.

Black clouds appeared over her mother portrait when Harvey Senior's foot hit the first step. I'm sorry mother, he won't be here long, I promised. She climbed the stairs to find out why Spencer was taking so long.

"What are you doing in my bedroom?"

"I told you I was going to check the house for intruders."

"Mr. Spencer," Ellie haughtily began, but was interrupted by a loud crash from the foyer.

"Wait here, I'll check that out," Harvey Senior commanded descending the steps two at a time. "Someone tried to steal a painting," he called to Ellie who held tight to the banister. "He must have dropped it in his haste. I'll rehang it." Ellie watched the hall light flicker flash, and explode.

"Power surges," Harvey said. "We get them all the time." He climbed the stairs, "Tell me where you keep your first aid kit and lie down on the bed."

Another loud crash issued from the lower floor. "What the hell? Stay here. Don't argue. This time I'll search the house from top to bottom."

Ellie winced and sat up. "I am not helpless, Mr. Spencer. I can take care of myself."

"Call me Spence. You always called me Spence," he urged, his voice seductive. Tender but firm hands caught her wrists. Harvey pressed her down on the bed, his hard body restraining hers. Eyes soft, he brushed a kiss across her lips.

"Oh gosh, I'm so sorry," blushing vividly Betty hastily backed out of Ellie's bedroom.

"Betty, come back! Mr. Spencer was tending my wound," Ellie struggled out from under Harvey.

"What happened to your head?" Betty demanded advancing on the Senior Spencer with the baseball bat she'd liberated from the umbrella stand in the hall when she saw the open door.

"Mr. Spencer arrived just in time to keep Jordan Platt from killing us," Ellie said. "Betty, stop poking Mr. Spencer with that thing."

Betty stopped poking, but held the bat ready. "Maybe you'd better start at the beginning."

"Do you mind if I get the Neosporin to treat her wound?" Harvey edged nervously past Betty.

Betty lowered the club, "Of course not."

"Spill it, girl" Betty said leaning on the bat, "Why was that man in your bed? How did you get hurt, and why are your mother and Aunt Emily's portraits on the hall floor?"

Ellie laughed until tears ran down her cheeks.

"She's hysterical," Spencer said. "She needs medical attention but she's too stubborn to listen to me. Help me get her into my car or should I have the doctor come here?"

Ellie mopped her face, "Betty please make two copies of the tape on the coffee table. You'll want a copy too, won't you Spence?"

Spence, Betty thought and wondered at the affectionate soubriquet. "Ellie honey, I'm not good at that sort of thing and I shouldn't leave you alone."

"I'll be fine, Betty. Just copy the tapes."

"You'll have a dandy lump Ellie, but the cut's shallow." They heard curses from the living room, "Sounds like Miss Betty needs help."

"She knows antiques and all about football." Ellie moved the baseball bat, "and she's added baseball to her repertoire, but electronics elude her." She stood; Spence steadied her, "Hurry before she breaks something."

Ellie labeled the tapes 'Jordan Platt's confession', firmly closed and locked the door, and with Betty climbed into the rear seat of Harvey Senior's car.

Harvey muttered under his breath. "Fifteen minutes ago I was Spence, and now I'm driving Miss Daisy."

"So you remembered you work here," Baker said sardonically when Jake took his stargazing seat on the bakery porch.

"Sorry, boss man," Jake tried to look repentant, but couldn't repress a broad grin.

"You look like Rex when he puts a dead mouse in my shoe. What have you been up to?"

"I've been working for a just cause. You'll agree when I explain."

"I'll be the judge of that. I should fire your sorry hide and I would too, if you didn't work cheap."

Jake ignored him, "Where do you suppose Derwood Day went and why did he go?"

Baker gave his answer some thought; Jake didn't ask frivolous questions. "Well," Baker grinned, "If I'd bigamously married four women and they came after me together, I'd get the hell out of Dodge." His grin was replaced by anger, "Rumor has it the bastard emptied Betty's bank accounts and sold everything of value. Her house is grossly under priced; Betty screwed that plan by coming home. Ranker likely told him the cops are looking for him. Why are you interested?"

"Baker, what I'm going to say is in confidence." Jake shifted uncomfortably, "It's not my story to tell, but I need a new perspective and I respect you," Jake paused, raked a hand through his thinning hair, and chose his words carefully.

Baker said, "Anything you tell me goes no farther. Spit it out. What's bothering you?"

"It's the money that bothers me. Doris' father sold his land to the government for a research station. He invested wisely and was always ahead of the pack consequently he left Doris a rich woman. I'm sure you've heard Doris is not, uh, academically inclined. Her father protected her inheritance well." Jake scowled, "It took Derwood nearly three years to break the trust and steal her millions. He sold the rest home her father bought for her, and dissolved a trust fund I would have sworn was unbreakable."

Baker refilled their coffee cups. "I didn't know Derwood was that smart. How did he manage it?"

"Thanks," Jake sipped absently, "I don't know, and it bothers me that I don't. He stripped Sue of every penny, every building, and every asset with little effort. A damn shame if ever there was one." He slapped the porch rail hard enough to rattle the cups, "But Valerie's the victim that effects me most, other than Betty of course," he said when Baker bristled. "The reason Valerie's victimization angers me is, her father started with nothing. He married above his station and was despised by his wife's family. He worked twenty-four/seven to build his business. Derwood enters the picture and Valerie's father unexpectedly dies leaving a girl ready for the picking." Jake poked his stubby finger at Baker, "Didn't Robert Archer die unexpectedly just after Derwood showed up?"

Baker's coffee cup stalled halfway to his lips, "Yeah, now that you mention it, he did."

Jake said, "Derwood kept a record of every transaction over the last fifteen years. Large or small he recorded them all." Jake laughed, "All those records were in the bag Lucy exposed her shapely assets to retrieve the other night"

Baker snarled, "The stupid bugger."

"Michael and I used his records to trace, recover, and return much of the money to the wives."

"That's great, but why didn't Derwood close those accounts when his records disappeared?"

"That's what bothers me," Jake said, "Either we didn't get it all or Derwood is dead, and if he is dead, who killed him, and where's the body?" Jake waited while Baker thought it out.

Baker spoke slowly, "You're right; he's dead, but the thing that boggles my mind is if he got millions from first wife, Doris, without danger to himself, why didn't he stop there? Doris couldn't go after him."

"Maybe he enjoyed the game more than the money, or it was the power to hurt and dominate women he craved."

"You must be right. The way he treated the women makes my blood boil. He's one contemptible bastard and if he's dead, good." Baker's teeth shone in the moonlight, "I say we keep this to ourselves."

"If he is dead I agree, but if he's exploiting another woman, do we have the right to keep silent?"

"The cops are searching for him. Let's let them do their job and we'll do ours."

"What do you see as our job?"

"As I see it, we protect those we care for or those that can't take care of themselves to the best of our abilities, that's pretty much what you and Michael did." Baker's dentures gleamed, "One more thing Jake, you strung more twenty-five dollar words together tonight than I've heard from you before. Don't let it happen again, I'm the talker, you're the listener, understand?"

Sirens wailed; Jake and Baker peered into the darkness.

Jake mulled over Baker's words, found them sensible and said, "Nice evening for a raid, but it's not our business. Hop to it Baker, doughnuts don't cook themselves."

"Mom what kept you? Brad was worried."

"That was very kind of you Brad, but with Betty's baseball bat expertise, I was well protected," she smiled mysteriously. "Mr. Spencer has notified the police and I believe that is a cruiser," Ellie clamped her hands over her ears.

"Eric," Betty gasped, "what are you doing here?"

"I am doing my damn job!" Eric Platt said for her ears only, "Jordan is my son, I have to be here," he walked slowly in Ruby's small room.

"Dad, did you call a lawyer?" Jordan whimpered. "Don't believe these liars. I didn't kill anybody. Make them untie me, my fingers hurt."

"This has been taken out of your father's hands," a police officer announced from the doorway. "You have the right to remain silent and refuse to answer questions. Do you understand?" the officer asked. "Anything you do or say can be used against you in a court of law. Do you understand? You have the right to consult an attorney before speaking," he continued reading the Miranda Rights from a small card while his fellow officer removed the stocking bindings and replaced them with shiny handcuffs.

"You know me, Dad. You know I wouldn't hurt anybody. These people are out to get me. Don't believe them; you know they'd do anything to make a cop's kid look bad."

"Get up Jordan, and for once in your sorry life act like a man," Eric ordered, profound sadness permeated his voice.

"Go home Eric. I'll take care of your boy."

"Thanks Ben," Eric said and watched the arresting officer close the cruiser door on his son.

Then he dropped heavily into the room's lone chair.

"The restorer did a great job cleaning Gran's portrait," Harv said having finally cornered his father. "What do you think of Lucy? She's perfect isn't she? This time it's the real thing."

"I'm glad to hear it, but I remember you saying similar things about several other women."

"I've grown up, dad. I did not know I could feel this way about a woman, but Lucy changed all that. What do you think of her?"

"She's perfect. She has class, poise and a fierce loyalty to those she loves, and she's beautiful even with the black eye. She's the kind of girl I'd have recommended if you'd ever asked my opinion, but if you marry her you get Ellie Wilson for your mother-in-law. You saw how devoted they are, and then there's good old Uncle Rodney who hates our guts."

"I don't think Mr. Wilson hates me anymore. He's very congenial at the cooking classes, and Lucy's mom says I'm her star pupil. I could take over cook's duties."

"We better talk about that," Harvey said his eyes straying to the contracts on his desk.

Harv turned the papers over. "Talk to me dad. Whatever that is will wait."

"Where did you get that ring?"

"Lucy gave it to me. I know she loves me because this ring is precious to her. It belonged to her father."

"Did it now?" Harvey drawled eyes locked on the restored portrait.

"Is something wrong dad?"

"No, I was just thinking about that the deal in the United Arab Emirates it's heating up and will require your immediate attention."

Lucy threw back the covers and flew down the hall. "Mom, are you awake?"

Ellie opened one eye, "I'm always awake at 3 o'clock in the morning. What's wrong?"

"Why was Hank cleaning Uncle Robert's shed?"

"Honey, you know I love you, but I'm not up to guessing games at 3 am."

"Mom," Lucy shook Ellie, "stay awake! Hank said he only worked when Derwood wasn't home. Hank knows Derwood's dead."

"Hank probably thinks *he's* running from the wives." Ellie yawned, "Why don't we talk in the morning."

Lucy climbed into her bed ready for sleep. But Hank's reaction when he'd seen her at Betty's puzzled her and kept her awake. He'd spoken to her like a stranger, when in fact he'd been her impromptu biology teacher and a lifelong friend. Why?

CHAPTER 27

"Don't sit down," he ordered.

She said insolently, "You won't fire me! I know where the bodies are buried."

He ignored her insolence, "You will fly to the U.A.E tonight. Accommodation is arranged. Harv will arrive tomorrow. You will keep my son in the Middle East and away from the Wilson girl. Do whatever it takes. Do you understand?"

"Yeah, I understand alright," she sneered."

"No one is to be damaged physically, do I make myself clear?"

"That might not be possible."

"Do it! If you can't I'll hire someone who can."

"I didn't say I couldn't, I said it might be risky."

He handed her a bulky envelope.

She tore it open and thumbed through banded bills. "I'll do it."

"You will keep my name out of it. You will report to me each day at seven a.m. my time. Have I made myself clear?"

"Crystal clear," she smirked. "I do the dirty work while you, as usual, stay clean."

He ignored her comment, "The money is a partial payment. You get an equal amount when you complete the job." He sneered, "Not what you earned in your former profession, but you get to keep your clothes on."

"I was never a prostitute!"

His burst of cruel laughter overrode her denial "Escort or hooker, same service." He turned his chair to the window. "Get out."

She slammed the door behind her, and Harvey Spencer Senior, captain of industry, master of all he surveyed, put his head down on his shiny, mahogany desk and wept.

CHAPTER 28

Nearing Eric's home Ellie's footsteps faltered. What could she say to him? Gee Eric, I know I helped trap your son but I'm really sorry, and here to cheer you up.

"Ellie, slow down," Betty gasped, "Lucy will meet you at the cooking class. Remember when Rex and Foster tried to attack Jordan at the bakery?"

Ellie nodded.

"Well when Lucy untied Jordan last night," Betty giggled, "that sounds kinky, anyway his jeans slipped up and he has cat scratches on both legs."

"Well that clears another loose end, Rex saw Jordan kill Rita, Foster smelled Jordan when he put Rita's body in Brad's closet. That's what they tried to tell us. Or am I anthropomorphizing the animal's actions? "

Betty grimaced, "I don't know, but since neither animal can testify in court, it's a moot point."

"I agree, but it is another piece of the puzzle neatly in place. Betty, you know we're stalling."

"I know. It might be easier if we visit separately." Betty disappeared around the corner, "I'll be on the back porch if you need me."

Coward, Ellie thought, her finger over the bell, but before she touched it the door opened and Eric, unshaven and haggard, slumped against the frame.

Ellie thrust the raisin spice cake at him. "I'll understand if you throw me off your porch."

"Yeah and sue me tomorrow," Eric said with the ghost of a smile. "Come in and say what you came to say, then go away."

"I've come to apologize and say how sorry I am for everything. I . . .
."

"Hell, Ellie, none of it's your fault! If I'd been a better father, Jordan wouldn't . . . but I can't go back. The job always came first, but dammit Ellie, I needed the job."

She longed to comfort him as he'd comforted her twenty years ago when she'd lost Charles. "Eric we each work with what we have that day. You have always been a loving father."

"I ignored all the signs, Ellie." Eric's fist hit the wall, "For the love of God, he hid the damn drugs right under my nose. How the hell could I have been so blind?"

"Eric, we all want to believe in our children."

"After his mother left and I caught him lying, I didn't call him on it. I knew he was stealing, but I didn't want to make waves. All those experts said to give him space, respect his privacy. I blew it Ellie, and the boy pays the price."

"You've made mistakes, we all have, but Jordan is an adult, and he's responsible for his actions; not you. I'll make coffee, you soak your hand. Hitting a wall may be therapeutic, but it hurts." Ellie scrounged for iodine, "Jordan is the same age you were when you joined the force. Think Eric, you gave him opportunities you never had, is that so bad?"

He took the cup of coffee she offered, "I'll move. I'll never live this down."

"Eric your friends will stand with you, and who cares about the rest!"

Betty's long pink nails scraped the window frame, her face pressed against the glass she signaled frantic warnings and sank out of sight.

The doorbell jangled raucously, moments later Eric's ex-wife's noxious presence filled the room.

"So this is why you didn't have time to keep my son out of trouble!" she spat. "You're busy entertaining your floozy. A fine example you set for my son," she loomed over Eric like an impending avalanche.

His voice dead, Eric said, "Get out, Babs. Take your foul mouth and get out."

"Where is my son?" she screamed. "Where is Jordan?"

"He's in jail."

"I knew you'd desert him," she reached across the table and slapped Eric's face.

Ellie grasped Bab's upraised arm and twisted it behind her back. Barbara screeched. "I'll break the damn thing off and beat you to death with the bloody stump if you touch him again."

Shaking her fist in Ellie's face, Babs shrieked, "Get your paws off me Ellie Wilson, what the hell right do you have to threaten me? If he wasn't messing around with you he'd have time for our son."

Betty stalked into the kitchen brandishing a corn broom, "I'm here Ellie, stand aside, let me at the witch."

"Thank you Betty, but I have this under control!" Ellie clasped Bab's upraised fist, tucked her right foot behind Babs left knee, and shoved. Babs hit the floor screaming. Ellie said calmly, "I warned you."

"My husband and I need to discuss our son. You take that witch," Babs jabbed her hooked talon at Betty, "and ride out on that broom she rode in on."

Ellie's mouth ran off with her brain, "The problem with your son is you. You flaunted one party boy after another in Eric's face, but he tolerated your behavior for the child's sake. Then you ran off with a snake oil salesman, abandoning that child you profess to love. You're a predator; you mistake decency for weakness, and while I loathe violence," Ellie paused for breath," I'll make an exception for you."

Eric dragged himself from his chair, effortlessly pulled Babs upright, bundled the screeching harridan to the front door, and thrust her out.

"Your son's at the county jail. Get off my property." The tinkle of breaking glass, the only sign of the anger he'd held bottled inside all those years. "I should have done that long ago. Maybe if I'd stood up to her, things would have been different"

"I'll clean up the glass," Betty shook her borrowed broom and fled.

"When did Betty get here?"

"She was on the porch trying to figure out how to approach you. I'll send her in and then get out of your way," Ellie strolled to the veranda, plucked the improvised weapon from her hand, and pushed Betty inside.

Eric waited inside the door, "I saw Babs hit you," Betty babbled against his chest. "Oh Eric, I'm so sorry, I had no idea what you endured."

"Why are you apologizing for something I should have stopped years ago?" Eric listened to footsteps on the well traveled porch. "Betts see who that is and get rid of them."

Betty caught the large hand reaching past the broken pane. "Stop! You'll cut yourself," she opened the door to Baker, flanked by Jake, and Rodney. "Sorry guys he doesn't want to see anybody."

"That's just too damn bad, because we want to see him," Baker pushed past her, a bottle of Scotch and a donut box in hand. Jake balanced a pizza and rum bottle while Rodney followed with pate', crackers, a cocktail shaker and several bottles of booze. "Brad's bringing the beer and pretzels, you know, healthy stuff to fill out the menu."

Betty made a production out of examining her wristwatch, "It's not even ten o'clock."

"Time waits for no man," Baker said puffing out his chest. "What Eric needs is a good bender and some guys around to share it. I don't want to hurt you feelings Betty, but when big trouble hits a guy he needs other guys, not dames."

Betty giggled and collected her purse, "Okay, but you all better be at Ellie's class tonight, and you'd better be sober."

Eric held Betty tight, "Thanks for coming Betts, I know how hard this was for you." He closed the door, turned to Baker, and with the shadow of a smile asked, "You guys sure you want to be seen with the outcast?"

"Yeah, and we brought good stuff," Baker watched Rodney fill the cocktail shaker and frowned, "Not real familiar with guy bonding rituals are you Rodney? No mixed drinks! You can add a little water to the Scotch, but that's all the mixing allowed."

Rodney stuck his nose in the air, "You bond your way Baker, and I'll bond mine." Everybody laughed a little too loud, and a little too long.

The bell rang; it was Brad with the pretzels and beer. The menu was complete.

After several drinks talk inevitably turned to Jordan.

Eric said, "They reviewed that tape. Jordan says killing Ms. Russell was an accident. He admits to taking your money Baker, but he denies offing Derwood. Ruby says he did, but I'm inclined to believe his story . . . what the hell am I saying? I don't know if Derwood ran because Jordan blackmailed him or not." Eric held his head in his hands to hide the tears.

"Nobody gives a damn about Derwood," Baker said dismissively. "In fact you should have heard Lucy put Ranker in his place when he yapped on about Derwood. If I hadn't been looking at her I'd have thought she was her mother." Baker hooted until his sides ached and his laughter proved to be contagious.

Brad handed Eric a stiff drink and talked about fishing.

Dressed in a scanty French bikini, obviously not chosen by her mother, Lucy decided to catch some sun and sketch. She donned cutoffs and a T-shirt over the swimsuit, don't want to shock the locals, and ignored Ellie's note. The lecture she deserved could wait. Maybe she was careless. Maybe she could have done things differently, but it worked and Jordan's in jail where he belongs.

Lucy locked the door; just a couple of short stops, and then sand and sun. She headed for Main Street and her aunt's shop. "Mikey, can you write a check?"

"Of course I can and I bet you can too, kid. All that expensive schooling wasn't wasted on you."

"Michael, don't be an ass." Lucy curtseyed, "Would you please write a check for Hank Parker, Aunt Betty's gardener? I'll take it to him."

"He usually picks it up, but if you're running a delivery service," he gave her a sealed envelope.

Certain she'd reached the wrong address; Lucy parked her bike on the gravel shoulder beside a neat split rail fence. In place of the dilapidated hovel she'd expected was a snug log cabin surrounded by gardens resplendent with flowers and vegetables that would turn Ellie green with envy. Intermingled sweet fragrances and brilliant, riotous colors made her wish she'd brought an easel and canvas rather than a sketchbook and charcoal. Hank Parker smiled and beckoned her in.

"Good morning Mr. Parker, I've brought your paycheck."

"Girl, you been calling me Hank for nigh onto twenty five years. Why'd you wanna to call me Mister now?" Hank's grin split his face from ear to ear, "Still wanna look behind me for my pappy when a body says Mr. Parker. Sit awhile, I'll make herb tea, knows all you ladies like tea. Don't take tea myself, like coffee fine."

"I'm a coffee drinker too," Lucy said quickly.

"Coffee it is then," Hank shuffled off to the kitchen.

The interior of Hank's house was wonderful, floor to ceiling bookcases filled to capacity, covered every square inch of wall. Next to the bow window stood an ancient, roll top desk and beside that a state of the art computer, on a Stickley Brothers mission library table. Dozens of black notebooks, like those Uncle Robert used covered every work surface. Lucy recognized Robert's unique hand writing, the margins were annotated in a much more fluid writing style. She replaced the book and stroked the fine polished desk.

"Likes my desk, does you? She's a beauty alright. Mr. Robert give her to me."

"She is beautiful. If you ever decide to part with her, I'll give her a good home."

"Might write you in my will; be good to know somebody'll give her love like I do."

"I couldn't help noticing your books. Were some of them Uncle Robert's?"

"Yeah, that no-good bugger Derwood, throwed them in the trash. I got them afore the garbage man."

"Lucky you did. I know you and Uncle Robert worked together. Are you continuing the foxglove experiments?" Lucy eased toward the reason for her visit.

"Yup and I almost got it. I'm fixing to present the flower at that fancy, highfalutin' flower breeders do next year. I'm set on calling it the Miss Betty. Drink your coffee."

"Hank, why did you decide to clean the shed?"

"It were messy, the numbskull cut all Mr. Robert's foxglove, strung them up on the ceiling. Weren't no call for it neither. Would a made Ms. Betty sad; got rid of them, didn't I now?"

"But how did you know Derwood wouldn't stop you?"

"I seen him dead, didn't I? Don't know where he got to, but he didn't move hisself. I knows dead when I sees it. Dimwit ain't gonna be beating on no more ladies. Whoever done him, done good." His left eye closed slowly and slyly.

"But why did you check on him?"

"I heard all that yelling, didn't I now?" his left eyelid dipped again. "Then a girl comes a running out of there like her tails afire. And holding herself like she hurt, but I expect you knows that. I kept an eye and listened real hard afore I went on in. There the sinner was alaying there stone cold dead he was."

"Was the woman alone? Did you recognize her?"

"She was all by her lonesome. If I knows her, I ain't saying." The eyelid came down again. "She done the town a favor. I ain't one to get a good gal trouble. Ain't nobody gonna think she done it, and I ain't never gonna tell nobody nothin'. Don't be getting all bothered 'bout that. I ain't talkin' to nobody," with that Hank blessed Lucy with another long conspiratorial wink.

Preoccupied by Hank's story and his many secretive winks, Lucy asked, "May I tell Aunt Betty you're carrying on Uncle Robert's work with the foxglove? I know she'll be thrilled."

A blush colored sun lined cheeks, "I reckon that'd be just fine."

"I don't want to keep you. Thanks for the coffee."

"You a running off already?"

"I want to do some sketching on the beach while I'm here."

"Saw you looking at my garden," Hank said leading the way out. "Mr. Robert said you was a fine painter. Ya'll come back anytime, paint the flowers if you wanna."

"I'd love that, your yard is fantastic."

"Remember that bugger ain't worth worryin' about, aint nobody gonna hear nothin' from me."

Her mind racing faster than her bike, Lucy worked to unravel Hanks convoluted conversation. There were all those enigmatic winks, weren't there now, she thought with a giggle. Hank thinks I killed Derwood and while I almost wish I had, I didn't, so who did? She cut through the woods, skidded to a stop, dropped the junction plate, made sure the kickstand landed on it, and ran to enjoy the sandy shore.

The secluded spot she loved was empty. Lucy spread her towel, dumped her pack and sketchbook on top, dropped her shorts and T shirt, and ran into the water. What I need is some real R&R, she thought, wading ashore. "And would that be rock and roll, rest and recuperation, rest and relaxation or rest and recreation?" she asked the seagulls circling overhead. "What do you think guys? Rest and recreation, you say? You're clever birds." She reached for her cell phone, hit redial and waited.

"Harv I'm sketching and need a model, are you available?"

"Sure baby. I'm on my way. Want me to pick you up?"

"No, I'm at the beach where we were the night of the lighthouse dedication. You remember, don't you?"

"Like I could ever forget, I'll be with you in fifteen minutes." Harv shoved aside the papers he'd been reviewing. "Dad, I'm going out."

"Have you finished with those contracts?"

"They'll wait. I'm on holiday and there's only so much sunshine."

"You've been working on this deal for over a year; why the sudden cavalier attitude?"

"I'm going to spend what's left of my vacation on the beach with Lucy."

"I need you in Dubai within the week."

"Send someone else."

Harvey Senior blocked the door, "This has been your baby from day one. There is no one else."

"I don't give a damn. I have enough money to last a couple of lifetimes; what I don't have is anyone to share it with. I'm not going anywhere except the beach." Harv pushed past his father and out the door.

"We will see about that," the Senior Spencer spoke quietly to the unyielding back so like his own.

BAKING POWDER CHEDDAR BISCUITS
(Not Baker's, but very good)

2 cups sifted all-purpose flour
2 teaspoons baking powder
½ teaspoon salt
1/3 cup lard or shortening
1/3 cup skim milk powder
1 cup water
1 cup grated cheddar cheese
Makes 12 to 15 biscuits
Baker will explain the method.

Ellie returned Baker's enthusiastic hug, "You're early, good!   Did you bring enough recipe sheets for everyone?"

"Would I disappoint the woman who solved the crimes at my bakery?" Baker enquired jovially, but sobered quickly when he thought of Eric.

Ellie read his face, "I regret the outcome too."

"There's nothing to be done except be there for Eric when he needs us," Baker said. "Now to prove I am a magnanimous man of my word, I've brought you my apple fritter formula as well as the biscuit recipe I'll be demonstrating tonight." He bowed from the waist and gave Ellie a sealed envelope.

"I can't accept it. I did not solve anything, Lucy did." Ellie shuddered, "I never want to profit from Eric's pain." She wiped away a tear and gave back the envelope.

"You make me look like a welsher. What if Jake quits on me?"

"Who's taking my name in vain?" Jake asked, "You talking behind my back, Baker?"

Baker quipped, "That'd be hard to do when I'm looking at your face."

"I wouldn't listen anyway, Jake," Ellie said. "Not after all you did for Betty and . . ."

Sue bowed to Jake, "And me, and Doris and Valerie." She turned to Ellie, "I hope you don't mind me sitting in, I thought I'd see how Lucy handles these rascals."

"I'm glad you're here," Ellie said frowning at her watch. "Lucy has a way about her that brings out the best in these fellows. I'm not sure what she does."

Harv took his usual place next to Ellie. I could tell her, if she wasn't Lucy's mother, "Good evening everyone, is Lucy here yet?"

"She's late again, but you, 'Mr. October', will be helping 'Mr. December', our celebrity guest tonight," Ellie slipped Sue a firefighter's calendar. "And Sue," Ellie pointed to Brad, "'Mr. May' will require special attention tonight."

"Wow, this is explosive stuff for a woman that hasn't had a beau in years," Sue stage whispered and then loudly added, "I can see there is a lot of talent in this town and I love all flowers, but roses and lilies are my favorites."

A dull blush colored Brad's dark complexion, but if a blushing trophy were awarded, Harv, despite the golden tan he'd recently acquired, won.

"Everyone's here so let me introduce our celebrity guest, a man who needs no introduction. A man who is responsible for the extra pounds we gain each summer. I give you Baker Wonder or, if you prefer, our wonderful baker. Prepare to be wowed by an expert in action." Ellie led the applause.

"All right men, listen up," Baker shouted, from the dais. "There will be no merriment, joviality, cheerfulness, gaiety, laughter, or lightheartedness while I am in charge of this here establishment," he stuck his tongue stuck out the side of his mouth and crossed his eyes. "I see my able assistant has arrived. Welcome Miss Lucy, you ready to beat these scoundrels into shape?"

Lucy saluted crisply, "Yes Sir."

"I expect Ellie's taught you all about the leavening agents, baking powder, bicarbonate of soda, and cream of tartar, I won't say anymore about that." Baker looked at the serious faces arrayed before him. Hell, some of the guys were even taking notes. Maybe Ellie had something when she said teaching could be a rewarding second career.

"Okay you've measured and been checked by my lovely assistants, so place all the dry stuff in your sifter, stuff that's a word we use in the profession for flour, salt and leavening," Baker joked. "Harv pay attention," he pushed Harv's bowl under his sifter. "Another important thing is that you keep at least one eye on the job," he pointed at a pile next to Harv's bowl. "Ellie maybe you'd better help this love starved youngster out."

"I wouldn't dream of interfering."

"Ah, so it's that way, is it, then Miss Lucy, you'd better sashay on up here to give this pilgrim a hand," Baker drawled.

"On second thought, I'm on my way," Ellie matched action to words. She smiled at Harv and quickly returned to her seat when Baker turned his back.

"Since the rest of you managed to get your stuff in your bowl, we'll work the shortening or lard in with a pastry blender. Why use this particular implement of torture? To keep the shortening cool and produce a light fluffy biscuit," he explained his eyes scanning the class for mistakes. "Don't overwork that shortening Brad. The resultant mixture should resemble peas not rice."

Sue moved Lucy aside, and grinned mischievously, "Brad might catch on quicker if I hold his hand,"

"Lucy, help your Uncle," Baker ordered. "You seem to distract these young fellows, I can't imagine why," his comment brought laughter. Baker pounded the table, "I said no frivolity. This baking is serious stuff!"

"He's making Ellie look like a pushover." Zack whined, "Lucy, make him stop browbeating us."

Hiding his ready smile Baker continued, "Now you gotta decide what extra ingredient, if any, you want to add. You might tart up your biscuits with raisins, cranberries, blueberries or any other dried fruit. Dried fruit is convenient and doesn't add moisture. Today though, we'll be adding shredded cheese. Mix it in well with your hands and at this point you can add fried, drained, crumbled bacon, sautéed, cooled onions or chopped ham." Baker paused to let them catch up.

"Thanks to your gentle tutelage, we're ready," Lucy said.

Baker dumped the water in all at once and mixed it with his hand. "You can use a fork if you're a sissy," he turned the moist mass onto a lightly floured table. "Do not overwork the dough," he cautioned, "or you'll end up with inedible biscuits." He folded over and gently pushed down on the dough once, turned it a quarter turn, folded and pushed down again and repeated his action ten more times. "Now roll or pat your dough out into a rectangle about 5/8 of an inch thick. Press your two inch cutter into the dough. Repeat placing each cut as close as possible to the previous ones without overlapping."

He waited while inexperienced hands clumsily shaped the dough. "Now I know you all have a dozen flawless round biscuits and a small mass of dough left over. Roll the remaining dough into a snake and put it across the pan behind your perfectly formed beauties. Why? Well, I'm rethinking my earlier assumption that you could read, because very few of you brought the suggested pan, so tuck the snake behind your biscuits to keep spread to a minimum. The snake bakes much faster and is inedible, but your biscuits will rise higher.

Jake, an old hand at biscuits, brushed his faultless efforts with a beaten egg, put a few shreds of cheese on the top, and placed the pan next to the preheated ovens. He pulled a chair close to Ellie and whispered, "He's a natural isn't he? He's serious about retiring. It's true he wants to fish and star gaze, but it's Ruby's betrayal that cut the heart out of him."

"She's had a difficult life."

"Haven't we all?" Jake snorted. "Baker trusted her and she betrayed him. The more we learn the gloomier he gets. She came to work all sunshine and cheek, like she wasn't the catalyst for Ms. Russell's death and Jordan's downfall. Not that Jordan doesn't deserve what he gets; Ruby's as guilty, but she'll walk away scot free."

"She'll be charged as an accessory. Jeremy Reese says the shoe bag I found at Brads belonged to Ruby, and that coupled with Jordan's confession, ties her to the robbery."

"Her type always comes out ahead. She'll plea bargain and walk. She started it, but takes no responsibility." Jake shook his head disgustedly.

Ellie thought a new subject prudent, "Perhaps we can ease Baker out of the bakery, and into teaching; he'd have more fun and less stress."

"That sounds good, but won't you miss teaching?"

"I love to teach, but I love writing my column more. I'll continue to shamelessly exploit you all by insisting you attend my dinner parties. I'll work on the novel I've promised myself I'd write," Ellie admired the expertise with which Baker handled her class. "Perhaps he and Sue could take the spring session," she speculated. "The pans are migrating to the ovens and that means it is work time for me."

Ellie stood next to Baker, "Biscuits have a short cooking time, 12 to 15 minutes so you can compare your efforts to Baker's before you leave tonight. Meanwhile Stan has something to say regarding the pies each of you generously donated for his family reunion. He kept track of the comments, so get ready to hear unbiased opinions." She rose to pour coffee and arrange Baker's biscuits.

"Mom, the guys can't wait to hear the complaints, uh, comments Stan's relatives made." Loud groans erupted around the table.

Stan grinned impishly, "The pies looked and smelled so good everybody thought I bought them. I had to show them my dish pan hands to prove I didn't, and then they weren't sure they wanted to try them."

Brad said, "I bet they flashed back to the Cajun catfish, stomach ache incident, and were afraid of death by chicken."

Stan glared, "Anyway after some coaxing, they took tiny slices. There was absolute silence and then 'pass me that pie.' It was hard to hear what they were saying with all the chewing going on. They wolfed down every pie and sniffed around for more." Stan handed Ellie a list, my aunts and cousins signed up their men for your next class and I'd say that's the best comment of the night."

Mac asked, "When is the next class Mrs. Wilson?"

"I'll plan for another in the spring, Ellie smiled at Baker, "Unless Baker retires and takes over."

"Who knows what the future holds," Baker philosophized. "Are those biscuits cool enough to taste yet? I'll only taste Jake's at my age I can't afford to break a tooth."

Clean up finished, Lucy said, "Harv will help pack up if you want to go home mom?"

"Thank you dear. We need to have that talk we missed this morning."

"I won't be too late," Lucy promised.

CHAPTER 29

Betty had a pot of Earl Grey waiting when Ellie got home.

"Give me a minute to record my thoughts on tonight's class," Ellie said, gratefully accepting the tea. "Ah, blast!"

"What's wrong Ellie?"

"The virus control program Lucy installed," Ellie spat and slapped the cumbersome old monitor with the flat of her hand. "It always updates and scans, when I need to work. I wonder if it's worth the aggravation."

"Michael says unsafe surfing is a major cause of disease among computer-kind," Betty giggled, "Maybe you should buy a new computer, like maybe one made in this century?"

"This one still works; what would I do with it?"

Betty dead panned, "Use it to anchor the boat."

Ellie ignored her, "Sometimes I long for the days when paper and pen were all I needed."

"Or," Betty said, "You could write your columns on clay tablets, use a stylus, or maybe resurrect cuneiform or pictograms."

"You're certainly in a good mood tonight. What happened? Did Mrs. Hooper take a round out of Sammy Ranker?"

"No nothing near that good, Ellie." Betty bit her last Luscious Kiss Candy truffle in half and put the rest in Ellie's mouth, "We had a super day at the store; small items are selling fast. I'll ask Lucy to watch for small French and English pieces for us." She smiled happily, "I don't want to travel for a while."

"That's nice," Ellie said absently, "Have you seen this file Lucy downloaded?"

"Not me, I wouldn't touch that relic, but Lucy found some crystal to replace the pieces *Derwood* sold."

"Pull up a chair and I'll help you choose."

Betty gasped as her bedroom and Derwood's battered body filled the screen.

Ellie's stiff finger closed the file. "I'm sorry, honey. Lucy must have copied those pictures from her camera phone; you don't have to see them."

"I want to see them." Betty shivered, "No I **need** to see them."

"Are you sure you're ready?"

"I have to know who killed *him*."

"The police suspect Jordan, but without a body . . . " Ellie hesitated.

"Stop stalling and open the damn file."

The image of Derwood, lifeless and bloodied appeared.

"It's worse than I remembered," Betty whispered.

Ellie clicked through one gory frame after another, increasing the pace as the camera zoomed in on Derwood's face. She begged Betty to let her sort the relevant shots and delete the rest."

"There might be a something the killer left that only I would notice."

Ellie nodded, but breathed easier and slowed her scan when the final images showed Betty's vandalized bedroom sans Derwood. "I wish we knew what to look for."

Betty unclenched her fists, "I was in a daze and don't remember." She frowned, "If only we knew who Baker saw in my house."

"Could it have been Jordan? The timing is right and Jordan Platt is capable of murder."

"Betty sighed, "Baker would have recognized Jordan, and although Ruby is a long haired blond, she's too short."

"I suppose you're right, but if not Jordan, then who?" Ellie sighed, "Maybe Derwood had a girlfriend?"

"He often compared me to tall, young blonds and made coarse remarks. He fancied the new beautician until she put him in his place with a word, well two words, neither of which I'll repeat."

"Oh Betty, how awful for you, he was an intolerable man and I'm glad he's dead."

"That makes two of us, but it gets us no closer to his killer."

"And you're not free until we do."

Betty took advantage of Ellie's preoccupation to slide Lucy's sketchbook out of sight. Lucy's mother doesn't need to see her new sketches just yet, or ever, Betty thought. "More tea?" she asked innocently.

"That would be lovely, thank you," Ellie replied, snatching the book Betty had not quite hidden. "Oh my goodness, so this is what my naughty child spent her afternoon doing." She hurriedly paged through and closed the sketchbook with a finality that didn't bode well for Lucy.

"Nude studies are an important part of an artist's development, Betty said, "and these are excellent, plus they fill out her portfolio. Just look at this musculature," she enthused, "notice the detail. How he seems to float and she's captured his expressive face perfectly."

"His face isn't what keeps drawing my eye," Ellie grimaced. "And stop justifying; Lucy is a grown woman. I wouldn't be upset if the subject weren't a Spencer! I'm not a prude you know."

"Or course you're not, Mrs. *Laissez-faire*. I recall your reaction when you saw her drawings of Brad!"

Ellie grinned. "That was different. She was thirteen years old and it was obvious Brad kept the crucial clothing on when he posed for her. As I recollect she filled in the gaps in her knowledge from her imagination."

"Remember how proud she was when she showed her sketches to Robert. He seriously critiqued each one, and promptly signed her up for 'Anatomy in Art' classes," Betty reminisced. "I miss Robert so much." A lone tear escaped from eyes that struggled to find peace.

Though Betty's grief tore at her heart, Ellie forced a smile, "Did I tell you what Robert said to me?" Betty shook her head. "He said, 'Ellie dear, if you thought there was anything other than friendship between those two, note certain anatomical depictions and reconsider,' and he said it all straight faced and in his stodgy, professorial manner." She laughed heartily; happy memories would in time ease the sorrow that Derwood's abuse hadn't allowed to heal.

"Robert had a wonderful, dry wit, didn't he Ellie?"

"He truly did."

Betty giggled. "He regretted taking her to that stud farm, he told me that if her education wasn't improved she'd be a terribly disappointed young lady one day." Her giggles intensified, "I'm happy to see that she's toned down her expectations," they laughed until tears rolled down their faces; Betty reliving a happy memory, Ellie with relief.

"I'd better finish what I started," Ellie sat at the computer," the phone rang.

"I'll get it," Betty said. "Oh hello Baker, how did the teaching go?" she listened, and gave the phone to Ellie, "He wants to talk to you."

Baker waxed poetic, and said he thought he could stand to try it again some time. Ellie suggested a combined class until he was comfortable, Baker agreed and said goodbye. "Wait, don't hang up,

Betty wondered if you remembered anymore about the woman in her house? Like what she was wearing. Ellie listened, "Really, that is strange. I look forward to working with you too." she replaced the receiver. "Betty, I wish you could have seen Baker, he's a natural."

"That is good news; you can enjoy life, and Lucy can actually rest when she's home; what did he say about the woman?"

"He's convinced he saw Lucy, but he admits she was in silhouette. Still, he's positive she was wearing a skirt or a dress and had her hair up in a bun of some kind, but Lucy wore slacks and her hair was down."

"I wonder," Betty said, "where all Derwood's other victims were?"

"That you, son?" Harvey Senior called, "Come in, we didn't finish our conversation."

"We finished," Harv said deadpan. "You want a cheese biscuit?"

"The deal in the Emirates is shaky; you need to be there tomorrow. Don't shake your head; we've got too much invested to watch it go down the drain. You insisted on absolute secrecy, so it's your baby."

"I'm on holiday, I'm going to spend my time with Lucy; I'll go next week."

"What the hell is wrong with you? Business comes first!" Harvey Senior stalked around his desk, "you have responsibilities!'

"Dad, for the first time in my life I know what I want, and I won't chance screwing it up. You know Talltree is waiting for me to mess up with Lucy."

"Lucy has a demanding career of her own. Don't you think she'd go if a lucrative contract were offered?"

Harv dropped onto a leather chair, "Okay, you made your point, I'll go. I should have it wrapped up in a week."

Harvey Senior relaxed, "Good, and Harv, Lucy will wait. She's a sensible girl with impeccable breeding and, a great track record."

Harv shook his father's arm off his shoulder. "For God's sake Dad, she isn't one of your damn racehorses. I'm in love with Lucy and I intend to spend my life with her. Why can't you understand?" belligerence sharpened his tone. "Stupid question, you've never been in love."

"That was uncalled for!" Harvey Senior snapped, he strode stiffly around his desk. "You're booked on the ten a.m. flight. I'll drive you to the airport."

Shoes in hand Lucy tiptoed across the foyer.
"Lucille Amelia Warden Wilson, come in here!"
"Mom, you shouldn't have waited up."

"Yes, I certainly should have; how could you have left those horrendous photos in plain sight?"

"What photos?"

"Derwood! Dead!"

'The file was closed I thought you might want to see them so I didn't use a password."

"I don't think your aunt benefited from that experience."

"I'm fine," Betty said.

"Well I am not," Ellie snapped. "Lucy, I'm extremely aggravated that you didn't trust me enough to tell me about that cursed bag, or your foolish plan to ensnare Jordan Platt. I can't believe you'd put yourself in such danger. If Brad and Harv hadn't arrived when they did, you and Ruby could have been killed. And then, to make the entire repulsive circus even more ludicrous, you put me in the position where I was forced to rely on and thank the Senior Spencer."

"Mom, if we're indebted to Harv and Brad, logically we must also be grateful to Mr. Spencer."

"That fact galls me almost as much as your lack of trust in me," Ellie screeched.

"I am not a child!" Lucy cried, "All I wanted to do was keep you safe and furthermore I would have handled the situation with Jordan if you hadn't rushed in to throw yourself at him like some crazed berserker."

"Do not speak to me in that tone of voice! If you had confided in me we could have properly prepared and the situation would not have become a mockery more suitable to a stage lampoon. But it's that furtive investigation of yours that rankles me most," Ellie drew a quick breath and overrode her daughter's attempt to speak. "First there was that absurd, salacious retrieval of that bag, and then your antics with Jordan and now these atrocious pictures. Why didn't you show them to me before? It's obvious they weren't taken yesterday. Don't bother to explain, it's just another of your idiotic secrets. You said you wouldn't be late, so what were you doing with that Spencer boy? And what is this hedonistic trash?" Ellie demanded, slamming Lucy's sketchbook to the table.

"That, Mother, is art and it is none of your business. As for Harv, I can't believe that you have the nerve to talk to me about secrets, you who are the queen of secrets." Lucy lowered her voice, "I love Harv Spencer, and I mean to marry him and no ancient, family grudge can change that."

A crash from the foyer made her pause, Lucy shook her head and bolted out the door, Barefoot and jacketless; she straddled her bike, and raced away.

Ellie, shadowed by Betty, took several steps toward the still vibrating door, she wanted to apologize, to hold Lucy, to explain her anger; but instead she trudged back to the kitchen, dropped into the worry chair, and hid her face with her hands.

Betty checked the hook and rehung Aunt Emily's portrait before she positioned a chair in front of the rocker. She tugged Ellie's chilled hands down and held them tight. "Ellie, look at me," she ordered. "You know you're my best friend and I love you, but you're wrong. Lucy is a well-balanced, young woman with a wealth of talent and you, who should be her most devoted fan, called her art hedonistic trash."

"But Betty . . . ."

"Let me finish. This young woman, your only child I might add, has given up her vacation to help us. I know her heart is with Harv, yet she's spent countless hours trying to solve a problem that she shouldn't have been saddled with in the first place. She has tried to protect us, yet you called her foolish, irresponsible, absurd, salacious, and if I remember correctly, idiotic. I'd also like to point out that she's tirelessly aided you with your cooking classes, all the while enduring the worst kind of prying interference from us. She works very hard and she deserves a vacation, but she never complains. I am not surprised she lost her temper, I'm amazed it took so long."

"I said all that to my child?"

"Yes you did. Now, I'll make some fresh tea and we'll figure out who killed *him.* Then we will tell Lucy so she can enjoy the balance of her vacation unencumbered."

"Harv, I'm at our spot on the beach, can you come?" Lucy, her voice husky with unshed tears, asked.

"I'm on my way," he replied, and was in his car before she'd hung up. He found her gazing at the lake with unseeing eyes. His footfalls silent on the sand, he held her in his protective arms. "Lucy baby, I'm here with news that might cheer you up."

She snuggled close, "I had a big fight with mom," Lucy sobbed, "I've agreed to find a property in Spain for friends of Aunt Betty's. I leave for Paris tomorrow morning, and then I'm going to drive to the Costa Brava. I booked two tickets. We can be together without our families and . . . ," she let her sentence peter away.

"I didn't know you located real estate."

"I don't usually, but I have to get away, and the commission is generous," she sensed trouble, "don't you want to come with me?"

"Baby, there's nothing I'd like more, but I have to go to Dubai. My project is in trouble. You could come with me; Dubai is the shopping capital of the world. I won't have a lot of free time, but all the major designers are there, you could shop."

"Didn't you hear me?" Lucy said stiffly. "I *promised* to find property in Spain for a client. Are you'd suggesting I renege on a promise to—shop. Or do you consider my career unimportant when compared to yours?"

"I'll pretend you didn't ask that question if you forget my stupid shopping crack. Let's kiss and make up." He drew her taut body tight against his.

Lucy sighed, "I would so much rather kiss you than fight you."

"I'll come to Spain every chance I get," he murmured.

"What am I going to do with that extra ticket?"

"Take your mother."

"She isn't speaking to me. I'll ask Brad."

"Why Brad? Why not ask Valerie?"

"You're jealous. Brad and I are best friends; he even knows where the bodies are sunk."

"Baby, he's got a thing for you and I don't like it. Why don't we hook him up with Valerie?

She looks enough like you to be your sister."

Somewhere in Lucy's brain, an idea sparked, Baker, Hank, and now Harv saw the sisterly resemblance.

"I said Brad's my best friend! If you can't stand me having friends, we're done." Lucy jumped on her bike and raced recklessly over the stump filled ground.

Harv stared at the lake and wondered what the hell had just happened.

She woke with her knees pressed tight to her chest. The dream so real her ribs ached. She closed her eyes and memories washed over her like storm tossed waves.

"How did you get in?" Day snarled, "You're a damn, stupid, loony bitch and I can't get rid of you. Is this the gratitude I get for taking care of you when your old man croaked, for listening to your whining?" He turned his back, "You're just like all the rest, you don't get it. I'm done with you. I hate the sight of you. You're skinny, ugly, and stupid. Get the hell out of my house."

She struggled to remain calm, "I'll leave when I get my money."

"You forgot you signed it over to me, you stupid slut. You're a weakling like your old man. You make me want to puke; sniveling over the schmuck's carcass, ruining my suits. You two-bit whore, I don't owe you, you owe me."

"I am not a whore," she said, "but you are wicked and immoral. Just give me my money and I'll go."

"Your money? I earned every cent putting up with you and your old man. Brainless bastard was glad enough to take my help when you, you damn, stupid, loony bitch weren't around. Don't whine to me about the money. I earned it putting up with your shit. You're a stupid, ugly forgetful slut."

"You are an evil piece of trash. You exploit one woman after another. You have to be stopped!"

"Yeah, and you're gonna' stop me, a crazy bitch that can't even take care of herself." He loomed over her, "You forgot who's boss again. I'll remind you," he grabbed her chignon, pins flew, long, blond hair cascaded over his hand; he reveled in the fear he saw in her eyes, and slapped her face, a forward slap, and then a backhand.

He let go of her hair, her raised arms covering her head she fell awkwardly, his heavy boot gained speed toward her unprotected ribs, and stopped, she let herself breathe, then with the speed of a viper he kicked her, drew back and struck again, "Stupid loony bitch, I'll give you a lesson you won't ever forget." He feigned a punch to her head, she cringed. "Always forgetting," he mocked, as his boot met her unprotected stomach, she whimpered. He chortled while he cursed and kicked, each blow designed to destroy her body, each word uttered to destroy her soul. He grabbed her hair and lifted; her groping hand felt a chunk of Betty's shattered bed, she swung; and through pain clouded eyes saw him flail trying to stay upright. With strength born of rage, she struck him until her fury induced strength faded and died. The sound of solid, ancient wood striking his unprotected head gave her a moment's pleasure before she fell. Seconds later he crumpled and fell on top of her. Fighting for breath, she crawled out of his reach and rested.

He lay ominously still. She rolled him over and still clutching her club gingerly touched his neck.

Dillon/Douglas/Daniel/Derwood Day was dead, she was safe. She searched until she found every hair pin, twisted her long blond hair into the chignon that gave her strength, found the bathroom, and was ready to face life without fear.

The old worry chair rocked at a pace not seen since Gertrude intercepted Ellie's letters. "She winced when I hugged her," Ellie said

Betty's tear filled eyes meet Ellie's. "That saddens me."

"We have to confront her."

"Let's sleep on it. If what we're thinking still makes sense in the morning we'll know what we have to do."

"I'll wait for Lucy," Ellie said, she massaged her temples and wondered when the Jordan induced headache would ease.

"I'll wait with you. Aspirin and tea should help the headache you say you don't have. I hear Lucy's bike," Betty ran to the window. "Now, we can apologize and make up." The motorbike roared past the house and on out the driveway.

The jangle of the service bell broke the nightmare's hold. Grateful, she rushed to answer it.

"Lucy, I wasn't expecting you. What's wrong?"

"You are! You killed him. Your PI found him and you brought all the wives here to confront him. But that wasn't enough for you, was it? You lurked outside Aunt Betty's house waiting for your opportunity; you killed him and ran away. You left Aunt Betty holding the bag." Lucy saw the smiley faced orange pumpkin bag with Derwood's remains inside and grimaced, bad analogy.

"Lucy, it wasn't like that."

"Tell me how you killed him."

"I didn't."

"Do not lie to me;" Lucy shook her head disgustedly; "I finally figured it out."

"I didn't mean to kill him. I swear I didn't."

"Tell me."

"I went to get my money back, he was horrid." She related the nightmare episode as if speaking of someone else. "She used the washroom to clean her swollen face and touched up her makeup from the stockpile she found in a drawer. Then she used clean towels to wipe away her prints. She was meticulous, she wiped every surface she may have touched, then backed from the room, closed the door, wiped the knob and continued on to the banister working her way down the stairs. She entered the study hoping to find some remnant of the life he'd stolen from her, but stopped short when a late night walker saw her and waved. She waited until he turned the corner, gave the front door knob a swipe; trudged to her car and drove home. She felt free for the first time since Daniel violated her life,"

"I did not mean to kill him, but I am not sorry he is dead," Valerie Tate said. "I am grateful that the nightmare is over.

Betty saw Lucy's bike roar past, "There goes Lucy. She knows, I wonder what triggered it for her."

"Are you certain she knows?"

"Yes, she's mad as hell, and there was air between her and the bike seat."

Ellie moaned, "If only I hadn't lost my temper, we would be confronting her together."

Betty showed uncharacteristic resolve, "You're right! But the fact is Lucy is confronting a killer alone. Like I said, she's angry and likely to be foolhardy. So get a move on."

"I see Derwood's death as a weird sort of blessing," Ellie said. "If she hadn't killed him, you would be dead and I on trial for your murder."

"Yes we owe her, but my bones say hurry."

"Then just this once we'll listen to your bones."

Ellie drove recklessly and in minutes pulled into the lot. "Lucy will not thank me for interfering."

"We have no choice. You said she winced when you hugged her; after I fell *he* always kicked me in the ribs. She must have fought back, but I don't believe she . . . ," Betty paused and Ellie finished her thought.

"Planned to kill him," Ellie said and climbed out of the car.

Betty inched the door open. "Derwood is a problem I brought on myself. I cannot let Lucy deal it with alone."

"Shush!"

"Don't try to explain or lie. I know what you did. You watched the house; saw Aunt Betty arrive. You heard them argue; and you saw her hit him. He was alive when Aunt Betty left."

"Yes he was alive," Valerie whispered.

I know he was, Rodney saw the bandages." Lucy shuddered, "Uncle Rodney came and you watched them quarrel, you saw my uncle punch Derwood, and leave."

Valerie tried to explain. "Shut up Val, it is too late for excuses. Next came Jordan and Ruby to blackmail Derwood. Jordan chased Derwood up the stairs. You saw Ruby take off with that damn duty-free bag. You waited for Jordan to leave and you killed *Derwood*."

"I didn't see Jordan leave."

Lucy shrugged. "That's not important. What is important is that you murdered him, you removed the bandages he'd applied and you walked away leaving the mess for Aunt Betty. You freaked when Baker waved at you, but your luck held; He thought you were me." Lucy paced angrily, "You saw me at the cafe, fed me a line of crap, and manipulated me into asking for your help." Lucy Laughed bitterly, "The master stroke was offering to clean Betty's house; you thought you missed something, so you charged in first."

"You can't substantiate any of that."

Lucy ignored her, "I cut my foot; and you picked the bathroom from a line of seven identical closed doors." Lucy shrugged dismissively, "But that doesn't matter now. Someone else saw you, and since we look alike, he thinks I killed Derwood."

"Everyone else sees the resemblance."

"Oh shut up! You stuck us with his rotten corpse; we stuffed him in that damn pumpkin bag and hauled him away."

"I helped get rid of his body."

"You did, as I recall the incinerator was your idea. When we had him on your table," Lucy gestured toward the gurney, "You clouded the issue with technical talk when you could have told the truth."

"Lucy, that's not fair. You didn't want to hear anything I tried to tell you."

"You obfuscated! You killed him. You knew we wouldn't let Betty suffer for his death. You knew and you played us like a two dollar fiddle, you abused our friendship. You let us suspect Sue and Doris."

"I wouldn't have let them be convicted."

"Right and when did you plan to step in, when they were charged, or convicted?"

"There can't be charges without a body."

"Wrong! Conviction without a corpse has happened." Lucy leaned toward her, "I can understand wanting to kill him, hell everybody did. But you involved mom and Aunt Betty, and should the truth ever come out; we'll be charged right along with you. And that Valerie Tate, I will never forgive."

"I wouldn't let that happen," Valerie began, "Lucy wait, let me explain!"

"Valerie the time for explanations is over." Lucy strode to the door, "Like our friendship is over and as dead as Derwood/Daniel /Dillon/Douglas, or whoever the hell he was."

Ellie blocked the doorway, "She's your friend Lucy. She's hurt and frightened. Let her explain."

Lucy slid past, "I have to pack, I leave tomorrow morning."

"Lucy?" Betty said, "She was desperate."

"I see neither friend nor desperate injured party. I see a liar."

"Lucy, this is not like you."

The sound of a spurting gravel almost drowned Lucy's, "Live and learn."

"Don't cry Valerie," Betty soothed, "Lucy will forgive you. She's angry and not thinking straight."

Lucy never quite knew how she got to the beach or why Harv waited, "I'm glad you're here"

"Baby," he dried her tears, "I'll wait forever for you. I'll always be as close as the phone. Call, close your eyes and I'll be there, I swear."

"That means a lot to me, Harv."

"I leave tomorrow; I wish you were coming with me."

"I wish I were too." Lucy sighed, "I have to mend fences with mom."

"Yeah my dad was unreasonable too," Harv gazed at the black water, "I know he's right. I have to go and straighten things out."

"Mom over reacted, but so did I. I should pack, my plane leaves early."

"Mine too. A kiss until we meet again."

Her face radiant in the moonlight, Lucy met Harv half way.

"Betty, I have to go to Lucy."

"She' needs time."

"I hurt her. I cannot let her leave angry."

"Five minutes Ellie, give me five minutes with this child."

"You heard Lucy! She said some miscreant thinks she killed *Derwood*. What if she's charged with *his* murder?"

"Ellie, you're not thinking straight. This child," Betty said, hugging Valerie, "we owe our lives. She foiled *his* plot to poison me and blame you, remember." She spoke softly for Ellie's ears only, "We owe Valerie, and Lucy when she cools off will remember that too."

"This is my night for stupidity." Ellie said, "Valerie, don't cry," Ellie hugged both women. "Give Lucy time, then tell her exactly what happened and why."

"She got most of it right, except I didn't plan to kill him. I didn't, but he kept hitting me and kicking me." Valerie sobbed, "I just wanted him to stop hurting me."

"Just like me," Betty whispered.

"I should have told you, but I thought Lucy would tell Platt." Valerie sighed, "Anyway she wouldn't have done for me what she did for you Mrs. Archer."

"You are so wrong," Ellie said, "Lucy does not abandon her friends. She would have helped you."

Betty said, "She hated Derwood for what he did to us."

"It has been a long night," Ellie said.

"Let's drop Val at home," Betty said, "She shouldn't be in this gloomy place. How bout I come spend the night with you Valerie."

Val's eager expression lifted Betty's heart.

Lucy called Brad, and told him everything as she always had. They talked until sunrise. Lucy rode home with a clear head and a forgiving heart. Ellie waited, their mutual love made forgiveness easy.

EPILOGUE

"Thanks for the lift, Uncle Rodney."

"Driving you is my pleasure, Lucy."

"She means she's grateful I'm not behind the wheel."

"'I did not say that, mom."

Ellie sighed, "I'm joking Lucy. Huron Shores will never be the same; Rita Russell's death and *his*, uh, disappearance changed everything. I may sell the house and move back to the city."

"Mom," Lucy cried, "Our roots are here and realistically, what's the chance of two unnatural deaths involving us ever happening again in Huron Shores? One in a million," Lucy grimaced, "I should have told you about Ruby," she did her perky act, "but I meant well." She shifted closer to Ellie, "I thought I could protect you and Aunt Betty and in my defense it did happen pretty fast."

"I was wrong. I treated you like an adolescent, but I wanted you to be as carefree as you were during that period of your life. You know I love you more than life itself."

Lucy giggled, "If I ever doubt that, I'll close my eyes and picture you riding Jordan like Porter riding Yellow Jacket with one second to the big money." Mischievously, she continued, "Uncle Robert called us salt and pepper, complimentary, but fundamentally different. He was right. I love you Mom, and I do like to be coddled when I'm home with you."

Ellie shook her head to clear the vision of a luggage handler riding a wasp, "Why would a porter ride a bee," Ellie sighed, "or was that a sports analogy?"

"We're here and there's never a porter around when I want one," Betty groused.

"There is a cart; and Uncle Rodney is capable of getting my puny, little bags out of the trunk."

"Puny?" Rodney grunted, holding his back.

Lucy checked in and they made their way to the passport control booths and metal detectors.

"This is goodbye, until Christmas," Lucy said, she hugged Betty who reminded her to call Val. Rodney simply held her and said he'd see her in Spain. She reminded Ellie of their unstoppable love and promised to be home for Christmas.

Ellie wiped away a tear and watched her daughter pass the passport checkpoint. They kept waving until Lucy turned a corner.

Rodney stiffened and snarled, "We cannot get away from that reprobate."

"Ellie stop pulling me you'll dislocate my shoulder. Oh, hello Spence, what brings you out so early?"

"Harv is off to U.A.E, I drove him down."

Before Betty could reply he was gone and if looks could kill, we would be giving Ellie CPR. Two nights ago I used a baseball bat to get him out of her bedroom. What changed, how much has he guessed? What will Ellie do now?

"Lucy, I'm glad you've got your phone on. I'll meet you at gate thirteen. I'm coming to Paris.'"

"Harv, that's wonderful."

"And I have a fifteen hour layover."

"I just love long layovers," Lucy said, sprinting to gate thirteen.

ABOUT THE AUTHOR

Eleanor Wood Mason, a writer of mystery novels, has been a closet writer for years, she has now decided to come forth into the light and publish her work. This novel is the first in a series of Huron Shores mysteries in which the principal characters evolve as their relationships deepen when they tackle new mysteries in subsequent volumes. Eleanor Wood Mason, now retired after running her own successful food processing business for 18 years, spends her summers in Sauble Beach, Ontario and escapes winter wherever she can; steamy Florida, sunny Spain … wherever… In any locale, she converts her diverse life experiences into compelling plots and infuses her characters with mystery, vitality and excitement. Wherever life leads her, she's sure to find fodder for new mysteries!

Email: EllieWardonWilson@yahoo.com